KISSING THE CHAMPION

"Your words are bold," Nick said, sidling closer to her until he could feel her heat. "'Tis a shame for a woman of such passion to be paired with one so aged and dwindling—he will never make you burn."

"Do you think you might accomplish that task if given the chance, Nicholas FitzTodd, Baron of Crane?"

Nick was shocked into silence. Then, reaching out a hand, he laid it alongside the warm, soft skin of her neck, forcing her to look up at him. He heard her soft breath at the physical contact and smiled when she would not meet his eyes.

"Verily, Lady du Roche," he began, "I—"

"Simone," she amended in a husky whisper, glancing into his eyes for only an instant. "My name is Simone."

"*Simone,*" Nick repeated, drawing out the syllables of her name even as he pulled her closer. "Shall I demonstrate my abilities for you?"

Just when Nick expected her retreat, Simone reached her hand from beneath the confines of the cloak and laid it upon his chest. Her eyes found his, and the invitation he saw there, the raw need, tested his resolve to move slowly.

She licked her lips, a fleeting dart of pink tongue. "Please do . . . *Nicholas.*"

He dropped his mouth to hers and pulled her fully against him. She tasted of honeyed wine and autumn's chill, and the sweetness of her small hands cupping his face shook Nicholas in a way no other dalliance with a woman had . . .

The Champion

Heather Grothaus

ZEBRA BOOKS
Kensington Publishing Corp.
www.kensingtonbooks.com

ZEBRA BOOKS are published by

Kensington Publishing Corp.
850 Third Avenue
New York, NY 10022

All Kensington titles, imprints, and distributed lines are available at special quantity discounts for bulk purchases for sales
promotion, premiums, fund-raising, educational, or institu-
tional use.

Special book excerpts or customized printings can also be created to fit specific needs. For details, write or phone the office
of the Kensington Special Sales Manager: Attn. Special Sales
Department. Kensington Publishing Corp., 850 Third Avenue,
New York, NY 10022. Phone: 1-800-221-2647.

Zebra and the Z logo Reg. U.S. Pat. & TM Off.

ISBN-13: 978-0-8217-8007-7
ISBN-10: 0-8217-8007-7

First Printing: April 2007
10 9 8 7 6 5 4 3 2 1

Printed in the United States of America

For John Scognamiglio
It is a pleasure to work with you.

For Diana Belcher
Who told me so.

And for Tim
A hundred lifetimes wth you would never be enough.

into his guts with a soothing heat. He handed the flask back to Randall and then urged Majesty down the narrow, rocky path that led to Obny.

Randall continued from behind. "You should be relieved to take a bride as well met as Lady Evelyn. Most only meet their wives the day they wed—you've known the lady since her birth."

Nick merely grunted.

"You've spent much time in each other's company. You get on well, hold many of the same views—I fail to see what catastrophic difference making her your wife will cause. Save that she will share Hartmoore with you." Randall paused, as if carefully considering his next words. "And your bed, of course. But I doubt you would consider that a great hardship."

Nick said nothing.

"She's quite easy to look at," Randall continued, now in an almost goading tone. "Her beautiful wavy hair, skin like cream. Not to mention her great, round, plump br—"

"Enough!" Nick shouted, but he could not keep the laughter from his voice. The path had widened to a sandy ledge and Obny lay before him, twinkling in her candlelit robes, Nick's future—wanted or nay—safe within. Nick paused on his mount to stare grimly at the border town. "There is no blight upon Lady Evelyn, in body or mind. She is a good match for me, and in truth, I would have no other."

Randall's smile faded. "Then why rail so, my lord?"

"Because a woman—*a wife*—is a shackle." Nick shook his head and snorted. "This is all Tristan's doing. Had my brother not become so fully ensnared, Mother likely would have let me be to decide the time to take a wife. Now I feel obligated to appease her."

"Lord Tristan does not seem shackled by Lady Haith. He—"

Nick waved a hand to cut Randall off. "Be not fooled, my friend. He is shackled, as well as any beast of burden." Nick's bark of laughter jarred the starry stillness. "*Saddled.*"

Nicholas abruptly swung down from Majesty, looked around, and then scrambled up a jumbled motte of boulders—

a mountain of sorts. He turned slowly, taking in the shallow bowl of the valley, draped in winter black.

He, by God, would not be saddled.

Nick spread his arms wide, drew a deep, aching breath of the frigid air, and called for any and all to hear.

"Nicholas FitzTodd answers only to God and King William! No woman will own me! I swear it!"

His words echoed over the valley and died away, and Nicholas felt cleansed. He was in control once more and could now face the chore ahead of him. Marriage would not change him, for good or ill. He was the Baron of Crane, and all within his demesne would still bend to his will.

Nick was off the boulders in two giant leaps, and he looked up at Randall's quirked brow.

"Feeling better now?" his first man asked.

"Aye, better." Nick swung up into Majesty's saddle with a grin and wheeled the beast to once more face Obny. "I'm ready to tell Lord Handaar the good news, that I have chosen his daughter for my wife."

And with that, Nick spurred Majesty in a gallop toward the border town.

"Lord Nicholas." Handaar rose from his chair before the hearth as Nick entered Obny's great hall. The elderly lord of the small town bowed slightly at Nick's approach, and although the man's smile seemed genuine and welcoming, he appeared to have aged a number of years since last they met. "'Tis good to see you again, son."

Nicholas reached Handaar, and the two embraced as old friends. At this close range, Nicholas saw more clearly the deeply etched lines on the man's face, the thinness of the white hair that ringed Handaar's shining pate.

"And you as well, Handaar." Nick clapped the old man's bony back and drew away. "How fare things at Obny?"

"Well. The border is quiet and my scouts report no sign of

trespass." Handaar gestured to the pairing of chairs before the hearth. "Sit, if you would."

Nicholas gratefully complied, sinking into a padded chair near Handaar's. His eyes traveled to the small table between them, on which sat a carafe and two chalices—the one closest to the old man already half-full of deep red wine. Nick's leg bounced on the ball of his foot several times before he took notice and stilled it. He knew it was a nightly ritual for Handaar and his only child to share a drink and talk of the events of the day before retiring, and as thoughts of Evelyn crossed Nick's mind, his tongue seemed to dry up completely and swell against his teeth.

As if Handaar had noticed Nick's longing glance at the carafe, he filled the empty chalice and handed it to Nicholas with a weary smile.

"To warm you from your journey."

"My thanks." Nick drained the vessel and was immediately obliged with more. He gestured toward Handaar with the chalice. "I vow Lady Evelyn will be much put-out with me for claiming her comfortable perch and cup."

Nicholas thought he might have seen Handaar flinch before he spoke. Slowly, as if choosing his words with great care, Handaar said, "Evelyn will not be joining me this evening."

Nick's brow lowered. "She is not ill, I hope."

"Nay." Handaar gazed into the blazing hearth, and the firelight danced across his worn countenance. "She is not ill."

"'Tis well, then." Nicholas could not fathom the root of Handaar's melancholy from the blunt statement, and so he pressed on. "I do hope to speak to her this night if she can spare me a moment. I did not send word of my visit as I wished to surprise her, but mayhap I should have."

The old man shook his head, his gaze focused on the brilliant flames. "Nay, 'twould have mattered not that you sent word." Handaar looked directly at Nick now, and his face took on a pained expression. "Two days past, she told me you would come."

Nick's eyebrows rose. "Did she? But how . . . ?"

Handaar shrugged. "You know as well as I that Evelyn has always possessed a keen ability to sense certain events. Just as she seems to know what any lowly beast would think."

Nick chuckled, even though his discomfort with the task before him was being compounded by Handaar's strange behavior. Something was about in Obny's keep.

"Yea, you are right, Handaar. Did I not know otherwise, I would wager she calls Majesty to her, therefore requiring my presence as well." He took a sip of his wine. "Oft times, I suspect she cares more for my horse than for me."

Handaar's gaze sharpened. "Evelyn cares for you very much, Nicholas."

Nick's stomach clenched like a tight fist at the man's grave tone. Now was as good a time as any would be.

"Lord Handaar, I—"

Handaar rose abruptly and strode to face the hearth. "How fare your brother and his wife?"

"Well." Nicholas frowned at being cut off. The subject was difficult enough to voice without being forced to begin again. But mayhap 'twould be better to humor the old man. "They have a daughter now—Isabella. Mother has recently returned from Greanly and brought word that Tristan's town prospers."

Handaar nodded but did not turn. "Then the baroness is in good spirits as well?"

"Yea." Nicholas chuckled and relaxed a bit. "As beautiful and overbearing as ever, and still hounding me ceaselessly."

Handaar did not laugh at the jest, nor did he make any reply at all.

Nicholas placed his chalice on the small table with unnecessary care and leaned forward in his chair, his forearms braced on his knees. He took a deep, silent breath.

"Her hounding has relevance to my visit to Obny this night."

"Of course it does."

Nick frowned at the man's back. "Handaar, I must speak with you in seriousness. I—"

"Do not, Nicholas."

Nick's nerves were wearing thin. "Please, friend, hear me out. This is not a thing I would take lightly and I think 'twill please you."

After a moment of silence, Handaar sighed, and his words were curled with sorrow. "Go on, then, if you feel you must."

"Very well." Nick cleared his throat, rubbed his hands across his thighs. "Since my father's death, it has been fully realized to me the responsibilities I now hold. Barring Mother's nagging, I know that for my father's line to be continued, I must marry. As you know, I am the last FitzTodd."

He cleared his throat again. "I have known Lady Evelyn since her birth. You were like a brother to my father and a second father to me." Nick's voice grew a bit hoarse with his last words, so he stole another quick gulp of wine before continuing.

"The baroness loves Evelyn as she would her own daughter, and I care for her as well." Nick took a deep breath, his heart kicking against his ribs as if it would burst from his chest and gallop from the hall without him. "As my wife, Evelyn will want for naught. I swear it to you."

"'Tis not possible," Handaar said, his voice gravelly and low.

Nick paused a moment to collect his thoughts. He had expected this, and he was prepared. "I know that she is promised to the convent, but Handaar"—Nick rose—"I will secure her freedom. I will pay the abbess her dowry so that Evelyn may marry."

When no reply came, Nick's nerves were outrun by his growing frustration. "Do you not see? She need not throw her life away by joining the order. You must admit that you are loathe to send your only child from you, and now, 'twill be avoided. She will be close at hand for the rest of your days and cared for by one you claim to be as your own son." Nick felt confident in the logic of his argument. "It only makes sense that we wed."

"I made a vow to Fiona," Handaar said. "I beg of you, Nick, let us not speak of it further."

"Evelyn's mother is dead, Handaar," Nick said as gently as possible. "Though do you not think if she were still alive, if she could see what a companionable match your daughter and I make, that she would bless this union?"

"Mayhap," Handaar said quietly. "But it matters not. As I've said, 'tis impossible."

Nick felt his choler rising as it never had before with the old warrior. "Nay, 'tis not impossible. As baron, 'tis my responsibility to see to the welfare of my people, and I will not have Evelyn waste away in a moldy priory when she could live in comfort, among family and friends."

Nicholas stepped closer to Handaar's back. His next words would be difficult to say to the elder lord, but Nick felt his authority in this matter need be exercised.

His voice was steady now, deep with resolve. "Handaar, as baron, 'tis also my right to take a bride of my choosing. I have made my choice, friend, and there is naught you can do to sway me." He placed a comforting hand on the stooped shoulder. "Fiona would understand, I am certain. Now, let us seek Lady Evelyn and share with her the good news."

Handaar turned under Nick's palm, and Nick was shaken and disturbed to see streaks of wet glistening on the wrinkled cheeks. Handaar's voice was strained but, aside from the tears on his face, his expression was stony.

"Evelyn is already gone, Nick."

Nicholas took an involuntary step back as Handaar's words hit him like a physical blow. "Gone? What do you mean?"

"She has left for the convent." Handaar swiped a hand over his face. "Two days past, when she foretold of your arrival."

Nick returned to his chair, stunned. "But . . . but why would she go if she knew I was coming? Were we not always friends?"

"That is the very reason," Handaar said, as he too regained his seat. He poured more wine into the chalices. "Although I am certain you perceived your hints about the matter as subtle, Evelyn knew you would offer marriage. As you your-self said, it only makes sense."

"But . . . *she knew?*" Nick asked, his thoughts tripping over themselves. He looked at Handaar and at the old lord's ex-pression of sympathy, Nick knew that his bewilderment must have been evident on his face. "She would choose the convent over me?"

Handaar shook his head and looked to a spot between his boots. "She had no wish to marry, to bear you the children she knew you would require of her. Evelyn took the vow I made to Fiona most seriously."

Nick felt his jaw harden until he thought his teeth would crack. "Then she is selfish and stupid. There is no guarantee that her fate would have been as Fiona's—that she would die in childbirth. She has thrown her life away and abandoned me."

Handaar sighed quietly. "In her heart, she felt she was free-ing you."

"*Freeing me?* For what purpose? To be forced to take a stranger for a wife?" Nick's bark of laughter was bitter and jagged. "Ours would have been a union of friendship and trust. That she would leave me is unforgivable. She never cared for me at all."

"Evelyn loves you very much, Nick."

"Nay!" His palm sliced through air thick with tension. "Nay, you do not treat one you claim to be in love with in such a manner as this—with deceit."

"I said that she loved you, not that she was in love with you. There is a difference." Handaar looked weary now to the brink of collapse, but Nick's hurt was not considerate of the old man.

"Love, in love." Nick waved a hand. "What does it matter?"

"Mayhap that is the very core of why she left—to give you the opportunity to see how much it truly does matter."

Nicholas stared at the old man for several moments, and Han-daar stared back. He had already told his mother, his brother, and several of the other underlords of his plan to take Evelyn as his wife. He'd even told his first man. What would they think of him now, when a woman Nick had known the whole of her life would prefer a convent before him as her husband?

Never had he felt such awkwardness, such humiliation in this place that was as familiar to Nicholas as his own home. He could no longer sit under its heavy weight, and so he stood.

"Very well, then. I bid you good night, Lord Handaar." After a curt nod in the old man's direction, Nick crossed to the great hall's doors.

"Nick, son." The sounds of Handaar rising and calling out chased Nick's retreat. "Let us not part on poor terms. Stay at Obny tonight. Would that I could have spared you this hurt, but in truth, I am not certain I can bear it myself."

At Handaar's words, Nick paused in his stride.

"Please, Nick." Handaar's voice hitched on the plea. "I have no one left now."

Nick turned, and at the sight of the old warrior, his once broad shoulders stooped with age and sorrow, Nick's chest tightened. He recrossed the hall and embraced Handaar while the man's shoulders shook.

"Ah, Nick," Handaar gasped, "I miss her so already."

"Forgive me, old friend, for my callousness," Nick said. "Never would I want to further your grief. But I cannot stay within these walls when every stone carries Evelyn's memory."

Handaar nodded, clutching Nick's arms and drawing away to look at him. His voice was gruff when he spoke. "Of course I forgive you. But 'tis my hope that you'll not stay from Obny forever."

Nick shook his head. "I will return."

Handaar nodded and released Nick, his wide, gnarled hands suspended in the air for a moment, as if reluctant to let him go. Nick saw their tremble. "Safe journey, my son. Godspeed."

With a final squeeze of Handaar's shoulder, Nick spun on his heel and departed Obny's hall, leaving Handaar alone with only the ghosts of his wife and daughter for company.

Chapter 1

September 1077
London, England

Simone du Roche perched upon her gilded stool in the king's grand ballroom, her rich velvet kirtle puddling in deep, green pools at her feet. Her black mane was intricately braided and twined around her headpiece, held at a lofty angle, and her cat-green eyes beheld the other guests with barely concealed disdain as they pranced about to the twanging music.

'Twas the third and final evening of King William's birthday celebration, and Simone was infinitely glad. With the conclusion of tonight's fete, she would finally be freed from the curious stares and hushed whispers aimed in her direction by the petty and spiteful lords and ladies that infested the English court.

Simone ground her teeth into a tight smile as a flabby noble nodded toward her.

He tries to be charming, Simone fumed to herself, *and yet the dunce knows not that I understood every scathing word his companion said about me.*

"He is too fat, Sister," Didier whispered to her in their native French tongue. "He would smash you, were he your husband."

Simone hid a wicked grin behind the veil attached to her headpiece and whispered back, "Didier, quiet! You are too young by far to have such knowledge of a husband and wife." Keeping her head turned to hide her mouth, she added to the boy, "Would that you had stayed behind in our rooms as I asked. I cannot help but feel you will yet cause me trouble this night."

Didier merely shrugged his bony shoulders. His elfin face was a younger version of Simone's, with identical green eyes and a mop of unruly, raven hair.

"I dislike being left alone, and no one has noticed me thus far," the boy reasoned.

"Regardless, you must not speak to me so freely here. 'Twill draw attention I do not wish." Simone smoothed her veil back into place and rested her hands demurely—she hoped—in her lap.

The set ended and the soft, old lord who had earlier caught Simone's eye parted from his companion. His fine, fur-trimmed tunic billowed from his considerable backside as he waddled toward her. *At least he has a kind face,* Simone conceded.

Didier snickered beside her. "Speaking of unwanted attention, the fat one cometh."

Simone steeled her face into a calm mask as the short, round noble bowed before her. He addressed her in French.

"Lady du Roche, it does not seem appropriate for one of your beauty to sit unattended at such a celebration. Your father has given permission for you to join in the next dance."

Of course he has, Simone thought to herself. *You are a rich old man and 'tis my duty to display the wares.*

But aloud, she said only, "The pleasure is mine, Monsieur Halbrook." And then she placed her fingers into his damp, thick palm with an inward shudder.

He would smash you, were he your husband.

As Halbrook led her to the center of the ballroom and the opening notes of the next set began, Simone struggled not to bolt from the line of ladies she joined and run back to the relative safety of her rented rooms.

Armand du Roche caught Simone's eye as the women sank into a low curtsey. Simone's father inclined his head ever so slightly, his auburn hair falling across the wicked scar on his forehead, to indicate the portly lord opposite her. He raised an eyebrow.

He will do, non?

Simone broke gaze with her father to plaster the required smile to her face and concentrate on the set.

Oui, Papa, he will do.

It no longer mattered to Simone whom Armand chose as her husband. Simone, her father, and even young Didier were outcasts in this foreign country, oddities to be whispered about by the gluttonous English. Her entire life was a lie.

Her feet followed the steps mechanically, and she wrapped the coldness of the truth around her like an icy shield.

"You are late, Brother," Tristan scolded as Nicholas approached. When Nick stumbled into a tall, delicate urn near them, Tristan added, "And also quite drunk, 'twould appear."

Nick caught the teetering vase just in time and sent Tristan a lopsided grin. "I had some rather pressing business to attend to, I assure you. Lady Haith, you look ravishing this evening. Mother sends her love."

Nicholas took his sister-in-law's hand and leaned in to peck her cheek. His lips barely landed on her ear and Haith rushed to steady him.

"Lord Nicholas," she choked. "Would this business entail dousing yourself in a vat of ladies' cologne?"

"My apologies, m'lady." Nick grinned despite Tristan's glare, as his brother caught wind of him.

"Good God, Nick! You might have at least bathed. 'Twill not be good for William to see you in this state. You know he will wish to meet with you while you're in London."

Nicholas shrugged. "'Tis no matter. William will care not

that I have raised a cup or two—only that I bring word that his border is safe."

Nick's beautiful sister-in-law looked to her husband. "My lord, mayhap 'twould be best if we accompanied Nick to his rooms. 'Twill not do for him to be seen in this condition."

"It cannot be helped, my sweet," Tristan replied to the red-haired woman with chagrin. "The ladies have already spied him. He is trapped, I'm afraid."

Nick turned to the room behind him and indeed saw several pairs of feminine eyes pinned to him as the ladies impatiently finished the current set.

He chuckled with unabashed glee. "Yea, I am trapped, and what a gentle snare it is!"

"Nicholas," Tristan warned, "the purpose of your attending the king's birthday celebration—of which you've not deemed worthy of your presence until now—is to find a suitable bride. Not to bed the entire female population."

Lady Haith rolled her eyes at the crude conversation and turned her back to the brothers, sipping her wine and admiring the dancers.

"'Tis only what I've been doing, Brother," Nick insisted. "I've been most harried, attempting to determine each lady's worth." Nick wiggled his eyebrows. "My investigations have been quite thorough."

Tristan leaned closer, and through the haze of drink, Nick caught a glimpse of concern—or was it disapproval—in his brother's blue eyes.

"This is no good, Nick," Tristan advised quietly. "You can drink and wench until the end of your days and 'twill not bring Lady Evelyn back to you."

"Do not mention the cow's name to me," Nick growled, all tipsy good humor gone. "Her deceit has no bearing on how I choose to entertain myself. She means naught to me."

"Really?" Tristan raised an eyebrow. "Is that why all the ladies presented to you thus far have been too dark or too wide, too tall, or having eyes of the wrong shade?"

Nick glared at his brother. "Mind your own affairs."

"I am merely suggesting—"

"Well, do not." Nick seized the chalice Tristan held and took a healthy gulp. His eyes scanned the bobbing, twirling crowd with less enthusiasm now, his earlier joviality diminished after his brother's meddling observations.

Many of the ladies in attendance openly stared at him, their eyes issuing blatant invitations—particularly those whose favors he'd already sampled. There were some new faces among the dancers, he noticed—young girls recently put out to market by their families and eager to make a profitable match. Although several were quite fetching and would make for enjoyable sport, none sparked any real interest in Nicholas.

'Twas as if he gazed over an open field dotted with cattle— each cow having slightly varying features, but when viewed as a whole, none were discernable from the herd.

Evelyn's face came to his mind's eye totally unbidden, as it was wont to do. Heavy shocks of wavy, auburn hair framing the calm, blue eyes of a winter sky. The delicate constellation of freckles across her rosy cheeks haunted him here when faced with the carefully composed masks of the ladies before him.

For the thousandth time, he scolded himself. *Would that I had seized her from the convent,* he thought. *The very night I learned of her flight, I should have ridden to the priory at Withington and brought her back to Hartmoore, willing or nay.*

But just as quickly as the thought blossomed, it withered and died. He would not press his suit to a woman who so obviously didn't want him. Even now, Evelyn's messages to him remained unopened. He could not bring himself to read the excuses and apologies the letters surely contained. She had deserted him, refused him.

Humiliated him.

The set ended then, and the crowd was dispersing evenly from the floor. Nick raised his commandeered chalice to his lips, but his arm paused halfway as he glimpsed the delicate creature being led from the crush by elderly Lord Cecil Halbrook.

She appeared impossibly tiny, even when paired with her portly partner, and Nick fancied that the crown of her head would not reach his shoulder. Her green gown trailed behind her in a regal swath, and when her downcast face tilted slightly in Nick's direction, his breath seized in his throat.

The greenest eyes he'd ever seen pierced him with their gaze. The lady only glanced at him, a fact that pricked at his pride, before bowing her raven-tressed head once more.

"Fetching, is she not?" Lady Haith asked lightly, once more addressing the brothers.

"Hmmm," Tristan replied.

Nick shook his head slightly as if to clear away the cobwebs that had enveloped it. "Who is she?"

"Lady Simone du Roche," Haith said. "Arrived recently from France with her father."

"Is she game?" Nick's eyes followed the beauty as Halbrook deposited her on a stool some distance away. Her partner immediately dismissed her and stepped away to speak to a tall, bullish man standing nearby. Left to her own devices, the woman averted her face into her veil, hiding her porcelain features.

"Indeed, she is game," Tristan replied. "The odd-looking brute to her left is her father, Armand du Roche. 'Twould seem her most recent dance partner has taken more than a passing interest in her."

"But why would she be presented at English court?" Nick asked. "Surely there was no dearth of French suitors for a titled lady as lovely as she?"

Tristan shrugged and then inclined his head toward his wife. "My lady?"

Haith's eyes sparkled as she leaned closer to Nick. "There was a fantastic scandal in her homeland. She was betrothed to an old, noble family, but the contract was broken by her intended on the very day they were to wed." Haith lowered her voice even further. "'Tis said she's quite mad."

"Mad?" Nick was only partly listening to the information about the woman he could not take his eyes from.

"'Tis rumored that she hears voices in her head—speaks to people who aren't there." Haith sniffed. "But I do not believe that for an instant. I think—"

Nick shoved his brother's chalice at Haith, effectively silencing her. "I must speak to her," he said before straightening his slightly rumpled tunic and striding in her direction.

After Nick had departed, Tristan turned to look down at his wife, who still stared intently at the dark-haired woman.

"What think you, my lady?" he asked. "Will Nick make yet another conquest out of the girl?"

A devious smile curled Haith's lips. "I think mayhap if he is not wary, Nicholas could find himself the one conquered."

"Might I visit the other hall, Sister?" Didier asked as soon as Simone was returned to her stool. "I saw some wondrous cakes I'd care to sample."

Simone dropped her chin and turned her head slightly before murmuring, "Nay, Didier. You shall remain here with me until Papa says 'tis time to depart."

"*Why-y-y?*" the boy whined, causing Simone to wince. "I've not had a sweet in so long—none shall notice me, I swear!"

Simone gave an unladylike snort. "Oh, verily, no one at all would notice tiny morsels of food rising from the buffet and then falling upon the floor." As soon as the words left her lips, Simone regretted her sarcasm. She softened her tone. "You've told me before that you can no longer taste, Didier—what would be the purpose?"

"I can imagine it," the boy said, casting hurt eyes to the marble floor beneath his feet. "If I try very hard, I can almost recall the taste of honey."

His words wrenched Simone's heart, and she smiled sadly at him through her veil. "Mayhap when we return to our rooms, I will have a tray sent up and then you can play a bit."

Didier sighed. His head popped up once more, and a devilish smile lit his gamine face. "Who's this coming to visit, I wonder. I've not seen *him* before."

Simone glanced out of the corner of her eye to see whom Didier was referring to, and nearly gasped aloud.

A large man, easily a half-head taller than Simone's father, was weaving his way through the crowd toward her. She noticed with an odd sensation in her middle the way the ladies he passed followed him with their eyes in a most familiar manner.

And it was no wonder that he held the female guests' attention—he certainly had Simone enthralled. From the dark hair curling to his shoulders, the penetrating gaze of his blue eyes that captured Simone's and held them, the hard line of jaw that chiseled the planes of his face into a sculpture, the man was a god.

His full lips cocked at one corner into a sleepy smile, and the warmth it created in Simone was as delicious as it was unsettling. His fine tunic and cloak indicated that he was a man of wealth and status—or had been, at any rate. The embroidered cloth was stained and wrinkled, and Simone thought she might have glimpsed the straggling threads of a poorly repaired hem. But his gait was confident—even a bit arrogant—as he drew nearer and nearer Simone and her brother.

"Didier," she hissed in warning. "Not a *word*." Simone calmly turned her face from her veil to look at the magnificent man who had stopped before her and was now bowing deeply. He nearly tipped sideways.

"My lady," he said, the rich timbre of his voice sending warm ripples over Simone's skin. "I hope you do not perceive me as bold in approaching you without introduction, but I fear I could not restrain myself. Your beauty drew me to you like the lowly moth to a brilliant flame, and I felt I must seize the opportunity to speak to you lest you vanish like the vision you appear to be."

"Oh, la-la!" Didier laughed directly into Simone's ear. "Methinks the man wishes your gown to vanish, the way he ogles you!"

Simone's smile faltered at Didier's bawdy comment, but she quickly recovered and placed her fingertips in the man's offered palm.

He bent once more to brush warm, dry lips across her knuckles, his eyes never leaving her face. Simone's skin tingled even after his touch, and when he spoke again, her stomach felt as though a litter of piglets had been set loose within.

"I am Nicholas FitzTodd, Baron of Crane," he offered, flashing a glimpse of white, even teeth.

"Oooh," Didier said in a singsong voice. "*A baron!*"

Simone stopped gritting her teeth to open her mouth and give the man her name, but he raised a silencing hand.

"Again, forgive me, Lady du Roche," he offered with a boyish grin. "I must admit that I asked after you upon my arrival." He gestured discreetly across the breadth of the hall toward a handsome couple. "My brother and his wife are my informants."

Simone eyed the large blond man and striking redhead warily and was quite disarmed when the woman raised a hand near her face and wiggled her fingers at Simone. Simone inclined her head in acknowledgment before turning her attention once more to the baron.

"Then I must be sure to extend my thanks to them before departing London," Simone said, her voice husky with the enchantment the man's very presence seemed to cast over her.

On the floor near her stool, Didier howled. The boy clutched at his ribs and hiccoughed with laughter.

"Do you thirst?" the baron asked. "Might I fetch you some wine?"

"*Merci,*" Simone replied. The man nodded with a heart-stopping grin and disappeared through the throng once more, and Simone whipped her head about to glare at her brother.

"*Didier!* Get up from the floor this instant!"

Fat, silvery tears of mirth rolled down the boy's cheeks. "*M-m-merci,* lover!" he cried, reaching a spindly arm after the departing man.

"Stop it, I said!" Simone felt the heat of her flush to her hairline.

Her brother finally pulled himself together enough to stand, wiping at his cheeks with the backs of both hands. "Ah,

Sister—that was wonderful! You forgot yourself so that you spoke English!"

Simone cringed. That the guests assumed she spoke only French was her single defense among the enemies. Should their hosts find out her deception, her chances for a profitable match would dwindle against their bruised pride.

"If you would cease goading me so, mayhap I would not forget myself," she snipped. A groan of dread escaped her as Armand limped toward her. "Now, do be good—here comes Papa and that Halbrook man."

"Simone." Her father towered over her, but Simone could not help but notice how much more of her view of the hall had been blocked by the Baron of Crane's muscular form. "You are enjoying yourself?"

"*Oui,* Papa."

Lord Halbrook hovered on the perimeter of Armand's presence, casting grandfatherly smiles in Simone's direction, and she gave an inward shudder.

"*Bon.* Lord Halbrook and I would find a more private area to discuss . . . ah, a *business matter.*" Armand's emphasis on his last words caused Simone's heart to skip a beat and her eyes to fly involuntarily to the round noble at her father's side.

Armand's nod was nearly imperceptible, and his mouth twisted into an awkward smile. "Are you able to entertain yourself if we leave you for a time?"

"Of course." Simone dropped her gaze as her father moved away in his hitching gait, Halbrook waddling along after him. She barely acknowledged the man's stumbling "Mademoiselle" in parting.

"Simone's getting married, Simone's getting married," Didier sang, skipping circles around her stool.

"'Twould seem so," Simone sighed. And while the thought of becoming the wife of an aged, pot-bellied dwarf of a man did not please her in the least, she knew she would comply.

"Oh, Didier," she said quietly, not bothering to shield her mouth. "If only *Maman* were still alive. We would be at home in France and I would, by now, be Charles's wife."

"Charles never cared for me," Didier said, his tone more subdued now as he sat at Simone's feet and rested his small head against her leg.

Simone ached to brush her hand over Didier's springy curls but, displayed as she was, she knew she could not. "Charles did care for you, Didier, he merely did not know what to do with you. There were not many children at the Beauville estate."

She caught sight of the Baron of Crane snaking toward her once more, a chalice in each hand and that private, sleepy smile across his face. Her stomach fluttered. Perhaps it was only Armand's recent disclosure of Halbrook's intent to offer for her, but the sight of Nicholas FitzTodd sparked a myriad of forbidden images to singe and sparkle through her mind.

Thoughts of pressing her body against his solid form, of letting him touch her lips with his own. To have one perfect moment within strong, muscled arms, refusing to think further than his next kiss, his next touch, his next scandalous whisper in her ear.

"Sister, you're trembling," Didier said before looking up and spying the baron's approach. A sly grin split his face, displaying proudly the gap where he'd lost a tooth more than a year ago. Simone was not charmed by his impish good looks, however, and sent him a withering warning glare.

"Lady du Roche," the baron said as he handed her a cup. "Perhaps you would care to take some air? It has grown rather close in here, do you not agree?"

Simone caught the sparkle of wicked intentions in those hopelessly blue eyes over the rim of her chalice, and a reckless abandon pulled at her—a nearly frantic desire to steal away with him, if only for a moment or two. Simone had heard tales of men of the baron's ilk, knew that he wanted nothing more than to seduce her. She also knew that any impropriety on her part could bring Armand's plans to see her wed crashing down.

But visions of a future with the pudgy Halbrook loomed in her mind and, suddenly, Simone simply did not care. This could very well be her first, her last, her *only* chance to experience passion. To make memories of one night's folly to sustain her through her lot as a bartered bride. And the baron's smile was too tempting by half.

Didier's urgent whisper of "Go on, Sister" seemed to echo in her own heart's rapid tattoo, and she rose from the stool on trembling legs.

"There is naught I would enjoy more."

Chapter 2

Nick's heart thudded in anticipation as he steered the diminutive Lady du Roche through the mazelike passages. He'd been correct at guessing her size—her complicated coif barely topped his shoulder as she glided along silently beside him. His mind filled with the possibilities of how their differences in size would play out within the confines of a bed.

He guided her through a gilded doorway and across a sparsely furnished chamber to a set of double doors. A private balcony lay beyond, sheltered on three sides from the brunt of the night's brisk breeze. Lady du Roche left Nick's side to stand at the carved stone railing and gaze across the night-soaked gardens below, her chalice gripped tightly in both hands.

And so the hunt begins. Nick grinned in the shadows as he shrugged out of his cloak and moved to stand behind the shapely woman.

"Are you chilled?" he asked softly, swirling his cloak about her.

She glanced at him over her shoulder and pulled his cloak closed with one hand, her cool flesh just grazing the insides of his palms. *"Merci."*

The warm scent of musky lavender wafted up from the delicate curve of her neck, and Nicholas moved away a step. The combination of her heady fragrance and the sight of her enveloped in his cloak was prompting his baser instincts, and Nick knew it was necessary to cool his urges if he was to woo the lady properly. He could not lift her onto the railing and disappear beneath her skirts, where the scent of lavender would surely be—

He took a deep gulp of the cold air and sent her a friendly smile. "You did not seem to be enjoying the celebration as I imagine most ladies do," he offered, attempting to set her at ease with light conversation.

Lady du Roche shrugged and sipped from her chalice before speaking. "What is to be enjoyed? Dancing with fat old men whom I hold no liking for while they grope me to determine my worth as a brood mare? 'Tis barbaric."

Nick's eyebrows rose. Such fire! He never would have guessed from her cool exterior. "The rumors are true, then?"

Her head swung to face him, green eyes flashing in the dim light of the balcony. "Of what rumors do you speak?"

"'Tis said you come to London to find a husband," Nick explained, wondering at her hostility.

"Oh." Lady du Roche visibly relaxed and then looked away from him again. "*Oui.* 'Twould seem that search is nearly at its end—even now, my father makes arrangements with my future husband."

"*Halbrook?*" Nick asked, remembering the aging lord whom he'd seen speaking to the lady's father. "He has grandchildren older than you!"

"But he is very wealthy," Lady du Roche sighed. "And that is the only criterion on which there seems to be no compromise."

"Have you an affection for him?"

Nick was surprised at her laugh—clear and bubbling, like water tumbling over rocks. "Nay, my lord. I have learned that affection plays no part in this business of marriage." She glanced at him again. "If I were in love with him, why would I be here with you now?"

Her words were painfully honest and brought to Nick's

mind Evelyn's betrayal. Perhaps this woman had been burned as well—hadn't Lady Haith mentioned a broken betrothal?

"Ah, beautiful *and* wise," he murmured, his eyes roving her delicate features. "You do not dread living out your days with a doddering ancient?"

"As you said, he is old. With luck, I will outlive him and one day be left in peace." She turned to him, leaning her hip against the railing, her features shadowed by the moon over her shoulder. "Perhaps he is not so old that he might yet give me a child to keep my company."

"Your words are bold," Nick said, sidling closer to her until he could feel her heat. "'Tis a shame for a woman of such passion to be paired with one so aged and dwindling—he will never make you burn."

He saw her smirk in the intimate space between them, and she chuckled. "Do you think you might accomplish that task if given the chance, Nicholas FitzTodd, Baron of Crane?" It was almost as if she mocked him.

Nick was shocked into silence for a moment. He tugged the chalice from her grip and set it on the railing. Reaching out a hand, he laid it alongside the warm, soft skin of her neck, forcing her to look up at him. He heard her soft breath at the physical contact and smiled when she would not meet his eyes. Nick thought it best to teach the girl to what ends teasing would gain her.

"Verily, Lady du Roche," he began, "I—"

"Simone," she amended in a husky whisper, glancing into his eyes for only an instant. "My name is Simone."

"*Simone,*" Nick repeated, drawing out the syllables of her name even as he pulled her closer. "Shall I demonstrate my abilities for you?"

Just when Nick expected her retreat, Simone reached her hand from beneath the confines of the cloak and laid it upon his chest. Her eyes found his, and the invitation he saw there, the raw need, tested his resolve to move slowly.

She licked her lips, a fleeting dart of pink tongue. "Please do . . . *Nicholas.*"

He dropped his mouth to hers and pulled her fully against him. She tasted of honeyed wine and autumn's chill, and the sweetness of her small hands cupping his face shook Nicholas in a way no other dalliance with a woman had.

He slipped his free hand beneath the cloak to find her waist, then wrapped his forearm behind her, lifting her slightly. Simone's hands smoothed to the back of his head, holding him to her mouth as tightly as Nicholas himself clung.

Nick wrenched his mouth from hers. "Lady Simone, have a care. I am not known for my restraint," he said, giving her opportunity for escape.

He could feel her breasts pressing against him with each breath as she looked up at him. "Then why did you stop?"

The sight of her lips parted like wet rubies and the innocent impatience flashing in her eyes destroyed any thought of return for Nicholas. He pulled her head to his to once more seize her mouth. His hand dropped to her collarbone, smoothed over her shoulder, and down to cup her breast.

Simone gasped at the intimate touch, and he raised his head slightly. "I should warn you," he whispered, "if this is some intricate plot to ensnare me as your husband, 'twill not work. I do not yield to feminine trickery."

Simone's eyes sparkled and one delicate eyebrow arched. She even huffed a short breath of laughter. "Fear not, Lord Nicholas. My betrothal is all but sealed, and any matter, you would not be a suitable match for me."

She leaned forward and closed her eyes as if eager for the kiss to continue, but Nick avoided her lips.

"Why do you say that?" he demanded, feeling a frown pull at his mouth and brow. She opened her eyes with a sigh of impatience, and he continued. "Because I am younger than four score?"

"Nay." Simone blinked, as if surprised. "'Tis because I think you a drunkard and a braggart and, most likely, you do not possess the wealth my father requires of my husband." She leaned in once more, but Nicholas retreated further.

"What in God's holy name led you to those conclusions?"

"Simple observation," Simone said, quite matter-of-factly. "When first you approached me, you stumbled on your feet and your tunic looked as though it had been used to clean a privy." She bowed her nose to touch his chest and sniffed. "You smell of cheap woman and drink. What else am I to assume but that you are a penniless womanizer?"

She must have mistook the choked sound Nick made for a different emotion, for she placed a silencing finger across his lips and continued.

"Be not shamed, *mon cher,*" she whispered. "I care not for your wealth."

Nick shook his head to rid himself of her pitying touch. Was he not good enough for any woman? First Evelyn, and now this pixie of a girl thought him unworthy? Mayhap his costume was a bit bedraggled from his earlier festivities, but God's teeth! Cecil Halbrook was one of Nick's own under-lords and he could buy the old codger a hundred times over.

"'Tis well then, my lady," he growled. "For on this night, I will leave you with such memories that even all the king's riches could never erase me from your mind."

He seized her again, this time roughly, grabbing her upper arms in viselike fists and dragging her against him. Simone's head reeled from his assault on her mouth. There was not a spot within that remained untouched by his hot tongue, and when he pushed her back against the railing, his hands roaming her body freely, she could not stifle her groan.

It was so very exciting! Sensations flooded Simone beyond her expectations—her legs were heavy and weak, and a warm ache began to wind in her midsection. Charles had kissed her before, even touched her leg on occasion, but not like this.

Never like this.

"Simone!" The whisper hissed directly in her ear—Didier's voice—but Simone only squeezed her eyes more tightly shut and willed him to disappear.

"*Sister!*" Didier implored. "You must listen to me!"

"Not now," Simone groaned against the baron's lips.

Nicholas raised his head slightly. "Of course," he breathed, his gaze devouring her face. "I will take you to my private rooms."

Simone shook her head and pulled his lips back to hers.

"Sister—"

"*Go away,*" she mumbled.

"What say you, Lady du Roche?" Nicholas demanded, his voice ragged. He made as if to draw away from her. "Would you now refuse me after leading me on your merry chase?"

Simone made a small mewing sound in her throat and pulled the baron's hand beneath the cloak. "Nay, my lord. I—"

"*Papa is coming!*" Didier shrieked.

The double doors to the balcony burst outward and Armand du Roche stepped through, Lord Halbrook close on his heels.

The blond man from the ball and his wife also appeared, the red-haired woman looking decidedly worried. Her husband, however, seemed not at all surprised.

"Simone!" Armand hissed, causing her to realize she was still pressed intimately against the Baron of Crane. She started, pushing away from Nicholas and frantically straightening her gown. She shrugged out of the borrowed cloak and shoved it at its owner.

"Papa, I—"

"*Non!*" Armand shouted. The right side of his face spasmed beneath his age-whitened scar, and his right arm was drawn against his side. He continued his rebuke in rapid-fire French. "No excuses! You were to remain in the hall and yet, the instant I am gone, you abscond with this . . . this"—he sneered in the baron's direction, spittle flying from his lips—"*rogue* to play the harlot!"

Simone dropped her eyes to the flagstones beneath her slippers, a hot sweep of embarrassment burning her ears. "I am sorry, Papa."

"And *you!*" Armand switched to English as he addressed

Nicholas. "You should be whipped for assaulting a lady in such a manner!"

"I do beg pardon, Lord du Roche," Nicholas said easily, donning his cloak and fastening it with care. "But perhaps you should know 'twas your daughter who propositioned me."

Simone gasped and whirled to face him. "Liar! You lured me here!"

"Ha! I had to run to keep up with you!"

The red-haired woman turned to her husband. "Can you not do something?"

The man shook his head and chuckled. "Ah, Nick. So you strike again."

"And with my betrothed, no less." The portly lord elbowed his way into the midst of the fray.

Armand turned to look down at the old man. "You know this fop, Halbrook?"

"Yea, the baron and I are acquainted."

Nicholas extended his hand to the old man. "Cecil, you're looking well. My deepest sympathies on your impending nuptials."

Simone shrieked in wordless rage.

Halbrook released Nick's forearm with a flustered look at Simone. "Ah, er . . . my thanks. Good to see you again, my lord."

Nicholas then turned to Armand. "I don't believe we've met. I'm Nicholas Fi—"

"I heard who you are," Armand ground out, cutting Nicholas short and ignoring his proffered hand. He spoke to Simone over his shoulder, as if he could not bear the sight of her. "Fetch our cloaks and wait for me."

Simone reached a hand toward her father's back. "Papa, you must not believe a word he says! He—"

"Go now, Simone!"

Simone dropped her hand and turned toward the doors but, in her fury, paused long enough to toss at Nicholas, "You are naught but a . . . a cowardly beggar, and I shall hate you forever!"

Nicholas growled and took a menacing step toward her, but the redheaded woman intervened, taking firm hold of Simone's arm and dragging her from the balcony.

Once inside the chamber, Simone jerked her arm free and stormed toward the corridor, the woman close on her heels.

"Lady du Roche, wait," she called as Simone gained the doors.

Simone spun around, her arm pointing toward the balcony. "That man," she said, "is a bastard!"

The woman gave her a sheepish "I know" smile. "I am Haith D'Argent, the baron's sister-in-law. Might I walk with you to retrieve your things?"

"*Non.* I wish to be alone." Simone wrenched the heavy chamber door open and disappeared into the passageway.

"Didier!" she hissed as she made her way—she hoped—toward the hall, trying to recall the correct turns. Right or left here? Her cheeks flamed when she realized she'd been too caught up in the baron's attentions to notice the way they'd come. "Didier, where are you?"

"Who is Didier?"

Simone jumped at the sound of Lady Haith's voice directly behind her. "I said I wish to be alone," she said over her shoulder before turning left and stalking in that direction.

"Very well," Haith called down the corridor, "but you're going the wrong way."

Simone stopped and closed her eyes, taking deep breaths and trying desperately not to cry. When she had composed herself, she turned to see Lady Haith still waiting, a sympathetic smile on her lips.

And Didier stood right beside the woman, staring up at the redhead as if she were some Celtic goddess of old.

Simone quickly made her way back to the intersecting passages, trying not to glance in her brother's direction. "Please forgive my rudeness, Lady Haith," she said. "I've had a trying evening and wish only to return to my rooms."

"Of course," the woman said kindly. "This way."

"I'm sorry, Sister," Didier said, falling into step between the two women. "But I *did* try to warn you."

"Wait." Haith stilled and looked to Simone. "Did you hear that?"

Simone's heart skipped. "Hear what?"

Haith frowned. "Naught, I suppose." To Simone's relief, they began to walk once more.

"Can you *hear* me?" Didier asked, his voice incredulous.

"There it is again!" Haith again halted and turned wide eyes to Simone. "Did you not hear it? 'Twas almost like a whisper!"

"*Non,*" Simone said, a trifle loudly for the close space. "I heard naught."

"She can hear me, Sister!" Didier cried.

"Please," Simone said to Haith. She could feel the panic begin to creep up. "If you could but point me in the direction of the entry hall, I really must go. My father will be along and he is already quite angry with me. I—"

"But, Sister—"

"Lady du Roche—"

"*Non!*" Simone interjected, cutting off both the woman and the boy. "I'm sorry. I heard naught."

Haith stared at her for a long moment. So intently, in fact, that Simone fancied the woman was trying to discern her very thoughts. She could feel cold beads of sweat blooming along her hairline and upper lip.

Finally, the woman sighed and gestured down the passageway. "A left, and then a right turn."

"My thanks," Simone breathed and moved away as quickly as she could without running. But she was not to escape before hearing Lady Haith's parting words called down the corridor after her.

"I do hope to see you again, Lady du Roche," she said. "And Didier as well!"

Chapter 3

Simone sat curled in the upholstered armchair in her chamber, awaiting her father's return with no little trepidation.

After what had seemed like hours in an empty receiving hall, a footman had arrived to see her to her father's rented rooms and told her that Armand would join her later.

That had been near midnight, and now, dawn wavered on the horizon.

She wondered for the hundredth time what could be keeping him. Any number of scenarios she crafted in answer struck fear in her, and she sank deeper under the robes piled over her.

The small fire in the hearth crackled and popped as it devoured the stout wood lengths and sent a cozy glow creeping across the rug, but Simone's tiny bedchamber was frigid. Didier was highly agitated following the evening's events and whenever that occurred, a deep chill descended around his presence.

The boy paced the room in his own strange manner, flitting from one corner to the next—appearing first on the wide, canopied bed and then, in an instant, seated cross-legged before the hearth. His darting about grated on Simone's already-worn nerves, and she scrubbed her hands over her face before giving a frustrated shriek.

"Didier! Can you not be still for one moment?"

Her brother said nothing, merely sent her a glare from his seated position in front of the—

No, now he scowled at her from the window ledge.

"You are making my head spin," she pleaded, noting with bad temper that she could now see her breath when she spoke. "Do you not calm yourself, I'll likely freeze to death before Papa returns."

"Good," the boy spat. "Mayhap then you will know what it's like."

"What *what* is like?" Simone sighed, rubbing her arms vigorously beneath the robes as another icy blast curled around her chair.

"Being ignored!" Didier now stood before her, his small fists planted on his hips. "Why did you not explain to the lady that the whispering she heard was me?"

Simone shook the fine layer of frost from her blankets. "Is it your wish to see me locked away for madness?"

"How could she accuse you of madness if she could also hear me?" Didier reasoned. "The moment I saw her, I felt she might be able to help us."

The temperature of the room had risen slightly, signaling to Simone that Didier's fit of pique was subsiding. Her teeth no longer chattered, and she could almost feel her fingers.

"How do you mean?"

"I know not, exactly," Didier said, a frown wrinkling his face. He flapped a hand at Simone's robes. "Let me sit with you."

Simone lifted the covering aside with a grimace as Didier climbed into the chair beside her, bringing a little extra chill with him.

"I'm sorry 'tis so cold," he offered, snuggling as best he could to Simone's side.

"No matter." Simone tried to give him a reassuring smile. "'Twill soon pass, as it always does."

Didier was silent for several moments as the pair stared into the hearth, waiting for the room to warm. When he did speak, his tone was filled with concern.

"What do you think Papa will do now?"

"I have no earthly idea," Simone sighed. "I suppose 'twill depend on Lord Halbrook's reaction."

"Will he still marry you?"

"For all our sakes, I hope so." Simone's mouth thinned as she thought of the scene on the balcony and the baron's blunt admission of her willingness to yield to him. Her ears burned once more as she recalled the wanton embrace the pair had been caught in.

Cad. Traitor. Drunken, selfish fop!

But, oh, how she'd felt in his arms! Free and treasured and desirable. Simone wondered if she was incredibly naïve for a man's attentions to affect her so. She also wondered if Lord Halbrook's embrace would elicit the same reaction, but the possibility was squashed as a vision of the fattened elder filled her mind.

She shuddered.

When she had been betrothed to Charles Beauville in France, she had, over time, granted him certain privileges with her person: a kiss here, an embrace there. She had known Charles her entire life and, if not passionate, his touch was comforting and safe. If there had been one person besides her mother that Simone felt she could trust with her greatest confidences, it had been Charles Beauville.

And still, he had betrayed her.

Tonight, the Baron of Crane—a veritable stranger—had kissed her and touched her and made her feel terrifying sensations. He had been crass and painfully blunt in stating what he wanted from her. He did not love her, would not court her, yet she would have given herself to him readily.

And he had betrayed her as well.

"Do you care for the baron?" Didier asked in a small voice, interrupting Simone's visions of blue eyes and damnably soft, masculine lips.

"What?" Simone sent her brother a frown. "Of course not. Why would you ask such?"

"I've not seen anyone kiss like that." He grinned up at

Simone before adding, "Save for the tavern wench in the village at home."

"Didier! That woman was a prostitute!"

The boy giggled. "I know."

"So you would liken your sister to a common harlot?"

"Then explain why you went off with him," Didier demanded. "Why risk Papa's plans with a man you care naught for?"

When Simone hesitated, Didier offered her a sympathetic smile. "Sister, are you in heat?"

"*Didier du Roche!*" Simone shrieked and bolted from the chair. She stalked to the bed, and her cheeks throbbed as she crawled upon the mattress.

"Well, are you?" Didier appeared, seated, on the bed. "That's how horses and dogs—"

"I am neither a horse nor a dog and I most definitely am not"—she sputtered—"*in heat!*"

"Very well—calm yourself, Sister. 'Twas merely a question."

"If I could, I would smack your backside for asking it."

Didier guffawed and stretched out alongside Simone. "So then, tell me: why Lord Nicholas?"

Simone stared up at the canopy in the flickering quiet for a long while. How to explain her reckless impulses to an eight-year-old boy who was, in truth, no longer a boy, but a ghost. She could not grasp the reason herself why she chose to behave with such reckless abandon on the eve of what could possibly have been the most important night of her life.

Of all their lives.

After her mother's and Didier's deaths and Charles's betrayal, rumors of Simone's descent into madness had quickly spread. Portia du Roche had been quite liberal with the funds of Saint du Lac, and after her death it was discovered that there was no coin left to solicit a family of even modest means. Should she not marry well in England—and soon—she and her father would be paupers at the mercy of a foreign people.

With this weight resting solely on her shoulders, that she

would jeopardize her father's efforts for a few moments in the arms of a known seducer baffled her.

The Baron of Crane is not worth the dust on my slippers, she reasoned. *So why? Why?*

"I know not, Didier," she finally sighed. Her answer seemed to leave the boy unsatisfied, so she reached for any possible explanation. "Perhaps 'twas because he was so handsome and I was so miserable at the feast. Perhaps, for once, I merely wanted to do and say what I pleased."

"You chose a poor time to do so."

Simone sent her brother a wry smile.

Didier gazed thoughtfully at her. "Would you do the same if given another chance?"

"*Oui.*" The answer passed her lips before she'd taken time to think on it properly, and Simone was surprised by the truth of it. "*Oui,* I would do the same. I cannot explain it to you, or even to myself, really."

The memory of the baron's kisses flooded her mind so that she rose up on her knees and began untying the bed curtains to distract herself. She could feel Didier's gaze on her back as she struggled with a knot.

"Perhaps you needed his touch," Didier offered in a small, uncertain voice.

"What do you mean?" Simone let the freed curtain fall and crawled to the next post at the end of the bed.

"'Twas something *Maman* used to say," he replied. "When she was feeling sad or out of sorts, she would hold me very tightly." Didier's voice grew wistful. "She would say, 'Come here, my lovely boy, and sit upon my lap.' She told me that, oft times, when a person is lonely, they need only the touch of one they love to make them feel happy again."

Simone let the second curtain fall and sat back on her heels, tears welling in her eyes. She turned and crawled back to Didier, the remaining ties forgotten, and slid beneath the furs. She held up a corner of the coverings, and Didier joined her.

"Didier, I do not love the baron," she explained softly. "He was merely . . . convenient."

"I know." He avoided her gaze, smoothing his hand across the soft fur. His small fingers disappeared as they passed through a fold and reappeared on the other side. "I miss her."

"You will see her again, *chéri*," Simone encouraged. "We must simply bide our time until we can learn why she passed on and you did not."

"Do you think I'll go to Hell, Sister?" he asked in a small voice. "Is that why I am still here? Because God does not want me in Heaven?"

"I most certainly do not!" Simone whispered fiercely. "God and *Maman* will welcome you into Heaven, into their arms, one day very soon. You must believe that."

Didier nodded half-heartedly and then looked into Simone's eyes. "I think Lady Haith can help us. Truly. She is . . . different."

His gaze was so earnest, so hopeful, Simone was tentatively won over. "Very well, Didier," she acquiesced. "If I happen to encounter her again while we are in London, I will confide in her, if 'twill make you happy."

Didier's answering smile was radiant.

"But I hope you realize the danger telling another of your presence holds for me," she warned, thinking of Charles and his disgusted horror at her confidence.

"Lady Haith will not betray you, Sister," he promised solemnly. He looked as if he was going to say more, but then thought better of it as a rap sounded at the chamber door.

"'Tis Papa," he whispered. He placed an invisible kiss on Simone's cheek and then, in a blink, was gone.

Simone's stomach clenched when she heard the key scraping in the lock. She sank down into the soft mattress and pulled the furs to her chin as the door swung open and her father stepped inside the room, carrying a single candle.

"Simone? Do you sleep?" Armand asked in a low voice.

"*Non*, Papa." Her heart raced as he shut the door quietly behind him. His full, ruddy face was etched with fatigue, the

ever-present tic around his eye jumping wildly as he limped
across the chamber and placed the candle on a small table.

He is too calm, Simone thought as Armand came to stand
at the foot of her bed. His arm was drawn against his side and
he stared at her intently. *Something is terribly wrong.*

Her imagination ran unchecked: Lord Halbrook had called
off the betrothal and they would be forced to leave London
because of her scandalous behavior. Where would they go
now? The meager funds Armand had managed to gather for
the journey were nearly depleted and they could not return to
France.

"Simone, have you an explanation for your behavior?"

She swallowed, and the hairs rose on the back of her neck.
"*Non,* Papa."

Armand rubbed his withered arm and rocked on his heels.
His lips moved soundlessly as he stared at her, forming inaudible words.

And Simone stared back, too frightened to look away for
even an instant. Armand was eccentric, and not a little intimidating. His one quest since Simone could remember had
been to find some mysterious treasure, its worth reported by
Armand to be quite priceless. Her father was largely a
stranger to her, always away searching for his elusive prize
while Simone was growing up. When he was in residence at
Saint du Lac, he was brusque and moody, and not unlikely
to punish a misdeed with his fists. Even now, in his advanced
age, he was large and strong. Simone knew her rash behavior
this evening was beyond forgiveness, and she wondered if
he would whip her.

Finally he spoke. "You cannot reason to me why you deliberately disobeyed me? Why, the instant I left your side, you
sneaked away with a known seducer to let him fondle you for
any who may pass by to see?" He moved around the end of
the bed toward Simone.

Her voice was barely a whisper. "*Non,* Papa."

"Come to me," he commanded, standing at the bedside
now and beckoning to her with a finger.

Simone's entire body shook as she crawled from beneath the covers and sat on her heels before her father. She was eye level with him now, and she couldn't help but flinch when he raised his good hand to grasp her chin.

"I have an idea as to why you behaved as you did," he said.

Simone's throat barely allowed her to reply. "You do?"

"*Oui.*" The corner of his mouth not frozen into place crept upward. "'Tis because you are very, very clever."

Simone's eyes widened. "I am?"

Armand abruptly kissed both of Simone's cheeks and then crushed her to him with one arm. "So very clever!" he repeated with a laugh. He held her away again, beaming at her in a way Simone could not recall him doing the whole of her life. "When Halbrook saw you in the arms of the young baron, he tripled the amount he'd offered for you!"

Simone closed her eyes, her relief dizzying. "Oh, thank God."

Armand chuckled again, and when Simone opened her eyes, she saw him hovering over her dressing table. He searched among the items scattered there, mumbling to himself, before selecting one and returning to the bedside. He perched on the edge of the mattress and held up the item he'd chosen from her toilette.

A small, silver reflecting disc.

"Look, and tell me who you see."

Simone frowned and then glanced at her miniature reflection—her hair hung down in black sheets around her near-colorless face.

"Me?" she offered weakly.

Armand shook his head with a sly smile. "Who is 'me'?"

Simone gave a frustrated sigh. He father was eccentric to the point of exasperation. "Simone du Roche of Saint du Lac. Papa, I do not understand—"

"Say *au revoir* to this girl," Armand interrupted, "for she will soon be no more."

"Papa?"

Armand rose from the bed awkwardly, leaving Simone

with the mirror. He limped to the window and looked out over the soft dawn, washing the rather seedy street where their inn was located in flattering light, and then he smiled.

"I have done it, Simone—England is mine!" He turned to her, shaking a fist in the air and laughing as if he could not help himself. "In two days' time, you will become the Baroness of Crane!"

Simone's world tilted. "What?"

"You are to marry Nicholas FitzTodd, here in London, with William's own blessing!" Armand clarified, obviously pleased.

"*Non,*" Simone whispered, horrified. She instantly recalled with startling detail the warning Nicholas had whispered in her ear: *If this is some intricate plot to ensnare me as your husband, 'twill not work. I do not yield to feminine trickery.*

Armand beamed. "This is better than I ever could have hoped for!"

"But . . . but Nicholas FitzTodd is penniless!"

"Oh, not so, not so! Although he may appear to be a ne'er-do-well, the baron is actually one of the wealthiest nobles in England. His demesne stretches the whole of the Welsh border and he is one of the king's most trusted men."

Simone could barely think. "But how, Papa? Lord Nicholas himself told me he had no desire to marry."

Armand poured a cup of watered wine and sat in the upholstered chair with a contented sigh. He raised the cup to his lips as he answered, his words sounding oddly hollowed as they echoed into the vessel. "He simply has no choice." He took a sloppy gulp and swiped his lips with his sleeve. "I petitioned the king on behalf of your tarnished virtue, and 'twould seem that William has a desire to see the baron wed."

"My tarnished virtue?" Simone cried. "Papa, how could you? Naught of consequence occurred!"

"How am I to know that?" Armand held the cup out to her, his useless arm resting in his lap. "Or good Lord Halbrook, for that matter? You were wrapped up in the man's clothing, for God's sake—"

"His *cloak!* 'Twas cold!"

"—and he looking as though he'd just crawled from a brothel. Smelling like it, as well." Armand added, giving her a pointed look. "What else would I think?"

"But," Simone sputtered, "'tis your word against his!"

"Ah-ah," Armand corrected. "You forget that the baron's own brother was also witness to your display."

"Of course his brother would not condone this farce," Simone reasoned. "Surely he will speak to the king on the baron's behalf."

"He already has," Armand offered easily. "Although what was said is a mystery to me—the man spoke in private audience with William."

Simone sat dumbfounded for a moment. "Well, I care not. I'll not marry him, Papa."

Armand looked amused. "Don't be ridiculous—of course you'll marry him."

"*Non!*" Simone shrieked and beat a fist into the soft bedclothes. "He is vile and I hate him!"

"Ah, *quel dommage, ma petite fille.*" Too bad, my little girl. "Would that you had thought your plan through more fully, eh?"

"There was no plan," Simone cried, frustration and panic causing her to feel nauseated. "I was merely trying to escape for a time—to gain a reprieve from being traded like an animal at market!"

"Have a care for your tongue, Simone," Armand warned. "You seem to have forgotten that had you not convinced the Beauvilles of your madness, claiming my dead son spoke to you, we would have had no need to come to this barbaric city."

Simone knew it was of no use arguing yet again over Didier. Truthfully, Armand was right—had Simone not trusted Charles Beauville with her grief-stricken confidences, she would most likely be his wife now, and Armand would be far away, on another leg of his grand quest. Didier may have frozen them all to death by now, but that fate seemed infinitely preferable to the future she now faced.

"Please, Papa," Simone said, resorting to begging. "The baron will hate me for this. I will be miserable as his wife."

"You'll make the best of it, I am certain." He stood, signaling that the discussion was over. He limped toward the bed. "I will make arrangements for your possessions to be delivered to the baron's suite."

"Why there?" Simone asked, thinking of the tens of trunks that held the precious belongings of her mother's and Didier's. She had begged her father to allow those most personal items to accompany her to England, at the sacrifice of leaving most of her own possessions behind. Armand had complied, although now, the impoverished estate could not afford the considerable added cost. The trunks were still being held at the docks for payment until the time Armand could sell her to the highest bidder.

"Because, *enfant*," her father spoke to her as if she were once more a small child, "after you are wed, you will stay in your husband's apartments before you journey to his home. You do wish to have your things with you, *non?*"

Simone nodded.

"*Bon.* Now, go to sleep." Armand crossed the chamber and opened the door, pausing to speak to her once more over his shoulder. "For once, you have served me well, Simone."

And then she was blessedly alone.

Simone knew 'twould be impossible to convince Nicholas that she'd had no intention whatsoever of trapping him into marriage. He had suspected it from the first, and although she'd thought she'd made it clear that she was resigned to wed the elderly Halbrook, these new circumstances would do much to persuade him to believe otherwise. She could only hope that the baron had not yet heard the rumors that had chased her from France.

'Twas as if fate were out to thwart her at every turn.

Simone let the candle gut out on its own as she lay alone in the early morning light and cried herself to sleep.

Chapter 4

A great pounding filled Nick's skull, as if God's own fist struck the earth, threatening to rattle his eyes from their sockets.

He rolled over with a groan and felt a yielding cushion of warm flesh against his bare knee. He raised a hand to cover his still-closed eyelids and his elbow brushed against more skin near his shoulder.

When the pounding began once more, he cracked open one eye and growled. Surely 'twas not yet dawn—

He heard a soft mewing to his right and gingerly turned his head to encounter the frowning, sleeping face of a comely blond woman. Apparently, Nick was not the only occupant of his bed unimpressed by the tremendous noise.

"What'n God's name izzat?" a sleepy voice demanded, from his left this time, and he turned his head gently. A scowling brunette was raised up on her elbows from where she'd been slumbering on her belly, her heavy brown curls only partially concealing her nude breasts.

"Shhh," Nick chastised, wincing. The sound of her voice so near his ear sent long, needle-like spikes into his head. While the two wenches' boisterous voices had delighted him in their play last eve, Nick vowed he would sell his soul for a moment of perfect silence. "Do not trouble yourself—" he began through clenched teeth, each syllable increasing the length of the assumed crack in his skull.

But his words were unnecessary, as the wench had flopped back down onto her face and was now snoring softly.

"Nicholas! Open the door!"

Tristan.

Why must I have a brother? Nick wondered pitifully as he struggled to sit. *He is good for naught but chastising me and stomping about.* And he very obviously had not aided Nick's plight with the king two eves past.

The banging on the chamber door began once more in earnest.

He must cease, was all Nicholas could manage to think. Anything to make that hellish din quit. He spied a clay jug amongst the tangled furs and drew it toward him with his foot. After grasping it carefully in one large palm, he hurled it at the door where it splintered into countless shards.

Only silence followed—blissful, empty silence. Nick sighed and sank back into the mattress, pulling the coverings high to shield his aching eyeballs.

The sound he heard next should have been barely audible, but Nick's overly sensitive ears registered clearly each distinct click and scrape of a lock being breached.

He could not have obtained a key . . .

The sound of creaking hinges filled the room, and then a sharp, feminine gasp of outrage. Nick snapped the covers from his face and peered down the length of his body to discover not only Tristan but Haith as well, observing him from the end of the bed.

"Get. Out," Nick growled, and dismissed the pair of them by raising the furs once more.

Tiny, tapping footsteps sounded around the bed, and then Haith spoke from somewhere over his head. "A fine idea, Lord Nicholas."

A resounding slap and a female shriek followed her words, and Nick grudgingly peeked out of his warm—*quiet*—cocoon to see his brunette friend being dragged from the bed. Lady Haith had a rather impolite grip on the nude woman's hair.

"Be gone from here, harlot," she commanded, pushing the woman toward the open door.

"Ay!" the woman cried. "Who d'ye think ye are, ye fancy bitch, rousin' me from me sleep?"

"I am the woman who will gladly wring your neck should you not be gone from my sight in the next instant," Haith warned, skirting the bed once more.

The brunette woman must have seen the sincerity in Haith's eyes, for she uttered not another word, only sent her a pouting glare. She spotted Tristan as she bent to collect her discarded garments.

"Good morn to ye, milord," she cooed, trailing her wrinkled gown across the floor.

Had Nick been in his usual good humor, he would have laughed aloud at the expression of panic that crossed his brother's face. Tristan was looking rapidly between the nude wench advancing on him and Haith, who was currently occupied with rousing the blonde from Nick's bed.

"And you as well, you shameful tart," she said, sending the woman from her rest in much the same manner as her friend.

"Lady Haith," Nick offered, "I believe your husband requires your assistance."

Haith spun around to behold the brunette stroking the front of Tristan's tunic, he with his hands held out to his sides and a look of sheer horror on his face.

"Sweet Corra!" Haith swore with a stomp of her foot. She flung a hand toward the door, and suddenly the two women were tossed through it. She snapped her fingers and the door slammed shut on their stunned and outraged cries.

Haith turned toward Nicholas, her arms folded sternly across her chest. "Lord Nicholas, you should be shamed. Consorting with those—those"—she sputtered and tossed her head—"*whores* on the very day of your wedding!"

A timid tap sounded at the door, and one of the displaced women—Nicholas thought it might have been the blonde—

called from the other side, "Milady, if ye please, we 'ave need of our clothing."

Haith never turned, but after an agitated sigh, the door swung open of its own accord and a pile of garments skittered across the floor and through the portal to land at the women's feet. Nick only glimpsed their shocked expressions before the door once more crashed to.

"Well?" Haith demanded of him.

"Tristan, I beg you," Nick said, tucking the furs around his nude body, "control your wife. Should she be allowed to continue this tyranny, I fear I shan't have any friends left brave enough to entertain me."

"Nay, Haith is correct." Tristan came to stand next to his wife, and the pair peered down at Nick. "Today you wed, or have you so quickly forgotten?"

Nick grunted. Of course he hadn't forgotten. How could he? That green-eyed minx, Simone du Roche, had lied through her pretty teeth while teasing him with her willing lips and warm hands. She had sworn she was content to marry Halbrook—right before her father had caught them *en-flagrante* in what Nick had been certain was a suitably secluded location.

The wench was unbelievably clever, Nick had to admit. She had laid a nearly undetectable trap, and Nick had offered himself up like a calf to the slaughter. Now he was fully obligated by William himself to wed the chit in order to placate her father and avoid yet another uproar at court.

"I still fail to see how my impending nuptials warrant the both of you bursting into my rooms like common thieves." Nick looked to his brother accusingly. "And just how did you obtain a key to the door?"

Tristan shook his head with a wry grin. "'Twas not I, Brother. I tried to break the door in." He raised his eyebrows and glanced pointedly to Haith, who was now flitting about the chamber. She mumbled crossly to herself while retrieving articles of clothing and emptied wine jugs from the floor.

"Of course," Nick groaned. "How could I have forgotten

Lady Haith's clever escape from Greanly's dungeon?" He instantly recalled the tale of how his sister-in-law had used her magical Scots talent to unlock her cell door and escape Tristan—a move that had very nearly led to disaster.

"Never you mind about that," Haith said briskly, a flush tinting her cheeks. She bent to capture a rent length of embroidered cloth. "Had we not admitted ourselves to your apartment, 'tis likely you would have missed your own—oh, Nicholas!"

Nick winced when he saw the ruined tunic Haith held. He must have been further into his cups last eve than he realized.

Haith turned wounded blue eyes to him. "Your mother and I labored over this piece while I carried Isabella—you were to wear it when you wed. And now look at it!" She held the tunic toward him, the wine stains and unraveling hem clearly visible.

"I am sorry, Lady Haith," Nick said, rising from the bed on unsteady legs and wrapping a fur about his middle. "Truly, I do not know what came over me. I had naught else to wear last eve and . . ." His voice trailed off at the sight of the tears in her eyes. "'Twas not my intention to hurt you."

"Enough," Tristan said, his voice hard. Nick turned to face him, and the tic along his brother's jaw indicated that he was struggling to keep control over his temper.

"Brother, I—"

"Nay, hold your tongue." Tristan approached his wife and steered her gently toward the door. "Wait for me in our rooms, my love. I'd have a word with Nick."

Haith's meek nod sent a pang though Nick's heart, and when she spoke, the hitch in her voice made him feel like a complete fool. "I shall see what can be done to repair this before the ceremony."

While his brother saw Haith through the portal, Nick hurriedly donned his chausses—an exercise that increased the pounding in his skull tenfold. He was trying to focus on the tangled laces when he heard the sharp click of the lock being engaged, and he chuckled half-heartedly.

"'Tis rather pointless to attempt to lock your wife from my chamber, Tristan. Should she desire entry, she will merely—"

Tristan's blow caught Nick squarely in the mouth, sending Nick flailing onto his back and releasing a myriad of colorful starbursts before his eyes. Reality wavered as he rose up on one elbow and stared at his brother. Tristan stood over him, the picture of serenity save for the jumping muscle in his cheek.

"You selfish, spoiled child." Tristan's voice dripped disgust. "Get yourself up so that I may have the pleasure of putting you on your pampered arse once more."

Nick spat to the side to clear his mouth of the metallic-tasting blood, lest his already turbulent stomach revolt. He slowly gained his feet, straightening with great care.

"Brother, I have no wish to quarrel with you, but I will not tolerate—"

Tristan was upon him again in an instant, driving a hamlike fist first into his stomach and then his ribs. Nick grunted and doubled over before charging headfirst into Tristan's midsection, sending both men crashing to the floor.

Nicholas garnered strength from somewhere deep within his abused and wine-soaked body and returned his brother's punches blow for blow. The two men rolled the width of the chamber, crunching over broken pottery, toppling a table and sending splintered wood flying. When they collided into a halting wall, Tristan was atop Nick, and he braced a massive forearm against his brother's throat while glaring down at him through an eye that was rapidly swelling shut.

"What is *wrong* with you?" Nick choked out, and shoved at his brother's form.

"Listen well, Nicholas," Tristan growled, forcing Nick to hold his position. "You will marry this day, willing or nay. These childish piques of rebellion the past two days have clearly done you no good purpose."

Nick strained against his brother's bulk, trying not to admit to himself that he was now truly behaving like a wet lad. "Get. Off. Me!"

"Quiet!" Tristan thumped Nick's head soundly against the wall. "Once you have wed Lady du Roche, you must *forget* Evelyn—she is not returning to you."

"Evelyn has naught to do with this," Nick croaked and silently cursed the amount of wine he'd consumed last night—it had stolen his strength and effectively left him at Tristan's mercy.

"And you're a liar. Now, get yourself up, wring the drink from your addled brains as best you can, and prepare yourself for the ceremony." Tristan's voice brooked no argument, and he leaned even closer to Nick's face. "And should you ever, *ever*"—he emphasized with another thud to Nick's skull— "dare to cause my wife tears again, you will have no need to concern yourself with whom you've wed, because I vow to you that I will soon after make Lady du Roche a very eligible widow."

With those words, Tristan released Nick and dragged him to his feet. Nick gasped and choked as the air rushed into his lungs, and he glared at his brother.

"I should kill you for that," Nick wheezed. "Brother or not, you have no right." He spat on the floor again.

Tristan walked calmly to a basin in the corner of the room and splashed water on his swelling face. "I have every right— and an obligation." He straightened from the bowl and tossed a soaking wet cloth to Nick. "You'll realize it once you emerge from this self-pitying fog you've created."

Nick touched a corner of the rag to his distended lip and winced. Had he been in a fog? Perhaps he'd been a bit rash in some of his recent actions, but—

'Twas all Simone du Roche's fault. If not for her conniving to ensnare a baron for a husband, there would have been no cause to worry over a simple tunic, and Tristan would not have felt it necessary to take him to task for what was very typical behavior for Nick.

Yea, Nick reaffirmed to himself, *the blame is to be laid at the tiny feet of my betrothed.* If only she had not been quite so shapely and soft in that green velvet gown which had matched her eyes to perfection. If she had not smelled of warm lavender and touched him in ways that made his heart pound and caused him to forget his wits . . .

"Nicholas?" A frown wrinkled Tristan's brow. "Are you injured overmuch?"

Nick's head snapped upward, causing his ears to ring, and he winced. "Nay, Brother. I scarcely felt your affectionate scratching." Nick chose to play off their altercation as meaningless, although his pride stung at Tristan's rebuke. Nick had already had one father—he'd no need of another. "You, however, are quite fetching. That violet hue rather enhances the color of your eyes."

Tristan laughed, but after a moment his face grew solemn. "This is the right choice, Nick. 'Twas time you wed, and left to your own devices, you may have never settled on a bride. Mother will be pleased."

"Yea, I suspect she will be," Nick answered mildly, but to himself, he railed, *As is Lady Simone, Lord du Roche, King William, Haith, and Tristan. Perhaps even Evelyn would be pleased to know I am taking a wife—she certainly did not want me.*

"I'll fetch you when 'tis time to depart," Tristan said, and then left the chamber.

Nick pulled the cloth from his tender lip and viewed the bright red blood that stained it. "I'm certain all will be pleased, save for myself."

Nick was glad to have his brother in his life after years of separation, but he would not be bullied—after all, Nick outranked him by several stations. He may be obligated to wed Simone du Roche, but he did not have to claim to be happy about it, nor would he break his back attempting to please his new wife as his brother did with Haith.

If Simone du Roche fancied the Baron of Crane as her lord and master, then she would have him—but on his terms.

And then Nick did smile to himself.

Chapter 5

Outside the dwelling in which their rented rooms were housed, Armand assisted Simone in mounting the dappled gray that would carry her to the ceremony. She had done naught but cry bitterly the past two days, and now, dressed in her finest saffron kirtle, the effects of her misery were clearly felt.

Her entire skull throbbed and her eyes ached from the near-continuous flow of tears that had plagued her. Her nose was red and raw, and her chest and neck were mottled with angry blotches. She sniffed and dabbed a wadded kerchief at her nose. The tears had finally ceased this morn, although Simone suspected the reason was not because she no longer felt like crying but that her body was exhausted.

Inside, her heart still wailed.

As her father conveyed orders to the man hired to transport their few belongings, Simone looked at her surroundings numbly.

Busy merchants called out to passersby, hawking their goods; the squawking of birds and the rumbling of hooves thrummed in her ears. Smells of cooking meat warred with an underlying sickly stench that caused Simone's empty stomach to spasm. All around her were people, scurrying to and fro like a churning sea, intent on their daily lives and the business thereof.

A glimmer caught her eye, and Simone turned her head to spy Didier dangling by his knees from the roof of a vendor's stall. On the ground beneath him were two mongrel hounds, painfully thin, sitting on their haunches and eyeing the boy with interest, their heads cocking first one way then the other. Didier saw Simone watching him and gave an impish, upside-down smile and wave before knocking a pile of dried meat strips to the street below.

The dogs attacked the charitable windfall with snarls and yips, causing the ruddy-faced merchant behind the stand to screech in rage. He chased the mutts away, but not before each had filled his jowls with venison. The man stomped and cursed as he surveyed his ruined goods, and Simone could not help but smile when Didier thumbed his nose at the fattened peddler.

Simone's horse lurched forward, signaling that Armand had mounted and was now moving, as her horse was tethered to his. She grabbed at the pommel and glanced back at Didier, who was now sitting beneath a large cart filled with apples. The boy was valiantly trying to eat one, but the fruit only fell to the ground with each attempt to cram it into his mouth.

Simone faced forward once more, unconcerned that they left Didier behind. She and her brother had discovered shortly after his death that horses could sense the boy's presence intensely and would go into fits of wild kicking and screams should he venture too near—a fact that broke Simone's heart; Didier so loved the beasts.

She knew that her brother would eventually find his way to their destination, and the thought gave her some comfort. His would be the only sympathetic face at the ceremony, she was certain, even if Simone would be the only person in attendance who could see him.

Panic seized her once more as they drew near the abbey and the throng of people crowded around the entrance, packed tightly along each side of the wide steps and even spilling out into the street. Simone gave her horse a gentle kick and drew alongside Armand.

"Papa, who are all those people?" she asked under her breath.

"Guests of the king, I presume," he replied nonchalantly. "Mayhap 'tis not often a wedding is held at his command. They are merely curious." Then, to her horror, her father raised his good arm and actually waved to the crowd, as if they had been awaiting an audience with him. "*Bonjour!* Good day! Thank you for coming!"

Simone felt as if a million eyes were picking her apart as they neared the base of the steps. The crowd stared openly at her, and she saw more than one pair of ladies with their heads bowed together, whispering to each other and smirking in her direction. Some women even openly glared at her.

But then the critical bystanders were wiped from her mind as her gaze traveled up the broad steps, and there he was.

Nicholas FitzTodd's eyes never left Simone as he descended to meet them. Armand had dismounted and was now standing at the head of Simone's gray, reins in hand. As her betrothed drew near, she could not help but be stunned once more by his appearance.

His tunic eerily complimented Simone's gown—cut from a fine, ivory cloth and embroidered heavily at the neck and hems with shining gold thread. His chausses were brown, as were his soft leather boots, and the tip of his broadsword fairly grazed the ground with its massive length.

She allowed the weapon to lead her gaze upward once more, traveling the length of its gilded sheath to the sparkling sapphire that adorned the hilt. Up his arm, clothed in a creamy undershirt, his shoulder, the tanned skin of his neck, brushed by raven curls . . .

"Du Roche."

The baron's voice hummed with animosity as he acknowledged her father, and Simone could not bring herself to meet his eyes.

"Baron," Armand replied robustly, and from the corners

of her downcast eyes, Simone saw her father hand her horse's reins to Nicholas. "May you be blessed with much prosperity."

Simone heard Nicholas's answering grunt, and then Armand's lower half disappeared from her field of vision. An ivory tunic brushed against her knees. Simone realized she was shaking terribly and did not know how to proceed. She could not bear to look at him, could not—

"Lady du Roche," Nicholas said, his voice so low and deep that its timbre seemed to increase her trembling.

Simone closed her eyes briefly and steeled herself before slowly turning her head and meeting her fate directly.

He stared at her for a long moment, and Simone thought she might scream from the tension. His eyes gave nothing away, sparkling like jewels in the bright afternoon sunlight. Just as it was upon their first meeting, Simone felt mesmerized by the blue depths. She noticed with an odd pang of concern his scraped cheek and the swollen cut on his lower lip—almost reached out to touch it before catching herself and clenching her fists tightly.

When he spoke again, his words were meant only for her. "You've been weeping."

"You've been fighting." Her voice sounded husky and strange to her own ears.

His expression did not change. He let the reins drop from his hand and raised it to her hip. The contact burned through Simone's gown, and she drew a wavering breath.

"Come to me," he commanded in the strange silence that had descended around them.

Oddly grateful for the direction, Simone complied, placing her hands on his wide shoulders and allowing Nicholas to swing her easily to the ground. She swayed slightly as her feet found purchase, and Nicholas seized her upper arms in a firm grip, steadying her. He then placed one of her hands atop his forearm, effectively turning them toward the steps, and together they began to climb.

Simone felt for a moment that perhaps the ordeal would be

bearable after all. And then the whispers along the front lines of the crowd reached her ears.

"—voices in her head—"

"—drove her mad—"

"—denied by her betrothed—"

Simone cringed and glanced up at the baron's profile, but he was stoic, slowly leading her up the seemingly endless staircase.

"—father a cripple—"

"—penniless—"

"The poor baron. Why, I'd—"

Simone turned her gaze forward once more, determined to block the hurtful words from her mind, even as her cheeks burned and her throat tightened. The doors to the abbey swung wide, and she saw Nicholas's brother and his wife standing just inside. It was obvious by the blackness around one eye that Tristan had been involved in the same brawl that had resulted in Nicholas's injuries, and Simone wondered what kind of family she was marrying into that such violence did not warrant some comment.

She and Nicholas gained the wide landing before the ornate entrance, and the smile Haith greeted them with caused Simone to feel a pinch of regret for her earlier rudeness. Now more than ever before, Simone knew she would have need of a friend, and she hoped that Didier's prediction that Lady Haith could be trusted with their secret was correct.

The startled shrieks of what sounded like every horse in London shattered the silence, and Simone cringed as Nicholas turned her toward the commotion.

Each beast that occupied the wide street, whether beneath the rump of a traveler or tethered to a cart, was rearing in fright, rolling his eyes and fighting his bonds. Several steps below Simone, Didier clomped up the stairs, a wince on his heart-shaped face and his hands held open beseechingly.

"Odd," Nicholas muttered, scanning the scene below before turning them to enter the abbey.

Simone tossed a warning look over her shoulder for

Didier's benefit and then passed into the darkened interior on the baron's arm.

The ceremony was short, and for that, Nick was grateful. His skull had ached since awakening—whether due to his overindulgence or Tristan's chastising—and Nick had no other wish but to get this ridiculous farce over with.

The high-ceilinged chamber was crammed with onlookers, making the air close and humid. William and Matilda sat regally on a dais behind the altar, placing the royal couple higher than the aging priest, as if assuming God's place. Tristan stood at Nick's elbow like some grim warden, and Haith took a similar stance on the far side of Simone.

The woman who, but in a few short moments, would become his wife.

The paleness of her skin seemed to glow above her yellow gown, and Nick could feel her trembling through the sleeve of his undershirt.

And frightened she should be, he thought. If not for the innocent-looking siren's trickery, Nick would likely still be abed, having his pains tended to properly. Instead, he listened to the droning Latin of the disinterested clergy as the priest draped a holy cloth over their joined hands, blessing the union.

If not for the king's insistent request that Nick and his bride remain royal guests for a fortnight after the nuptials, Nick would perform his husbandly duties and then pack Simone off to Hartmoore and hope that he'd gotten a child on her. Because of Lady du Roche's beauty, Nick would not balk at their physical relationship, but he vowed that she would never hold his heart.

Simone's gaze as the priest spoke the final words joining them for all eternity startled Nick with its solemnity. Her green eyes were wide and glistening with unshed tears, but within those emerald depths, he glimpsed a seriousness that hinted at her understanding of the verses said over them. Her gaze pinned him as if marking him for better or nay, and an odd heat suddenly spiraled in Nick's gut.

My wife.

The echo of the priest's words still hung in the heavy air as the first wave of guests surged forward, milling around him and Simone and effectively separating them. Nick caught only a glimpse of yellow gown and her panicked, sad face before he, too, was swept into a sea of forced joviality and hollow congratulations.

The feast lasted well into the night, and the only time Nick was in arm's length of his bride was at the meal itself. Even then, she was distracted by conversation with Haith, who never left her the whole of the evening. Nick found himself searching the crowd for her more often than he cared to admit.

His mood had significantly improved since the ceremony, thanks to His Majesty's generous casks, and Nick brushed off his awareness of Simone as a mere return of his baser appetites. When he did have a chance to glimpse her from afar, he noticed that Simone moved like sunlight through the hall, her gown trailing behind her like a wave sliding from the shore back to the sea. There was a pointed demand for her attention by the male members of court, and jealousy twanged within Nick like the discordant strum of a lute.

"Easy, Brother." Tristan appeared at Nick's side and gestured toward Simone with his chalice. "I doubt any of those dandies are brave enough to usurp your place so soon after you've won her."

Nick snorted. "You've imbibed overmuch of the king's fine brew, Tristan, if you think me concerned about my wife's admirers. 'Twas not my wish to win her in the first place."

"Ha. Your scowl says otherwise."

Nick spied Armand du Roche speaking to Simone, and she raised her head just then, her eyes finding Nick's briefly before looking away. He saw fatigue there, and worry. Haith appeared at her side, and after a moment, the two ladies moved away from Armand, deeper into the crowd.

"Any matter," Nick said, "I shall be quit of her soon enough. Once William releases me from London, I'll return us to Hartmoore and continue on as I have before." He tore his searching eyes from the milling crush. "Will you and Lady Haith travel with us?"

"Nay. We depart for Greanly on the morn. Haith longs for our daughter and worries what mischief Minerva has introduced her to in our absence."

Nick ignored his brother's jest about Haith's great-aunt— the news that Tristan was leaving him to entertain his new bride alone soured his humor.

And now he could no longer locate Simone within the hall.

"So you would encourage my capture and then abandon me to see to my own release," Nick muttered. *Where was she?* "My thanks, Tristan."

His brother laughed. "I believe you shall endure. Nick?"

Nicholas started as Tristan shook his shoulder. "*What?* What is it? You blather senselessly while it seems my bride has absconded without me."

'Twas only then that Nick noticed the large congregation of men gathered around him and his brother. At his side, Tristan grinned like a fool.

"Fear not, my brother, for we mean to reunite the both of you posthaste!"

Nick was grabbed and thrown into the air, his chalice teetering drunkenly as he was hoisted along on hands and shoulders. A bawdy song filled the hall as he was juggled from the feast and through a maze of interior corridors.

"Release me!" he roared, struggling futilely against his captors. His chalice found purchase against one abductor's thick skull, but still they carried him onward. He felt one of his fine leather boots tugged off by unseen hands, but Nick's vitriolic curses were muffled as his tunic and undershirt were yanked over his head.

The belt holding his sheath loosened, and Nick sent out a sincere cry of protest. Tristan appeared on the fringe of the crowd, holding Nick's sword safely aloft as the mob halted before the door to his suite.

"I'll wager you won't be needing this," Tristan laughed, spurring comments from Nick's tormentors.

"Nay—he'll be thrusting with a different weapon this eve!"

"And what a comely sheath he's acquired!"

Nick's face reddened, but he could not help himself from grinning. Memories of Simone's willing lips flooded his ale-fogged brain and he struggled comically to gain his feet, joining the play.

"Right you are!" he bellowed. "Send me into the fray, then, for I am well armed!"

The door to his chambers burst inward and the rowdy legion of men flooded through, jostling Nick to the fore and tossing his commandeered attire in after him.

A crashing silence fell upon the crowd as all took in the scene before them. Simone sat propped in the middle of the wide bed, thick, white furs piled around her. Only her face, framed by long, inky tendrils of hair and one creamy shoulder, could be seen of her. Her green eyes, like beacons, widened at the male invasion of the room and she gasped, sinking deeper into her shielding coverings.

Nick's own breath caught in his throat. That he'd had his share of comely wenches was not to be disputed, but this vision of female and ermine filled him with a possessiveness that he had never before experienced. Desire flared within him at the sight of her ruby lips and flushed cheeks. The fire crackling in the hearth like seductive music cast a dreamy glow over her features.

A female voice shook the invaders from their stupor, and Haith appeared from the shadows of the room. "Yea, you've had your play. Be gone with you now—shoo!" She strode toward the group, flapping her hands at the men behind Nick, and they began to trickle back into the corridor, most glancing over their shoulders for one last covetous glimpse of the vision upon the bed.

Only Tristan remained, and he, not for long. He leaned

Nick's sword against a near wall and joined his wife at the door. "Good eventide to you, Brother," he said with a grin. "I'm certain we shall see you both upon your arrival at Hartmoore." He bowed toward Simone. "Baroness."

Then Tristan closed the door, leaving Nick alone with Simone. He turned back to the bed, feeling somewhat foolish clothed only in his chausses and one boot. The silence was heavy around the fire's staccato chant, and Simone's eyes seemed to burn across his skin.

He cleared his throat. "How fare thee, Lady Simone?"

"As well as can be expected, I suppose," she said, her voice low and wary. "'Twould seem you've lost some of your clothing since last I saw you."

He was sure she'd meant it as a flip retort, but as Nick let his gaze roam over her bare shoulder, a fire was stoked in his belly. "As have you," he replied, and couldn't help but chuckle at the wild blush that colored her face.

He began to slowly approach the bed, but his seductive advance was hampered by the awkward hitch in his stride, thanks to his missing footwear. He cursed softly as he kicked off the remaining boot. He had composed himself by the time he stood over the bed, forcing Simone to raise her face to meet his gaze.

"'Tis time for you to claim your prize, my lady," he said, and began to untie his chausses, his eyes never leaving hers.

"My prize?" she whispered. Her tongue flicked out over her full bottom lip, and her eyes dared a peek at his busied hands.

"Yea, your reward for your very well-executed plan." Nick's temper flared for an instant as he recalled Simone's neat scheme to win him, but his anger was a mere flicker compared to the burning want he felt.

A frown creased Simone's fine brow, and she looked away as Nick let his chausses fall around his ankles. He picked up a corner of the fur and climbed into bed, his hand shooting out to ensnare Simone's arm when she would have skittered to the far side of the mattress.

"Nay, milady—do not flee," he cajoled. The skin beneath his hand was warm and smooth, like sun-kissed silk, and his fingers met themselves around her slight bones. "I see no reason why we both should not profit from your good fortune."

Nick was not expecting the slap that left his already tender lip throbbing. Fury ripped through him so that he seized her with both hands, dragging her to him, her bare breasts flattened against his chest. Simone was no longer meek and nervous but glared daggers into him.

"That is for humiliating me before my father and Lord Halbrook," she said. "And if you are *my prize,* then I would argue that the nature of my fortune is quite otherwise."

"Do not toy with me, Simone," Nick warned, his eyes roaming her face. He could feel the heat of her soft belly against his skin, and his loins responded despite his anger. "We are both full-grown. I know that you schemed with your father to discover us on the balcony, and your neat speech on how you were content to marry an old nanny goat will do you no good now. Better you admit your deception so that we might proceed in this marriage with some semblance of good will."

"Rot in Hell, you pompous, selfish jackass," she hissed, shoving away from him.

Nick let her go, partially out of shock at being called selfish for the second time that day. Simone took the opportunity to scoot off the edge of the bed, dragging a fur around her body and forcing Nick to scramble to cover his nudity.

She spun on him. "Pray tell why I would desire to marry the likes of *you,*" she demanded, looking at him from head to toe as if he were a pile of fresh dung. "No woman would hope to become the wife of a raging womanizer who, on each unfortunate instance of our meeting, has reeked of drink and who entertained not one but *a pair* of prostitutes on his wedding day! In this very room!" Simone flung out an arm, sputtered, then stomped her foot. "*In this very bed!*"

"They weren't prostitutes," Nick said, somewhat taken aback at her knowledge of his activities. His erection shriveled.

One of her delicate eyebrows arched.

Nick stuttered. "Well, I didn't pay them." He, too, stood, dragging a fur about him and mirroring Simone's pose across the bed. "How did you learn of that, any matter?"

"Lady Haith thought I should know."

Nick growled, marveling at the size of his sister-in-law's mouth. "'Twas *before* we were wed. As you can plainly see, you are the only woman in my suite now."

"So you will no longer partake of strange women now that we are wed?" she challenged.

"Most likely none stranger than you." Nick nearly laughed aloud when Simone's eyes narrowed. "Yea, I've heard the rumors—how could I have not?" He edged around the foot of the bed, causing Simone to retreat. "So, is it true? *Are* you mad?" he asked, reaching for her.

She jerked away, but not quickly enough. He pulled her closer, trailed a finger along the ridge of her collarbone. The woman was irresistible. Already, his ire was fading. "Tell me, Lady Simone," he whispered, "shall I be forced to restrain you?"

"I'm not mad," she replied, and Nick could clearly see the gooseflesh his touch raised.

"Then let us both throw off this insanity that plagues us," he said, allowing his fur to drop to the floor. He wrapped his arms around her lightly and dropped his mouth to her shoulder. "My desire for you led me to that balcony that fateful eve and, for all your innocent protests, I believe you desire me as well."

He tasted her warm skin with his tongue, felt her shiver. "Deny it, then," he dared. "Tell me you do not want me. Mayhap you now regret making me your prey, but it cannot be undone. Let us seek a little pleasure in each other." His mouth moved to her neck. "I still find you very, very beautiful, Simone."

He heard her sigh, felt her yielding to him, but only for a moment. A freezing chill raced up his spine, and Simone went stiff. Nick raised his head and peered down at her, confused.

"Simone?"

Chapter 6

"He certainly is hairy, is he not, Sister?"

Simone felt as if she had been languishing in a deep, warm pool under Nicholas's damnable kisses, and Didier's voice was like a bucket of icy water, tossed in just for spite.

Her eyes darted beyond the baron's wide shoulders, searching the chamber's darkened corners for the imp. Her view was hampered by the massive male body before her, prompting Simone to lean slightly to the side in his embrace.

Still, she did not spy Didier.

The baron's arms tightened and he cocked his head, forcing Simone to look at him. She was surprised by the concern in his azure eyes.

"Did you hear something?" he asked.

Simone blinked. "Yea—hmmm . . . I *thought* I did."

The sleepy grin returned to his face. "'Tis merely nerves, I'd wager. I hear naught." He drew her close once more, and Simone could feel his heat even through the thick fur. He moved her closer to the bed. "Allow me to put you at ease."

Nicholas sat on the edge of the mattress and pulled her to stand between his knees. Simone's heart fluttered as her curiosity about Didier's whereabouts warred with her awareness of the baron's nude proximity. The man was impossibly arrogant, and still she ached for him to kiss her, to touch her again.

But 'twould not do to have one's young ghost witnessing the act. *Where was he?*

Nicholas began nuzzling the edge of the fur covering her breasts, kissing her skin with his open mouth, and the warm silence of the room combined with his tender attentions convinced Simone that Didier had politely left. She placed her hands on the warm, smooth skin of Nicholas's shoulders and breathed a delighted sigh at the contact. She had never been touched so intimately, and the baron was nudging her covering away . . .

"In truth, he has hair *everywhere*." The awed statement came this time from somewhere over Simone's head.

Simone squeaked and stepped away from Nicholas, hitching the fur around her. Her gaze flew upward and she spied Didier lounging on his stomach atop one of the canopy's wide beams. His chin rested in both hands, and he peered down curiously.

Nicholas blew out a frustrated breath. "Simone, this cannot continue. I understand your—"

"Lord Nicholas, a moment, I pray," she interrupted. "I have need of a bit of privacy." His frown clearly displayed his annoyance, and Simone's mind worked frantically to devise an excuse. She spied the chamber pot resting discreetly in one corner and glanced at it pointedly. "Please?"

Nicholas sighed. "Simone, we are married now. There is no need for—" Married or nay, he was mistaken if he thought to ever witness her using that base convenience. The horrified look on her face must have convinced him to humor her. "Very well. I shall wait just beyond the door." He rose and moved around the bed, where he scooped his discarded chausses from the floor.

Simone looked away as he adjusted himself to put them on. He did not look happy in the least. "My thanks," she called after him as the door slammed.

She spun to glare up at the boy now perched atop the canopy, his legs dangling below him. "Didier du Roche, get yourself down from there this instant!"

Didier reappeared in a blink, sitting cross-legged in the center of the rumpled bedclothes, his look of fascination making him wide eyed.

"Sister, mayhap the baron is half beast," he ventured in an excited whisper. "There are such things, you know—half beast, half man. His staff looked to be as long as my—"

"Nay!" Simone held out a hand and shook her head, squeezing her eyes closed briefly. When she opened them again, Didier was looking at her with an offended frown. "You cannot be here at the moment, *chéri.* This night is proving difficult enough without your spying."

"Where would you have me go?" the boy demanded, and then sat taller. "And you are upset. I want to stay and protect you in case the baron truly *is* half beast. What if he tries to eat you?"

Simone sighed. "'Tis very thoughtful of you, Didier, but I do not require protection from Lord Nicholas. The time we will spend together—as a husband and a wife—is very special and must be private."

"I vow I won't utter another word," he promised.

"Simone?" Nicholas's muffled voice called through the door. "Are you nigh ready?"

"A moment longer, my lord!" Simone turned back to Didier, frantic to convince him. "You cannot be here, little one. Please, try to understand."

"I understand that you prefer the baron's company to mine." Didier's face drew into a pout. "Why can I not stay?"

"'Tis unseemly for you to witness—"

"I won't look, then. Whatever it is, I'll avert my eyes."

"Nay, Didier! You must leave before—"

"Simone," Nicholas called. "I'm coming in, now."

Simone clasped her hands together before her breasts, beseeching Didier. "Please, *ma cher?*"

Didier stretched out on his back and interlaced his fingers behind his head just as Simone heard the chamber door creak open. She spun to face Nicholas as he entered, a wary frown on his face.

He glanced about the room before closing the door and locking it behind him. "Were you speaking to someone?"

Simone forced a smile to her wooden lips. "Nay, my lord— only myself." She cringed inwardly. Talking to oneself was not exactly indicative of sanity. *Brainless twit . . .*

The air in the chamber was becoming significantly more chilled, and Simone glanced at the bed. Didier glared at the baron.

Nicholas was silent for a moment, studying her with his hands on his narrow hips. She saw him give a shudder before he turned to the hearth.

"It grows cool, Lady Simone," he said, stooping to feed the fire. "Let us retire to the bed and seek some warmth. I've grown weary of chasing you about the chamber."

Simone looked to Didier, who was grinning broadly and patting the mattress at his side with one small hand. "Come, then—do as your husband commands."

Get out, she mouthed to him, but he merely wrinkled his stubby nose and shook his head.

Nicholas rose from the now blazing fire and rubbed his arms. He seemed a bit surprised that Simone still stood at the bedside. He slowly made his way toward her, his hands dropping to the ties at his waist.

"My lord," Simone stuttered, pulling her fur higher around her breasts and searching her mind for any excuse for Nicholas to remain clothed. "Perhaps we could talk for a bit—become better acquainted with each other?" She smiled brightly. "You could tell me about your home!"

His chausses were nearly undone as he reached her. "Let us not play games, Simone," he said, not unkindly. "'Tis no secret that we hold no great affection for each other and 'twill do us no good to attempt to induce such feelings now. Let us be satisfied with our physical attraction and perhaps, one day, friendship will follow."

Any hint of passion Simone had earlier felt for Nicholas vanished completely as Didier chortled on the bed behind her. She felt her ears burning in the cold air.

"Do not remove those!" she shouted when Nicholas brought his hands to the waist of his chausses.

"*Why not?*" Nicholas demanded, his frustration clear in his tone. He composed himself. "Simone, I understand your fear, but you must trust that I will be as gentle with you as possible."

Didier was laughing so hard that he fell off the far side of the bed. Simone felt sick to her stomach.

"Nicholas, you *do not* understand," she whispered. "We cannot . . . *be together* at this time."

Nicholas's eyes narrowed, and then comprehension dawned on his face. "Are you having your monthly?"

Simone's hands flew to cover her flaming face as Didier's head popped up over the side of the mattress.

"What's a 'monthly'?"

"Nay." Simone's voice was a muffled wail behind her palms. She dropped her hands and sighed. Her defeat was imminent.

Before her, the baron crossed his arms over his bare chest. "Then why in God's name can I not enjoy my wife on our wedding night?"

"Oh, I *must* hear this," Didier said, scrambling back onto the bed.

Simone took a bracing breath. "Very well. If you insist . . ."

"I do."

"Little more than a year past, my mother and my younger brother were killed in a terrible accident, at our home in France."

Nicholas nodded. "So I have heard. I am sorry for your loss, but—"

Simone squeezed her eyes shut. "We cannot be together this night because we are not alone."

"What?"

"*Mon dieu!*" Didier shrieked. "I cannot believe you're going to tell him!"

Simone straightened her spine and looked Nicholas in the

eye, trying to ignore her brother. The baron glanced around the room suspiciously.

She lifted her chin. "Our every move is being watched by Didier's spirit. He sits on the bed, even as we now speak." She waved a hand toward the aforementioned piece of furniture where Didier watched the exchange, enraptured.

"Didier is—*was*—your brother?" Nicholas asked.

"Yea."

"Your *dead* brother."

Simone nodded.

Nicholas's eyes roamed the rumpled furs, and Didier waved cheekily to him. "*Bonjour,* Lord Nicholas."

The baron's gaze pinned Simone once more. "I see naught."

"Yea, I know," Simone admitted, fidgeting with her fur. "Only I can see or hear him, but you must believe me. I—"

"You *are* mad," Nicholas said, slowly backing away.

"Nay!" Simone stepped forward, reaching a hand to him. "I know that you must now think the rumors to be true, but I swear to you, I'm *not* mad."

"'Tis little wonder your betrothed refused you," Nicholas muttered while gathering up his discarded clothing and dressing. "Your father should be whipped for this duplicity."

"Nicholas," Simone huffed, "hear me out—do you not think it strange that this chamber is frigid when the windows are shut tight and a fire blazes in yonder hearth?"

"'Tis merely a draft," he replied, pulling his tunic over his head.

Didier giggled. "A *daft* draft!"

Simone shot her brother a stern look before once again turning her attention to Nicholas. She knew she must convince him that she was quite sane or 'twas very likely she, Didier, and Armand would be tossed out of London on their backsides. Her mind latched on to the one person whom the stubborn man might believe.

"Lady Haith!" she exclaimed.

Nicholas paused in belting on his sword. "What of my sister-in-law?"

Simone rushed forward. "Ask her about Didier—she can hear him as well!"

Nicholas seemed to think for a moment, frowning at her warily, before shaking his head and finishing attaching his sheath. "Nay, you're mad alright." He picked up his boots with one hand and headed toward the door. "Rest assured that I will speak to William on the morrow—I'll not have a raving lunatic as the next Baroness of Crane. Good evening to you, Lady du Roche."

Simone spun to face Didier, her panic nearly out of control. Should Nicholas persuade the king to dissolve their marriage, Simone would truly be ruined. All of England would hear of the night's events and she would never marry.

Never be rid of Armand.

"Didier, help me!" she cried, no longer caring that she spoke to a figure invisible to Nicholas.

She heard the baron unlock the chamber door, muttering about a "demented female."

"Hurry!" she urged the boy.

Didier scrunched up his face and then spoke. Simone did not understand the meaning behind her brother's words, but her desperation knew no bounds. She turned toward Nicholas to see him stepping across the threshold.

"Didier wishes your permission to ride Majesty as you allowed Evelyn!"

Nicholas froze in the doorway and slowly turned to face her. His eyes blazed so that Simone took an involuntary step back.

"How do you know of Evelyn?" he asked in a deadly whisper.

Simone swallowed convulsively, and she opened her mouth to speak, but no words issued forth. Nicholas reentered the room, dropping his boots as he strode toward her.

He reached her and seized her roughly by the elbow,

shaking her. "How do you come by this personal knowledge of me?"

"Let go of me! I know naught of any Evelyn," Simone insisted. "I am merely repeating what Didier told me!"

Nicholas hesitated, glaring at her with a fire that should have turned the chilled room to sweltering. Finally he spoke, and the disgust in his voice wounded Simone more than she ever could have imagined.

"Why, you manipulative viper." He dropped her arm and backed away. "Of course you learned of her from Lady Haith. You are not so clever as you would have me think, Simone—nor I so dense."

"You shall not speak to my sister in that manner!" Didier shrieked and rose to stand on the bed. The fire in the hearth released a curled lick of flame with a loud crack. Simone gasped as the red-orange finger flicked the hem of Nicholas's chausses and set them alight. The baron jumped and stomped his foot with a hoarse shout, stumbling backward over his discarded footwear.

"Didier, good heavens!" Simone cried, rushing forward to slap at the flames. When the chausses were extinguished to little more than a fringe of blackened, smoking hem, she spun back to face the bed.

"That was entirely unwarranted!" she scolded the boy.

"He said hateful things to you," Didier replied, his expression not in the least repentant. "You have done naught to deserve such name calling."

"You cannot go about setting people afire merely because you do not care for their words, Didier, and I would think that by now you had learned to what ends arson should bring you. Lord Nicholas clearly does not understand our predicament. My lord—" Simone turned to apologize to Nicholas and to try to convince him that the strange events he'd recently witnessed were but a tiny sampling of the fantastic reality of Simone's life during the past year.

But the room behind her was empty, the door left standing ajar.

Chapter 7

Nicholas maneuvered the winding corridors feeling as though he'd been dropped from a great height. Beads of sweat dotted his forehead and his heart pounded. How the wench had managed to nearly burn him alive without Nick seeing her so much as move toward the hearth, he did not know.

He halted before a chamber door identical to his own and raised a fist, pounding insistently. "Tristan! Tristan, open the—"

As if his brother had been waiting with his hand on the latch, the door swung wide. Tristan was still dressed for the feast, and Nick charged past him into the room.

"Good eventide, Nick," Tristan said lightly, closing the door after his brother's entrance. "How goes the wedding night?"

Nick halted in the center of the chamber, his breathing labored. Haith sat calmly in a dressing gown, brushing her undone mane before the fire.

"Lady Haith, I've an issue to take up with you," he said through clenched teeth. "Several issues, actually."

Tristan appeared at Nick's side, a frown darkening his features. "Nicholas, I warn you—you have already upset my wife once this day. Should you value your comely face from further damage, you will guard your tongue."

Nick opened his mouth to tell his brother that he could take his threats to the devil, but Haith spoke instead.

"'Tis alright, Tristan." She rose from her seat and placed the ornate hairbrush on a small table. "'Tis my guess that Nick is merely confused and seeks us for answers. Although, in truth, I did not expect him so soon."

"Confused?" Nick railed. "As I stand here, my new bride flies about our chamber speaking to herself. She tried to set me ablaze!" He shook his foot forward in example. "She's mad, I tell you!"

Haith looked at Nick's proffered hem with wide eyes and then brought a hand to her mouth to hide her smile.

Tristan's mouth also twitched. "Nick, why would my wife have understanding of your troubles? She has already spoken to Lady Simone—surely we do not need to school you as well about what is to take place on your wedding night."

Nick growled and thought briefly how he would relish twisting his brother's head from his shoulders. But Haith intervened once more, drawing near to Nick and placing a hand on his forearm.

"I can only assume you've met Didier."

Tristan frowned. "Who is Didier?"

"So she has dragged you into this farce as well, has she?" Nick shook his head. "And I thought you to be a sensible woman, Lady Haith."

"Oh, but I am," Haith said. "Highly sensible."

"Who is Didier?" Tristan demanded once more.

Nick snorted. "No one."

"Simone's younger brother."

Tristan's gaze flew between his wife and brother. "Lady Simone has a sibling?"

"Nay."

"Yea. But he's dead, I'm afraid." Haith's words were so matter-of-fact that Nick growled again.

Tristan threw up his hands. "Now *I'm* confused." He walked to a table holding a wine jug and chalices. "Drink, Nick?"

"Yea." Nick kept his gaze on the calm redhead. "Are you saying you believe this drivel?"

"Of course." Haith passed a filled chalice from her husband to Nick. "In truth, she did not wish to confide in me. Would not have, I'm certain, had I not heard the boy myself."

Nick felt the bottom of his stomach give way. He shook his head to clear it. Surely he could not have heard his sister-in-law correctly. "You mean to tell me that, at this very moment, a ghostly presence resides in my chamber, conversing normally with my wife."

"I do."

Tristan chuckled and claimed Haith's vacated armchair. His chuckle grew into a hearty laugh, and he threw back his head in obvious glee.

"I fail to see the humor in this situation," Nick muttered before taking a healthy gulp of wine. His whole bloody family had apparently gone mad.

"Forgive me, Brother." Tristan chuckled, wiping at the corners of his eyes. "'Tis just so reminiscent of my initial disbelief of my own lovely wife's . . . er, *talents*."

"Nicholas," Haith said, tossing her husband a private smile, "I know this must be very difficult for you to accept, but accept it you must. Doing otherwise would ruin Simone."

"What do I care for that viper's welfare?" Nick asked. "'Twas her machinations that led us to this night—let her suffer the consequences of her duplicity. The king will see reason, if you do not."

Haith let loose a feline growl and tugged at her hair in a mockery of frustration. "Have you no feelings at all? Should you have the marriage dissolved, none would dare wed her after the rumors of her madness are confirmed by your charges."

"What of it?" Nick was trying to retain his indignation, but the image of a gamine face with wide, pleading eyes plagued him. "She brought her troubles on herself."

Haith shook her head. "I think not. Spirits of the departed do not linger except for a purpose, and it seems odd that the boy's spirit is attached solely to Simone. I think Didier has a mission."

"This is ridiculous." Nick drained his chalice and walked to the hearth to stare into the flames. The room fell silent as his pride warred with his conscience.

She had lied and manipulated her way into becoming his wife. She had struck him and then tried to set him ablaze! 'Twas quite possible she was mad as a privy rat.

But she was lovely. And quick. And she had appeared so very forlorn at the wedding feast, when any other woman in her position should have been triumphant. Something about the distorted tale of her and Armand du Roche's exodus from France had left a foul taste in Nick's mouth from the start.

"'Tis too fantastic to easily believe, you must admit," Nick said, and then glanced over his shoulder. "And if—*if,* I say— you could hear him, Lady Haith, why cannot I?"

Haith only smiled prettily and fluttered her eyelashes.

But Tristan was obviously intrigued. "What mission could the ghost of a young boy possibly have?" he murmured, then looked to Nicholas. "Revenge? How did he die?"

Nick shrugged. In truth, he knew not the first thing about his wife, other than her name, that of her father, and where she'd come from.

"'Twas a terrible accident—a stable fire," Haith supplied, easing herself onto her husband's lap.

Nick gave a short bark of dark laughter as he recalled Simone's rebuke about arson to the vacant room. "Fire. Of course."

"But perhaps 'twas no accident at all," Haith said thoughtfully, "and Didier is trying to protect his sister from the same fate that befell him and his mother."

Nick frowned. "The two of you spoke at length this eve. Did you learn naught else of import?"

Haith shook her head, and her lips formed a thin line. "But that I cannot help her. If you wish to know of Lady Simone's plight, you should hear it in her own words."

Nick sighed. Was he losing his mind as well to even consider returning to his chambers?

Tristan wagged a finger at his brother. "Beyond the fact that Lady Simone may be in need of a champion, an annulment would reflect very badly on you, Nick. Already there is talk at court of your recent rash behavior. Wallace Bartholomew and some of the other lords think you too young, unstable, and the king is listening keenly. 'Tis why he had want to see you wed—in hopes that it would settle your wildness."

"That's rubbish," Nick scoffed.

Tristan merely shrugged.

Nick did not want to return to his chamber, but what choice did he have? Did he request a dissolution, the king may take it as a further sign of his incompetence. Besides, William might merely be moved to find Nick another—less attractive—bride.

Nick decided that no real harm could come from indulging in Simone's tale for a short time more. "Very well." He set his empty chalice on the table and walked to the door. "I shall see the pair of you when I return to Hartmoore."

"Good night, Brother." Tristan gave a sly smile. "Sleep well."

"Good night, Nick," Haith called. "Mayhap I will have some answers for you when you arrive at your home."

Nick paused on the threshold, the door latch in his hand. "But you said you could not help her."

"I cannot," Haith agreed. "But there is one at Greanly who can."

"I'm sorry, Sister," Didier said for the tenth time since the baron had left. "I've ruined it all, have I not?"

Simone sighed and straightened from the trunk she'd been packing. She pressed the heels of both hands to her pulsing eyes. She hated to cry, and she'd wept so often the past three days that she had no tears left to offer. Her skull ached.

"I don't know, Didier." She'd donned a light underdress

after Nicholas's hasty retreat and now tried to smile at the boy, perched atop the dressing screen she'd vacated.

"Papa will be furious," Didier whispered.

She could think of no comforting reply. Armand would indeed be furious if her marriage to the baron failed. Her father would be forced to search for another wealthy match, if any would even consider her after tonight's tale was told. And all because Simone had not heeded Armand's warning at the marriage feast.

Make no mention of your penchant for the absurd, Simone. No mention of Didier, no apologies for your failed betrothal or the reasons thereof. With luck, FitzTodd will get you with child this night. I will have my coin, and the past will be behind me.

But Simone had not listened. She did not know why she had not taken the escape offered to her by the baron himself. Although a humiliating condition, experiencing her monthly cycle was a completely believable and reasonable excuse not to consummate the marriage. Instead, she'd felt it necessary to reveal Didier's presence to a man she barely knew and did not trust in the least. Why had the man warranted her confidences?

"Perhaps you are in love with him," Didier suggested.

"Stop plucking at my thoughts," Simone snipped.

"You won't speak! How else am I to know what will happen to us?"

"Didier, I do not know what our future holds, so invading my mind will do you no good. And, any matter, 'tis rude— I forbid you to do it again."

"*Do you* love him?"

"Nay. And you will apologize to Lord Nicholas if he should dare to ever be in our presence again."

Didier made a strangled sound of protest. "Why? *He* was being rude to *you!* And he wouldn't be able to hear me, any matter."

"I care not," Simone said, placing the last carefully folded gown atop the pile in the trunk and closing the lid. "Just because you are dead does not give you leave to forget the manners *Maman* taught us. You will apologize for my benefit. Do you understand?"

"What did he say?"

Simone spun around with a gasp as the deep, masculine voice filled the room. In her irritation at Didier, she had not heard the chamber door open and close, and now the baron leaned against it, a shuttered expression on his face.

"My lord," she breathed. "I did not think you to return."

"Neither did I," Nicholas said, his tone flat. "Again, I ask you: What did he say?"

"Forgive me, but"—the man's very presence rattled Simone. How much had he overheard?—"What did whom say, my lord?"

"Your otherworldly companion." The baron's eyes roamed the chamber as if searching for the boy. "You bade him apologize to me and I'd hear it now, if he would."

Simone looked from Nicholas to her brother and back again. Was the baron admitting he believed Didier spoke to her, or was this merely a bit of subterfuge to further implicate her in her madness? She chuckled to herself—it mattered not. Better to pull the man fully into her and Didier's world and see the strength of his mettle. At least she would have the satisfaction of shrugging off the tired ruse of his nonexistence, if only for a moment.

"You heard Lord Nicholas, Didier," she commanded, her spine growing taller. She pointed to a spot on the floor before the large man. "Come down and make your regrets."

"Surely you jest," Didier said, his small features skewed into an expression of distaste.

"I do not." She pointed to the floor again.

Simone caught Nicholas squinting toward the top of the dressing screen as Didier jumped from his perch and swaggered to stand before the baron.

"He's directly in front of you, my lord," Simone offered, feeling foolish for the man as he leaned forward at the waist.

Nicholas was peering intently at the floor as if Didier were the size of a mouse.

Simone's brother cast a disparaging look at her over his shoulder and rolled his eyes.

The baron cleared his throat and spoke rather loudly. "Very well, er . . . boy. Let's have it, then."

Didier sighed. "Lord Nicholas, I am very, truly sorry that you behaved so badly that I was forced to put fire on you," Didier said with such solemnity that Simone could feel his sarcasm. "I certainly do hope for your sake that it will not happen again." He turned to Simone. "There. Are you satisfied, Sister?"

"I suppose it will suffice." She fought to hide her grin when Nicholas turned questioning eyes to her. "My lord, Didier says that he is very sorry to have burned your chausses. 'Twill not happen again."

The baron merely grunted at her translation. He stared at her—through her, it seemed—for several uncomfortable moments before speaking again.

"Prove him to me."

"My lord?" Simone's eyes flew to her brother, who had turned from them in obvious disgust and now lay across the bed. She looked once more to the baron, leaning against the door again as if unsure that he would stay.

"Prove to me that Didier exists—that he is in this chamber, right now." His eyebrows rose. "Surely you do not expect me to take you at your word—if that were so, I'd be addressing you as Lady Halbrook."

Simone's cheeks burned. She returned his hard stare even as she gave her command.

"Make the flames dance again, Didier."

In an instant, the glow inside the hearth flared to a crackling display of red and gold. She tilted her head. "Is that proof enough?"

"Merely a draft from the chimney," Nicholas reasoned, although Simone could detect a flicker of shock in his eyes.

"Very well," she said smoothly. "What would you have him do?"

"Ay, now!" Didier sat up in the bed. "I'm not here for your entertainment!"

"Hush," Simone hissed. She turned back to the wary Nicholas. "Well? What will convince you, my lord?"

She watched the baron's eyes roam the room, as if searching for just the thing. Apparently he found a suitable task, for his mouth quirked in a sly grin and his eyes challenged Simone.

"Have him bring me that brace of candles," he said, gesturing toward a weighty-looking, iron candelabra, holding three long, unspoiled tapers. Then his finger whipped around to point at Simone. "And you stay where you stand, Lady Simone—I'll have no sleight of hand from you this time."

She gave him her sweetest smile. *Too easy, by far,* Simone thought to herself. Aloud, she said, "Didier, fetch the candles to Lord Nicholas."

"Didier, fetch the candles. Didier, do be quiet. Didier, get down from there," the boy mimicked. "I vow 'tis more work for me to be dead around you, Sister, than when I lived."

"Just do it," Simone said, her eyes never leaving Nicholas's. "Please."

Simone knew the instant the candelabra took flight by the stunned expression on the baron's face. A moment later, the heavy object floated past Simone's left shoulder and hovered, weaving hypnotically, before the baron's chest.

One by one, the tapers flamed to light.

"My God," Nicholas breathed. He waved both hands over, under, and around the piece, as if checking for hidden supports. Finding none, he looked to Simone, his face not a little pale under his swarthy skin.

Simone shrugged and turned to walk back across the chamber to her trunk. She knelt before it and eased open the lid.

"Sister, have him seize it—I'm tiring."

Simone glanced over her shoulder at Nicholas, who still

stared at the now wildly bobbing brace. "My lord, take hold of it, if you would. Didier can only suspend heavy items for a short time."

Nicholas turned questioning eyes to her, as if he did not understand her request. The candelabra fell to the floor with a great crash, snapping each of the waxen stems and dousing the tiny flames.

"Oh, he could not—" Nicholas broke off abruptly and shook his head.

"No matter." Simone dug in the depths of her trunk until she found the item she sought. She turned on her knees and, seeing that Nicholas had made no move farther into the chamber, gained her feet and crossed the room.

The baron's complexion was as waxy as the broken candle pieces littering the floor, and his eyes darted about the room. Simone felt a pang of sympathy for him.

"There is naught to fear, my lord," she said, giving him a smile.

Although her intention had been to put him at ease, her words seemed to have the opposite effect.

"Don't be ridiculous, Lady Simone," he said so gruffly that she flinched. "I am a battle-seasoned warrior—'twill take more than a mere trick of light to frighten me." He strode past her, giving her a wide berth, to a table holding a jug of wine and a selection of chalices.

Simone watched him tilt the jug skyward and drink—what seemed to be—the majority of its contents. The fine linen of his undershirt strained against his chest muscles, his tanned throat working convulsively to accommodate the liquid, and her stomach fluttered. She tentatively approached.

"My lord," she said, and when he half-turned, she held forth the small, cloth-wrapped object she'd retrieved from her trunk.

Nicholas looked at her hand for several moments, and Simone held her breath. Finally, he took it from her and, with a sigh, made to sit on the chair next to the small table. He paused in a half-seated pose and glanced over his shoulder.

"Didier isn't . . . ?"

"Nay, he's not under you." In fact, Simone could no longer locate the boy within the now cozy-warm chamber. She wondered briefly where he'd gone off to.

Nicholas sat, the wine jug still hooked in one hand, and looked at the cloth-wrapped object he held in the other. Simone watched him closely as he set the jug aside and unfolded the rough rag.

Inside was a charred chunk of wood, blackened and hardened by fire and barely discernable as the wooden hilt of Didier's play sword.

Nick's face gave nothing away. "A wooden sword?"

"*Maman* bought it for him on our last trip to Marseilles, only weeks before the fire," she said. "Didier was to be sent to his fostering soon, and she wanted him to have his own special playthings."

Nicholas raised his eyes from the ruined toy as Simone lowered herself to sit on the edge of the chair opposite him. "'Tis a costly piece, for a toy."

"Yea, and that is not even the whole of it. There was a shield, a helmet . . . a pouch with a flint, and small blade. It was his soldiering outfit. Our mother and Papa argued over it for days, but *Maman* eventually won." Simone could feel a melancholy tug at her mouth. "She usually did. And Papa always doted on Didier, much more so than he ever did me."

Nicholas glanced again at the last toy Didier ever touched while alive before laying it—almost reverently, Simone wanted to think—in the center of the table between them. He drank again, from a chalice proper this time, and drummed his fingers on one knee as if waiting for her to say more.

And so, because Simone needed to tell someone, she did.

"Didier was being punished. He'd been caught in the village setting fire to bits of brush. Naught of consequence, until one of the sparks lit upon a privy and burned it to the ground." Simone studied her dressing gown, picked at a loose thread as the memories of those days fell upon her as clean and clear and cold as winter rain. "His playthings were confiscated, and he was made to ride in the carriage with me and my maids to the Beauville estate." She looked up at Nicholas. "My betrothed's home. I was to marry the next day."

Her eyes fell back to her lap. "Papa charged me with his care. I was quite trepidatious about becoming a married woman and had no wish to add Didier to my list of burdens that day."

Nicholas nodded.

"Didier was furious at being forced to travel with us, like an infant. He wanted to follow on his own horse, with *Maman* and Papa, and with his soldier things. So when the carriage slowed to round a bend still some short distance from our home, Didier escaped the carriage and ran back to Saint du Lac."

"You did not follow him?" Nicholas asked quietly. His tone was not accusatory, but Simone bristled all the same.

"I was young. So very much younger than I am now, it seems, only a year later. As I said, my head was filled with thoughts of my upcoming nuptials and, in truth, I was piqued at Papa for forcing me to play nursemaid." She swallowed. "So, yea, I let him go without chase."

After a moment, she continued. "I was already abed that night, in my guest chambers at the Beauville's. Not long after I had fallen asleep, Didier pounced upon my bed—although I had been certain the door was bolted—pale as could be, soaking wet and shivering. He would not speak." Simone could hear her own voice growing quieter, smaller. "I railed at him for invading my chamber. Then, Papa entered, covered in soot, raving and sobbing, 'Where is Didier, Simone? Where is my son? Where? Where?' I had to tell him of Didier's escape from the carriage.

"Then, because my father could not, Charles told me about the stable fire. My mother was dead—trapped inside. Didier, missing."

Nicholas poured another chalice of wine and handed it

to Simone. She took it with a trembling hand and drank gratefully.

"Did you tell them that you had seen Didier in your chamber?"

She nodded.

"What did they say?"

Simone gave a rueful chuckle. "Charles was horrified. He told me I was mad with guilt for allowing Didier to escape." She looked at Nicholas. "Charles called off the betrothal and I never saw him again."

Nicholas nodded once more. "And your father? What did he do?"

Simone looked down into her lap again. The truth was painful, humiliating. "He scoured the countryside for Didier, for days, although I told him Didier would not be found. When Papa finally accepted that his worst fear had come true, he . . . he beat me. Told me that if I ever again mentioned the name of his son whom I murdered, he would set me from him. That he has worked so hard to see me secured in marriage, come all this way . . . I am grateful."

Nicholas frowned. He gestured toward the charred piece of wood still resting on the table. "Where did you get this?"

"Several days after the accident, Didier had mastered speech. He told me he'd gone to the keep to get his things and then to the stables to fetch his mount—'twas as much as he could remember before the fire. I went to the stable ruins at night and dug through the ashes." She looked at the small piece of wood, made to fit a young boy's palm. "'Twas all that was left."

"You didn't give it to your father." It was not a question, but an observation.

"Nay. I've told no one how I know for certain Didier was lost in the fire. Save for you, this night." She looked at him and tilted her chin. "It's mine now. Didier wanted me to have it."

Nicholas was silent for a very long time, staring across the chamber, drinking from his chalice.

Simone could stand the tension no longer. "Lord Nicholas, do you still intend to have our marriage dissolved?"

He looked at her. "Nay. It no longer suits me to do so."

Simone's heart skipped. "You believe me, then?"

Nicholas set his empty cup on the table and rose from his chair. "Not necessarily," he said, moving away from her and toward the bed. "It is—"

"Why?" Simone cried, also coming to her feet. "What else must I do to—?"

The baron's frown silenced her. "I am not accustomed to being interrupted, Simone."

"I'm sorry. Do go on." She clasped her hands before her.

He cocked a wry eyebrow at her cheekiness but continued, undressing casually as he spoke. "Only hours ago, I would not have believed what I've witnessed tonight was possible. Although, my sister-in-law *is* a witch, so it should not surprise me that things beyond reasonable explanation exist. Even so, I still know not what to make of them."

"Lady Haith is a . . . a witch?"

"Yea, but I would not use that term in her presence," he advised. He paused, his hands at the waist of his chausses, and looked directly at her. "You have lied to me, and I do not enjoy being manipulated, but if I must be married, I see no reason why it shouldn't be to you."

"Oh, that is lovely, my lord. Very romantic."

Nicholas lifted a corner of the fur and climbed into bed, still wearing his chausses. He shook a pillow out and tossed it behind his back, and then beckoned to her. "Come to bed, Simone."

She hesitated for only an instant before crossing the room and joining him. She faced him on her side, hugging the very edge of the mattress. Her pride still stung, but she could not help but feel an immense sense of relief. For whatever reason, Nicholas needed this match to work as badly as Simone did.

"What are we to do about Didier?" she prompted quietly. "Obviously this will be quite an unusual marriage, if we are unable to be . . . intimate."

"We shall deal with that once we return to my home," he said simply.

She wanted to smile from the glimmer of hope he'd given her. Simone felt cleansed after telling her tale to this man, although why she should, she knew not.

Nicholas yawned. "Put out the candle, Simone. On the morrow, I will show you London."

She twisted around and reached out an arm, and an instant later, the chamber was dark. The fire in the hearth was a mere suggestion now, the flickering coals throwing off the most meager glow.

Simone chewed on her lip in the silence. "Good night, my lord."

Nicholas grunted, and the mattress bucked as he rolled over.

She sighed, smiled to herself. "Good night, Didier."

Chapter 8

Nicholas was true to his word. The fortnight following her wedding was a whirlwind of activity for Simone. Her new husband was a most accommodating host, touring her through shops and markets, feasts at countless nobles' homes, and even several meals with the king and queen. He seemed to enjoy showing her off at every opportunity. Nicholas bought her trinkets and baubles, ribbons and bolts of cloth, and the strangest item of all: a small, slender feather from some exotic bird.

Simone had looked to him in bewilderment when Nicholas handed her the near-weightless gift outside a dressmaker's shop.

"Thank you, Nicholas. 'Tis beautiful." She frowned and spun the feather between her thumb and forefinger. "But what is its purpose? 'Tis too small for writing."

Nicholas grinned down at her, causing her heart to flutter. "Nay, it is not for writing, nor is it for you. I purchased it for Didier."

"For me?" Didier crawled from beneath a merchant's cart and scrambled to Simone's side. "Let me have it, Sister!"

Simone shot her husband a confused look before holding the feather out to the boy. Didier whooped with glee, shouting, "*Merci,* my lord!" before bolting through the crowd, waving his prize over his head and making wild bird noises.

Simone laughed. "Didier thanks you, Nicholas, but I don't—"

"Oh, now." A fat, friendly-looking maid carrying a basket of turnips on her hip clucked her tongue. "The wind's done stole yer lovely feather, milady. Look"—she pointed a plump finger over the sea of people—"there it goes, for certain. What a shame." The woman moved on, leaving Simone to stare wide-eyed at Nicholas, a smile dawning on her face.

The baron's own grin grew even wider. He took her elbow and began walking once more, following in Didier's wake by the wildly tumbling, white feather.

Simone laid her hand atop her husband's and squeezed briefly. How ingenious the man was, she was discovering. And thoughtful, when he was of a mind. While Didier could not support items of weight for any length of time, the feather would not prove a burden for the boy.

Nicholas was sly as well. Simone suspected that the root of the baron's generosity was so that he could detect Didier's presence himself. The past several nights of sharing a wide, warm bed with her husband in only the most platonic sense was proving much more of a challenge than Simone would have ever guessed. At times she felt certain that Nicholas would kiss her, wanted to, but then Didier would appear, dousing her passion like a spill into the icy Thames.

In truth, Didier had been busy creating mischief wherever he accompanied Nicholas and Simone: at a noble's home, where two regal, white hounds were found mysteriously painted with jam; in any crowded marketplace, where sudden gusts of wind were often blamed for tossing a fattened lady's skirts over her head; during a royal feast, where beautifully dressed fish seemed to regain life and flop from their platters to swim in the rushes.

Yea, a feather to track the prankish boy was a fine idea.

Except for Armand's odious company—forced upon them on a handful of outings, begging coin from her husband and spoiling her carefree moods—the past two weeks had been like a dream for Simone. She had noticed on occasion the familiar manner in which some of the noble ladies addressed her husband, and she was disconcerted by the pinch of jealousy she felt, but Nicholas never acted inappropriately while in Simone's presence. Already, the initial attraction she'd felt for him was blossoming into a friendly affection.

The only instance since their wedding night that Simone had observed Nicholas less than jovial was on an outing to an open air bazaar. Simone had mentioned a desire to peruse the heavy woolen fabric offered in a nearby stall. Nicholas had immediately obliged her but, upon reaching the stall, sponsored by the nuns of a local convent, he had suddenly become tense and distant. They had returned to their rooms shortly thereafter, and Nicholas had immediately excused himself, stating he had some forgotten business to attend to. 'Twas well past midnight when he finally returned, and as Simone had feigned sleep as he crawled in bed beside her, she could smell the strong drink and cologne on him.

She had no idea what had affected him so that day and was too fearful of breaking the spell of camaraderie to pry into matters Nicholas clearly wished to keep private. She was shamed of her reluctance to inquire about the particularly feminine scent clinging to his clothing. Simone did not think Nicholas had sought another woman, but . . .

Any matter, he was his same pleasant self the next morn, and he even allowed Simone to read the letter his mother had sent to him. A messenger from Hartmoore had arrived that day, bearing not only the message for Nicholas but also a small chest. The words scrawled gracefully across the parchment buoyed Simone's hopes for a strong marriage even further.

> *My dearest son,*
> *'Twas with great pleasure and surprise that I read of*
> *your unexpected detainment at court. I am delighted*

that you have wed and have prepared your chamber to accommodate the baroness.

I look forward to your homecoming with great anticipation and feel certain that I shall be as enchanted with your new bride as you seem to be.

Your loving mother,
Genevieve

"Do I enchant you, Nicholas?" Simone asked, handing the parchment back to him. She knew her smile betrayed her pleasure.

"You do." He set the missive aside. Reaching for her, he pulled her onto his lap. "Would you prefer to call me Nick? My family does."

"I would like that very much. Nick." She felt a silly giddiness at his nearness, and when his name rolled off her tongue sounding more like "Neek," they both laughed.

"I think you will get on well with my mother," Nick said through his smile.

"Oh?" Simone was fascinated by the texture of his skin.

"Mm-hmm. She is French as well."

Simone raised her eyebrows. "Verily? Would that she had been in attendance at our wedding. Why did she not accompany you and your brother to London?"

The small muscles around Nick's mouth seemed to tense for a moment before he answered her. "Mother does not often come to London. She left France on rather bad terms and has no wish to encounter anyone from her past."

Now Simone was intrigued. "Your brother's surname is D'Argent—is he not also French?"

"He is." Nick was silent for a long time, so long, in fact, that Simone thought him not to elaborate further. But then he did speak, his voice strained. "I've only known Tristan for two years," he said. "In truth, he is my half-brother, born in Paris and left behind when my mother came to England and married my father. D'Argent was my mother's maiden name."

"She abandoned him?" Simone asked quietly.

Nick shook his head. "She thought him dead. Tristan was abducted as a young boy, sold into slavery by my mother's first husband—he was not Tristan's father. When my mother discovered Tristan missing, when her husband boasted of what he'd done"—Nick looked away for a moment—"she killed him. Fled France a murderess."

Simone's shock knew no end. To look upon the Baron of Crane and his brother, one would never think that roots of such a sinister nature grew beneath their shining exteriors. "King William knows this?" she asked.

"He does, and he's absolved her of any crime."

Simone was quiet for a time, digesting this very personal confession, and was started back to the present when Nicholas asked, "Does this change your opinion of me?"

"After what I have told you of my own family? Of course not," Simone insisted. "I admit that I am quite surprised by your mother's past, but I admire her for her strength. Not many women, I think, could bear such a burden. You must feel very lucky to have them both.

"My mother is a treasure," Nicholas admitted, and then winced. "Tristan and I are . . . still becoming acquainted. He feels he needs protect me since my father's death. Mother dotes on him, in recompense for the many years they were separated."

"You're a good man, Nicholas," Simone said. "And so is your brother. I am certain you both will work out any differences between you."

Simone felt closer to Nick since they had shared so much, and she wanted to scrape up her courage and ask him of his exploits of the previous night—she felt she had to know. But then Nick's gaze grew warm and he brought his head down to Simone's. She turned slightly to deepen the kiss, and her worry was forgotten.

Simone felt his hand rise up over her hip to her waist. Up her back, into her hair, now smoothing over her shoulder and sliding down to the side of her breast. Her heart raced, and a small purr of pleasure escaped her throat into Nick's mouth.

She'd not seen Didier in over an hour, when he'd raced from the chamber with his ever-present feather. Perhaps now . . .

. . . he could finally take his wife.

Nick groaned as Simone's passionate mew vibrated inside his skull and she arched into his chest. He brought the arm not behind her back under her knees and stood, lifting her easily. Without breaking contact with her mouth, he carried her the length of the chamber before depositing her gently on the furs.

Nick pulled away and stood at the side of the bed, drinking in the sight of her flushed cheeks, like pink flower petals floating on fresh cream. Her lips were full and parted, and Nick pulled his tunic over his head. He kicked off his boots as his hands went to the laces at his chausses.

And then Simone's face fell.

Nick could not stifle his frustrated sigh as he turned his head to follow Simone's gaze.

A tiny white feather bobbed in an odd fashion around the opposite side of the bed. Up, down, pause. Up, down, pause. Up, down—

"What is he *doing?*" Nick asked, his voice tight.

Simone's hand flew to cover her eyes. "He's attempting to sneak up upon us, I can only assume." She dropped her hand and turned her head. "We can see you, Didier. What is it you want?"

Nick watched Simone's forehead crease as she listened to her brother's reply. She turned back to Nick. "My father approaches."

He cursed under his breath just as a knock sounded on the chamber door. He extended a hand to assist his wife from the big, comfortable—much unused—bed, and turned to grudgingly thank the boy for the warning.

Didier's feather was gone.

Nick shook his head and stepped into his boots. He didn't bother with his tunic, but was content in his billowy undershirt. "Simone, why is it that Didier is never in the same room as your father?"

"I know not," came the answer from behind him. "I've not noticed it before, but you are correct. 'Tis odd."

Nick grunted and crossed the chamber where he unbolted the door. Armand du Roche stood in the corridor, just as Didier had predicted. Simone's sire was a large man, a trait Nick guessed Armand used to his advantage at every opportunity. But unlike Nick's own muscular build, Armand's girth was composed of mostly flab where perhaps muscle used to lay. His strange afflictions of person—the scarred and oddly dented forehead, facial spasms, stunted right arm, and slow right leg—gave him a ghastly appearance. He was as tall as Nick, a fact that clearly irritated the man, as he was forced to address his son-in-law eye to eye instead of looking down upon him.

"Du Roche. Is aught amiss?"

"Naught of consequence." Armand's permanent expression of distaste was more pronounced than usual, and he dabbed a kerchief at the drooping corner of his mouth. "'Tis with regret that I must seek your assistance."

Nick stepped away from the portal, admitting du Roche into the chamber. He closed the door reluctantly and turned to see Armand standing between him and Simone.

"Good day, Papa." Simone sent her father a hesitant smile. "I hope you are well."

"Simone. You look"—his eyes flicked over Simone's wrinkled gown—"disheveled."

Nick's anger bubbled at Simone's flush and downcast eyes. "What is your problem, du Roche?"

"'Tis the servants," Armand began, dismissing his daughter completely and facing Nick. "I went to the docks this morn to arrange for Simone's belongings to be separated from mine and readied for our journeys, but they refused.

They said they would not so much as lift one trunk before payment."

"'Tis strange, no doubt. William employs only the most capable and loyal of men." Nick frowned. "Have they not already accommodated you in moving your possessions once?"

"*Oui, mais,*" Armand faltered and his complexion grew ruddy. He dabbed at his mouth again, and his shoulder hitched. "'Twould seem I had not the coin to fully compensate them."

Nick heard Simone's gasp, and when his eyes sought her, she was staring at her father in horror.

"Papa, you did not pay them?"

Armand's eyebrows drew downward and he spun on Simone. "Do not rebuke me, Simone. If not for your emptyheadedness, I would not be in this humiliating position."

Simone flinched as if struck, and Nick drew a deep breath to prevent seizing the man by his thick throat.

"Du Roche, guard your tongue when speaking to my wife."

Armand opened his mouth as if to reply, but apparently—wisely, in Nick's opinion—thought better of it. Instead, he bowed almost imperceptibly in Simone's direction and all but sneered. "My apologies. Of course."

Simone swallowed and winced before she asked her next question. "But you did pay the innkeep, did you not, Papa?"

Armand's jaw clenched, and the leather strip holding back his stringy brown hair trembled. He ignored Simone's query and turned back to Nicholas. "If you would be so kind, Fitz-Todd. Had I the payment agreed upon for Simone's hand, I would not require your assistance."

Nick's stomach soured at the greed and illogical actions of his wife's sire. What had the man planned to do had he not quickly secured a match for Simone? If word had gotten around that a certain penniless lord left his debts unpaid, Armand could have easily been tossed in the gaol. And then what would have become of Nick's raven-haired pixie, alone in London and without coin or even a lady's maid to assist her?

"Then you are in luck, du Roche," Nick said grudgingly, walking to the table where the small chest from Hartmoore sat. "Your coin arrived this very morn." He rapped his knuckles across the top of the wooden trunk, then shoved it the length of the table.

Armand's eyes widened, and he seemed to be frozen in place for a moment. His mouth twitched, and his arm drew tighter to his side. When Armand dabbed at his lips yet again, Nick got the distinct impression the man was drooling over the trunk's contents. It was disgusting to watch.

Armand covered the few steps to the table in an excited, hitching gait and then sat in Nick's recently vacated chair without invitation. He pulled the box toward him with his good hand and maneuvered it onto his knees.

"This is the whole of it?" he asked, his tongue flicking over his lips as he flipped open the clasp with a tiny click. He raised the lid to reveal stacks of shining coin.

"Yea. All of it after your debts," Nick replied easily. "You'll find them accounted for on the note within."

Armand frowned as he lifted a folded square of parchment from the box, clinging awkwardly to the trunk with his misshapen arm. "Of what debts do you speak?" he demanded as he shook open the page and scanned it. His complexion darkened. "This is an outrage!" Armand bellowed. He shot to his feet, knocking the coin box from his lap and sending a shower of shushing, tinkling gold to the floor. Simone gasped and backed away. Armand still clutched the piece of parchment and now he read aloud from it.

"Accommodations at Stag and Stern Inn, livery hire of one gelding, walking stick from Petra Bazaar—" Armand slurred the words, and he raised blazing eyes to Nicholas. "How *dare* you deduct such frivolous expenses without my council!"

Nick's voice brooked no apologies. "If you will note, I deducted none of Simone's expenses from prior to our marriage, as was my right."

"This is absurd," Armand sputtered, his eyes skittering

over the parchment once more. "Would that I had known of your miserliness beforehand, FitzTodd. I would have—"

"What?" Nick prompted. "Objected to the match? Not been as liberal with your drink or purchases? Not presented me with every bill for your care while in London?" His chuckle held no humor. "I think not."

Nicholas could feel Armand's anger radiating like an evil blaze and was not surprised when Simone stepped forward to attempt to placate her father.

"Papa," she cajoled, "surely you did not intend to accept the lord's coin with an air of charity—your pride would not allow it."

Armand looked at Simone as if she'd sprouted horns. "'Tis neither pride nor charity of which I speak, you empty-headed brat," Armand raged. He shook the parchment at her. "I need every c-coin, every farthing. M-my treasure demands it! I am close—I can feel it!"

Nick had quite enough. "I tire of your company, du Roche. Collect your spoils and be gone from this chamber. Simone and I depart London on the morrow, so you may say your farewell to her as you go."

Armand stared at Nicholas for some time, saying naught but speaking volumes with his eyes. Then he dropped awkwardly to his knees and began scraping the spilled coin back into the box with his useful hand. Simone joined him on the floor, attempted to assist him. "Touch it not! Get away," he shouted crouching over the puddle of coin. "You'll poison it!"

Simone jumped to her feet again, a hurt frown on her face. When Armand had closed the lid and hefted it awkwardly under his afflicted arm, he stood.

"We may not see each other again for many years, Papa," Simone ventured. "Fare thee well."

"Let us hope not," Armand sneered. He looked her up and down. "You are your mother's daughter, for certain. Good riddance, Simone." Armand swerved around Nicholas, wrestled with the door handle, and then was gone into the corridor, leaving the door swinging wide behind him.

Nick shut the door quietly, and when he turned back to the room, Simone had thrown herself onto the bed, sobbing.

She screeched into the coverings. "Oh, I hate him! I hate him!"

Nick sat on the side of the bed and gathered Simone to him. "Shhh. He's gone now."

"Why must he still look to me as if I am to blame?" she demanded through angry tears. "Have I not done all that he's asked of me? And yet he cannot treat me with the most meager kindness!" She scrubbed at her nose.

"Shhh," Nick said again, rocking her gently. "He'll not cause you further pain. He has his beloved coin now, and is gone."

After several moments of sniffling and hiccoughs, Simone grew still. "I am surely going to burn in Hell," she murmured into Nick's shoulder, "for I wish with all of my being that he would have died instead of my mother."

"Nay, you'll not burn in Hell," Nick replied lightly. "Your beauty would turn that fiery pit into Eden, and then what would Satan do, hmm?"

Simone giggled half-heartedly, and it encouraged Nick. Tears were not common for Simone. Nay, not only tears, but any weak emotion, and he would resort to whatever trickery at his disposal to see her smile again.

"He'd have to close up shop. Relocate. Perhaps to Wales," he said, and then nodded. "Yea, I'd wager Wales to be an ideal location for Hell."

Simone's giggle evolved into a chuckle and she pulled away from him, swiping at her eyes. "But, Nick, does not Hartmoore lay near the Welsh border?"

"Why, yea, it does," he said, a grandiose expression of shock on his face. "How fortunate for me—I shan't have a lengthy journey."

Simone sent him a genuine smile this time, and Nick was immanently relived. "Thank you," she said. "For so much."

"Perhaps you should not thank me just yet," Nick said, his voice serious.

Simone gave him a wary frown. "Why not?"

"For if I ever have the opportunity to get my hands on that scamp, Didier, I'll blister his rump for interrupting us."

Simone leaned forward, enveloping Nick in her heady, unique scent, and he breathed it in. She kissed him lightly, a devilish gleam in her eyes.

"And I shall hold him down for you."

Chapter 9

The first day of travel on the journey to her new home passed more quickly than Simone had expected, even though Nicholas had told her it was the longest stretch of the two-day ride. They followed the Thames westward at first light, leaving the closeness and stench of London behind like a fever, gradually acclimating their ears to the quiet of ever-increasing stretches of countryside. They passed through small villages, spread farther apart as the day grew longer, where young children would dart from doorways of humble cottages at the sounds of jingling tack and the rumbling of cartwheels on the packed dirt road.

Nick had warned Simone of the beggars before leaving London and had handed her a weighty sack of coin to dole out at her discretion. More often than not, after depositing a coin into the grubby hand of a child and seeing him sprint away, kicking up dust with bare, blackened feet, a peasant woman would catch up with the group, offering fresh bread or a small sack of dried fruit in thanks for the gift. Simone was touched by the friendliness and generosity shown by these bucolic clusters of the English workforce and marveled at their fortitude. 'Twas never far from her mind that she had been a mere hair's breadth from such poverty herself, and she wondered if she could have accepted such circumstances with the same no-nonsense contentment.

Simone adjusted in her saddle while the gray beneath her traversed the sloping plains and shallow, green valleys. Wide squares of cropland, intersected by lines of scrubby brush and copses of beech and oak, divided the thick forests the party often skirted. Nicholas had been accompanied to London by only a handful of his men, and their numbers were not increased overmuch by the three hired to transport their belongings in a similar number of carts. Not including Didier—who, of course, kept his distance from the horses and remained unseen by Simone since leaving London—their caravan numbered under a score. Five soldiers each to the fore and aft of the party gave them significant protection, but still the baron preferred to avoid long stretches of dense wood.

Simone was not afraid.

Her mind went briefly to her father. Was he still in London? Or had he departed the city as well that morn? She had heard tales of his treasure since she was a young girl— Armand's description always cryptic, never revealing the true nature of the prize, only hinting at its enormous value. In truth, Simone doubted the thing—whatever it was—even existed. Perhaps 'twas just a mental game Armand played with himself, to give him the life of adventure his injuries had long-denied him.

Urging her gray over the crest of a low ridge, Simone forgot Armand for a moment to smile at the view below. A small village, nested along the banks of a bright ribbon of water, lay like a gem between the rolling hills. Nicholas brought his horse even with Simone's and gifted her with a grin.

"Do you tire?" he asked.

"A bit," Simone admitted, pushing down the grimace brought on by her tender bottom. "What is yonder village?"

"Withington, and the river is the Coln. There is a small inn where we will pass the night before continuing on to Hartmoore on the morrow."

Simone breathed a measured sigh of relief at the rest she now knew they neared. "And the morrow's journey—'tis as lengthy as this one?"

"Yea. The distance is less, but the riding more difficult. The land between Withington and Hartmoore is thick with forest. We'll pass near a band of mountains"—he pointed a long arm to a bumpy shadow crawling across the horizon—"and the River Severn, laying farther west."

Simone's excitement grew. Nick had told her tiny bits about his demesne butting the rugged Welsh border, and her imagination toyed with what her first glimpse of Hartmoore and its wild terrain would reveal.

"I can hardly wait for morn," she breathed, staring off at the faraway mountain range, the childlike exclamation out before she could catch herself. She flushed.

Nick laughed, then reached across the space separating their mounts and seized her hand. He brought it to his lips, kissed it, and gave it a reassuring squeeze.

"I'll send a man ahead to announce us," he said, and then spurred his horse forward.

Simone watched him ride to the head of the party with an irrepressible smile. 'Twas as if she'd stepped from her miserable circumstances and into a fantasy. Nicholas's demeanor had changed drastically since their row over Didier on their wedding night, and now he was naught but kind and attentive to her every need. For the hundredth time, Simone wondered if he would be thusly when he finally took her to bed.

She felt slightly naughty at such lurid musings, but her husband's very presence was driving her to distraction. She could bring to mind vividly now the taste of his mouth, the texture of his palm on her skin, the masculine smell of his dark, curling hair where it met the tan cording of his neck. She knew by heart the order in which the smooth muscles rippled across his back when he bent over a basin to wash, and the way his arms—

Good heavens! Simone shook herself from her rapidly

deteriorating thoughts. Perhaps Didier had been correct in his innocent guess. Maybe she *was* in heat.

But nay, 'twas not only Nick's physicality she admired. It was also his wit, his rumbling laugh, his generous nature.

Simone's thoughts turned in comparison to Charles, the man she'd been slated to marry since girlhood, and her perception of him now surprised her. She recalled his yellow hair, pleasant if not exotic features, and his soothing manner. For years, Simone had regarded Charles as a shining example of manhood, the perfect model of a noble husband. But now, she guessed her early opinions of him had been colored by her lack of worldly experience and few others besides Armand to measure her betrothed against.

Charles had lacked fortitude and passion. But Nicholas— oh, Nicholas!—he had plenty of both.

There was no more time for lurid thoughts as Simone halted her gray before the inn. A two-story, daubed structure snuggled beneath a steep, thatched roof, the inn squatted at the head of the dusty track that led through the village. A handful of similarly constructed dwellings lined the road, with more cottages sprinkled over the fields beyond. A large, stone edifice lay some distance beyond the village, the tall, square towers topped with crucifixes clearly indicating the building's holy purpose. While the priory was certainly meant to house those whose lives were slated for a pure, higher service, Simone could not help but shiver at the compound's bleak appearance.

Nicholas was at her side then, and Simone noted the strained expression on his face as she pulled her gaze from the priory. She rested her hands atop his shoulders gratefully as he lifted her from the horse and set her on her feet. Her lower back, buttocks, and thighs groaned as they were forced to perform.

"*Merci,* Nick." She smiled up at him. "I fear I'll not prove an attractive sight in the days to come, hobbling about in my stiffness."

"You look fine," Nick said abruptly. He took her arm and

led her through the darkened doorway of the inn, leaving the dismal view of the convent behind but causing a worried frown to crease Simone's forehead all the same.

He led her straightway up a steep, narrow stair along the inn's common room and into a chamber directly at the top. The room was cramped, a narrow bedstead pushed under the sloping ceiling; the only other furnishings consisted of a basin on a small table and a chipped pot. A tiny window afforded a view of the wood behind the inn, and Simone was oddly relieved that she would not be forced to look upon the forbidding priory.

Nick's words drew her attention from the forest. "I'll see to your meal," he said, and Simone noticed his guarded glance out the window. "Is there aught from the wagons you have need of?"

"I would change my gown and clean the dust from myself," Simone replied. "If one of my trunks could be sent up?"

Nick moved toward the door. "I shall see to it directly."

Simone's call of thanks was disrupted by the closing door, and she frowned again. Nicholas was clearly displeased, and she replayed the events since their arrival in Withington but could not fathom the source.

Taking advantage of the privacy, Simone made use of the pot and then returned to the window. The western woods ringing the village stretched out before her, dark with autumn's damp colors in the quickly fading light, and an oddly ominous feeling crept around Simone's shoulders. She suddenly wished for Didier. She hadn't seen him all day and wondered if he would show himself by nightfall, as was his habit. Or perhaps he would stay away, affording husband and wife a night of peace—and perhaps the opportunity to become intimate.

"I vow *that* would raise Nicholas's spirits," she said aloud, and then giggled at her scandalous self to throw off the sliver of disquiet the view of the woods had slid across her throat.

A rap sounded at the door. "Lady FitzTodd? I've yer trunk, 'ere."

"Come," Simone called, and one of the burly drivers shoved open the door, hefting the large trunk as if it weighed naught. Simone thanked the man as he set the cumbersome item in the middle of the floor and turned to go.

But he had brought the wrong one, Simone realized as she neared the piece. This trunk, with its age-colored brass hasps and ornate carvings, was Portia's—Simone's own containers were infinitely plainer and smaller than her mother's.

"*Pardon,*" she began, but the driver had already gone. "No matter," she said to the empty room. She stared at the trunk with a feeling almost akin to fear. She had not looked upon her mother's possessions since before Portia's death. These trunks had been packed by Simone's mother herself, anticipating the journey to Simone's wedding celebration. "*Maman* had lovely gowns. And since they now belong to me, I see no reason why I should not wear one."

She dropped to her knees and fished the ring of keys from her chatelaine. Her hands trembled as she searched for the correct key, and her fumbling fingers fit it into the lock. The clasp let loose smoothly, but the sound it made was like a crack of lightning in the tiny chamber. Simone's heart fluttered and her breathing came in short gasps. Steeling herself, she raised the heavy lid.

Portia's scent hit Simone like a physical blow. In an instant, she could recall her mother in the most minute detail: her long, dark hair, her sparkling eyes with their tiny, fascinating creases at the corners. Her no-nonsense manner and secret smiles when she surprised Simone with yet another gift. All of these memories and countless more from the simple, musky-feminine scent wafting up from the trunk.

"*Maman,*" she breathed, and reached for the topmost gown as if in a dream. Slowly, she pulled the rose-colored material up and out of the trunk and crushed it to her face, inhaling deeply.

Simone, would that you wear rose more often. 'Tis my favorite shade and it becomes you so.

She let the gown fall into a puddle on her lap and reached for the next.

Do you like the trim? I'll have one made for you if you desire.

With each kirtle or underdress pulled from the trunk—whether rose or green or midnight blue—snippets of Portia danced through Simone's memory, spinning her emotions to the tune of bittersweet loss.

Where is Didier? Where is my darling boy?

Simone, Charles has arrived. Will you go riding today?

Go to your chambers, Daughter. Your Papa is displeased with me and I must speak with him.

'Tis merely a bruise—fear not. Your father cannot harm me, darling.

When Simone finally surfaced from the deep, cold pool of the past, her mother's gowns were piled high on the floor around her. She had emptied the trunk of clothing and yet there were still items within.

Stacks of folded parchment, cracked and yellowed with age and tied with ribbon into thick bundles, lined the bottom of the deep trunk.

Simone forgot her sorrow for a moment as curiosity gripped her. She reached into the trunk and pulled out a stack, taking care not to bump the already crumbling sheaths. Rising, she picked her way amongst the discarded gowns and sat upon the bed. Simone tugged on the ribbon, and it fell loose easily, allowing her to remove the topmost square. She pulled the edges apart, once, twice, revealing a single sheet of her mother's swirling handwriting.

1 July, 1068

I have a son. Didier Anton Edward du Roche came into this world early this morn, wailing as though it offended him highly to do so. He is a darling, though, perfect in every way. At first sight, he reminded me of his sire, and that thought did comfort me greatly. Simone is rather unimpressed, but even she had to smile and coo at his handsomeness. I do believe they will be great companions one day. When I am free from my childbed, I shall take them both to Marseilles. My children are my only joy.

"'Tis a journal," Simone whispered, setting the page aside and rifling cautiously through the remaining stack. The sheets in the bundle were dated through the end of 1069, and Simone's melancholy lifted. Here, perhaps at last, was a way to learn of her mother, as Simone had neither the opportunity nor the inclination to do while Portia lived. Perhaps in this way Simone might learn how the family's fortune was decimated. Already, the first entry mentioned Marseilles—certainly there would be further insight in the remaining bundles.

And 'twas also a way she could once again feel close to Portia. As Simone had read, it was almost as if her mother had been speaking directly into her ear.

Simone rose from the bed and took two more bundles from the trunk, setting them on the thin mattress. She scooped up the gowns littering the floor, dumped them unceremoniously back inside the trunk, and dropped the lid closed. The tiny sleeping chamber had grown dark with shadow as the sun was nearly set, and Simone lit the thick, crude candle on the bed-side table.

A tap on the door startled Simone into remembering her husband. She quickly crossed the room and swung the door wide.

"Nick! I've found—" But 'twas not Nicholas who stood in the corridor beyond, only an old, stooped woman bearing a tray.

"Good eve, milady." The woman smiled, and Simone noticed that she had only three front teeth. "The lord bade me bring ye yer supper an' tell ye he's takin' a cup or two before retirin'."

"Oh." Simone blinked and then stepped back, admitting the

inn's mistress. The woman placed the tray of dark stew, bread, and wine on the bed, carefully avoiding the pages strewn across the coverlet.

She straightened with a grunt and showed Simone all three of her teeth once more. "Is there aught else ye be needin', milady?"

"*Non. Merci,*" Simone said, shaking off her disappointment. She gave the woman a smile before closing the door after her.

Apparently, Nick was indeed in a foul humor again, and if the episode in London was any indication, he would not return to the chamber until dawn. Simone wished that her husband would trust her with his troubles, but she felt that pressing him now would only cause him to further withdraw. She hoped that, in time, he would not retreat from her when burdened, but to her.

Simone sighed and walked to the bed. After climbing upon it, she pulled the tray of food to her side and picked up the remaining pages from the first bundle. At least with the bulk of Portia's journals lying unsampled, she would not pass the eve entirely alone.

Chapter 10

Night settled around Nick like a heavy cloak as he sat on a knoll some distance away from the small inn, his back pressed against the gnarled skin of an ancient oak and a wine jug pressed against his thigh. He felt foolish and angry at himself as a handful of darkened windows on the convent's south side were lit from within the thick stone walls. A bell tolled, each deep, echoing clang reaffirming his recklessness.

He lifted the jug and drank deeply, wiping at his mouth with his sleeve when cool rivulets ran down his chin. How could he have forgotten the close próximity of Evelyn's chosen haven to the route his party traveled? Silky dark hair and glittering green eyes sprang into his mind, but he pushed the vision of Simone away. He could not think of his pixie bride in this place, not when Evelyn had him once more in her grip. Though, in truth, thoughts of one woman were as damning as thinking upon the other.

Evelyn, with her face and disposition like a calm, sunny afternoon, whom he'd known her entire life. She, who had abandoned him and removed herself from his reach in yonder, dismal walls.

Simone, as sparkling and deep as the midnight sky, who gathered her fear of Armand and her love and mourning for those long dead around her like a fortress as impregnable as any stone keep.

And was Nick partly to blame for her sporadic aloofness? He knew she wondered about his late-night excursion in London. She'd been awake when he'd returned, although she'd feigned sleep well. He would not allay her fears—could not. How could he explain his weakness, his need to be alone with his black thoughts? Had he assured her that he'd been quite without intimate female companionship, she might have probed deeper. And he would not humiliate himself further by trying to explain a situation he himself did not understand.

He drank again. 'Twould be easy enough to retrieve Majesty from the stables and ride to the priory under the cover of night. His station would demand admittance. He could seek Evelyn and have his answers. But what good would it be? 'Twould not change the fact that she'd left him without word, that she had thrown their friendship and Nick's offer of marriage back in his face.

Bah. Foolish fantasies. Nay, he would not seek Evelyn but hope that the memory of her betrayal would fade in time. As it were, Nick had not been to Obny since that fateful visit with Handaar, a fact that caused him deep shame and made him consider the validity of the rumors circulating with the other lords. He vowed to himself that he would make amends to the old warrior as soon as he returned to his home. Perhaps he should also call a meeting of all the marcher lords, to solidify their defense and make clear to all that he was in control of his demesne.

The wine jug was nearly empty now, and the windows of the convent were finally dark. The silence of the night around him was soft and comforting in his self-enforced solitude, and he didn't even mind the frigid breeze that washed over the knoll, causing his hair to lift and the few dried leaves above his head to whisper conspiratorially. A glimmer of white danced in his peripheral vision, and he turned his head to see a small white feather circling and swooping toward him.

"Ah, young Didier," Nick said, noting with dark humor the

slur in his words. "Chastity itself. I'd think you'd be sitting faithfully at your sister's side, preventing me what little comfort I have in this world."

The feather neared Nick and sank to the dried grass at his hip. "You'd rather torment me directly? Very well, I have naught else to occupy my time."

Nick reached for the wine jug, but it toppled over abruptly as if kicked, sending the last dark trickle of Nick's anesthetic bubbling down the knoll.

"Ay!" Nick cried. "That was mine, you little meddler. Now I shall have to return to the inn to get it filled." He started to roll to his feet, but the jug gave a violent start as his fingertips grazed the handle, and it tumbled down, down the hill. It disappeared into the night before a faint splash was heard.

"And who are you to tell me I cannot?" Nick demanded, his voice rising. Then he felt his face warm. He must truly be pissed, carrying on an argument with a ghost who was unable to argue back. He settled against the tree once more with a sigh.

The feather rose up from the ground and swooped in front of Nick's face, tickling his nose. He swatted at it and growled.

"Cease, Didier. I'm in no mood."

The feather wiggled before his nose again insistently.

"What?! What is it, then?" Nick asked, frustration and drink making his words sharp. "Why do you not float back to London, or however it is you travel, and torment your father so that I can be alone with my wife, for God's sake?"

The feather stilled briefly and then the tip moved slowly, deliberately, in a side-to-side motion.

Nick paused, eyeing the bright piece of fluff warily. "You do not wish to visit Armand?"

The feather moved up and down.

"He *is* rather poor company, is he not?" Nick tried to shake off the wine-induced sluggishness that mired his thoughts. Either he was hallucinating or the boy was trying to communicate with him. He cleared his throat and glanced about the knoll, as if any were about to spy on him.

"Didier, are you a boy?"

The feather moved slowly, up–down, up–down.

Nick's eyebrows rose. "Have you a tail?"

Back and forth, quickly.

"My God," Nick breathed. 'Twas ingenious, really. It crossed his mind that he would have liked this boy in life, resourceful as he was. Nick cleared his throat again and leaned to the side, propped on one arm. "Is there something you wish to discuss?"

Yea.

"Alright. What is it?" Nick waited, but the feather did not move. He then realized that his question required a more involved reply than the boy was able to give. "Sorry. Is it about Simone?"

Yea.

"And yourself? Is it about the accident?"

Yea, yea, yea.

Nick thought for a moment on how to best continue. His only information about Simone's family's deaths had come from Simone herself. He did not know what to ask.

"Do you recall what happened?"

A slight hesitation, and then, *Nay.*

Nick sighed and scrubbed one hand across his suddenly weary eyes. "I don't understand. How am I to help you if you don't remember any of the accident?"

Nay, nay, nay.

Then the feather took off down the knoll and disappeared into the darkness. Nick growled and looked toward the convent, silhouetted in a blackness darker than the night sky.

"I do hope you are pleased, Evelyn."

Something cold and wet slapped Nick's cheek, leaving fat droplets of water behind before falling into his lap. He looked down and saw Didier's white feather, matted and dripping a dark pool on his chausses.

Nick looked up, around him. "Water?"

A sinister cold seemed to wrap itself around Nick, so sudden and frigid that his teeth began to chatter. The damp spot where the feather lay on his thigh burned with cold, as if ice had formed there. Nick's breathing became labored and he could not draw sufficient air. He raised a hand to his throat, panic seizing him.

But then, quite suddenly, 'twas gone, and the feather hovered once more before his face, damp now, but no longer dripping. Air rushed into his lungs and he gasped a hoarse breath. It had almost felt as though he'd been dr—

"Didier," Nick began slowly, testing his raw throat, "did you drown?"

The feather remained still.

Nick frowned. "But Simone said you and your mother lost your lives in the stable fire. That you were trapped inside."

Yea.

"There is only one way to find out for certain," Nick said, his anger rising. "As Armand was the only survivor, I shall summon him from London and demand an explanation. He may have been able to bully Simone, but he'll not fare so well with me." He rose from beneath the tree and began striding back in the direction of Withington. But before he had taken a score of steps, Didier's feather swooped before his face in wide, wild arcs.

Nay, nay, nay!

Nick stopped. "You do not wish for me to summon Armand?"

Nay.

"Why not?"

Nay.

He was on the brink of ignoring the boy when the scent of warm lavender filled his senses. His wife's unique fragrance brought her instantly to mind, and Nick recalled that Didier had answered affirmatively when asked if the matter concerned Simone.

"Is Simone in danger?"

A hesitation, and then, *Yea.*

Nicholas placed his hands on his hips and stared at the earth between his boots for several moments. Clearly, Didier did not wish for Armand to know he possessed this information, and in truth, what could Nick charge the man with if he did summon him? There was no proof of Armand's wrongdoing.

He sighed and looked up at the feather once more. "Very well. I shall keep my own council for now. I assure you, you were no more glad than I to have seen that pompous miser's departure."

Yea.

The feather twirled away in the direction of the crude animal shelter near the inn, prompting Nicholas to call out, "And stay away from the horses!"

Nick turned to look one final time at the night-draped convent. On the morrow, he would pass by that place with his wife, on their way to Hartmoore. His thoughts turned briefly to Tristan's warning about Nick's foolish pining, and his conscience tugged at him.

He turned back toward the inn and 'twas just then that the humor of the situation struck him. He chuckled as he passed through the dim, quiet common room and mounted the rickety stairs. His chuckle broadened into a low laugh.

"A nun, a ghost, and a Frenchwoman arrive at an inn . . ."

Nick eased the door of the bedchamber open and stepped inside. The scene that greeted him caused an unexpected warmth in his gut.

A thick candle splattered its dying glow over the plaster walls and the large trunk in the center of the room. Nick spied sleeves and fancy trim where 'twas pinched in the seam of the trunk lid. His wife lay sprawled across the stingy bed, amongst a scattering of parchment and ribbons. The tray bearing her evening meal sat upon the floor, barely sampled.

Simone's face was turned toward him, her delicate features relaxed in sleep. Her lips were parted, and her eyelashes lay thick and dark upon her cheeks. In spite of the trunk obviously brimming with gowns, she still wore the dust-caked kirtle from the day's journey. One hand lay upon her stomach, pressing a cracked, yellowed page to her body.

Her quiet breathing filled the room, and Nick closed the door behind him with care. 'Twas well past midnight, and he had no wish to wake Simone and answer questions about his absence.

He unbelted his sword and leaned it against the wall near the bed and eased out of his boots, all the while his eyes never leaving the form of the woman before him.

So beautiful, he thought, *and yet in her trials she's shown strength few men would possess.* Nick's eyes lingered on her soft lips, and he remembered the easy way she could be stirred to passion. His want for her grew to a bittersweet ache.

Would their tentative friendship grow into something more? Nick did not know, but he was curious to learn more of the true Simone du Roche FitzTodd, when she was no longer saddled by the sorrow of her family.

Simone's eyelids fluttered open, and her gaze was soft and unfocused. "Nick? I—"

"Shh." He crouched down at the bedside. "I did not mean to wake you. All is well, go back to your sleep."

"*Non.* I have something to show you." She rolled to her side and sat up, handing the parchment she'd be clutching out to him. There was a hopeful gleam in her eyes. "Look."

12 December, 1069
Marseilles was wondrous, as expected. A fortnight of escape from this dreary existence at Saint du Lac. Simone thoroughly enjoyed herself, indulged as she was by Jehan. Young Didier's first journey was a success and he proved quite content on horseback, slumbering nearly the whole of the way. Our friends took much delight in his good nature, and we were pressed by many to spend Christmas in Marseilles. But I returned for my children's sakes. As it were, Armand had depleted his funds and arrived at Saint du Lac before us, and I do believe he has broken two of my fingers. I shall not be able to get away now until spring. O, frigid winter, how I wish for your speedy end!

Nick looked to Simone. "Your mother?"

"Yea." She smiled and began gathering the scattered pages together. "There are stacks of them I've yet to read." She paused in her tidying and looked up at him, her face radiant. "Is it not wonderful, Nick? I never knew my mother kept note of her thoughts and activities. 'Tis almost as if I have a small piece of her with me again."

"I'm glad it pleases you." Nick was more than a little troubled by the blasé manner in which Simone had accepted the horrific account of her mother's injuries. He sat on the bed next to her. "But are you not troubled to read of her abuse at Armand's hand?"

"It saddens me that he caused her pain, yea," she replied, a curious frown on her face. "But 'twas common enough. My parents' arguments were oft quite violent." She shrugged. "Papa has a fierce temper when crossed, and *Maman* was never one to take orders. Many times, when they rowed, I would ride the countryside for hours. Sometimes with Charles, sometimes alone."

Nick frowned. Before, he could only imagine the turmoil of Simone's childhood, but now, reading a firsthand account of the viciousness, Nick was truly sickened.

And he cared not at all to hear what a comfort Simone's betrothed had been to her.

A look of concern crossed her lovely face, and she laid a hand on his arm. "Fear not for Portia, Nick. She meted out her own share of punishment. Verily, Papa is missing several whole teeth and his hearing is impaired on his right side."

Nick cocked one eyebrow and could not help the snort of laughter that escaped him. "Is that how Armand came by the afflictions that plague him? The scar, his lameness?"

Simone's nose wrinkled while she thought. "'Tis possible, but I think not. Papa was in a great battle before I was born. He's been that way as long as I can recall."

Nick shook his head and sighed. "'Tis a wonder one of them did not kill the other." The words were out of his mouth and Simone was chuckling before the implications of what he'd said struck Nick.

Was it possible that Armand du Roche had killed his wife? His own son? 'Twould explain Didier's reluctance for Nick to consult the man about the accident—and perhaps also why Didier was never in the same room as his father—but why would any man want his only heir, one he claimed to adore and an innocent, bright boy at that, dead?

"Nick? What is it?"

He pulled himself from his wildly tumbling thoughts. There was no cause to alarm Simone needlessly when all Nick knew for certain was based on speculation. Indeed, if Simone's father had a hand in his wife's and son's deaths, she may well be in danger, and the less she knew of Nick's ripening theories, the better.

"'Tis naught," he answered, forcing a relaxed smile to his lips. "Tell me about Marseilles."

She smiled then, and a faraway look came into her eyes. "*Maman* called it the city of dreams," she said. "We traveled there often when Papa was away on one of his adventures."

"He did not accompany you on your trips?"

"Oh, nay. Never." Simone shook her head. "Papa detested Marseilles."

"Why?"

Simone lifted a shoulder and gave a crooked smile, as if to say, "Who can know?" "Perhaps 'twas because *Maman* was so different there—carefree and merry. She had many, many friends, and the shops were divine."

Nick's mind worked methodically, seeking ways to wheedle tidbits of information from Simone that may lead to clues about her mother's death. "Is that where you believe Portia spent the du Roche fortune?"

"I know it for certain." Simone rose from the bed, clutching the precious pages, and crossed to the trunk. She dropped to her knees and, setting the stack aside, lifted the heavy lid. She continued to explain to Nick over her shoulder as she began tidying the rainbow of gowns within.

"When we traveled to Marseilles—she and I and Didier, and often Charles, would come as well—*Maman* would bring coffers filled with coin. Upon our return, we would have trunks of gowns and ceramics. Tapestries, carvings, furnishings, and often a new horse or two for Didier." She paused, lifting a bright azure gown and admiring it for a moment. "But the coffers were always emptied."

Nick nodded slowly. 'Twould seem that Portia du Roche had set out to deliberately destroy the family's wealth, but certainly no amount of clothing or horseflesh should render a healthy estate penniless. "Who is Jehan?" he asked, recalling the name from the entry he'd read.

"*Oncle Jehan,*" Simone sighed, and Nick could hear the smile in her voice. She craned her neck to give him an impish smile. "Not my uncle, really. A commoner—a wealthy merchant in Marseilles and a great friend of my mother's. We would stay at his château when we visited."

The more Nick learned of Simone's life in France, the more twisted and tangled the threads leading to Portia's and Didier's deaths became. Secret trips to Marseilles, a city Armand abhorred. Disappearing coin. A wealthy merchant. And Charles Beauville—where exactly did he fit in all of this? Nick decided to let the subject go for now. Once they were settled at Hartmoore, Nicholas would feel more comfortable about sorting out the clues in earnest. Simone was his responsibility now—a beautiful, sensual, nearly irresistible responsibility—and Nick was determined to protect her as best he could.

He stood from the bed and extended a hand to assist Simone from the floor. Once she was on her feet, Nick pulled her into his arms without thinking. He dropped his head and kissed her as he'd wanted to do since first seeing her sleep amongst the scattered sheets of her past. The fire that was always at a careful bank blazed out of control as he felt her lips answer his. This night had been a trial—the long journey from London, wrestling with Evelyn's memory once again, Didier's cryptic clues, Simone's bittersweet discovery. Nick felt the eagerness in his loins, the impatient cry of his body to possess her.

Then Simone pulled away from his mouth, prompting Nick to crush her close once more, "Nay," on his lips. He needed her tonight. But she resisted yet again, a small mew issuing from her throat. "What is it?" he asked, and was almost shamed by the husky need in his throat.

Simone rolled her eyes and wiggled a finger over Nick's shoulder. He turned his head and immediately saw the small white feather, leaving a ghostly, damp trail on the trunk lid, back and forth.

"We can see you, Didier." Nick sighed and leaned his forehead against Simone's. "'Twould seem it is time for us to retire."

Simone sighed and gave Nick's midsection a squeeze. "My thanks for listening to me this night, Nicholas."

"You are most welcome." He returned her embrace, his arms lingering about her for just a moment longer than was necessary.

In his mind's eye, he could still see Didier's feather, dripping and cold, feel the air shrinking from his lungs.

And he was infinitely glad that Armand du Roche was far, far away from his wife.

Chapter 11

Simone's aching muscles felt each plodding step of the gray she rode on the second day of travel. She'd fallen asleep in the small hours of the morn, pressed close to Nicholas almost as soon as her head had touched the pillow and, by the sore state of her body, hadn't moved until Nick woke her before dawn. It had taken until nearly midday before her eyelids ceased trying to close of their own accord.

They rode northwest into a brisk breeze, but the sun was bright, warming Simone's cheeks and shoulders. Her spirits were also warmed as she glanced repeatedly at Nicholas, who was never far from her in the party. She felt as though she'd been given a second chance, by God, perhaps, on this journey to Hartmoore. At her side was a handsome, caring husband. Her mother's journals—a written remembrance of Portia— lay tucked deep within the trunks that followed her. Armand was in faraway London, soon to return to France, leaving her in peace at last.

The only stain on Simone's bright new tapestry of future was Didier's restless wanderings. She saw him frequently, if only briefly, during the journey that day, and always at a safe distance from the caravan. She would have felt guilty at his solitude if not for the fact that he seemed to be enjoying himself quite thoroughly. Through patches of forest he would shimmy up tall trees to chase squirrels from branch to branch, and in open fields, the delicate butterflies were his constant companions, fluttering around and landing on him in such great numbers that even several of Nick's men were moved to point out and admire the fantastic sight of so many of the beautiful creatures seemingly paused in mid-flight.

They'd spoken of it as a good omen, and Simone prayed they were correct. She was very much looking forward to speaking once more with Lady Haith. Perhaps then, too, Didier could find peace.

But what shall you do when he is gone? The dark whisper crept across her sunny thoughts unexpectedly, like a menacing cloud, and for a moment, Simone was chilled to the bone by its shadow.

But the upsetting turn of her thoughts was cut short as the party rounded a bend into a stretch of deep forest and was faced with a large group of mounted men blocking the road. Simone gasped and reined her horse with a jerk, looking worriedly to Nicholas. Good omen, indeed.

But he smiled at her. "Fear not. They are but Hartmoore's own, sent by my mother, no doubt, to lead us on."

Simone felt the tension leave her with an odd urge to laugh, and she nudged her gray forward alongside Nick's mount. The men awaiting them in a wide spot in the dirt road appeared to be from a race of lean giants—rugged, hard men dressed in full battle gear, atop barrel-chested steeds obviously bred for their substantial girth and muscle. Their drapings bore the now-familiar crest of Nick's demesne, and Simone's excitement grew.

The soldier to the fore of the group approached them at a canter and swept his halberk back from his head, revealing white-blond hair falling over hawklike features. He grinned and drew near to Nicholas.

"My lord, welcome home."

Nick turned his horse to grasp the man's forearm. "Randall. I see that Lady Genevieve received my message."

"Yea, Sire. The keep is in a frenzy most dire. No man of

battle dares enter the hall for fear of being set to some maid's task. Already, guests arrive for the wedding feast." Randall glanced at Simone, and his grin turned self-conscious.

Nick, too, looked toward Simone and chuckled. "I can only imagine. Randall, I present my wife and Hartmoore's new mistress, Lady Simone FitzTodd."

To Simone's surprise, the man promptly dismounted and knelt, bowing his head. "My lady, 'tis my humble honor to serve you."

In an instant, the remaining soldiers had done likewise amongst the nearly deafening sounds of clanging metal, and 'twas Simone herself who felt humbled.

"Your homage is well met, Sir Randall," she said with a nod and seemed unable to banish the delighted smile from her mouth as she looked across the kneeling company of men. She caught a glimpse of Nicholas from the corner of her eye, and the look of pride on his face thrilled her.

The men returned to their mounts and broke rank, consuming the small party from beginning to end. Randall, however, stayed at Nick's side as they once more began moving forward through the wood. Simone listened unabashedly to the exchange between lord and general.

"How fares the border?" Nick asked.

"Mostly quiet, my lord. We received word from Lord Handaar of a small band of raiders just beyond Obny, four days past."

Nick grunted. "Damages?"

"Slight," Randall assured. "'Twas but a skirmish at best. A score or less Welsh doing little more than hurling rocks were no match for Obny's men."

"'Tis odd there were so few," Nick mused. "What clan? Donegal's?"

"We know not. Handaar's message did not specify."

"That does not bode well." The rough timbre of Nick's voice sent gooseflesh springing on Simone's arms. "What of captives?"

"None. All were killed." Randall glanced to Simone. "Pardon, my lady."

Simone's eyes widened slightly, but she said naught, waiting for Nick's reply.

"Good." His jaw was set, the muscles working just under his skin. "It seems as though I will journey to Obny sooner than anticipated upon my return. This attack was strange by your account, Randall. We must be on our guard."

Simone let the men's conversation fade from her attention as the talk digressed to such topics as arrowheads and armor, of which she had neither knowledge nor interest. She instead occupied her mind with scanning the road ahead, seeking a break in the treeline through which she might spy her new home. She frowned to herself as she thought of the wedding feast awaiting them at Hartmoore. Would the arriving guests hail from the surrounding countryside within Nick's demesne? Or would she also be plagued with the nobility from London once more, with their sharp eyes and even sharper tongues? She certainly had not expected to be put on display so quickly, instead hoping her first days on the Welsh border would be quiet, peaceful, with time to learn of her new family, Nick's mother included.

She killed him. Fled France a murderess.

Nick's words describing his mother's past suddenly troubled Simone. Should she be fearful of this woman who had killed for her son? Or proud to be now allied with such a strong maternal figure? Nick seemed to love Genevieve very much, and her message to him in London was filled with words of only delight and praise. But the dowager baroness was obviously very protective of her offspring. Perhaps she would not welcome Simone's intrusion.

Then there was no more time for worries, for they had quit the dense wood and 'twas there, sprawled in the valley below, that Simone laid eyes upon a fortress of such scale that she had never imagined its equal.

Large, square stones comprised the castle, the sheer height of its outer walls reaching up to Heaven as if rebelling against the docile fields surrounding it. Simone counted seven square towers ringing the main complex and two low wings, recently built by the looks of the crisp lines glittering in the late sun's hazy glare. The wings stretched to the north and south of the keep proper, as if bracing it in a readied stance of attack.

The village huddled on the east side of the fortress, cottages and huts tossed about like giant boulders down the sloping motte to the wide wooden bridge over the river, winding around Hartmoore and snaking out of the valley. On the far side of the bridge, Simone saw a large gathering of people, and her stomach fluttered.

"'Tis not much," Nick's voice rumbled playfully, intruding on her fascination. He laid his wide, warm palm upon her arm. "But I vow 'twill keep you safe within its walls.

Why, of course she would be safe here. What could possibly harm her, in a place such as this? Surely God himself must beg entrance at Hartmoore's gate.

A choking laugh escaped her, and she shook her head in wonder. The billowing treetops lining the river and tucked around the village sparkled dazzling reds and golds, lit by autumn's fiery torch.

"'Tis beautiful, Nicholas," she breathed, and then turned to him. She covered his hand with hers. "You must show me every corner."

Nick's eyes sparkled, and his smile told Simone he was pleased with her reaction. "And so I shall," he promised. Gathering her reins with his, he said, "Would you care to ride ahead with me and meet your people?"

A spiral of nervous excitement coiled within her. *This is your new life, Simone, where all will be different, better. Seize it.* Tossing her husband a grin, she abruptly kicked her mount into surging gallop away from the treeline and down the wide dirt road leading to the bridge, grabbing for her reins as they were jerked from Nick's loose grip.

He gave chase with a whoop and was at her side in moments, their horses matching strides. As the sweet-smelling breeze rushed over her face and into her ears in a deafening roar, Simone could not help but laugh aloud.

Nicholas was pleased to have Hartmoore in sight again, but what pleased him more was Simone's reaction to his home.

He reined Majesty to keep pace with Simone's gray, and her shout of laughter seized his heart. Their thundering hooves reached the wide bridge spanning the River Teme, and as they slowed their pace, the echoing beats were overcome by excited "huzzah"s from the crowd of villagers and guests awaiting them on the far side.

Nick seized Simone's reins and edged slightly ahead of her, maneuvering the pair of them through the crowd. The villagers bowed deeply and stared at their tiny new mistress, and he heard more than one hushed whisper of "She's so lovely!"

Simone smiled at them all, extending a slim hand from serf to nobility, murmuring, "*Bonjour.* Good day to you. I am most pleased to be here. How lovely to see you again."

Nick was also accosted with greetings.

"Good to have you back, milord."

"The grains from the final harvest are nearly milled, milord. Miller says—"

"Finally caught, are you, FitzTodd?"

Nick's attention jumped from one person to another, just as Simone's, as they seemed to be addressed by each person gathered beyond the bridge.

He could not recall a more joyous homecoming.

He urged Majesty forward, drawing Simone deeper into the village, the crowd following eagerly. Within moments, they had passed through the deep barbican and into the bailey. Nick saw Genevieve dart from the doorway of the keep, and she was before them even as Nick assisted Simone from her horse.

"Nicholas, my darling!"

He kept a grasp on Simone's hand as he acquiesced to his mother's welcome. She kissed him on both cheeks and then drew away, her eyes instantly finding the small woman at his side.

"Lady Simone, oh, but you are lovely!" Genevieve abandoned Nick to grasp Simone's hands, pulling her from Nicholas and consuming her in a statuesque embrace. "Welcome to Hartmoore, my daughter."

Nick cleared his throat. "Mother, you're crushing her."

The two women drew apart, laughing, and Nick saw wetness in both their eyes. Simone's face bore an expression of immense relief. Had she been nervous to meet his mother?

"Thank you, Lady Genevieve. I am most pleased to be here."

Genevieve glanced around Nick's wife. "But where is your father, my dear? I assumed he would want to see his daughter to her new home."

Simone's smile faltered. "Nay, he . . . Papa had some pressing business to attend to in London before returning to Provence. I hope his absence does not offend you."

"Offend me?" Genevieve said, shaking her faded blond head. "Of course not. Why, I"—Nick's mother paused, a frown creasing her high forehead—"did you say Provence?"

"*Oui,* do you know of it?"

Genevieve nodded. "I once knew of a family du Roche of Provence, long ago. What is your mother's name, darling? Perhaps I know of her as well."

Simone looked decidedly uncomfortable, so Nick intervened. "Portia du Roche is dead, Mother. Simone lost her and a younger brother in a fire last year."

"Oh my." Genevieve blanched. "Forgive me, Lady Simone."

Simone smiled and squeezed Genevieve's hand. "Do not trouble yourself about it. But does her name seem familiar? Could you have known her? From Marseilles, perhaps?"

The tense look darkening his mother's face dissipated, leaving an odd wash of relief in its place. "Nay, I'm sorry. The family I knew had no married offspring—and certainly no children of your age." Genevieve looked from Simone to Nicholas. "But why do we stand about in the bailey? I'm certain you have want to refresh yourselves before seeing to your guests."

Hartmoore's great hall was as grand and intimidating as the castle's exterior. Beyond the thick double doors lay a cavernous, square room with a gigantic hearth opposite the entrance to warm the lord's table on its raised dais. Two additional hearths commanded a wall each to the left and right, garlands of dried oak leaves and fall flowers snaked over and around the armament and banner displays decorating the hearths, adding a crispy, tangy fragrance to the acrid smell of woodsmoke and aroma of roasting meat billowing from the room.

Ten long trestle tables were divided to each side of the hall, their benches nearly half-full of celebrants. Loud chatter punctuated with shrieks of laughter, and good-natured barbs echoed in the empty space above the tables, the guests washed in easy evening light by the windows set high up in the walls. In the far left corner of the room, Simone saw the curling end of a set of stone steps twisting away to an upper floor. Everywhere, the hall sparkled and shone with the light from what seemed to be a thousand candles.

Everyone quieted and stared as Simone entered the hall on Nick's arm. For one awful moment, the room was as silent as a tomb.

"Brother!" Tristan shouted, raising a chalice high from his seat at the lord's table. Simone spotted the red-haired Lady Haith to his left, and the woman sent Simone a friendly smile. "The miscreant baron returns! Huzzah!"

The rest of the crowd erupted with echoing cheers, and Simone could feel Nick's laughter at her side. Several of the lesser nobility who had greeted them at the bridge flowed into the hall behind the couple, finding their seats once more. Nicholas led her through the center aisle created by the tables, and as they passed, Simone surveyed the guests, responding to greetings and calls of congratulations. The hall seemed mostly composed of strangers until they neared the rear of the room and she saw Lord Cecil Halbrook, the old man she was to have wed, and several other lords from King William's feast. An aching void grew in Simone's stomach as they neared, and her ears burned as she remembered the vile whispers she'd endured in London.

"Lady FitzTodd." Lord Halbrook gave her a kindly smile and shallow bow as she passed. "A pleasure to be in your home."

She nodded to him and smiled, thankful for his graciousness. And even more thankful she was not being addressed as Lady Halbrook.

"FitzTodd." A skinny, gray string of a man angled his chin toward Nicholas. "I suppose I should extend my congratulations, as you were gracious enough to have me in your home."

Simone felt Nicholas tense under her hand. "Bartholomew. 'Twas not my doing, I assure you. You may give your thanks instead to my mother."

Simone could almost smell the animosity between the two men and was relieved when Nick guided her past the table before Bartholomew could respond to the slight. He brought her to stand before his family, where Lady Genevieve had already taken a servant in hand and was quietly giving instructions.

Nick released her then, and she felt chilled by the removal of his steady presence. He clasped forearms with his brother before leaning down to peck Haith's cheek. Simone thought Haith may have whispered something in Nick's ear and waited for his inaudible answer, but it happened so quickly that Simone couldn't be certain. Simone smarted for a moment when faced with the easy intimacy of the close group. She felt like an intruder.

Finally, Nick turned his attention to her. "Simone, of course you remember my brother and Lady Haith," he said.

"Of course." Simone forced her lips into a smile.

Nick looked to Haith. "But where is young Lady—"

His question was cut off by a child's delighted squeal, and

Haith laughed. "Speaking of the little minx, she's playing under the table, as usual."

Nick turned to Simone, a grin on his face, and she couldn't help but note how different Nicholas seemed here—other than the encounter with Lord Bartholomew, she hadn't seen him scowl once.

"Lady Isabella is a lover of caves and hidey-holes." Nick crooked his finger at her and squatted down.

Simone hesitated for only a moment before following suit, one hand grasping the table's edge for balance. A striking infant under a year old, with coppery curls and creamy skin, sat happily in a white gown, her fists clasped together, squealing in amusement—

—at Didier's feather swooping in circles before the child's face.

"Hallow, Isabella," Nick called. "Have you a kiss for your uncle?" Nick's smile faded when he too saw evidence of Simone's brother. He looked to her accusingly.

Didier chortled in French at the baby and glanced at Simone. "Isn't she keen, Sister?" He tickled Isabella's nose with the feather. "Was I ever this small?"

"Would you *do* something?" Nick whispered to Simone.

"What would you have me do?" she hissed in return. "Paddle him?" She looked at her brother. "Didier, shoo!"

"I beg your pardon." The boy looked highly offended. "I'll not hurt her, Sister."

Simone looked back to Nick, helpless.

Nick growled, snatched the baby from the floor, and rose. Simone followed, pasting a smile to her face.

"What are you about, my girl?" Nick laughed and tossed the babe into the air until she giggled. "Staying out of mischief?"

"How rude!" Simone heard Didier's offended cry and felt a rush of cold air whoosh around her ankles.

"Lady Simone," Haith asked, her eyes narrowing, "are you unwell?" She leaned back on the bench slightly and glanced under the table. She straightened quickly, her face blank.

"Ah . . ." Simone swallowed with some difficulty as Didier crawled from beneath the table, his feather gripped in his fist.

"I'm certain she is merely fatigued," Nick intervened. Obviously, he'd seen Didier's emergence as well. He handed a wriggling Isabella to her father and grasped Simone's elbow, his fingers biting into her flesh. "Lady Simone?" he prompted darkly.

"Oh, yea." She forced a laugh. "The journey . . . I *am* weary." She tried not to let her gaze follow Didier, who was now crawling in the direction of Lord Halbrook's table. "Mayhap I should retire."

Lady Haith's eyes darted about the room as if searching for something—or *someone.* "Of course," she said distractedly. "We'll have time a plenty to"—she paused as a shrill scream pierced the hall—"become acquainted."

Nearby, Lord Bartholomew had shot to his feet, and Simone realized where the rather feminine shriek of horror had come from. The stingy-looking man continued to yelp, shaking one leg and then stamping his foot. A manservant rushed to attend him.

"Something's tried to crawl up my pant leg! I daresay 'twas a rat!"

"Well, that's not all bad, then," Simone heard Nick mumble before clearing his throat and speaking loud enough that all gathered could hear. "If you'll excuse us, friends."

As he half-dragged Simone away from the table, a ringing crash sounded behind her. She craned her neck to see a round, ornately made battle shield skid down the center aisle of tables, Didier sitting upon it as if it were a sleigh. Lady Genevieve stood transfixed, her fingertips pressed to her lips.

Nick's fingers dug deeper into her elbow. "That was my father's shield," he growled in her ear. "Call him to you before he destroys the entire hall!"

"But, how—"

"*Call him!*" Nick shook her arm.

Simone pressed her lips into a thin line. "Didier," she hissed from the corner of her mouth.

The heavy iron chandeliers bearing hundreds of lit candles began to sway like pendulums, dripping hot streams of wax on the guests below, and their surprised cries filled the great hall.

"Simone," Nick warned.

She knew she had no choice. "Didier!" she said sharply, her voice ringing among the confused murmurs of the guests.

"Coming, Sister!"

A man sitting close by looked at Simone with a perplexed expression. "Dee-dee-yay, Baroness?"

"Pardon me?" Simone asked airily.

"Ah, well," the man fidgeted, and Simone was appalled to find the other occupants of the table looking to her now as well. Lady Haith had left her seat altogether and was slowly circling the perimeter of the hall, eyes moving to each gently swaying light fixture.

"You said 'Didier'," the guest continued, flushing. "Were you seeking someone?"

Simone's mind worked furiously. The only excuse she could fabricate was out of her mouth before she could think. She let her accent thicken.

"Oh, *Didier!*" Simone laughed gaily.

"What is it, Sister? I'm right here."

"'Tis . . . 'tis a custom of my home," Simone explained, exploring the outrageous lie as it formed and ignoring her brother. "Similar to *au revoir,* but . . ." she stuttered, swallowed, then smiled, "reserved only for dear friends."

The man's face broke into a smile as his tablemates murmured amongst themselves, testing the phrase on their tongues. "Of course! Forgive my ignorance—I am honored." He rose from the bench and bowed. "*Didier* to you, as well, Baroness."

Simone huffed out a shaky laugh as Nick pulled her to the stone steps in the corner of the hall, amidst calls of "Didier! Didier!"

Simone was mortified. Didier followed them up the winding

stairwell, walking backward and blowing kisses to the crowd. "Yea, yea—I am the prince! Bow down to me, loyal subjects!"

Simone was very much aware of Nick's cross mumblings above her. "I do apologize, my lord," she said.

Nicholas half-turned to glance down at her as he continued to stomp up the stairs. Ah—*there* was the scowl Simone was accustomed to.

"Can you not control him, Simone?"

Simone paused in her climb briefly, her mouth agape. She skipped up the stairs to catch up one more.

"Nick, he is a *ghost*. I cannot control his actions anymore than I can yours."

They had gained the upper level and Nicholas turned to her in the stone corridor. "And what is that to mean?"

Simone lifted her chin. "You do what you please, when you wish. You have yet to explain your whereabouts the night you left me in London, or your absence from the inn last eve— you weren't in the common room," she accused. "I checked."

Nick blew a scoffing breath through his lips before turning and disappearing around a corner.

Simone followed, determined to not let him escape without an explanation and worried at what his answer would reveal. She trotted along behind him, her eyes on his wide, stiff back. His silence only served to increase her dread.

"You were with a prostitute, were you not?"

He did not turn. "Nay."

"You lie!" she accused.

"God's teeth," he muttered, and then stopped before a massive carved door at the corridor's end. His expression was impassive.

"Then *tell me,*" she demanded. "How am I to trust you if you will not confide in me? If you keep secrets?"

Nick looked at her for a long moment, as if debating on whether to answer her, and Simone held her breath. She wanted to have faith that he had not betrayed her, would not betray her, despite his promiscuous reputation. She just needed his assurance.

Simone's hopes crashed.

"You shall have to solve that riddle on your own, I'm afraid," he said, and then grasped the door handle and pushed open the door. He swept his arm toward the open portal, and Simone had no choice but to enter.

The Baron of Crane's suite was beyond spacious. The large, square chamber was nearly the size of the great hall at Simone's childhood home. Not one but two hearths faced each other from opposite sides, their openings so tall that Simone fancied she could stand in them upright.

Thick, sculpted rugs in bright blues and golds covered the smooth wood floor and two long, deep windows, complete with wide stone seats, welcomed the crisp night air. There were two silk dressing screens in opposite corners; chests and tables and sidechairs; tapestries and candelabras gracing the walls. But the centerpiece of the chamber, the item that took Simone's breath, was the bed dominating the floor. She walked toward it with a gasp of pleasure.

"Oh, Nick!" She forgot her anger at him as she reached out to stroke one of the tall posts, intricately carved from a wood so dark—or so old—it appeared black. The post stretched up what seemed twice Simone's height, and at its narrowed tip perched a carved, winged creature, seeming to peer down at her.

Simone could hear Nick's smile in his voice. "You like it?"

"I've not seen its equal," she breathed, craning her neck to admire the figures on the remaining three posts. The carvings adorning the bed were all fantastical: unicorns and other horned beasts chased each other around the wood in a slow spiral, frolicking, it seemed, with merfolk and fiery birds, minotaur and dragons. But the faeries were reserved for the tops of the posts, each one with slightly differing features and expressions, overlooking the chamber.

Nick moved to her side, and Simone shivered when he rested his hand on the small of her back. "'Twas my parents', and my grandparents' before them. This chamber was theirs as well."

She turned her head to look up at him, expecting to see

sadness at the mention of his deceased family, but his lips were curved in a faint smile.

"I love it. Truly, *c'est magnifique*."

Nick raised a hand to brush at a wayward lock of hair framing Simone's face. "I'm glad you are pleased. I wish for you to be happy at Hartmoore."

Her heart beat heavy in her chest at Nick's nearness, the solitude of the chamber. She wanted to close her eyes and freeze this moment in time, preserve the peace and intimacy she felt standing at the foot of this most symbolic piece of furniture, her husband at her side. He spoke of her happiness as if he truly meant it. An odd situation for Simone—no one had ever concerned themselves with her happiness before.

She took a deep breath, tucking the moment safely away in her heart. She rose up on her toes before she could stop herself and pressed her lips to the corner of Nick's mouth. "Thank you, Nicholas," she said before quickly retreating, her impetuous action causing her face to heat.

But before she could escape completely, Nick wrapped his arms about her, drawing her against him fully. Peering down at her, he asked, "So, you trust me not, Simone?"

She tilted her head and met his gaze. "Nay. How can I?"

His fingertips grazed light circles on her shoulder blades, and he nodded. "We have known each other only a very short time, and there are still many things you have yet to learn about me."

Simone could barely think as his hands widened the path of his caresses. "What sort of things?"

Nicholas was silent for several moments, his eyes searching her face while his fingertips played their silent melody over her waist and ribs. "Naught of considerable import," he said. "But a man must have council with his own thoughts. I will not bare my soul to you—it belongs only to me." His hands paused. "I will never lie to you, though—this I vow."

Her eyes dropped to his chest, and she was surprised to see her hands resting there, her fingernails skimming the dusty embroidery. He did not trust *her*. That was clear.

"Simone," he commanded softly, "look at me." She raised her face. "*I will never lie to you.* And I have had no woman since we were wed."

"I know that we have much to learn of each other, Nicholas," she said, her heart fluttering with need and not a little hurt. But she believed him, God help her. "But I hope that, one day, you will have want to seek my council with your burdens. Already, you hold my highest regard for believing in Didier—even if you do not understand that I cannot foresee or forestall his impetuous actions."

Nick huffed a breath of laughter and cupped her cheek in one large palm. He kissed her softly. "Your highest regard?" he asked against her mouth.

Simone swallowed, her eyelids sliding closed and her knees trembling. His touch was . . . intoxicating. "And affection," she whispered.

"That is much more to my liking." Then he kissed her again, slowly, while pulling her closer. Simone wanted to melt into him, be absorbed by his masculine scent, his solid presence. Even though she knew 'twas folly, she felt safe in Nick's arms. Safer than she'd felt for many, many months.

But then he drew away abruptly and stared into her eyes, his desire sparking icy blue flecks within his own. "I have spoken with Lady Haith."

Simone frowned. It seemed an odd comment for such an intimate moment. "Lady Haith, my lord?"

Nicholas turned her chin gently with one long finger, and Simone saw Didier marching in circles around the perimeter of the wide mattress, his feather held above his head. She was more than a little shocked that Nicholas had noticed her brother's presence before her. In truth, she had forgotten about Didier completely as soon as they'd entered the chamber. Simone sighed.

Didier paused in his play to look at her. "Oh, do carry on, Sister. I'll not make a peep." He took up his happy march once more, humming a jolly melody.

"As I said," Nicholas continued, "I've spoken with Lady

Haith. You'll soon have assistance with our young mischief maker here."

Simone's eyebrows rose. "Really? How?"

"Minerva is coming," Nick said simply.

Chapter 12

The next morning found Nick seated at a wide, planked table in the small ground-floor chamber under the stairwell where he conducted Hartmoore's business. He'd spent the remainder of the previous evening with Simone, settling her into his chamber, and except for the awkward moments after Didier's enthusiastic arrival into Hartmoore's great hall, it had been a most relaxing homecoming.

His new wife had two distinct personalities it seemed to Nick: open and caring when shown tenderness, but reserved and defensive at mention of Didier or Nick's actions. Surely his life would assume some semblance of normalcy after the arrival of the old healer, Minerva, and after he was rid of all the blasted guests infesting his home. What had his mother thought, inviting that bastard Bartholomew? Nick grinned to himself as he recalled Didier's antics with the man.

Rat, indeed.

Now a steady stream of laborers and overseers flowed in and out of the chamber, pressing Nick for decisions or reporting on the state of Hartmoore's various industries during his recent absence. His crops had flourished and were harvested, calling for another storehouse to be constructed; several head of sheep had been lost to wolves due to a less-than-vigilant—and now disposed—herd. One birth, two deaths of old age, and one handfasting were chronicled in the clerk's ledger, and by midday, Nick had grown weary of accounts and chores. His mind wandered once again to the dark-haired beauty who was his wife, while Randall droned on about weaponry repair.

Nick had left Simone early this morn in his—nay, *their*—chamber, dressed in a pretty rose kirtle and surrounded by the precious stacks of her mother's journals. He'd itched to pull her from the dusty pages and steal away for a ride through the countryside, even as Didier's swooping feather had chased him from the room. Nicholas had the, admittedly juvenile, urge to do the things Simone had spoken of doing with Charles Beauville—he wanted to erase any memories of the man from his wife's mind, replacing them with his own presence.

Today though, he must ride over his lands without her, to Obny—a journey he did not relish—to learn firsthand of the ineffective Welsh raid on Handaar's keep. He had neglected his duty for far too long, and was shamed. Evelyn was gone. So be it. Nicholas was married now, and 'twas past time for him to renew his vow of protection and service to his father's closest friend. And besides, with Bartholomew in residence at Hartmoore, 'twas impossible for Nick not to have heard the insinuating rumors of why Handaar had not answered the invitation to the wedding feast.

"And so, my lord, by spring we could be equipped with newly fashioned vests, in the latest style of weave," Randall said, winding down his lengthy lecture on chain mail and stroking a sample of the new armor. He sat across the wide table from Nicholas, casting the frowning clerk a warning glare. "The cost will surely be accounted for by lives saved."

Nick leaned back in his chair with a sigh and rolled his head to relieve his stiffening neck. "Very well, Randall. You've made your case. What say you, clerk?"

The thin, wiry man grimaced and peered down at his ledger, his nose fairly brushing the page. "I know not, Sire," he muttered. "It seems a large sum for new armaments when we yet have useable—"

Randall stood abruptly, knocking his chair backward. "And

what do you know of proper battle gear, you spineless scribbler? 'Tis my men who fight to keep this hold secure, and they warrant only the best protection!"

The clerk sat up and sniffed in Randall's direction. "And 'tis *my* duty to manage the lord's accounts. If not for me, your spending would surely—"

"I'll have your arse for a saddlebag, you—"

"Enough!" Nick's command cut the argument before his very capable clerk incurred physical harm. "Randall, you may have your new equipment, but only by half. Give it to the first line archers and send any mail past its prime to the apprentices." Nick shook his head at the smug smiles on the faces of his clerk and first man. Apparently, both felt victorious in his decision.

Randall righted his toppled chair. "My thanks, Lord Nicholas."

"Yea, Sire," the clerk chimed in. "If that's all, I'd be off to the mill." He bowed in Nick's direction and scurried from the chamber, passing Genevieve in the doorway. "Good day, m'lady."

"Good day, clerk," she replied. Genevieve entered the room, and Nick immediately noticed the folded squares of parchment in her hands. He groaned to himself.

"Good day, Nick, darling. Randall." She approached the table with a nonchalant air. "Have you a moment to conduct a bit of business with your mother?"

Nick's eyes darted once more to the letters she held. He knew by the telltale cross embedded in the wax seal that the missives were more offerings from Evelyn, and suddenly Nick longed for a skin of wine, a tankard of ale—

A sharp blow to the head.

"Of course I have time for you, Mother," he said as an idea came to him. "In fact, I have need of those."

Randall cleared his throat. "I shall leave you to your privacy, my lord."

"Hold, Randall," Nick said, pulling the letters from a wide-eyed Genevieve. "I require your assistance as well."

Nicholas walked to the small chest tucked away in a corner

behind the table and knelt, unlocking the small clasp holding
the lid closed. Inside the miniature trunk lay stacks of parchment, identical to the two squares he now held. Nick tossed
the folded pages on top of the others and closed the lid, locking it once more. Then he rose, bringing the chest with him
and holding it toward Randall.

"My lord?" Randall's brow furrowed as he took the small
container.

Nick returned to his chair with a satisfied grunt. "We leave
for Obny within the hour. Summon Lady Simone at my request, then ready a score of men for the ride." He waved a
hand at the chest. "And burn those."

"Nicholas," Genevieve chastised. "Have you not even
read one?"

Nick glanced at Randall, who hovered in the doorway.
"That is all."

Randall hesitated. "Shall I destroy the chest as well, my
lord?"

Nick paused, his eyes roaming the hand-tooled leather. It
had been a gift from Evelyn, more than two years past, when
he'd inherited the barony upon his father's passing. He
grasped at his ring of keys, jerking the small heart-shaped one
that unlocked the chest free, and tossed it to Randall.

"Burn it all."

"Yea, Sire." When the guard had quit the room, Nick
turned to his mother, and her faded blue eyes revealed her
hurt.

"Did she mean so little to you that you would destroy all
memory of her?"

"Nay, Mother," he sighed, his anger draining away. When
he next spoke, his voice was low, controlled. "There is naught
else for Evelyn and I to say to each other. 'Tis over."

Genevieve stepped forward and opened her mouth as if to
argue the point, but Nick silenced her by holding up a palm.

"Do you wish for my match with Simone to be agreeable?"

His mother tilted her head. "Of course I do, darling."

"Then I must do what I must do." Nick scrubbed a hand

across his face. "I cannot help but suspect that I failed Evelyn in some way that she would refuse me as she did. If I am to be an effective liege to Obny, I must pretend that Evelyn is dead. Bring me no more of her missives, should any arrive."

Genevieve swallowed and then nodded. "I understand. I love Evelyn as if she were my own, but I vow to you that I will go to whatever lengths necessary to encourage your and Lady Simone's happiness." She held out her hand with a melancholy smile and Nick took it.

Speaking—nay, even *thinking*—of Evelyn had soured his humor, and 'twas no help that the task of visiting Obny lay still ahead. He sought to shake off his black mood before telling Simone of his overnight journey.

"Now, tell me," Nick said, releasing Genevieve's hand after a squeeze, "have you seen my rogue brother this day? I'd command he accompany me to Obny, since he is in my home and I outrank him by a league. I know how he adores taking orders from me."

Genevieve laughed, the first sincere smile from her since she'd entered the chamber. "I have. And you may command him all you like, but you know 'twill mean naught to Tristan. He'll do as he pleases, whether here or at Greanly." Her voice carried more than a touch of pride, and Nicholas felt stung. When Nick did as he pleased, everyone frowned upon him.

But then Genevieve changed the subject. "Lady Simone, she is *different,* is she not?"

"How do you mean, Mother?" Nick's eyebrows lowered. "Simone has had a series of misfortunes befall her within the past year; she is in a foreign land, in a foreign hold filled to the very rafters with strangers, no family to speak of." Nick waved a hand.

Genevieve nodded, but frowned. "There have been rumors—"

"Oh, Mother," Nick groaned.

"Wait, wait," Genevieve hastened. "Then, her arrival in the great hall yesterday . . ." Her eyes narrowed and she peered at

Nick as she had when he'd been a troublesome lad. "What are you not telling me?"

Nick immediately thought of Didier's white feather. How would his mother react if Nick told her that he had returned to Hartmoore with not only a new bride but a ghost as well?

"You of all people should know better than to listen to gossip," Nick chastised, and was satisfied with Genevieve's flush. "'Twill take time for Simone to adjust to life at Hartmoore. I would hope you will be an aid to her instead of a hindrance by propagating rumors."

"Nicholas," Genevieve said, offended, "I would never—"

"Very well then." Nick rose from his chair and skirted the table. He held an arm toward the doorway, indicating Genevieve should precede him from the room. "Let us seek my brother."

She pursed her lips at him and sniffed, her nose in the air. But she walked past him into the great hall without another word of the happenings of yesterday.

Nick could only hope that Minerva did hurry and that she would be able to give Didier the peace he sought, before Hartmoore was turned inside out.

22 June 1075
I do hope that Hell is not as bad as I have been taught, for surely that is where I shall spend eternity. I believe Armand has discovered my secret and now I can only pray for his death.

Simone gasped, her hand flying to cover her mouth as her mother's words jumped from the page.

"What is it, Sister?" Didier lay stretched on his back near where Simone sat cross-legged. He'd been occupying himself by floating his feather from one hand to the other while Simone read to him from Portia's journals—the only way she could think to keep him away from the guests that lurked about Hartmoore's chambers and corridors. He turned his head toward her now with an annoyed expression. "Why did you stop?"

Simone swallowed, and her eyes quickly skimmed the rest of the entry. Portia's shaky writings of that day were unlike any that Simone had read thus far. Until now, the accounts had been rather tame, mentioning Marseilles often, relating minor accomplishments of her children, humorous anecdotes of the townsfolk. But this entry was beyond vitriolic, cursing Armand with such viciousness that Simone was left stunned.

But the writing gave no explanation of the cause of her ire or the nature of the secret Portia believed had been found out.

"Sister, have you been struck deaf?" Didier floated the small white feather across the short span separating him and Simone and wiggled it under her nose.

She swatted at the tickling distraction. "Cease."

"You stopped reading."

"I know." Simone refolded the parchment quickly and placed it on the small stack of read entries. She would not voice Portia's wrath to the boy who adored her. She tried to hang a bright smile over her frown. "My eyes grow weary. Let us explore the keep instead."

"You lie—your eyes aren't weary. Any matter, you told me that I cannot"—his voice became an eerie mimicry of Simone's—"'flit about the keep, disturbing Lord Nicholas's guests.'" Didier stared at her accusingly. "What did you read that you do not wish for me to know?"

Simone searched for a plausible excuse, but any that came to mind sounded blatantly contrived, even for a young boy. She sighed. "Didier, oft times adults say—or write—things unsuitable for young ears."

"What things?"

"Adult things." She stood from the bed and began replacing the journals in the trunk still filled with her mother's gowns.

"Curses? Blasphemies?" Didier sat up, his already luminescent face bright with salacious curiosity. "Tell me!"

"Nay." Simone's legs felt weak. Although she had been delighted with the discovery of the journals at Withington's small inn, she'd had no illusions that her mother's private writings would lend any insight to the combative nature of Portia's relationship with Armand. This most recent entry, though, had opened a small fissure in Simone's perception of her parents' lengthy marriage and left her shaken and wary.

Would future entries reveal the secret Portia suspected Armand had discovered?

Did Simone truly want to know?

Didier huffed and flung himself onto his back once more when he realized that Simone was not going to accommodate his demands. "You treat me like a child."

"You *are* a child."

A knock sounded at the chamber door, causing Simone to jump. She gave Didier a warning look before calling out, "Come."

The door swung open, and her husband's towheaded first man, Randall, stood in the doorway. He bowed, and Simone immediately noticed the small leather chest under his arm.

"Good day, my lady. The lord requests your presence in his accounts chamber."

A tingle of excitement teased Simone's stomach. It seemed the more time she spent with Nick, the more she looked forward to seeing him again. When they weren't having a row, she was happiest in his presence.

Be wary, a quiet voice inside her whispered. *Charles made you happy as well.*

"Of course, Randall. My thanks." The man bowed again and turned to go, but Simone realized her predicament and stepped forward. "Er . . . Randall?"

He halted, and although his face was a mask of respectful patience, Simone could sense an urgency to be away.

"Yea, my lady?"

"I fear I do not know the location of the accounts chamber." She felt a blush creep over her cheeks. "Would you be so kind?"

Simone thought she saw the flicker of a grimace touch the man's face, but then he inclined his head graciously. "'Twould be my honor, my lady."

"A moment, I pray." Simone flashed him a smile and then crossed to the small dressing table. She picked up her polished reflecting disc, smoothed her hair, pinched her cheeks. Replacing the mirror, she began a thorough inspection of her kirtle for lint, shaking out the wrinkles, checking for the hem of her underdress.

"Sister," Didier called to her.

She glanced out the corner of her eye, raising one eyebrow as if to say, "What?"

"Good Sir Randall seems to be in a bit of a rush."

Simone turned and caught the guard rolling his eyes heavenward. "Am I keeping you from some other business, Randall?"

The soldier started. "Oh, nay, my lady. 'Tis no matter," he said, shuffling his feet. He hitched the small chest higher under his arm and glanced at it.

"You must tell me," she urged, stepping toward him. "You are very kind to assist me, and I'd not delay any important task the lord has set you to."

"'Tis of little import, really." Randall cleared his throat. "I am to ready some of the men for duty and then dispose of this chest before reporting back to the lord. Er, within the hour." He winced. "I was unaware that you did not know the way. But 'tis no matter," he hurried to add once more.

"And I am delaying you." Simone smiled and reached both hands for the chest. "Allow me to assist you."

Randall jerked the vessel out of her reach, his face pained. "My lady, Lord Nicholas would have me thrown in the dungeon should I allow you to perform a duty he set me to."

Simone frowned, her fists on her hips. "Don't be ridiculous, Randall. You have graciously agreed to aid me, at the lord's *request,* I might add. 'Tis no fault of your own that you are pressed for time. I am fully capable of disposing of . . . of"—she flapped a hand at the chest—"*that*. And Lord

Nicholas need not know about it, if you so wish." She smiled then. "Consider it repayment for your kindness."

Didier's voice rang out from behind her. "This is a bad idee-aaa."

Simone ignored her brother and instead hopefully watched the clearly uncomfortable Randall.

"I don't know, my lady," he said, wincing.

Didier tsk-ed. "Don't do it, Randall."

Simone sent the soldier what she hoped was her most persuasive smile. "I'll take care of the chest, and you can be about your other duties without delay. I'm certain you are very busy with the lord's return, being his first man."

Randall's chest puffed slightly. "I *am* a bit harried of late." He glanced at the chest held to his side, as if debating. Then Randall gave a short sigh. "Alright, then."

Simone clapped her hands together and beamed even as Didier groaned behind her.

"But you must destroy it completely in fire, my lady," the soldier warned, handing her the intricately decorated leather box. "There cannot be one splinter remaining."

"Of course," Simone promised, taking the chest. Its weight was surprisingly light for its sturdy appearance, and she wondered at its contents, hidden behind the small dangling lock.

As if Randall had read her thoughts, he pressed a tiny key into her palm. "This as well," he instructed. He paused, winced. "And you won't open it?"

"I wouldn't dare," Simone assured him, and now that she had sworn it, she wouldn't.

Simone turned to face the room, her eyes ignoring Didier's disapproving frown and searching for a suitable place to hide the chest until her return. Moving to her dressing screen, she tucked the chest and key under yesterday's discarded clothing. Satisfied with the effect, she returned to Randall's side.

"There you are," she said. "And you need not think upon it again."

"You have my undying gratitude," the soldier said, bowing. He offered his arm with a smile, looking much more relaxed.

Simone felt she had done a very good deed. After all, she wished Nicholas's men and servants to like her. "Now, allow me to escort you personally to the lord."

Simone took Randall's arm and, turning to pull the door closed, paused to point surreptitiously first at Didier and then at the floor: *You stay in this chamber.*

"Oh, alright," the boy sighed. "But don't be long."

Simone winked at him, and then closed the door after her.

"Sister, Sister," Didier muttered to the empty room. "What have you done?"

Chapter 13

"You wished to see me, my lord?"

Nick looked up from belting on his sheath to see Simone standing in the doorway, as fresh and pretty as he remembered. He sent her a smile and motioned for her to enter.

"I did." He watched her sink gracefully into a straight-backed chair before his accounting table, hands folded in her lap, a gentle curve to her lips

But was that a shadow of disquiet in her eyes?

He did not want to leave her so soon. Even with her many eccentricities, Simone was like a cool woodland brook, soothing and fragrant, lending a quiet vibrancy to Hartmoore's vast, gray canvas. He must have stared for several moments, for Simone flushed and prompted him.

"My lord?"

"Hmm? Pardon me." Nick shook himself and walked around the table to stand before her, resting his backside against the table's edge. "And how have you faired this morn?"

"Quite well. Except I—" she shook her head, chewing at her bottom lip, and her eyes flashed again with uncertainty. "My . . . my mother was keeping a secret."

Nick tried to keep the frown from his face, his tone neutral. "A secret? Of what?"

Simone shook her head again. "She only alluded to it in the last entry. I was reading them aloud to Didier to keep . . . to keep him occupied. I was forced to put the journals away before I could learn more."

"You do not wish for him to hear what your mother had written?"

"Nay. *Nay.* The things she wrote, the foul words she used"—her full mouth thinned into a grimace—"I cannot imagine my mother merely *thinking* such vile things, never mind putting them to paper."

Nick leaned back and crossed his arms over his chest. "This frightens you."

"Yea. If you had known my mother, you would understand. Even in her most raging temper, she never—" Simone broke off, pausing to collect herself. "She wrote that she prayed for my father's death."

Nick raised his eyebrows. "'Tis serious, indeed."

Simone nodded, and Nick saw the plea for help in her eyes before she spoke. "Would that you read the entry yourself, my lord. I cannot—" She paused again. "I fear any conclusion I would come to would be colored by my emotion."

"Of course I will read it." To himself, Nick added another clue to the riddle of his wife's broken family. Perhaps 'twas no simple marital animosity that sparked Portia and Armand's violent battles but some terrible secret Simone's mother harbored. Something Armand had learned. Could that knowledge be so threatening that he would be moved to kill his own wife?

But what role did the boy play in this deadly tragedy? Surely Didier must have posed some threat to have his young life snuffed short. But why then spare Simone? Of the two offspring, Simone would likely be the most dangerous if only because of her advanced age and comprehension.

Nick recalled Didier's offering of the cold water, the feeling of falling, drowning . . .

He pulled himself back to his wife's concerned face. "Unfortunately, though, the journal must wait until I return."

"Return?" Simone's expression turned from dismay to surprise. "Where do you go?"

"To the village of Obny, but a half-day's ride."

"Of course—the attack." Simone's eyes fell to her lap. "Will you be long away?"

"Nay—but overnight." Nick could plainly see the disappointment on Simone's face, and his conscience spasmed. In truth, he would like nothing more than to remain with her at Hartmoore, read Portia's cryptic journal entries, and see that Didier did not cause any more mischief. But this journey was much delayed already. Obny's minor assault by the renegade Welsh was a final, dire warning to Nick that he must set aside Evelyn's betrayal to serve his barony and his long-neglected friend.

"I shall return on the morrow, and by then, Minerva should have arrived." Simone nodded at his explanation, but her mouth was set in a grim line. He knew she did not relish being left alone in a keep full of strangers. Nick dropped to one knee before her and took her chin in his hand.

"Simone, I have no wish to be away so soon after we have arrived, but it cannot be helped. 'Tis my duty as Obny's liege, and I will not shirk it. My mother and Lady Haith will be here to keep you company and help you find your way—you shan't be lonely."

She frowned and jerked her chin from his grasp. "Good heavens, Nicholas. I am no child, in a temper at the prospect of one evening without anyone to entertain me—Papa left me alone enough for me to be accustomed to it by now. I am sad because I will miss you, you buffoon."

Nick felt as though he'd been kicked in the stomach at Simone's admission, but she gave him no opportunity to relish her tender remark.

"But if that is how you think of me—a brainless, spoiled ninny"—she stood—"then I shan't miss you after all. In fact, I'm glad you're going. Good day."

Nick watched her struggle against tears and once again felt

the pinch of his conscience. She'd had a trying morning and he'd just made it worse. Would he never learn a woman's mind?

He rose to his feet and took Simone's hand, drawing her to him when she would have pulled away. "I did not mean to imply that you were spoiled, and you certainly aren't a ninny," he said solemnly. "I apologize. I was merely concerned that you would be uncomfortable alone at Hartmoore after only one night."

Simone's petulant frown turned remorseful, and she unexpectedly threw her arms about his neck. "Oh, Nicholas, I know." She had released him before he'd had time to return the embrace. "I do not intend to cause you worry over my acclimation to your home. Lady Genevieve and Lady Haith and I will get on splendidly. I feel that I love Hartmoore already and will be quite content here."

Her words touched Nick. He wondered, though, if she would feel the same should she learn of the woman whom Nick had always assumed would be in Simone's place. His thoughts went briefly to the small leather chest so recently disposed of by Randall, and he was glad the reminders of the woman who'd wounded him were no more. Better his wife learn of Evelyn much later, when Nick's hurt had subsided and Evelyn at last meant no more to him than a stranger.

"Good," he said finally. "The time grows near when I must depart. Would you see me off?"

Simone accompanied Nick to the bailey where a score of soldiers waited with their mounts. Tristan was there, Majesty's reins in hand, as were Lady Haith and Genevieve. Many of the noble guests milled about the departing group, ladies in festive costume conversing and laughing in the bright sunlight. She snugged closer to Nick's side.

Had Nick slept with any of them? All of them? The thought chilled Simone, and she quickly shut it from her mind as she neared Nick's family.

"Simone, darling," Genevieve called, bouncing the child, Isabella, in her arms. "Good day."

"Good day, my lady," Simone replied, and nodded to those gathered.

Nick removed his arm from Simone's grasp and stepped to his mount, checking his horse's trappings.

At her side, Haith touched Simone's elbow, drawing her attention. The redhead lowered her voice. "How fare thee, Lady Simone?"

Simone knew the question was more than a polite inquiry. "Things could be worse, I suppose," she murmured.

Haith's eyebrows rose. "Yea, mayhap Didier could have set the great hall afire."

Simone sighed, nodded. She glanced at Genevieve, satisfied that the dowager baroness was occupied with handing a giggling Isabella up to her father. Simone leaned toward Haith.

"This Minerva Nicholas has mentioned—who is she? And when will she come?"

"She is my great-aunt, a powerful healer," Haith replied. "I expect her in a day—two, mayhap. She was attending my sister's childbed and should be en route to Hartmoore this day. She is elderly and needs travel slowly."

Simone frowned, the information doing more to worry her than allay any fears. Heaven only knew what havoc Didier could wreak in a pair of days. "Do you truly believe she can help us?" Simone asked, hearing the desperation in her voice.

"If anyone can, 'twill be Minerva." Haith squeezed Simone's arm and gave her a kind smile. "We shall do what we can in the meantime."

Simone was unconvinced that the two women could do anything to curb the boy's prankishness—even if one of them *was* a witch. But then Nicholas turned toward her and held out a palm. Simone immediately moved to him, happy in a catty way that the ladies in the bailey watched them still.

"But overnight," Nicholas reminded her. The bright sunlight gilded his jaw, and Simone had the urge to kiss him there.

But she only nodded. "Safe journey, my lord."

Nick's family moved away, and Simone felt a slight tug on her hand. She stepped closer to Nick, giddy with anticipation that he would kiss her.

He embraced her briefly, laying his cheek against the crown of her head. Then he released her and stepped away, dropping her hand. Simone tried to squelch her disappointment.

"Lady Haith," Nick said to the redhead, who was just now releasing her own husband from a passionate kiss. "I do hope you and Lady Simone will become . . . *better acquainted* during our short absence." He glanced at Simone, and his meaning was not lost on her.

"Not to worry, Nick," Haith answered. "We shall—"

Her reply was cut off by a commotion across the bailey, beyond the raised portcullis, and Simone prayed Didier was not the cause.

"What now?" Nick muttered as a guard crossed the dusty expanse toward the group.

"My lord," the young man called. "A visitor at the gates for Lady Simone."

"For me?" Simone asked, her surprise evident in her voice. "Who?"

The guard had reached them and waited for Nick's slight nod before continuing. "'Tis your father, my lady."

Nick could not suppress the curse that issued from his mouth. He threw his gauntlets to the dirt even as Simone turned to him, a childlike brightness lighting her green eyes. The bastard.

"My father? Nick, did you call for him?"

Nick snorted. "Nay." To himself, Nick surmised the miser was looking to wring more coin from him. But still, he was rather surprised that Armand had tracked them all the way from London when he was to return to France soon. His arrival at Hartmoore could only spell trouble. Even now, muffled snatches of the man's blustery argument for admission reached them.

Nick turned to the guard. "Deny him."

"Aye, my lord." The young soldier began to walk away.

Simone gasped, and Nick looked at her, impatient to be done once and for all with Armand du Roche and be about his duty to Obny. Nick did not trust the man and was yet unconvinced he'd not had a hand in his wife's and son's deaths.

"I am sorry if this displeases you, Simone," Nick offered, "but your sire has not endeared himself to me. He's gotten all the spoils that he would, and I'll not have him in my home."

Simone only blanched, but Genevieve was more forthright in voicing her displeasure.

"Nicholas, how dreadful," she exclaimed. "Surely you did not expect Simone's father to leave England without saying farewell—he may never see her again."

"Actually, Mother, I expected exactly that." He looked to Simone and was not surprised to see her staring toward the barbican. His wife so wanted the love of her father, and yet Armand threw his daughter's affection in her face time and again. Even after his gross mistreatment, Simone still held out hope that Armand would soften toward her.

Tristan drew near Nick. "Brother," he began, but one more glance at Simone's sad face had Nick cursing once more, cutting short Tristan's lecture before it could begin. He would not allow his brother to chastise him in his own bailey.

"Thomas!" Nick called to the retreating guard. The man paused, turned. "Give Lord du Roche entry."

Simone smiled at him and then craned her neck to search the barbican for signs of her emerging father. Nick swore he could almost hear her hopeful thoughts—that her father had come to Hartmoore because he missed her, because he loved her. Nicholas would not allow Armand to crush Simone again. Although wary of du Roche, Nick did not worry for his wife's safety at Hartmoore.

"Wife," Nick called, drawing Simone's reluctant attention. Her eyes shone.

"Yea, my lord?"

"You know full well that I have no desire for Lord du Roche's presence at Hartmoore while I am absent, but I cannot delay my errand. Have your visit, say your farewells, and heed my command that he be gone by morn."

Simone nodded. "Of course, my lord. As you wish."

Nick saw the man riding into the bailey, and his stomach churned. "And he's not to receive any gifts while here. From anyone. I know not why he's come, but knowing Armand du Roche as I do, it can only be for some gain."

Genevieve turned startled eyes to Nicholas. "Who?"

Simone replied for him, a sweet smile on her lips. "Armand is my father, Lady Genevieve. I thought he would leave for France from London, but . . ." She gave a happy shrug.

Genevieve's face paled. "Armand du Roche is your father."

Simone turned to Nicholas, her eyes showing a growing concern.

"Mother, what is it?" He grasped Genevieve's elbow. "You're making Simone quite uncomfortable. I told you Lord du Roche is Simone's father."

"Nay. Nay, you"—Genevieve's eyes flicked from Nick to Simone, Haith, and then finally Tristan—"you did not give his Christian name."

"Lady Genevieve, are you unwell?" Simone asked tentatively, stepping closer to Nick's mother.

But Genevieve did not respond, only brushed between the two couples, her fingers fluttering against bloodless lips. Nick turned and watched his mother stop and stare at the dusty cloud heralding Armand's mounted entry into the bailey. The man in question spotted them and dismounted, tossing his reins to a nearby lad before limping stiffly toward them, his right arm drawn against his side.

Simone touched Nick's arm, drawing his attention. He looked down at her worried face and shook his head in answer to the question in her eyes.

"'Tis not possible," Genevieve whispered, her gaze pinned to the large man approaching.

Armand called out as he drew nearer. "Simone, would that you not abandon me to the company of such crude laborers in eagerness of your station," he chastised, slapping billowing sheets of dust from his tunic. "I vow they would have kept me standing about like a common beg—" Armand halted in his stride and words simultaneously, not ten paces from where Nick and his family stood. His eyes first narrowed, then went wide.

"Genevieve," he breathed.

Nick stepped forward and glared between his mother and Armand. "Do you mean to tell me that the pair of you are acquainted?"

Genevieve ignored her son and backed away, first just a step, then two more, her heels slipping and dragging in the fine silt. "It cannot be," she whispered. Tears sprang into her eyes, unblinking, as she searched Armand's face. Her next words were nearly inaudible through her constricted lips.

"You're . . . *you're dead.*"

Nick heard Simone's gasp, and he quickly took hold of Genevieve's arm once more, this time none too gently. "Mother, you are confused. 'Twas Simone's mother who was killed in the accident—not her father."

Armand shook himself from his own stupor and slowly walked toward Nick and Genevieve, a strange, half-smile on his twisted lips. "How fortunate our reunion is, Lady D'Argent. In truth, there has not passed a single day since last we spoke that I did not wonder at your whereabouts."

Nick frowned. "She is now called Lady FitzTodd, du Roche. My mother is the dowager Baroness of Crane and commands your respect."

But to Nick's growing rage, Armand was oblivious to the reprimand. He now stood before Genevieve and pulled her hand to his lips, his eyes never leaving hers as he kissed her fingertips. "I cannot tell you how it gladdens me to see you once more."

A strange gurgling was Genevieve's only answer as she

snatched her hand from Armand's and wiped it against her skirts. "*Non, non . . .*" She backed up into Nick's chest.

"Mother." Nick grasped her shoulders and turned her, and the raw terror in her eyes shook him. "What on earth is it?"

Genevieve stuttered, a single tear sliding down her cheek. She glanced at Simone and then fell against Nicholas, unconscious.

Chapter 14

Simone waited in the lavish great hall for her husband's return, her stomach in knots. Her first full day as Hartmoore's mistress had been going quite well until the moment Armand had arrived.

How very typical.

She sat in an upholstered chair, her muscles turning to cold iron, and eyed her father as he moved about the cavernous room, inspecting the ornate tapestries and weapons displays decorating the walls. Her mind went to the journal entry she'd read this morning—what secret had her father discovered? Would he tell her if she asked? She chuckled to herself. Of course he would not. She felt the ultimate fool for hoping, even for an instant, that her father had come to Hartmoore to reconcile with her. His attitude toward Simone had not softened in the least.

So be it. But Hartmoore was *her* home now, Nicholas her husband, Genevieve *her* family. Armand would not ruin it. He would not.

Drawing a deep, silent breath, Simone rose from the chair and crossed the hall to stand at her father's side. Armand stood with his head tilted, admiring a mounted shield embossed with the FitzTodd crest, a jagged scratch now marring its surface, thanks to Didier.

"Papa," she ventured, "Lady Genevieve seemed rather distraught at your arrival. How is it that you know her?"

Armand's jaw muscles flinched under his sagging jowls, making him appear to tremble. "Ah, we met long ago. In Paris. I was quite enamored with her at one time."

Now 'twas Simone who flinched. "Did *Maman* know of her?"

"*Non.* Genevieve D'Argent had fled France before I met Portia."

"You know that she fled France?" Simone asked, unable to keep the surprise from her voice.

"Of course—who did not know? The woman murdered a nobleman, on their wedding night, in fact." His voice grew low, as if sifting the memories from a dense fog. "'Twas the scandal of the decade at court."

Simone swallowed, gathering her courage into a meager pile. "Were you in love with her?"

Armand snorted. "You think too much on that fantastic emotion, Simone. Love is merely a meeting of lust and opportunity. It has no place in reality, for the more you seek it, the better it eludes you. Love . . . love is a myth. A fabled treasure."

Simone shivered, gooseflesh washing over her like a blustery wind. "I don't believe that," she blurted.

Armand merely shrugged. "You will learn."

Simone's bravado had more or less run out, but she could not keep from pressing on. "Then you did not love *Maman* either?"

Armand turned to look down at his daughter, a bemused smile twisting his face. "Of course not."

A lump caught in Simone's throat and she fought to break it to pieces by swallowing hard. She could not block the implications of Armand's confession: neither of his children had been conceived in love. She was infinitely glad Didier had not been present to hear the blithe admission—surely all of Hartmoore would be incased in ice if he had.

But now was not the time to shed tears over Portia's loveless union, not when Simone's future teetered on Lady Genevieve's return. Nick's mother's demeanor would likely set the tone for Simone's life at Hartmoore, and Simone could only hope that whatever past lay between the dowager baroness and Armand, it would not taint Simone's relationship with Nick.

And she was unable to wait any longer for her husband's return. Simone straightened her spine, composed her face. "If you will excuse me, Papa, I'm going to find Lord Nicholas." She turned to go, but Armand's hand snaked out, staying her.

"*Non.* You will wait here with me and we will hear Lady Genevieve's explanation together."

Simone wrenched her arm from his grip and backed out of his reach. "I will not. I am worried for the lady and wish to speak to *my husband* privately."

Armand's face darkened, and the skin drew taut from his eye to his chin. "Don't threaten me, Simone. You'll do as I say, and I'll have no argument from you."

"Is aught amiss?"

Simone nearly wept with relief as Nick's strong voice filled the hall. She spun to see him crossing the breadth of the chamber, a very pale Genevieve between him and Tristan.

"My lord," she breathed. She took a step toward them but then hesitated, glancing at Nick's mother.

Genevieve must have seen the uncertainty in Simone's eyes, for she smiled then, and beckoned to Simone. "Come, darling. All is well."

Simone reached mother and sons in a score of steps. "My lady, how do you fare?"

"I am much better now." Genevieve glanced up at Nicholas. "'Twould seem I became overexcited at the surprise arrival of . . . an old acquaintance." She released her sons' arms, and Simone thought she saw a look of determination harden the woman's eyes.

Had Genevieve been trying to convince Simone or Nicholas with that neat explanation? Simone could not tell.

The dowager baroness pulled Simone to her and tucked her

into her husband's side. With an oddly bright smile, she turned toward Armand.

"Lord du Roche, I do hope you'll accept my apology for my earlier behavior."

Simone rose slightly on her toes and tilted her head closer to Nick's. "What is this?" she whispered.

Nick frowned and shook his head, nodding toward Armand's approach, as if to say, "Watch and see."

"Please," Armand said, reaching Genevieve and bowing. "I can only imagine the shock it must have been."

Lady Genevieve's nostrils flared. "You are very gracious. Indeed, you also must have been taken by surprise."

Armand shrugged. "I always knew we would meet again. But what matters now is that our children have happily joined in marriage. How fortunate for us both that we will not be relegated to being kin to strangers, eh?"

"Fortunate. Of course."

No one in the hall moved, and Simone felt the tension gripping them all like a giant fist. If someone did not say something to disrupt the terrible silence, Simone felt as though she would scream.

Nicholas cleared his throat. "Well, then. We must be off. Tristan?"

The large blond man to Simone's left nodded, his eyes never leaving Armand. "Yea. Mother, do you require assistance in settling . . . your guest?"

Genevieve did not turn when she replied to her elder son, but continued to stare at Armand. "The pair of you go on, and have your farewells with your wives. I shall see to Lord du Roche personally."

Simone glanced to Nick, urging him with her eyes to intervene. For reasons unknown to her, she did not like the implications behind Lady Genevieve's words, nor the very manner in which her father stood before the woman, as if poised to pounce on her at first opportunity. She suddenly wished more than anything that she had quietly acquiesced to her husband's initial command to bar Armand from Hartmoore.

Nick frowned. "Are you certain, Mother?"

"Of course," Genevieve replied distractedly. "Lord du Roche and I have much to discuss after the passing of these many years. We shan't bore you young people with our reminiscing."

Haith took a fussing Isabella back inside the hall for her afternoon feeding, leaving Simone alone to watch Nicholas pass through Hartmoore's gates with his brother and small band of men with more than a little pang of sorrow.

And worry. What was she to do now, alone, and with Armand at Hartmoore?

Simone drew herself upright and took a deep breath. Nick would return on the morrow, and by then, her father would be gone.

"*Non!*" The cry sounded directly in her ear, and Simone could not help but shriek. She spun round to find Didier standing several lengths behind her in the dusty bailey. His unearthly pale face wore a look of ghastly horror as he stared after the lord's party, riding away from the town.

Simone walked quickly toward where he stood, her eyes scanning the busy enclosure for eavesdroppers. Several villagers and guests glanced at her curiously.

"Didier, what is it?" she hissed through tight lips as she neared him. "Lord Nicholas will soon return. Fear not."

"*Non!*" he cried again, the sound filled with heartbreaking anguish. He swerved around Simone and ran toward the gates in his odd, skipping–floating manner. Tiny dervishes spun and then fell in his wake.

Simone watched her brother fall to his knees as if he'd run straightway into a stone wall. The wail he sent up was a keening, piercing sound that not only shook Simone's composure but sent the birds roosting on the battlements to flight. Deep within the town, the village hounds added their mournful howls to Didier's cry. Several villagers in close proximity paused, their heads cocked as if listening, before shrugging and continuing in their tasks.

Simone did not know what to do. Didier's bony shoulders heaved with his tearless sobs, and she longed to comfort him. But countless people milled about—she could not be observed speaking to thin air, especially with the many guests from London in residence and so soon after escaping that stigma of insanity.

But Didier needed her.

She casually made her way toward the gate, cringing inside as she realized it was the second time she'd crossed the bailey, alone and seemingly without purpose. As she neared the boy, his sobbing quieted somewhat, but still he stared at the now-empty road, snaking over the bridge and away from Hartmoore.

"Didier," she whispered. "Come inside with me. You mustn't draw attention in this manner."

Didier said nothing for a moment, merely stared off at the hilly horizon and sniffed. When he did turn to Simone, the sorrow in his eyes caused her breath to hitch in her chest.

"Come," she whispered again, indicating the keep with a flick of her eyes.

He shook his head and unfolded his legs beneath him, coming to rest on his backside before the wide barbican. "I'll not move until Lord Nicholas returns."

Simone growled in frustration and looked furtively around her. "Didier, please. I cannot stand here all the day. Lord Nicholas will return on the morrow—"

"He won't."

Simone blinked. The solemnity and dreadful certainty of her brother's words washed fear over her like a dark, swollen river. She forgot that she stood in a common area, where any could see her drop to her knees.

"What do you mean?" she asked, fear hushing her words. "Of course he will. The village to where he hies is but a half-day's ride. He shall overnight at Obny and return on the morrow."

But still, Didier shook his head. "*C'est mal.* The place he goes to is bad."

At the chilling words, unease crept around Simone's heart and squeezed. She was prevented from speaking further as the screams of a horse drew her attention.

A serf driving a horse-drawn cart filled with great, round wine casks waited just beyond the gates. The aging, bony beast had stalled and was now rearing and pawing at the air, fighting his harness. The driver of the cart gained his feet, and his ruddy face plainly showed his displeasure at the horse's misbehavior.

"Git on now, ye temperamental Hell beast!" he bellowed, raising a slim switch. The swishing sound of the crude whip licking flesh caused Simone to jump. "Out of the way, lass— I ain't got all bloody day!"

The driver struck the horse again.

"Didier, please," Simone pleaded, her tongue flicking over her parched lips. "The horse will not pass through the gates while you block the entrance. Do you truly wish to be the cause of a frightened animal's pain?"

Her reasoning must have touched him, for he turned his face to her, watching her warily.

"You must move. If no horse can enter, then neither can any depart. Papa has arrived, and Lord Nicholas has commanded he leave at first light." When the boy still stared at her, Simone closed her eyes and raised her face heavenward. "Please, Didier."

When she opened her eyes once more, Didier had stood and was walking to one side of the wide road. Simone scrambled to her feet as the panicked horse gave a final piercing shriek and lunged forward, knocking the driver from his perch with a strangled cry. Simone felt rooted to the ground as the beast and cartful of casks barreled toward her.

She flung herself to the side of the road only in the last instant, the wrenching wheels whispering against the soles of her slippers and showering her with flying debris. The renegade conveyance clattered through the bailey toward the sheltering haven of the stables, sending serfs diving for cover before its cacophony dwindled away.

Simone could not coax her lungs to draw breath as she stared across the settling dust to Didier. The boy returned her appraisal with no expression, his often merry green eyes blank. Blurry, black spots danced around the edges of Simone's vision, and she felt the ground beneath her tilt precariously. A great gasp filled her at last, relieving her straining lungs but doing naught for her dizziness.

Simone stood with care, dusting herself off and waving away a pair of approaching guests, concern and curiosity lighting their faces. "I'm fine, thank you. Really."

Her eyes found Didier once more. The boy no longer stared at her but directed his gaze to the hills rolling away in the distance. Not certain it would work, but desperate to try, Simone called to her brother with her mind.

Come inside with me, Didier. We must talk about this.

He was still for several beats, so that Simone thought she had failed to reach him. Then he turned his face toward her, a flickering yellow glow like a sickly fire filling his green eyes. The voice Simone heard in her head was deeper, guttural, and quite unlike Didier's tone.

Lord Nicholas does not return on the morrow. Papa does not leave Hartmoore. He waits for you in your chamber.

Simone's flesh seemed to turn to stone beneath her clammy skin. What did Didier mean? That Nicholas would never return? That she would forever be saddled with Armand? And why would her father wait for her in her and Nick's own chamber?

The journals!

Simone spun on her heel and raced toward the hall at a run.

Chapter 15

Simone skidded to a halt before her chamber door, not caring that she'd left a string of shocked manor staff in her wake. If Didier was correct—and he always was in regards to Armand's whereabouts—her father lurked just beyond the thick door, dangerously close to Portia's writings.

Her chest heaved from her flight and also her fear, and she stared at the door handle, curving toward her like a serpent poised to strike. She fought back a wave of nausea and opened the door.

Simone's breath caught high in her throat at the scene before her: Armand stood at the foot of Nick's intricately carved bed, his back to her. In his left hand was a stack of creased parchment, and he quickly scanned the sheets and then flicked the topmost away with his clawlike right hand, where it floated to land on the thick mattress. The bed and floor around Armand's feet were littered with the discarded pages. Tens of them—a hundred, it seemed.

"Papa?" she croaked. "What are you doing?"

Armand did not jump at the sound of her voice, merely turned slightly, tossing her a self-satisfied smirk.

"Ah, Simone. I was looking for you."

Simone stepped fully into the room, sending the door

closed behind her. How much of the journals had he read? Would he try to take them from her?

"What are you doing in my chamber?" she demanded, her brave words tainted by the warble in her voice. "You have no right to go through my personal belongings."

Armand chuckled. "Do not chastise me so soon after your husband has evicted me from your home, Simone. 'Tis quite offensive."

Her fists clenched at her sides. "Get out."

"Besides," Armand continued, ignoring her command, "these do not actually belong to you, do they? You certainly did not pen them, nor do I think they were ever meant for your eyes."

He tossed the sheaths still in his hand onto the bed, and some slid off the side like a waterfall. "Although, having read their contents, I can understand why you would be interested in them, and why you also found it necessary to hide them away." He flipped a small metal object in the air, and it arced and spun before also falling to the bed. He tsk-ed. "I did not think you so foolish as to leave the key alongside the prize, though."

'Twas only then that Simone caught sight of the corner of the small chest poking from beneath the flood of pages, the fine-tooled leather nearly causing her to sob in relief. 'Twas the small box Randall had given her charge to destroy, and the letters were not Portia's, but some other written account.

She couldn't help but glance to the other, larger trunk, still closed and resting near the hearth, just as she'd left it. With a quick prayer of thanks, she crossed the room to stand between Armand and the bed, crisp pages crackling beneath her feet. Her courage increased a bit, and she tossed him a glare before bending to sweep the discarded pages into a pile.

"These belong to my husband. The baron would be much displeased."

An incredulous bark of laughter drew her attention up to her father. Armand stared down at her in disbelief, a frighteningly pleasant smile on his thick mouth.

"*Mon dieu,*" he breathed. "Could you be so naïve as to have taken possession of the trunk without knowing its contents?"

"Of course I don't know its contents," Simone replied tightly, gathering up the pages and rising. "It is not my affair. In fact, I was given the task of destroying it."

After a long moment of staring at her in amazement, Armand threw his head back and laughed so loudly that Simone jumped. He hooted and chuckled his way to a chair near the bed, collapsing into it in his mirth.

"I fail to see the humor in my respect for others' privacy," Simone bristled.

Armand dabbed at his eyes with his sleeve, still chuckling spasmodically. He flicked a hand toward the chest. "Read them."

"Nay." She dropped the pages she held onto the bed with the others. After dragging the leather box from beneath the pile, she began stacking the notes inside, careful not to let her eyes linger on the writings upon them.

"They may change your opinion of the honorable Baron of Crane and his journey this day."

"Nay."

She heard Armand rise and turned to face him as he neared.

"You may feel differently about staying on at Hartmoore," he advised, his face serious now, although traces of his smirk still lingered. "Mayhap you would even desire to return to France."

Simone frowned. Her father was speaking in ridiculous riddles—he knew full well that naught could entice her to return to the people who had shunned her after Didier's death. She had a chance for true happiness at Hartmoore.

But a splinter of doubt pricked her curiosity. Didier had said that Nick would not return on the morrow as promised, and now even Armand had given mention to the journey. 'Twas as if something were about under Simone's very nose and she was the only one unaware of it. Her eyes flicked unwillingly to the trunk.

Armand stepped nearer, as if sensing her weakness, his voice low, persuasive. "Do you not wonder what secrets they must hold for the lord to command you to destroy them?"

Simone wavered for a moment, not bothering to disclose that it had not been Nicholas who'd given her the trunk. Her husband's face flashed in her mind's eye. How disappointed would he be if he knew that Simone had pried into a matter where he had not invited her?

A man must have council with his own thoughts. I will not bare my soul to you—it belongs only to me.

The pages were likely nothing more than an old accounting ledger. Of course Armand would be enthralled with them, greedy as he was.

"Nay," she said, pleased with the finality in her voice. She closed the lid with a snap and seized it from the bed. Turning away from her father, she headed toward the still-bright coals in the hearth.

With a growl, Armand was upon her, jerking Simone by her arm and causing her to lose her grip on the trunk. It fell to the floor and popped open, spraying the pages across the rug.

She struggled against her father's grip. "Release me, Papa! I will not dishonor Nicholas by spying on him—that is your manner, not mine."

Armand's slap effectively silenced her and set a loud buzzing in her ears. She blinked, trying to focus her eyes, and felt the telltale numbness in her lips.

"You simpleton," Armand grunted, bending to the floor while still holding her captive. He rifled crudely through the pages with his twisted hand. "You stand and spout righteous drivel of dishonoring your beloved when your very presence here hinges on what is in this chest—items the baron wished destroyed."

He selected a page from the floor, shook it open, and scanned it silently for a moment.

Simone gingerly touched her throbbing lip and winced. "Papa, do not. I beg you."

"Ah, *oui*," he said, almost to himself. He cleared his throat. "Eighteen April. My dearest Nicholas—"

"Nay!" Simone jerked away.

"—I fear that I have made a most dreadful mistake in refusing your offer of marriage. Papa—"

Simone covered her ears with her hands and turned to walk to the chamber door. But Armand followed, still reading aloud, his deep voice easily penetrating her weak barriers.

"—Papa writes that you no longer visit Obny and I know that I am to blame. How I must have hurt you—"

Simone jerked the door open, only to have Armand slam it closed once more with his palm and then lean his weight against it, preventing her escape from the damning words.

"How I must have hurt you in my choice of the convent. But, Nicholas, I do confess, I am most miserable in my decision and regret it with each beat of my heart."

Simone finally gave up the struggle to flee and instead let herself slide down the length of the door until she rested on her bottom. Armand followed her descent, crouching down on his heels, reciting each syllable clearly. The words sank into Simone's brain like rusty spikes, nailing themselves into her memory.

"How I miss our long rides and conversations, you can never imagine. Please, Nicholas, if you still care for me at all, send word to Papa. I will be at Hartmoore in a thrice and we will be married as you wished. Handaar but waits for your word as baron to release me.

"Yours with much affection, Evelyn."

The silence filling the chamber after Armand finished the letter bore down on Simone with suffocating weight.

It all made sense now—Nick's swift changes in humor, his aversion to their marriage; the nun's stall in London, the convent at Withington. He was in love with this Evelyn, and she had refused him.

The stupid, stupid girl.

Armand's voice taunted her. "Do you now see? Your baron

fancies another. Even now he rides to this Obny. Your place here is tenuous at best."

Simone shook her head and looked up at her father. "He called for the letters to be burned. He must no longer desire her, or why would he wish them destroyed?"

"Ah, poor Simone," Armand taunted, a sparkle in his eyes. "When I discovered the letters, all were still sealed."

Panic welled, throbbing and fierce within her. "If he's not read the letters, he does not know—"

"*Oui*. He does not know his long lost love wishes to return to him." Armand rose, tossing the letter aside, where it fluttered and twisted and floated to the ground. He looked down at Simone with a haughty contempt. "How long do you think it will take Lord Handaar to relay the happy news to his friend?"

Simone shivered, staring at the pile of hateful truth as if in a trance.

"Fear not," Armand soothed, his voice sounding abnormally comforting. "Once William is informed of the baron's abandonment of you, compounded with his initial assault on your person, the king will no doubt grant us a divorce with lands and money. After all, you may be with noble child at this very moment. And I"—he looked around the lavish chamber, a secret, terrifying smile on his face—"I have come to feel a sort of affection for England. Mayhap I will stay on awhile—take a bride myself, before returning to France."

Simone's dread increased tenfold. She raised wide, tear-filled eyes to her father, and her voice was a shaky whisper when she spoke. "There will be no divorce, Papa."

"What do you mean, there will be no divorce?" Armand cocked his head. "Surely you do not intend to remain married to a man who would bring his mistress to dwell alongside his wife?"

Simone shook her head. "There will be no divorce, for one is not necessary. 'Twill be an easy matter for Nicholas to be rid of me once he's informed the king that—" She broke off, closing her eyes while a blazing heat crept over her face.

"What? Once he's informed the king what?"

"That we have not made love."

Armand's face paled, and he returned to the chair near the bed. "*Mon dieu,*" he said, and continued speaking in a low voice, almost to himself. "This could ruin me. All that would be required to dissolve the union is a statement from the baron citing a lack of intimacy. She'd be examined by the king's physician. He would demand I return the bride price." Then Armand's eyes blazed. "What is wrong with you, girl? Why have you not given your husband his due?"

"Papa, please." Simone had never felt such shame. "Didier—"

"*Non!*" Armand bellowed. "Do not t-take his name in vain, not my beloved son whom you k-killed!" He calmed a bit. Beads of sweat tricked down the deep seam of scar on his forehead. "Your mad reasoning matters not. I must concern myself with securing your position. I cannot leave England just yet . . ."

Simone felt numb. Only hours ago, her life had been on the verge of blossoming into a happy and contented future. But now . . . now, perhaps Nicholas would return and demand she leave.

Simone licked her dry lips. "Perhaps naught will come of this. Lord Nicholas journeys to Obny on business, but surely he will tell such a good friend of his marriage. That will be the end of it. He will not forsake me."

Armand's eyes narrowed, and he perched his chin on his ruined fist. "What father would not scheme to have his daughter a baroness, hmm? Particularly if 'tis a love match between old friends?"

Simone rose slowly from the floor, her muscles twanging in protest so soon after her near miss in the bailey. "I'll not draw any conclusions until the baron's return."

"Very well." Simone was more than a little surprised at her father's easy acceptance. "And I, too, shall stay on at Hartmoore until such time."

"But, Papa, Lord Nicholas ordered—"

Take A Trip Into A Timeless World
of Passion and Adventure with
Kensington Choice Historical Romances!
—Absolutely FREE!

Enjoy the passion and adventure of another time with Kensington Choice Historical Romances. They are the finest novels of their kind, written by today's best-selling romance authors. Each Kensington Choice Historical Romance transports you to distant lands in a bygone age. Experience the adventure and share the delight as proud men and spirited women discover the wonder and passion of true love.

Get 4 FREE Books!

We created our convenient Home Subscription Service so you'll be sure to have the hottest new romances delivered each month right to your doorstep—usually before they are available in book stores. Just to show you how convenient the Zebra Home Subscription Service is, we would like to send you 4 FREE Kensington Choice Historical Romances. The books are worth up to $24.96, but you only pay $1.99 for shipping and handling. There's no obligation to buy additional books—ever!

Save Up To 30% With Home Delivery!

Accept your FREE books and each month we'll deliver 4 brand new titles as soon as they are published. They'll be yours to examine FREE for 10 days. Then if you decide to keep the books, you'll pay the preferred subscriber's price (up to 30% off the cover price!), plus shipping and handling. Remember, you are under no obligation to buy any of these books at any time! If you are not delighted with them, simply return them and owe nothing. But if you enjoy Kensington Choice Historical Romances as much as we think you will, pay the special preferred subscriber rate and save over $8.00 off the cover price!

We have 4 FREE BOOKS for you as your introduction to
KENSINGTON CHOICE!
To get your FREE BOOKS, worth up to $24.96, mail
the card below or call TOLL-FREE 1-800-770-1963.
Visit our website at www.kensingtonbooks.com.

Get 4 FREE *Kensington Choice Historical Romances!*

♥**YES!** Please send me my 4 FREE KENSINGTON CHOICE HISTORICAL ROMANCES (without obligation to purchase other books). I only pay $1.99 for shipping and handling. Unless you hear from me after I receive my 4 FREE BOOKS, you may send me 4 new novels—as soon as they are published—to preview each month FREE for 10 days. If I am not satisfied, I may return them and owe nothing. Otherwise, I will pay the money-saving preferred subscriber's price (over $8.00 off the cover price), plus shipping and handling. I may return any shipment within 10 days and owe nothing, and I may cancel any time I wish. In any case, the 4 FREE books will be mine to keep.

NAME_____

ADDRESS_____ APT._____

CITY_____ STATE_____ ZIP_____

TELEPHONE (_____) _____

E-MAIL (OPTIONAL)_____

SIGNATURE_____

(If under 18, parent or guardian must sign)

Offer limited to one per household and not to current subscribers. Terms, offer and prices subject to change. Orders subject to acceptance by Kensington Choice Book Club. Offer Valid in the U.S. only.

KN047A

"Is it your wish to be tossed on your arse in a foreign country, alone and without so much as a mount should the baron favor the reluctant nun?" Armand demanded. "Tell me now, Simone, that I might know the very depths of your madness."

Simone knew he spoke true. If Nicholas did usurp her position, where would she turn? She knew no one outside of Hartmoore and possessed not Armand's conniving charm, which easily opened doors and garnered aid.

"I understand, Papa," Simone said calmly. "But you cannot be here when Lord Nicholas returns. There is an inn at the village of Withington—"

Armand frowned. "I know of it, you addle-brained chit. Think you I slept on the ground on my journey to this hellish hold?"

Simone took a deep breath. She must remain in control. "Very well. Once Nicholas returns, I shall send for you and perhaps he will allow you respite. But you do goad him overmuch, Papa, and it would not aid my cause were I to deliberately disobey him."

Armand chuckled as if she'd paid him a grand compliment and rose from the chair. "If he does not banish you from his home, I do believe Lady Genevieve will be of assistance in endearing me to her son. After all, she is a widow now, and with both her sons married, she will likely have want of a companion."

Simone cringed at the thought of the graceful Genevieve and her father as a couple, but she made no comment as Armand passed her and crossed to the door. With his hand on the latch, he spoke a final time.

"We shall see if I go or nay."

After the door closed, Simone's trembling increased. She stared at the pile of letters at her feet and wondered at her fate. Would Nicholas refuse her, send her away in favor of his Evelyn? If so, Simone did not know what would become of her or of the eternally young boy standing watch at the gates, stubbornly awaiting the lord's return.

She knelt by the hearth with a shuddering sigh and stoked

the coals, adding ragged tufts of dry peat until a small fire blazed. Moving to a cross-legged seat, she stretched her arm to the scattered pages and retrieved a handful, wrinkling them hopelessly, but uncaring. She unfolded the topmost sheaf and read it through before slipping it into the flames. The edges quickly retreated with a blackened curl, and in seconds, the missive was devoured in a tiny burst of flame. She reached for another letter. Then another. On and on, she methodically sifted through the buttery pages.

My dearest Nicholas . . .

How I miss your company . . .

Do you remember when we were children . . .

My dearest Nicholas . . .

My dearest Nicholas . . .

When dusk finally blurred the corners of the chamber, there were no more letters and the small leather chest was disintegrating in a shower of sparks. The tiny, silver heart-shaped key was all that remained, and Simone raised her fist to hurl it in after the chest.

But her fingers would not uncurl. She felt the key's slight impression on her skin as if it were seared to her palm, each fine turn of metal clear in her mind.

The blaze in the hearth warmed Simone's body and evaporated the tears on her cheeks, but it could not dispel the cold fear in her heart.

Chapter 16

Nicholas could not suppress the sense of relief that enveloped him as he and Tristan led the men over the hilly terrain toward Obny. Behind him lay Hartmoore and his beautiful—if a bit unusual—new bride; around him, as far as his eyes could see, stretched a prosperous barony. By the time he returned to his home, all would be set to rights with Handaar, Armand would be naught but a distasteful memory, and Minerva would have likely arrived. Perhaps with the old healer's help, Simone could begin to make peace with her past as well.

Yea, this day signified a fresh start. He would show his underlords that he had ultimate control of his lands—they had naught to fear. Nick very much looked forward to reestablishing his connection with Handaar. He'd sorely missed the old warrior's council and had to restrain the boyish excitement that tumbled in his stomach as they drew nearer to Obny. He had much news to share, and much to ask of Obny's recent attack.

Beneath him, Majesty tossed his head and nickered softly, eliciting a chuckle from Nicholas. "Yea, boy—nearly there, now, are we not?"

Randall's shout drew Nick's attention from his mount. "Sire!" he cried, pointing to the rolling horizon.

The black tower of smoke boiling over the hills froze Nick's blood. He reined Majesty to an abrupt halt, prompting his men to draw near. Together they watched in horrified silence as the smoky pillar thickened and billowed.

'Twas Tristan who broke the shocked stillness. "Perhaps they are burning fields."

Nicholas shook his head, the movement little more than a twitch. "Nay." He watched the dark, angry cloud, and dread descended on him as cold and heavy as wet peat. Tristan had never been to Obny—he could not know that they were but halfway to the hold. The smoke from burning fallow patches of land would have dissipated from sight at this distance.

"'Tis a building that burns," Nicholas said, his voice jagged and catching in his throat. "A large building."

He knew he need not further clarify his meaning. The other men were all well familiar with the border town and would know that the only dwelling of a size to produce such a large indication of disaster was the keep itself.

Obny was under attack.

Randall shifted in his saddle, his unease representative of all the men in the party. "Do we send a rider to Hartmoore for reinforcements?"

Nick heard his first man's query but felt oddly mesmerized by the sight of the endless smoke. He was already too late to save Obny and he knew it. The burning of the keep would be the last action of any attackers.

The memory of each rumor doubting Nick's competence as baron flashed through his mind, accusing him.

"What say you, Nick?" Tristan prompted.

Nick swallowed the hard lump in his throat. "There's not time. We'll need every man we have."

He wheeled Majesty to face the men. "Circle wide and approach from the north. If any of the bastards remain, they'll expect approach from the south or east. Kill as many as you can, but keep together—if their numbers are too great for us to battle, try to run them back toward the border." Nick met each man's gaze, ending with his brother's, and was satisfied with the revenge-bright blaze in their eyes.

He turned Majesty once more. "Go!"

Nick's lungs ached as Majesty picked his way among the lifeless bodies tossed carelessly around Obny's burning shell. The sky above him was black with night and smoke, but his vision was regretfully unhampered. Flames still licked at the charred remains of the border town, casting the dead, the dying, in a maniacally gleeful glow.

He turned his horse to approach the opening where massive timber gates once stood. One of the huge pieces of wood lay to the side, unsplintered, the great beam that should have prevented entry unbroken. Few people milled about the carnage, most of them children and a handful of women—the attackers had meant to spare none. His own score of men were the only ones astride—even Obny's beasts were slaughtered, their steaming bodies devoid of tack and fallen in such a manner as to indicate they were trying to escape the flames when butchered.

When Nick and his men had arrived, the Welsh were already in retreat. The party had paused atop the final knoll in time to witness scores of Welsh fording the Wye, slinking back across the border and destroying all hope of immediate retaliation. For Nick to have ordered pursuit would have been tantamount to suicide. Their numbers were just too great.

"Mama! Mama!" a small girl shrieked.

Nick looked down and watched apathetically as the child pounded tiny fists on the chest of a woman severed cleanly in two at her waist. As Majesty carried him slowly past, the sightless eyes of the dead woman seemed to follow Nicholas, accuse him.

The horrific sounds swelling Obny's carcass invaded Nick's brain, swirled around it in a grotesque wail. Moans and cries and retching sounds flowed around the crashing of burning and falling timbers. Nick was no stranger to the carnage of battle, but this had been no real contest—the town's inhabitants slaughtered with such ferocity that many lay with their entrails exposed.

The only part of the town still actively burning was the keep, and Nick drew up before the hellish inferno with an absence of emotion. The great hall, where Nick's own father and Handaar had taught Nicholas to brawl and drink like a man, collapsed in on itself with a tortured wail of defeat and a shower of sparks.

As Nicholas stared at the gnashing pile of flaming timbers, Tristan drew his horse even with Majesty. Neither man said anything. Randall soon joined them and after a moment, he spoke.

"It's all gone, Sire," he said, and Nick noted the break in his voice. "I have counted but ten and seven survivors—mostly children."

Nicholas did not want to ask, but had to know. "And Lord Handaar?"

A beat of silence passed. "He is not among them."

Nick turned his attention back to the burning keep while Tristan asked Randall, "Stores?"

"Everything is gone, my lord. Burned."

Nick nodded to himself.

Randall cleared his throat. "I've ordered the living to be gathered at a cottage untouched, to the east."

Again, Nicholas nodded. He tore his eyes from the smoldering shell and slowly scanned what once was the bailey. Bodies lay nearly shoulder to shoulder, men and women, young and old, laid low within the very walls meant to protect them.

Nicholas felt each of their wounds on his own body, and his blood ran just as cold as the dead's, chilled by an anger and a guilt so fierce he could not fully comprehend the reality of it. Little more than a fortnight ago, he had been in London, at the king's birthday celebration, the only weighty thoughts in his head where his next bit of sport would come from, how he would escape matrimony's clutches among the marriage-hungry maidens. When he would have his next drink. He'd met Simone then, as well, not long before Obny was attacked by the small band of Welsh—seemingly of no consequence.

But now Nicholas knew it had been a scouting party—a preliminary raid to test Obny's fortitude. Had Nick been at Hartmoore, he would have come to Handaar's aid, scoured the border, routing out the instigators, possibly preventing this massacre. But Nick had been in London. In far, faraway London, dallying with Simone, getting himself wed.

His vision blurred with the thoughts and the smoke. Then a glimpse of white, a patch that should have been invisible from across the bailey, caught Nick's eye. He blinked. Beyond the wide, muddied rump of a fallen horse: a snowy fringe of hair ringing a smooth circle of flesh. A bloodied, crumpled leather coif lay near it. Nick slowly dismounted, dread eating a hungry spiral in his stomach.

"Nick?" Tristan called from behind him.

But Nicholas was moving, faster now. He neared the dead beast and steeled himself for what lay inevitably beyond.

Lord Handaar's prone form came into view, his right leg buried beneath the horse, his left tossed back at an unnatural angle. He lay twisted on his back, displaying clearly the bloody slashes in his tunic. One shoulder had been hacked clean to the bone and a wide, bruising gash marred his brow.

He was without mail.

Nick fell to his knees in the churning mud, a macabre combination of dust and blood. "My lord," he whispered hoarsely, reaching out a trembling hand to the man's chest. "Oh God, forgive me, Handaar."

The stuttering orange light fluttered over Handaar's craggy features, causing Nick to look more closely at the twitching of an eyelid.

"Handaar? Do you yet live, old friend?" He dropped his head to the man's bloodied chest and listened.

There! Faint and impossibly slow, a whisper of a heartbeat sounded. Nick scrambled to his feet and drew his sword.

"Tristan! Randall!" he roared, raising his weapon high and lunging at the dead horse. "Help me! Handaar is alive!"

Nick began hacking at the carcass pinning his friend, flailing with his sword and sending wide arcs of still-warm blood flying. His brother and his first man were at his side in a blink.

"What do I do, my lord?" Randall asked urgently.

"We must free him!" Nick never paused in his blows to the horse's limbs, but shouted to be heard over the thick, thudding cuts. "Take the head and neck!"

Without hesitation, Tristan had already begun the grisly task of dismembering the large war horse. Randall needed no further direction, and soon, two more soldiers had joined them in their efforts.

"Hold!" Nicholas fell back onto his knees in the warm lake they'd created, swiping at the blood dripping into his eyes. He dropped his sword and reached for one half of the portioned torso. "Take hold, men, and go with care. Now!"

The grisly part was raised with a powerful heave and rolled away, revealing the crater beneath, as well as Handaar's crushed leg. The chausses and skin covering it had split upon the horse's fall, busting the flesh and leaving thick splinters of bone protruding, Handaar's torn boot twisted backward in the mangled stirrup. None of the men witnessing the display spoke.

Nick crawled to the old man's head. "My lord," he called loudly. "Handaar!" He grasped the man's face and turned it toward him. "Handaar, can you hear me?"

Nick's heart leaped as a nearly inaudible groan escaped the man's bloodied lips.

Behind him, Tristan roared, "A pallet! And water—quickly!"

Nick jerked at his tunic, pulling it then his undershirt over his head as his brother and his men dispersed, leaving him alone with Handaar. Nick's body was wracked with tremors as the cold night air sluiced over his sweat-slicked back. Nick ripped at the undershirt, tearing wide strips.

"Handaar," he called as he worked. "Open your eyes, Handaar. Look at me!"

He pulled a slender dagger from his boot and leaned over the old lord's body, cutting away the bloody tunic. Handaar's pale chest was scored with slash marks, but the shoulder wound was most dire, still spurting blood when the fabric was peeled away. Nick eased the shoulder up, nearly giddy at the groan it elicited from the man, and wrapped several lengths of his torn shirt about the wound.

"Yea, cry out," Nick urged, breathless, working frantically. "Let me hear that you yet live." He tied the lengths in stiff knots and then lowered him back to the ground. "Handaar?"

"*Nick.*" The word was barely a whisper, but Nick's straining ears heard it clearly.

"Handaar, open your eyes, friend." He drew his face near to the old man's, willing him to speak again. *Please . . .*

"Nick," Handaar wheezed, his eyelids cracking open. He was so still. "Knew you'd . . . come."

"Of course, my lord. Of course I came. Stay with me, now."

"Dying."

"Nay!" Nick fought to squelch the foreign wave of hysteria that wanted to send him screaming from Obny's nightmarish bailey. "Nay, you'll not—I'll take you to Hartmoore, to my mother. Lady Genevieve will care for you there. We all will."

Handaar's eyes closed. "Obny . . . gone. Fiona?"

Nick's sob caught in his throat and he swallowed convulsively. The old lord knew his town, his home, was no more, and he was calling out for his long-dead wife. Nick prayed that she would not answer him.

Randall and Tristan reappeared, pulling a low, wheeled cart behind them.

"It's all we could find, Nick," Tristan said, dropping the long wooden poles of the crude conveyance.

Nick let his eyes flick to the cart. "I'll have to straighten his other leg before we move him."

"Do not." The strength of Handaar's voice startled Nick.

"We must get you to the cart, my lord. 'Twill be quick, I vow it."

Handaar's eyes opened slowly, rolled for an instant, and then seemed to pierce Nick's very soul with their intensity. The old man whispered something so low, Nick was forced to lean his ear directly over the man's lips.

"Say again, Handaar."

"Back broken." A wheeze. "Leave me."

Nick rose, swiftly shaking his head. He moved to Handaar's twisted leg, ignoring that the lord had closed his eyes and turned his head away. The limb was broken in several places, the myriad of angles making it difficult to ascertain the joints from the fractures.

Nick wrapped one hand around a boot-clad ankle and placed his other high up on Handaar's thigh.

"I'm sorry, my lord," he murmured, and then, taking a bracing breath, he straightened the leg with a swift, dragging motion. Nick's stomach knotted and cramped at the cracking and ripping sounds coming from Handaar's limb.

Handaar neither flinched nor cried out.

Nick looked up at the faces of the men standing around him. Each was grim, and one of the youngest men stumbled away to retch.

"Two men to each leg, two on each side." Nick rose to a squatting position. "I'll have his head. Steady now."

The soldiers stepped into position without hesitation, save Tristan, who went instead to his brother's side.

"Nick, we cannot transport him in this manner and expect him to live."

Nick looked up at his brother and was annoyed at the pity he saw. "I'll not leave him to die, Tristan. Do as I command or be gone from my outfit."

But Tristan did not heed the threat, only dropped to his knees. "His right leg is destroyed, Nick. Crushed. If he survives transport, the fever of it will kill him."

Nick stared at his brother with fury boiling inside him as

he realized Tristan's meaning. "I'll not take his leg! How will he fight again with only—"

"*He'll not fight again, any matter!*" Tristan grabbed Nick's head in both hands and pulled it toward him, their forehead's butting. Nick's breath heaved in and out of his body. "Listen to me, Nicholas. Handaar's battle days are past. If you wish to spare his life, he must lose the leg. I've seen it too oft, as have you. You *know* this!" Tristan gave Nick a firm shake. "Much as your heart would argue the contrary. Think, Brother."

The acrid smell of smoke and the sweet stench of torn flesh and sweat filled Nick's senses until he panted and shuddered, his fists clenching and unclenching at his sides. Tristan leaned his head back but retained his grip on Nick. He stared into his brother's eyes, and 'twas then that Nicholas accepted the truth of his words. Many a proud warrior had been laid in a grave with bloated and mangled limbs still attached. He knew what must be done.

Nick unclenched his fists a final time and raised his hands to mirror Tristan's hold on him. After a squeeze on his neck, Nick released him and moved away.

"I'll have need of hot tar."

Two soldiers quickly dispersed on that errand, Nick retrieved his discarded weapon and wiped it as best he could on his chausses, trying to remove the horse's thick blood. Tristan grasped his forearm.

"Let me, Nick. He was your friend."

"He *is* my friend." Nick shrugged off Tristan's hand and stared at Handaar's still form. "I'd have no other do it."

Tristan nodded and stepped away.

The men returned with the tar, placed it near Handaar's right leg, and quickly moved back. A queer calm seemed to descend upon Nicholas; his trembling ceased and his hands steadied. He sank to the ground at Handaar's hip, Tristan not far from his side. Nick hesitated when he saw that Handaar had once more opened his eyes and was now watching Nick closely.

"Don't," the old man breathed. "Please, Nick . . ."

Nicholas ran a gentle hand down the proud old face,

closing the damning gaze. Then he turned his attention to the split and mauled leg. He drew his sword high over his head and, with a cry that echoed through the dark marches, severed the useless limb with one blow.

Nick shot to his feet as a weak stream of blood spit across the dirt, and he turned away, leaving Tristan to the task of slathering the scalding tar over the stump. Nick bent at the waist, his hands on his thighs, while his stomach heaved painfully, yet nothing was spewed forth.

Tristan stood at his side when Nick straightened. "'Tis done," his brother said. "Would you have him moved now?"

Nick looked back at Handaar's broken body and saw that the old man watched him with bitter eyes.

"Yea. We'll take him to the cottage for the night, find him some ale. On the morn we'll start for Hartmoore. We may not reach it by nightfall." Nicholas knew that any movement of his men along the border this night was dangerous. With their small numbers, should any Welsh still be lurking about, their party could easily be overcome and slaughtered. "Send a man ahead to Withington—Evelyn must be told. And command that Randall travel to London as fast as the swiftest horse might carry him. The king needs be aware that we will retaliate against the Welsh."

Tristan nodded and for once did not offer an opinion differing from Nick's. The two men returned to Handaar's side, and the old man's body seemed impossibly light as they moved him to the cart.

Nicholas stood alone in the hollowed-out bailey as the cart rolled slowly away from the destruction that had once been Obny. The breeze wrapping around his naked chest chilled him, his bloody tunic crushed in one fist, his sword in the other, but still Nick stood in the cold wind, his heart crying out in unspeakable pain.

And he wished he had never laid eyes upon Simone du Roche.

Chapter 17

To Simone's great surprise, her father had been waiting for her in the bailey the next morn, ready to take his leave. Simone had fought the urge to disobey Nicholas and ask her father to stay. True, 'twas more dangerous to have him at Hartmoore, where he may stumble upon Portia's journals or further alienate Simone from Nicholas, but Armand was her only living kin. He was her *father*—who else could she turn to should her husband refuse her?

But she had bid him *adieu,* hoping that he would leave her with an encouragement or a kind word. Instead, Armand had only warned that did Simone not send for him within two days, he would return to Hartmoore regardless of Nick's orders and Simone would surely regret the repercussions. He had not embraced her, not wished her well, merely trotted through the gates eastward.

She had never felt so very alone.

Now Simone sat propped in the middle of Nick's wide bed, the mid-afternoon sunlight washing the scattered pages of Portia's journals with a cheery light. She hadn't slept well at all the previous night, her troubled thoughts chasing slumber away each time it neared. She yawned until her jaws ached and paused in her reading to rub her sandy eyes.

She tossed the most recent page aside, turning to stare out the deep windows toward Hartmoore's main gates. Simone could see no sign of Didier, but she knew he still kept his worrisome vigil.

Simone stretched her aching back with a groan and wondered for the hundredth time what Nick's return would yield. She was certain he'd intended for Simone to never see Evelyn's letters—Nicholas himself had no idea the woman regretted refusing his proposal. Perhaps he would return from Obny without mention of Lord Handaar or his daughter, and they could continue as before.

But could Simone keep the festering knowledge of a woman before her, a woman Nicholas loved and had voluntarily offered to take as his wife, to herself for all eternity? It felt dishonest somehow, but she could not tell her husband of the letter's contents—'twould be far too humiliating for Simone and would possibly cause kind Sir Randall hardship.

Simone groaned and rubbed her eyes again. Her mother's journals were not helping Simone's rocky emotional state. The dates of the entries had become more staggered, often leaving months between writings, as the content became more cryptic and confusing.

She picked up the most recently discarded sheaf and scanned it once more.

He left this morning and would not tell me to where he journeys. He must think me without brains that I do not guess his intentions. Let him seek as he would, though. He will never find it.

What does he plan? How much does he know? If I can survive these last few weeks, all will be well. Our fortune secure, our daughter married, our son nearby at his foster and safe. Armand needs remember that he too has his own dangerous secrets. He will not win. I swear it by all that is holy. On my very life, do I vow.

Simone shivered at the eerie words, wondering if her mother had had any idea when she'd penned them that her life would soon end. She set the page in the stack she'd finished reading and looked to the last bundle. It was tied with a thin cord—no ribbon for this lot. She picked it up and tugged at the twine, surprised at the packet's unusual thickness when only three folded pages were secured within.

The first two entries revealed nothing new. The first: *I will try to get away to Marseilles before Simone and Charles are wed to make my final plans. Armand is growing agitated. He knows he is running out of time.*

And the next: *He stopped me from leaving. Now all I can do is wait. And pray. We are so close.*

Simone looked at the last square for a very long time without touching it. It would be the last entry Portia had written before her death. Reading it would either reveal to Simone the secrets her parents were hiding or torment her for eternity with a myriad of unanswered questions. She picked up the folded page, pulled the edges apart.

The parchment was blank. But tucked into its fold was an additional sheaf, creamier than the pages that comprised the journals, thick and waxy smooth and obviously of greater age. Simone opened the letter, her heart pounding. Her eyes widened.

Decree of Marriage
'Tis witnessed on this third day of January, in the year of our Lord, 1058, that Portia Bouvier of Saint du Lac, ward of the Crown, has given oath of marriage to Lord Armand du Roche, an invalid.

Simone frowned. Why would her mother be named Lady of Saint du Lac before her marriage, and a ward of the crown? And why had her father been labeled an invalid? Armand had incurred his injuries before Simone was born, that same year, in battle for the French king.

She read on.

> *Upon this holy union, Armand du Roche accepts the charge of the town and lands of Saint du Lac and shall hold its possession and that of any heirs until the time of their majority, in lien of a debt owed to the crown of 10,000 gold coin.*
>
> *In return of this covenant, Portia Bouvier vows to protect from harm the demesne of Saint du Lac in her husband's stead, until such time that he is returned to health or until the time of his death, when the debt owed by Armand du Roche will be extracted from the funds of Saint du Lac and the manor handed to his widow.*

The bottom of the document was scrawled over with signatures, Portia's own a graceful swirl compared to the ragged X of Armand's, as well as royal and holy seals.

Simone stared at the decree, her mouth slack. Far from solving the riddle of her parents' marriage, the discovery of the contract had raised a score more questions. The wording was certainly odd—what of this debt owed to the crown? When Simone and her father had fled France, she'd been told that Armand was unable to pay the king's taxes because of Portia's loose purse strings.

But 10,000 gold coins was a fortune by any standard. 'Twas the French king's own missive that had garnered Simone and her father entrance to King William's birthday celebration. Now that Simone had married and gained Armand his bride price, 'twould be an easy matter for her father to stay on in England, build a new life, and forget the debt owed to the French crown.

Her mind picked at another disturbing revelation: Armand had been an invalid when he'd married Portia. Simone pressed her fingertips to her brows. She felt certain that bit of information was important to the riddle of her parents' marriage, but she did not know how to find out more. Certainly, Armand would not be amenable to answering such a personal inquiry and, in fact, would question where Simone had learned the facts of his and Portia's marriage contract.

Simone's head was spinning, tangled in the sticky web of her parent's half-truths and outright lies. She wished above all else that Nicholas would return so that she could seek his council. But Nick had yet to return from Obny. And Simone could not fathom his feelings toward her when he did.

So there was no one for her to turn to. Certainly no one who had known her father before—

Lady Genevieve!

Simone scrambled from the bed, leaving the pages of the journal scattered and fluttering to the floor.

Simone lost some of her bravado standing before Nick's mother's chamber door. What if the lady wasn't within?

What if she was?

Simone raised her hand, hesitated, then knocked.

"A moment, I pray," the dowager baroness called from beyond the thick door, and Simone took a deep breath.

"I can come back if you are indisposed, Lady Genevieve," Simone said, now wondering what exactly she would say when faced with the woman.

She heard the scrape of the bolt being drawn back, and the door swung open, revealing a pale Genevieve, a ghostly smile on her lips. "Of course not, darling," Genevieve said. "Come in."

"I did not wake you, I hope," Simone said, entering the chamber and eyeing the rumpled bed coverings.

"Oh, nay." The blond woman gave a weak laugh. "I must admit to merely being slothful." She shut the door after Simone and threw the bolt once more. Simone thought it odd that the lady would lock herself in her own chamber but said naught of it.

Behind Genevieve's easy words, Simone sensed a desperate panic, and she grew more nervous about broaching the subject of her father. She looked around the chamber instead, noting the soft buff color on the plastered walls, the small tapestries depicting scenes of battle and horses and scripture. The bed was significantly smaller than Nick's own, the wood polished to an almost red sheen, the headboard sporting the insignia of the Baron of Crane.

"This was Nick's room as a boy," Genevieve offered, moving to the bed and pulling the furs to order. "I spent so much time here when he was young, 'twas the only room I felt comfort in after Richard's death."

"It is a good room for a boy," Simone said, a genuine smile curving her lips. She could just imagine the dark-haired young rogue playing on the wide window ledge or pretending battles on the faded and scarred map of England painted expertly on the wooden floor. Genevieve had not changed the room to suit a woman in any way.

"He did love it," Genevieve admitted. "After Richard died, I could come in here and sleep, and pretend that Nicholas was still a boy. That he was having nightmares and needed me." She walked to the window and looked out, presenting her back to Simone. "It felt . . . normal. Sleeping in that big bed in your chamber without my husband did not."

Simone did not know what to say to the poignant admission. She had been without Nicholas for only one night—she could not imagine knowing he would never lay by her side again.

"You still miss him very much, then?"

Genevieve turned, her smile so achingly sweet that Simone felt tears welling in her own eyes. "With every breath." She sighed, walked to the bed to stroke one tall post. "He made this for Nicholas, with his own hands. Richard was considerably older than I when we wed, and he was resigned to the fact that he would never have an heir. When Nick was born, Richard . . . Richard thought the sun rose and set in that boy. As did I. We both doted on him, likely to excess. Look," she said, turning and crossing the room to the largest tapestry covering a far wall.

Simone followed the woman to the woven piece as she pulled it aside, revealing a short wooden door. "'Twas Nick's own secret passage to the bailey, only steps from the stables. He thought I didn't know about it, but Richard told me. Nicholas would be sent up for his nap by his nurse and then sneak away to wherever Richard was. In this hold, Nicholas was a prince, a king." Genevieve let the tapestry fall once more. "I fear we may have made him overbearing, and not a little demanding."

"Nicholas is a good man," Simone said. "He has shown me great kindness, and I admire him very much."

Genevieve cocked her blond head, meeting Simone's gaze directly. "But do you love him?'

Simone swallowed, opened her mouth to speak, but then closed it once more. This was not going at all how Simone had planned. 'Twas *she* who was supposed to be asking Lady Genevieve questions, not the other way around. Now it was Simone who walked to the window. "My lady, I—"

"I know the tale of your hurried betrothal." The strong tone of Genevieve's voice indicated that she still studied Simone. "I cannot claim that Nick's behavior on the night you met surprised me in the least. I am rather shocked, however, at the easy way you seem to have taken to each other's company."

Simone could not bring herself to meet the lady's eyes, and her cheeks warmed. "I hope we have reconciled our differences from our initial meeting, my lady. Nicholas is most companionable, and I am pleased to have married him."

A beat of silence, and then Genevieve repeated her earlier question. "But do you love him?"

Simone did not know why the lady was pressing her so about such a private and complicated matter, but it set her already raw nerves singing. How could she relate her feelings about Nick when she herself remained so tangled in confusion? Nothing was simple now, it seemed, and Simone was

unsure if or how deeply to bare her heart to this woman, still
so much a stranger to her.

"I do not judge you, Simone." Genevieve's voice gentled.
"And know that your answer is for my ears alone." Simone
glanced up as Genevieve joined her at the window. The lady
pulled Simone's hands from their viselike grip on each other,
holding them tightly in her own. "But I must know."

When Simone raised her head to fully face Nick's mother,
she was shocked at the hot, heavy tear that fell from her lower
lashes. "Yea," she whispered, meeting Genevieve's hungry
gaze. "I fear I do love him."

"Oh, my darling," Genevieve soothed. "'Tis naught to
weep for."

"He doesn't seem to trust me. I . . . I fear he will turn
from me."

Genevieve drew Simone into an embrace, her voice low
and steady over the crown of Simone's head. "There, now.
These things take time. Nicholas has had much weighing on
him since his father's death." She paused, patting Simone's
back, as if searching for the right words. "He was hurt very
badly by someone close to him."

Simone reluctantly pulled away from Genevieve. Although
the comfort was badly needed, Simone already felt the fool.

"Evelyn."

Genevieve's eyebrows rose. "He spoke of her?"

"Only briefly." Simone drew a steadying breath. "But I am
not so dense, my lady. I, too, have my own shallowly buried
heartaches."

"*Oui*. Nick told me of your broken engagement."

It was Simone's turned to be shocked. "He did?"

Genevieve nodded. "It was because of Didier, was it not?"

Simone grew so still, she felt as though time itself had
stopped. "You think I'm mad, don't you?"

"Nay, not mad." Genevieve smiled sadly, and in a gentle
motion smoothed a lock of hair behind Simone's ear. "I do
think you miss your mother and your brother very much,

though. Oft times, grief plays cruel tricks with our hearts and minds."

"He's not a figment of my imagination," Simone said, willing herself not to frown and move away from the woman. Genevieve's reaction to Simone's admission was surprisingly open, and she had no wish to alienate the woman. "But I understand that you do not believe me. No one else does either."

"Nicholas does," Genevieve said softly. "I have never seen a ghost Simone, nor have I ever conversed with the spirit of one departed. Although"—she gave a bittersweet chuckle—"there have been many times I've wished my Richard could answer me when I speak to him. I do seem to be in need of his wisdom of late."

Simone grew very still. "Lady Genevieve, may I pose a personal question to you?"

There was but the slightest hesitation before she answered. "Of course, darling."

"How do you know my father?"

Genevieve stared at Simone, the baroness's posture as rigid as Hartmoore's stone walls. A hollow pit grew in Simone's stomach at the ensuing silence, and she wondered that she had just made a dreadful misstep.

Or hit upon the very answer she sought.

Genevieve blinked and shook herself before reaching out to clasp Simone's hand once more. "'Twas so long ago—" She halted again, and Simone could feel her hesitancy. "I knew your father only briefly before I came to England. We met when we were both very young, before he received his commission in the French Army. We were reintroduced years later and spent some time together before he married your mother."

"Did you meet her? My mother?"

Genevieve shook her head. "Nay. I had already left France by the time your parents had wed. My relationship with Armand up to the point that I came to England would have made a meeting with your mother . . . highly inappropriate."

Simone's eyes widened as she stared at Genevieve's reddening face. "Oh," she whispered, bringing a hand to her lips. "Forgive me, my lady, for my prying."

"Think naught of it." Genevieve revived a brittle smile. "Now Armand and I are reunited. I am a widow now, and Armand may prove to be a welcome companion."

Simone's dread increased at hearing Genevieve's reply—so eerily reminiscent of Armand's words just the day before. She felt she had to press on, had to know fully, beyond all doubt. "But . . . you said"—Simone swallowed—"when Papa came to Hartmoore, you said, 'You're dead.' Why . . . why would you think that?"

Genevieve's eyes hardened, and Simone was not a little frightened at the fierce spark she saw in the faded blue depths. "I was very young and naïve, Simone. Someone had told me he had died, and I believed them. Obviously, I should have inquired further of that particular rumor before I left France." Genevieve's eyes narrowed. "Why do you ask?"

"Ah . . . no reason." Simone tried to laugh. "It is quite a co-incidence that I would marry your son, is it not?"

"Indeed." Genevieve's face relaxed after a moment. "Will you dine with the guests this eve?"

"Forgive my weakness, but would that you permit me to take my meal in my chamber, my lady."

"You may take your meal wherever you like." Genevieve sent Simone a worried frown. "Are you feeling unwell?"

"Nay, merely tired." Simone gave a sheepish smile. "I did not sleep well last night."

"Worried about Nicholas, are you?"

Simone doubted Lady Genevieve could ever fathom the true depths of her worry. "I am eager for his safe return, yea. I expected him today."

Genevieve nodded. "He and Lord Handaar are good friends and have not seen each other in many months. It does not surprise me that he is delayed."

"So you portend his return on the morrow?"

"Most likely." Genevieve smiled. "I'll have water sent to your chamber for a bath, if you like."

"I would. Thank you." Simone felt oddly traitorous, abandoning her kind mother-in-law to dine with the guests alone, but she had need to be alone and think before seeking Didier on the battlements. She felt that the pieces of the puzzle were all present now, and she only needed time to fit them together properly.

"Very well, darling. I'll see you on the morrow." Genevieve walked Simone to the door and then leaned in and kissed her forehead. "Good night. Sleep well."

Cheery fires blazed in each of the commanding hearths, and by nightfall, Simone had bathed and eaten sparely of the hearty stew. With her damp hair plaited and a fresh gown on, she set out from her chamber, stealthily making her way through Hartmoore's narrow stone passages to the wallwalk. In one hand, she carried a lantern to dispel the inky blackness of the night-cloaked corridors, and in the other she held a small chunk of bread—a meager peace offering to perhaps coax Didier from his perch.

Climbing a short flight of steps to a thick, metal-strapped door, Simone emerged onto the wallwalk near the rear of the keep. She saw clearly Didier's shimmery outline, sitting cross-legged on the moon-rinsed stone, his elbows on his knees, his chin on his fists. Near his far hip was a small, dark shape, blending into the shadows. She heard the mournful hoot of some night bird.

"Didier," she called in a low voice, closing the door carefully behind her and wincing at its creak. "I've brought you a gift."

He did not reply. Simone drew nearer to his statuelike pose and dropped to her knees. She was on her feet again in an instant, the short scream escaping her throat before her hand could cover her mouth, and she nearly dropped her lantern.

Her shriek bounced off the stone walls, echoing over the hills, and Simone hoped no one would investigate her alarmed cry.

The brown bird at Didier's side jumped a little on its feet, ruffled its wings, and gave a startled little coo but did not fly away. It stared at Simone with eyes seemingly the size of Didier's fists, giant black orbs ringed with eerie, dazzling yellow.

"Didier," Simone gasped, clutching at her chest. "What on earth is that?" The cold breeze cut to her damp scalp and smelled of ice, adding to the chill of fright the creature had given her and stealing her breath. She scolded herself for not donning a cloak. Her nose ran and she sniffed.

"*He's* an owl and his name's Willy," Didier said, staring at the invisible horizon. "He won't harm you."

Simone lowered slowly to her knees once more, keeping a wary eye on the bird. Willy was obviously leery of Simone as well, for he skittered and ducked away when she dropped to the wallwalk. Simone dragged her gaze from the owl.

"Didier, please come down from here," she implored. "I have discovered some things about Papa—about his treasure—that are quite disturbing. We may be forced to leave Hartmoore."

She thought she saw him glance out of the corner of his eye toward her, and so she pressed on. "Look what I've brought you." She laid the tiny chunk of bread on the rough stone near his knee. The owl hooted curiously and sidled closer. "And I've saved some stew in my chamber as well. Come inside with me so that you will be close at hand in case we must go."

The boy reached out a hand and fiddled with the bread. "I can't," he said at last. "I'm waiting."

"But Lady Genevieve says that Lord Nicholas will return on the morrow. Surely you can give up your vigil now."

But Didier shook his head. "*Non.*" He turned to Simone. "Why can you not stay here with Willy and me and we will all await the baron together?"

Simone hesitated, but then another frigid gust buffeted her body. "I'll freeze, Didier," she implored. "Besides, what if I am missed at the keep? There is no logical explanation for me to sleep atop the wallwalk."

"What of it?" Didier shrugged and picked up the bread. He held it out to the owl in his palm, and the bird picked it up daintily with his sharp-looking, hooked beak. "You are mistress here—you may do as you please. If it pleases you to stay, stay. Should it not please you . . ." He shrugged again. "I'll not be going with you, any matter."

Simone sighed, her teeth chattering and her muscles stiff with cold and fatigue. "Fine, Didier," she said, her ire rising. "Fine. Stay here for as long as you wish, while I must go inside and carry this burden on my own."

He did not reply, and Simone gained her feet with a huff. Her supper nearly left her body when she heard the door behind her creak. She spun around, but the corridor beyond was dark and unoccupied.

"Go, then," Didier said.

Simone looked down at the ethereal form seated below her, her heart still thudding in fright. She was hurt by her brother's cool dismissal. She picked up her lantern and turned to go.

"He *will* return on the morrow," Didier said from behind her, giving Simone pause.

A final plea begging him to come inside was on her tongue but she squelched it, sensing he would not be swayed.

"Very well. Then I shall see you on the morrow." She stepped into the corridor and bid him a whispered good night before closing the door.

Didier sat in the quiet night, alone once more save for Willy. "Good night, Sister."

Willy snuggled up to his side and sat down on his bony owl feet. Didier arced a hand down the bird's back, certain it would be silky-smooth if he could feel it. The bird hooted sadly.

Many people were coming to Hartmoore, of that he was

certain. A great storm would envelop them all soon, leaving some stronger and others to drown in the aftermath.

He shuddered, and Willy hopped over to sit where Didier's lap would have been with a sympathetic little cry.

'Twas a race, now—who would learn the terrible truth first and use it to destroy their enemies. Death was coming for Didier again, regardless—this time in the form of an old woman.

He tried to cry.

Chapter 18

Simone smiled as Isabella struggled to pull at each item set on the table before her mother. Haith never hesitated in the conversation she was holding with the other women, but calmly plucked each contraband from the babe's chubby fist and moved it farther out of reach, often with a colorful, mild scold such as, "Och, leave it be, lass."

Isabella squealed in three-toothed delight when Haith handed her a large wooden spoon. Simone wondered if she and Nicholas would ever have children.

Simone wondered if she and Nicholas would even remain married after she told him the truth about Armand. After Evelyn.

Genevieve looked tired this morn, her eyes puffy and glassy, but she shook off some of her apathy and was entertaining the younger women with a scandalous anecdote about a particularly amorous male guest and a kitchen maid when a horn sounded, heralding the baron and his party's approach of the town.

Simone's stomach fluttered as Haith and Genevieve each gained their feet. Today was the day, then. In a few short moments, she would know if Evelyn still held Nick's heart. And Simone would tell Nicholas that it was Armand whom his mother had thought she'd killed in France, Armand who had

sought to rid Genevieve of Tristan. It was very likely that
Nick would set Simone from him, but for Lady Genevieve's
safety, Simone knew it was a risk she must take.

She rose from the table as a soot-covered soldier burst into
the hall and raced to Genevieve's side. In an instant, the lady
had lifted her skirts and flew into a run across the hall and out
the door to the bailey, leaving Simone and Haith without so
much as a word.

Simone increased her pace, Haith close at her heels, and
dread gripped the back of her neck. She called out to the soldier. She shortened her strides into a skipping trot and drew
near the filth-covered knight. "What is it? Where is the
baron?"

The soldier seized Simone's elbow and pulled her along as he
spoke. "Obny was under attack when we arrived, my lady. Lord
Handaar is wounded most dire—we don't think him to live."

Simone could only comprehend that there had been a battle.
Nicholas!

She shook free from the hand that sought to steady her and
flew from the hall in much the same manner as Genevieve.

Once in the bailey, Simone saw the party of Nick's men
crowding through the gate, leading a ramshackle cart. Genevieve had already reached the men and had thrown her arms
about one—Simone now knew for certain that Nicholas was
safe, and her throat convulsed in hysterical relief. But as she
neared the somber cluster of soldiers, her pace slowed.

Genevieve drew away from her son, sniffling and framing
his face with her hands as she spoke to him, but Simone could
not hear her words over the roar in her own skull. She vaguely
noticed Lady Haith running past her, following Genevieve as
the lady stepped away from Nick to Tristan, who stood near
the cart. Simone could now view Nicholas's battered appearance fully.

His hair was dull and stiff-looking, creases of black filth
streaking his face and neck. His ivory undershirt was missing, revealing Nick's tanned arms turned crusty with mud and
debris through the sides of his tunic—once a vivid blue and

silver, now stained an ugly brindle. His chausses were in tatters around his boots, and resting near his toes was the tip of Nick's gilded sheath, now caked with—

Blood.

Simone's heart hitched in her chest, and her gaze rose to meet Nick's. The usually sparkling blue orbs were dimmed as Simone stared at him, aware that she had stopped several paces short but unable to command her feet to move closer. It was as if she could feel an energy radiating from him, and it was not good.

He looked ten years aged from when Simone had seen him last, and he faced her with no expression, his long, muscled arms hanging limp at his sides.

"Nicholas?" she whispered around the jagged rock in her throat. "Are you injured?"

Still he stared at her, motionless save for the tic in his cheek.

"Nick?" Her voice had risen to a barely audible squeak around her sob, and she took a step forward. A breeze sprung up around the bailey, stirring the sick, metallic stench of dried blood. It stung Simone's nostrils and caused her to sway on her feet.

And then, because she could stand it no longer, she flew to him, wrapping herself completely around him and pressing her face into his chest, uncaring of the prickly stench and filth that caked him. His arms did not come around her, but still she held him tight, tighter.

"Oh, Nick. Oh, my love," she whispered into his chest, uncaring whether he heard her or not, but speaking in gratitude to the heavens for sparing this man. "Thank God, thank God."

Nick could not help but inhale deeply of the warm clean scent of her, tucked into his chest. He heard her mumbled ramblings, but the meaning of her words did not reach him. The feel of her tiny body, her unique fragrance so familiar to him now, caused him naught but shame.

She is the reason I return to Hartmoore with Handaar's body. If not for Simone du Roche, I would have returned from London weeks ago. And still, the scent of her, the sound of her soft weeping, caused Nicholas to almost wrap his arms around her, hold her close, take greedily of her warmth.

Instead, he took hold of her shoulders and held her away from him, conscious of the black smudges his hands left on her gown. Her pale pixie's face was awash with tears.

"What happened?" she wailed.

Nick had no desire to explain the tragedy at Obny to her—it would humiliate him to admit that he had been too late to save his border town. And besides, guests and their soldiers now crowded the bailey, shouting curses upon the barbaric Welsh, moving the cart that carried Handaar's body toward the great hall. Many hailed Nick, seeking his direction. The town had grown to deafening chaos swirling around them.

"I must see to my men." He stepped around her.

"But," Simone turned and fell into step beside him, swiping at her tears, "Lord Handaar . . . is he—?"

"He lives," Nick said succinctly, striding toward the stables and soldiers' quarters. "But for how long, I know not. If he regains consciousness, I must discover the name of Obny's attackers."

She was nearly running now to keep pace with him. "You will retaliate?"

Nick could not look at her as his anger boiled precariously close to the surface again. To see her, remember lying in bed with her in London, escorting her to markets and shops, laughing with her, dining in lavish halls on fine food, while all the while the Welsh had stalked his lands, made their plans. He wanted to wipe the memories of her, his tender feelings, away.

He halted, turned to her. "Obny is destroyed. The Welsh killed the villagers, sparing not even children or animals." Nick flung an arm back toward the gates, saw Simone flinch, but he did not care. "See you those handful of serfs? They are all that remain. See you the blood that covers me? It belongs to Lord Handaar. The smell that haunts me is of burning flesh. Can you smell it, Simone? Could you smell it from Hartmoore?" he demanded. "Yea, I will retaliate. I will have my revenge, and well."

Tears filled Simone's emerald eyes once more, but behind them now lay a spark of fury. Nick waited for her to rail at him, for her to flee him, horrified by his blunt and callous description.

"Then let them reap what they have sown," she said in a low voice. "You need but direct me, and I will do what I can, my lord."

He had not expected this response, and for a moment, Nick was struck dumb, struggling with conflicting emotions. Tristan's voice carried to him across the bailey, and Nick raised a hand and called out for but a moment longer. He directed his attention back to his wife.

"Assist Lady Haith and my mother with Lord Handaar's care. She and my father were very close to Obny's lord, and his condition will be difficult for her to accept."

"Of course."

He seized her arm and turned her toward the keep, continuing. "When we have readied the men, we will depart for the border."

Simone slowed her pace, pulling him almost to a halt. "How long?"

"I know not—a day, mayhap." He tugged her forward again until they stood near the entrance of the great hall. A steady stream of serfs and soldiers flowed in and out of the doorway like angered bees to a hive, and from the darkened interior, Haith's strong voice could be heard, issuing orders.

"Do you recall us speaking of a Lady Evelyn while we were in London?"

Simone's lips thinned almost imperceptibly, and she nodded.

"She is Lord Handaar's only child, and I have sent word for her to come immediately. Would that you look after her should she arrive after I am away."

If this news disturbed Simone, she hid it well. "As you wish, my lord."

"Go," he commanded, releasing her and backing away.

"Nicholas, wait," she called, reaching out a hand to him.

He paused. "What is it, Simone?"

She glanced over her shoulder at the keep. "My . . . my father—there is something you should know—"

Nick felt his brows lower. "Do you wish to chat about your father's unpalatable disposition while I have a man dying in yonder hall? I have no time for your reminiscing and riddles, Simone. In truth, I have grown quite weary of them. Is Armand gone from Hartmoore as I commanded?" At her hesitant nod, he continued. "Then do as I ask and torment me no more with the strange tales of your kin. Not just this day, but all days."

Simone paled even further, and Nick could see her swallow. She said not another word, but turned and slipped into the doorway with a swish of her skirts.

Nick set off in a trot toward the soldiers' quarters, his mind spinning with the tasks ahead of him even as his battered body called out for rest.

And Evelyn was coming.

Chapter 19

Simone's heart felt as though it had simply stopped beating as she wove her way through the swirling throng of people in Hartmoore's great hall. She could feel tiny pearls of sweat along her hairline and upper lip, but her skin was chilled beneath the light gown where Nicholas had touched her. Her breath came shallowly.

She is Lord Handaar's only child, and I have sent word for her to come immediately.

Simone tried to smother the ominous words as she moved absently through the hall. She felt as though she walked in a vast sea, the sounds around her muffled.

I have no time for your reminiscing and riddles, Simone . . . torment me no more with the strange tales of your kin. Not just this day, but all days.

A very young soldier—barely more than a lad, really—collided with Simone in his haste to join the battle planning and did not so much as look back to inquire of her welfare. Simone moved on, her eyes skimming the frantic faces about her, not really hearing their shouts.

She is Lord Handaar's only child . . .

There, near the monstrous hearth, she caught a glimpse of Nick's mother and Lady Haith kneeling over a prone figure, several housemaids clustered around them. Simone slipped through the buffeting crowd slowly.

I have sent word for her to come immediately.

Simone broke through the ring of onlookers surrounding the ladies and their patient, and her shock left her as if landing on the hard earth from a fall of great distance, the sounds of chaos erupting in her ears.

The unconscious man sprawled on the thin, woven mat was not whole. His head and features lay indiscernible beneath the wash of blood that painted his skull; his wide, sunken chest bore evidence of the mighty battle waged upon him—a blow to the shoulder hidden by a tightly knotted length of cloth, perhaps once white, now a terrible ochre color.

The only clothing covering Lord Handaar was the ragged remains of his chausses, and 'twas this article that caused the bile to rise high in Simone's throat. The left leg lay bowed and serpentine within the woolen confines, sick splashes of blood soaked through the material from the twisted flesh within, staining the garment black. The right leg—

Oh God.

The right leg ended in a wide stump a handsbreadth below the hip, the tar slathered over it catching the torn placard of chausses in its cool mire and leaving Simone feeling as though her breath had been severed from her own body just as cleanly. Her stomach convulsed, and she gagged as the stench from the wounds billowed up.

Haith's hands flew over the man with a small dagger, cutting away soiled bandages and the remaining scraps of clothing with urgent efficiency. Lady Genevieve followed Haith actions, gathering up the remnants of the useless material and weeping silently. Haith's voice bore no tremble has she called out her desires calmly, firmly.

"Two braziers and a pail of water—from the brewer's well, not the stream," she ordered, cutting the cloth carefully along the tarred limb. "Also a large, smooth stone. Rose?"

"Aye, mum."

Genevieve gasped and averted her head as Haith peeled the

sticky cloth away. Haith did not flinch. "A fresh cake of strong soap and a clean farrier's brush. Go, child, hurry. Where is Tilly?"

"At your side, milady."

"All the clean linen you can quickly lay hand to and the black fur from my chamber. See Isabella to her nurse." She paused as one of the requested braziers and the stone were placed near her hip. She dropped the stone into the flashing coals. "And find Lady Simone."

"Aye, milady." Tilly popped to her feet and moved into the throng, mere steps from Simone, already calling out, "Baroness! Where is the baroness?"

Simone tried to open her mouth, willed herself to step forward, but 'twas as if her body were made of rotten wood. One movement and she feared she would crumble.

"*Baroness!*" A small, hard hand gripped her upper arm. Simone was spun about to encounter the maid Tilly, obviously adept at seeking out prey. The small woman's face was flushed, and her expression clearly betrayed her annoyance as she juggled a wailing Isabella.

"Yea, I am here," Simone said dumbly.

Tilly frowned and pushed her none too gently toward Lord Handaar. "Go on with you!" the maid scolded before disappearing once more into the crush.

Simone could feel every pair of eyes upon her as she stepped to the ladies' sides, and she wished with all of her being that she could simply dissolve into the stones beneath her feet. She cleared her throat.

"What can I do?"

Haith glanced up at her for but an instant. "Simone, good. I need you across from me.

Simone skirted Lord Handaar on shaking legs and dropped to her knees on the far side of him. Genevieve had retreated to the man's head and was cradling his face, stroking his bloodied pate and whispering fervent prayers.

Haith turned her head and called loudly over her shoulder. "Clear the hall! Unless I have given you a task, seek your duties elsewhere," she commanded, and the crowd immediately backed away and began to disperse amidst the cacophony of speculating comments.

"He'll not live. He's likely dead beneath their very hands."

"What's the baron to do now? Poor Lady Evelyn—"

"She's coming. The lord's fetched her from the priory and—"

"The new mistress'd better watch—"

"She's mad any matter—what would she care?"

Across from Simone, Haith snarled and turned on one knee. "Go or I shall banish the lot of you!"

Simone offered neither comment nor apology to the disparaging remarks, but kept her gaze pinned to the thin, scored skin of Handaar's chest. It barely moved with his slight, irregular breaths.

Simone heard a plop and a sizzle, and a large object crossed her line of vision. Haith was holding forth the pail of water into which she'd dropped the hot stone. Simone instinctively took hold of the handle and hoisted it over the body to her side. Several soft rags landed on her lap as Haith directed her.

"Begin at his head and work your way down," she said, slipping her blade beneath the stained bandage binding Handaar's shoulder. "When we have the soap and brush we will cleanse the wounds themselves."

Simone nodded dumbly and shook a rag free from the bundle, willing herself to move quickly even though her limbs felt mired in cold mud. She plunged the wadded-up linen into the pail and cried out when the water scalded her hand.

"Take care—'tis hot." Haith glanced up, the tip of her dagger still tangled in the knots of the expertly tied bandage. "Simone?"

"Yea?" Simone wrung the rag over the pail, wincing as the white-hot water sluiced over her throbbing skin. She applied it to the crown of Handaar's head between Genevieve's hands, and instantly, red rivulets ran wild down the man's face. A sob caught in her throat.

Haith's hand grasped Simone's wrist, stilling her actions and forcing her to meet the redhead's gaze. "Simone, can you do this?"

Simone shook free of the lady's grip and dunked only the rag this time into the pail. She wrung it out and began to wipe at Handaar's wrinkled brow.

If Haith detected the fear in Simone's actions, she chose to ignore it. Then the remaining supplies were delivered to Haith's side, prompting her to begin calling out orders once more.

"Thank you, Rose. Now, fetch a large jug of red wine and the nettle from my bag. Handaar has lost much blood and we need fortify him as quickly as we can." With a delicate huff, her dagger broke through the bandage on the man's shoulder. She lay the cutting tool aside and took ginger hold of the material's edges, slowly peeling them back as she spoke.

"Two more pails of water, and fetch the stone back to the brazier. Find a—oh my God!"

Simone looked up in time to see a thick, red stream of blood spurt and then bubble from the torn chasm in Handaar's shoulder.

"Nay, oh, nay," Haith muttered, splaying her already blood-ied hands over the font.

Simone's scalp began to tingle, and a queer itch sprouted deep in her ears.

Ye must staunch the flow. Both hands, lass. Faery needs hers to work.

Without thinking, Simone scrambled around Genevieve and pushed Haith's hands away. Stacking her palms, Simone pressed her hands into the gash, straightening her arms and bearing down with as much weight as she dared. Warm blood seeped between her fingers, pooled, ran across the backs of her hands and dripped onto the flagstones. A weighty calm enveloped Simone, drowning out the roar of flooding blood that had, a moment ago, threatened to deafen her. She spoke, but it felt as though the words came not from her own mouth.

"Bandage the wound once more, faery—quickly now," Simone said in an odd brogue that tangled her tongue. "Tie the knots over my hands. The Lady and the Hunter, lass." Simone had not the slightest idea what she said and, had she been in any other situation, would have likely fainted from the nightmarish events unfolding around her.

But she must have made sense to Haith, who nodded and began tearing long strips of linen, muttering to herself.

"The Lady and the Hunter, yea. The Lady . . . think, think!" Her breathing was ragged as she rendered fresh bandages. "*When my lady walked through the forest—*"

The pulse of blood beneath Simone's palms was weakening, although the flood still boiled. A chill enveloped Simone as Haith quickly positioned the first bandage under Handaar's shoulder.

"Dammit!" Haith muttered, her slick hands fumbling with the strip. "*When my lady walked through the forest, 'twas in the heat of midsummer . . .*"

Haith grabbed the next bandage, and Simone felt a queer humming, seeming to emanate from deep within Handaar's wound to travel the length of Simone's outstretched arms and into her aching shoulders. The tiny hairs on the nape of her neck tingled.

That's it, lass. Hang on. I'm nearly there . . .

"Hurry," Simone urged to absolutely no one.

"*. . . 'twas in the heat of midsummer and the blood* . . . the blood . . . I can't remember!" Haith cried, securing the linen at last.

The humming increased, and Handaar's chest jerked skyward, causing Lady Genevieve to cry out. Simone caught a glimpse of dull, gray eyes as the old warrior's eyelids jittered and then revealed naught but white. A great shuddering, like horses hooves on packed earth took hold of the man's body, forcing Simone to bear down with all her strength. His teeth gnashed, and a dreadful gurgling came from his corded and rigid throat.

"Nay, Handaar!" Genevieve sobbed, holding the old lord's head as still as she could.

Haith looked to Simone, and the fear in the redhead's eyes rocked Simone to the center of her soul.

Here is the threshold of death, all ye who would dare see it.

The spicy smell of green things burning caught Simone off guard and, as if some unseen finger turned her chin, she looked over her left shoulder.

A small, impossibly old woman with frazzled gray hair bore down on the group, her rough black cloak billowing around her like hellish wings. Eyes the color of the deepest well bored into hers. Simone wondered madly to herself if this old one was Death, come to harvest the life ebbing away there on the cold stone floor. She grew calm as the oddly life-like harbinger swooped to her side.

Then the phantasm spoke.

"Sweet Corra, move away, gel," she said, and Simone noticed hysterically that Death spoke with a Scot's accent and carried a large tapestry bag, embroidered with mysterious sticklike symbols. "Doona tarry, now." She flapped a hand at Simone with a frown.

Haith's cry was filled with relief. "Oh, Minerva! Thank God you've come!"

Simone's blood-slick hands slid easily from beneath the useless bandage, and she skittered backward away from the body, watching the hag from behind. Simone was drenched in sweat and blood, and trembling so that she felt she would vomit.

The old woman eased to her knees with a grunt and immediately opened her satchel. She all but ignored the man before her. "When did the fits start, faery?"

"But a moment ago," Haith answered. "His shoulder is— I'm sorry, Minerva—I don't know how I could have forgotten the chant."

"Doona fret. We must stop the blood, though." The old woman withdrew a black, cloth-covered object and an ornately handled dagger from the bag. She plunged the knife into the closest brazier and spoke without turning her head. "I see you have nettle—good, faery. Well done. Little one— Simone, is it? To me."

After an instant of hesitation, Simone joined the old woman who spared her not a glance.

"On my word, roll him this a-way and hold him on his side," she said in a no-nonsense voice. "Faery, you tend the nettle; Genny, you be keepin' his head still." She pulled the cloth-covered object close. "Do it now, lassies."

Simone strained with all her might to pull at Handaar's convulsing body, and Haith quickly scattered large handfuls of dried, crumbling leaves on the woven mat, whispering a string of unintelligible words.

"That's it. Now, ease him down."

Simone released Handaar and watched in frightened amazement as the next events unfolded before her eyes.

Minerva held her gnarled hands over Handaar's body and a soft, silvery mist began to envelop the old woman. When she spoke, her voice was strong yet quiet, melodious, ancient and with no hint of age.

When my Lady walked through the forest,
'Twas in the heat of Midsummer,
And the blood like a river.
Life of hare, buck, and owl.

Minerva wrapped her patched, dusty skirts around her hand and retrieved the now-glowing dagger from the brazier. She stroked it lightly across Handaar's shoulder where it sizzled, and the remaining bandage fell away.

And a hunter was welcomed by Her,
Even though forbade to linger,
And he took of the bounty
And he drank his fill.

The old woman set the dagger aside, and Simone noticed that Handaar's convulsions had slowed. Minerva then reached for the large object and removed the black covering to reveal a perfect hunk of blue and silvery ice. She held it in her cupped palms for but a moment before placing it on Handaar's shoulder.

My Lady cried for the slaughter,
And in Her wisdom, called the Winter,
To save Her children for a season,
Let the blood stop now!

The hag's ominous words died away in the silence of the hall, and Simone realized she'd been holding her breath. She let it out slowly, quietly, as Handaar's body stilled and a peace seemed to come to him. Wondrously, no more blood seeped from beneath the rapidly disintegrating blue ice, but the melt water seemed to coat the wound, soaking into Handaar's very skin.

What awful powers did this old woman possess that she should stop blood flow? Haith and Genevieve appeared quite comforted by her presence—even now, the dowager baroness had regained her composure and was embracing Minerva, murmuring her thanks.

The old one patted Genevieve's back briefly and then eased her away. "There, now. You'll have a bit of a rest. Go care for yourself—faery, tend your babe. Simone and me'll take care of him until you return."

Simone's eyes widened as she watched Genevieve look to Handaar uncertainly. Surely the women—Simone's only allies, now—would not leave her alone here with this dying man and frightening old woman. Simone's heart sank as Haith gained her feet.

"My thanks, Minerva. I'll be down to assist you in a thrice." And she left the hall without looking back.

Genevieve gave a moment's pause to look to Simone. "Will you be alright, darling?"

Simone opened her mouth to insist that, nay, she certainly would not be alright, but eerie words flooded her brain and flowed out of her mouth instead.

"Aye, milady. I'll be just fine." Simone slapped a hand over her mouth.

Genevieve did not so much as blink, but set off for the upper chambers.

"Alright then, lass," Minerva said, rummaging through the discarded supplies scattered around Handaar. "Let's get him cleaned up and warm."

Simone lowered her hand from her mouth. "You made me say those words! Just now, and before you even arrived!"

"Aye, I did." The old woman fetched Simone's discarded rag, wrung it out, and began wiping at Handaar's face. "I couldna get through faery's thick skull or I'd have used her."

Simone sat stunned as the old woman continued the chore. "Who are you?"

"Kin, of a sort," Minerva replied, dunking the cloth once more. "Give me that cake of soap."

Simone grabbed the bar and handed it to Minerva. "Are you the one who is to help me with . . . with my brother?"

"Not if you do naught but sit about chewin' yer own teeth," the old woman said, her black eyes flicking to the pile of rags.

Simone seized one of the cloths and began mopping Handaar's chest.

"How did yer brother die?" Minerva asked conversationally.

"He was trapped in a stable fire, along with my mother."

Minerva was quiet for a beat of time. "But yer mum, she doesna come to you?"

"Nay."

Within moments, Handaar's body was wiped clean of blood and dirt. He seemed to be resting peacefully when Minerva reached for the black fur throw and covered him. She looked to Simone with a weary-sounding sigh. Simone noticed that the old woman's costume bore not one speck of red, although Simone—as well as Haith and Genevieve—was covered in Handaar's blood.

"It shan't be pleasant," Minerva warned. "He'll be bound to me, and once we begin it, we canna stop. I"—Minerva glanced down at Handaar—"I doona know if I'd have the strength to start again. It'll likely be more of a trial for you than you think."

Simone shivered. "I understand."

"Do ye?" Minerva asked quietly.

After a moment, Simone shook her head. "Nay."

Minerva looked across the hall as if someone had called her name. "I'll be finding my chamber now," she said, turning back to Simone and gaining her feet with a groan. "Stay with the laird until faery or I return. Call out if he wakes." She grabbed up her odd satchel and walked toward the stairs, her unburdened arm held akimbo, palm out.

"Come on then, lad."

Simone's confused frown left her face when a silvery streak flew over the flagstones. Didier appeared at the old woman's side and took her hand. He glanced over his shoulder at Simone, giving her a sad little smile and an open-fisted wave as the pair left her in the hall, alone.

Chapter 20

Simone still sat at Handaar's side when Haith reentered the hall, her gown fresh, her hair damp, and her babe on her hip.

"Simone, my God!" Haith stalked to stand over her. "Where is Minerva?"

Simone gave a deep, shuddering sigh and began to rise from the floor. "She went above with Didier. I think to—"

"I'll have her leathery hide for a bag, leaving you like this," Haith growled.

"Nay, Haith." Simone reached out a hand to touch Haith's arm, but when she saw the brown stains covering herself, she let it drop. "She left only a moment ago. Rail not at her."

Simone was a bit unsure why she felt it necessary to defend the woman, except that had she not come to their aid, Handaar would have surely died.

Leaving Evelyn alone at Hartmoore with no kin.

Haith seemed ready to speak again but was interrupted by Tristan's entrance into the hall, followed in a moment by Nicholas. At the sight of her husband's familiar stride, Simone's heart lurched. He, too, was still covered in filth from the past days' events, and his brow was lowered into what seemed to be a permanent frown.

There was a skip in Nick's gait when his eyes met hers, but he recovered quickly and was soon at her side. Simone wondered if he would ask after her welfare, if he would apologize for his earlier words, blame them on his anger at the Welsh. She tried to give him a smile.

"Has he wakened at all?"

Her weak smile fell from her face. "What?"

"Lord Handaar, Simone. Has he spoken?" Nick's face was impatient.

"Nay. Nay—he's . . . he's quite ill."

Nicholas nodded curtly, and his eyes roamed Handaar's still form. "He looks better, I vow."

Haith broke the awkward silence. "His leg . . . was it the battle?"

Nick's gaze flicked over the old man's pieced lower half. "I had no choice. He would have died in Obny's bailey for certain."

Simone's chest contracted painfully as she realized what her husband's words meant. He'd had to amputate his friend's leg.

Lady Haith laid a gentle hand upon Nick's shoulder. "Oh, Nick, I am so sorry."

Simone wished she could touch her husband in the same easy manner, but since his return, she did not know how her advances would be received.

Torment me no more with the strange tales of your kin. Not just this day, but all days.

"'Tis no matter now," Nick replied brusquely. "Over and done. I can only hope now that he awakens so that I might avenge him as I crave to do." He looked to Simone once again, his features shuttered. "My mother?"

Simone cleared her throat. "Minerva sent her to her chamber to re—"

Simone's words were interrupted by a faint wailing, a screeching like a lone oak in the grip of a relentless storm. The sound grew louder, and chills raced over Simone's skin as she recognized its source.

She knew all too well the sound of grief.

"*Papa!*" The dreadful scream sliced up Simone's spine, and

she could feel the shift in the atmosphere of the hall as the door flew open and a figure stumbled inside. "Papa!"

The woman's puffy eyes swept the room before landing on Handaar's still form at Simone's feet. Evelyn choked back a sob before running across the rushes and falling to her knees. No one in the hall moved or spoke, but Simone instinctively took a step backward while the woman bent over her father and wailed. She was draped in yards of coarse brown wool— even her head and neck were covered—a rough wooden cross and primitive hemp belt holding a leather pouch, the ensemble's only adornment.

Simone swallowed as the woman abruptly clapped her hands together against her breasts and raised her sobbing face toward the ceiling. Her eyes were squeezed shut, belying the rivers of crystal tears that flooded over her pale cheeks, and Evelyn's lips moved frantically, speaking desperate, fervent prayers in Latin, her body rocking and trembling so that Simone did not know how the woman remained upright.

Simone felt gruesomely mesmerized by the sight of her and could not seem to drag her eyes from the slim nose, reddened at its tip and dusted with freckles, the dark fringe of lashes, clumped and spiky with tears, her wide mouth and lips moving with frantic pleas for mercy from her Creator.

My dearest Nicholas . . .

Even in the throes of grief, Evelyn's holy beauty, her purity, had no equal. She seemed to glow, like an ivory statue in some ancient cathedral, her eyes rolled heavenward.

The ground seemed to tremble beneath Simone's bloodsoaked slippers as her world began to crumble. This was the woman who held Nick's heart, his family's affection, and Simone could not help but realize how woefully lacking she was in comparison: mad, and French, and looking like some exotic peasant. Tears filled her own eyes at the sweet wails coming from the dedicant, stabbing viciously at Simone's heart.

And then Nicholas was there, but not at Simone's side. He dropped to his knees and pulled Evelyn into his arms, and she turned into him, sobbing. Nick's face was twisted painfully, and Simone felt herself growing lighter, as if she would soon depart from the stone hall and float away into the sky.

Nay. Nay, she would not give up yet.

"My lord," Simone called softly down to him, forcing herself to stay focused on his face. She would help him, if he would let her.

Nick's eyes opened, and Simone felt sick at the expression they held in their reddened confines. "Simone." He glanced over her sticky form and then looked away from her. "Go to your chamber. You need not be party to this."

She felt his dismissal like a blade to her heart, but Nicholas's attention did not linger on her as a clattering filled the hall. Simone turned and saw two stern-looking monks with neatly shaven pates and broadswords standing just inside the doors.

"Evelyn Godewin," one of the monks called flatly. "You have witnessed your sire's deathbed. We will now return to the priory."

Simone heard Evelyn's wild mew. "Nick, please, nay! I beg you, do not let them take me from Handaar!"

Nick shushed her gently. "Fear not, Evelyn." And then he released her and stood, drawing his own soiled weapon in one smooth movement and approaching the monks.

"Get thee from my hall, men of God," he warned, prompting the monks to lay hands to their sword hilts. "Lady Evelyn is most welcome to remain as she so pleases, and you will not move her."

"'Tis not your will to be done here, nobleman," one of the monks sneered. "Dedicant Sister belongs to the Heavenly Father, and her duties lay only in service to Him."

Nicholas raised his sword until it was held horizontally to his waist, and his pace quickened as he neared, ready to champion Evelyn's cause. A collision seemed imminent, and Simone held her breath.

"As do you too belong to God, you arrogant prat, and I shall send you to test his mercy *should you not leave us in peace!*"

Tristan stepped into the trio of readied, deadly weapons, and Simone's soiled hands flew to her lips.

"There will be no more blood shed in this hall," Tristan commanded. His voice lowered to mumbles, and Simone looked once more to Evelyn, still kneeling at her feet.

To her surprise, the woman was appraising her, her wide, powdery blue eyes taking in Simone's macabre gown. And then Evelyn spoke, and her voice was as gentle as rain.

"I thank you," she whispered, her lips trembling and her hand resting on Handaar's shallow chest. "I thank you for what you have done for my father. Here—" She fumbled at her small pouch for a moment and then withdrew a single, misshapen coin. She held it toward Simone. "Its value is not much, but 'tis all I have. Please, take it."

Simone stared at the coin, frozen.

"*Please,*" Evelyn repeated with a hitch in her voice and a nervous glance at the monks. "Before they see."

Simone held out her hand, stained and lined with Handaar's blood, and Evelyn placed the ragged, dull coin in it gently. "God bless you. Now go, and do as your lord commands lest he punish you for your disobedience."

Simone looked at the small circle in her palm, then back to Evelyn, before clenching her fingers around her payment until her nails bit into her flesh.

Haith appeared at her side, touched her arm. "Lady Simone, let me—"

Simone jerked away, not bothering to address Evelyn's questioning frown, and turned toward the stairs, fleeing the hall as quickly as her trembling legs would allow.

"I will handle this, Tristan," Nick gritted out between clenched teeth as he eyed the burly monks. "Step aside."

"Nay, Nicholas. You are not thinking clearly," Tristan said, and for an instant, Nick wanted to turn his weapon on his own brother. Hartmoore was his and Tristan had no right to command anything. Could he never live up to his brother's

shining example? 'Twas bad enough that Simone had witnessed his failures firsthand, now must he also bear Tristan's
reprimand before his wife?

"I said, step aside." Nick moved closer to the monks, his
shoulder pushing against Tristan's chest.

Tristan grasped Nick's upper arm. "I know you are angry,
Nick," he said in a low voice, "but put your anger aside for a
moment and think. These men are no match for you, and their
deaths would bring repercussions you do not desire." Tristan's
eyes flicked to the robed men. "*I stand with you*—they will
not take Evelyn before Handaar breathes his last, I swear it."

As if sensing Nick relenting, one of the monks announced,
"We have no quarrel with you, Nicholas FitzTodd, but we
have our orders and we will obey them."

Inside, Nick shook with rage and humiliation. Tristan—
damn him!—was right again. To challenge these monks was
folly—the king would hear of it, and combined with the dev-
astating loss of Obny to the Welsh, William would be furious.
Nick dare not lay further shame upon his family.

Nick sheathed his sword with a powerful thrust and a low
growl. "Get from my hall. You may bed in the stables until"—
Nick paused, swallowed the thorny lump in his throat—
"When he is dead, you may return with her to Withington. I
can assure you, you will not have a lengthy wait."

Both the monks sheathed their weapons, and one spoke.
"We must return this day," he said firmly, but his beady eyes
encased by plump flesh narrowed. "Mayhap we could fetch
Dedicant Sister in a fortnight had we coin to replace her holy
labors. You see, we are but a poor house of God . . ."

Nick could feel his mouth twitching in a disgusted sneer at
the monk's greed. He knew that, more likely than nay, the
monks were under no such orders to return Evelyn to Withington within any set time and that 'twas probable they would
spend the next two weeks drinking the payment they bar-
gained for.

"How much?" Nick asked. Tristan apparently felt the

situation had been properly diffused, for he moved from between Nicholas and the monks.

The robed men glanced at each other before the beady-eyed one answered. "Fifty gold pieces should fulfill Dedicant Sister's obligation for a fortnight."

"You'll get ten," Nick said. "Wait for my clerk at the stables."

The monks bowed and then made the sign of the cross in the air before Nicholas. "God bless you, nobleman, and may His divine mercy comfort you in this time of—"

Nick turned and walked away, dismissing both the swine and their false blessings. He heard Tristan volunteer—quite firmly—to escort the monks to the stables and the hall door close with their departure.

Evelyn still knelt by Handaar's unconscious body, and Nick crossed the hall to join her once more. That Simone had, for once, obeyed him gave him some measure of relief. Seeing her standing over Handaar, covered in the old lord's blood, and witnessing firsthand the devastation his inadequacies had brought to those he'd sworn to protect had been more than Nick could bear.

He'd made a grand mess of everything.

He neared Evelyn, whose tears had stopped and who was now sitting quietly on the rushes, smoothing the fur draped over Handaar's torso. He crouched down.

"The monks have gone," he said gently. "Not to return for a fortnight. You will have your time with Handaar."

"I thank you, my lord," Evelyn replied, her eyes not meeting his.

My lord? Evelyn had not used that title when they were alone for ten years or more. Was it due to the fact that he'd failed her—both as a potential husband and as her father's liege? "How fare thee, Evelyn?" he asked, willing her to look at him. "I had no wish to leave you alone—I thought my sister-in-law would—"

"She followed Lady Simone," Evelyn interrupted quietly, and then she did raise her eyes to Nicholas. "Your wife."

Nick stared at her for several moments, anticipating the pain he would feel at Evelyn's observation: he had a wife other than her. But the pain never came.

"Yea," he whispered. "Simone is my wife. We were married in London, only weeks ago."

Evelyn closed her eyes slowly, and a single tear fought its way from beneath her lashes to slide down her cheek. "After all my letters—why did you not tell me, Nick? Why would you allow me to humiliate myself again and again when you did not reply?" She opened her eyes, and Nick saw a faint spark in their blue depths. She glanced at Handaar and then inclined her head. "Is this my punishment, then? For leaving Obny and you? That my home is destroyed, my father dying?"

Nick felt his chest tighten. "Nay, Evelyn. You bear no responsibility in this matter, nor should you feel shame. I—"

"But each letter I sent—"

"I never read them." The silence after Nick's admission hung like a wet blanket, cold and heavy and miserable.

"I see." Evelyn dropped her eyes to Handaar once again. "I hurt you so much, then?"

Nick could not bring himself to admit to her that he now knew the gargantuan anguish he'd felt after Evelyn's flight had not been the result of heartbreak but of his badly battered pride at her rejection, his failure to wed and please his mother as Tristan had, to fulfill his father's legacy.

Nick could not tell her now, as Handaar lay dying beside them, that what he'd fooled himself into believing was love those many months ago was a pale shadow of the emotion he now realized he felt.

For Simone.

Evelyn looked at him, her gaze shrewd and searching. And if she saw the truth in his eyes, she hid it well, or she simply did not care. Her eyes went to the stairs, to where his accounting chamber lay.

"I'd like them returned to me. My letters," she said quietly. "'Twould not do for your wife to happen upon them."

"They are destroyed," Nick said.

Evelyn nodded once.

A clattering on the stairs drew both their attentions, and Nick looked up to see Haith descending. She approached.

Nick rose. "How fares Lady Simone?"

Haith's lips thinned. "I am calling for a bath to be sent to her. She has want to see to her brother before she returns to the hall."

"Minerva has come, then?" Nick felt some of the heavy burden lift at Haith's succinct nod, but it was not to last.

"Yea, Minerva has come. Excuse me, Nick—I have need to seek a house maid and then see to Isabella." Haith's words were icy, but when she turned to Evelyn, her tone softened. "I'll sit with you awhile when I am done if you like, Lady Evelyn."

Evelyn gave her a weak smile. "Lady Evelyn—I have not been called that in many months. I would like for you to sit with me very much. Thank you."

And then Haith moved briskly toward the kitchens.

"Leave me, Nick," Evelyn said quietly, turning her face to Handaar as if she could not bear to look at Nicholas. "I would make peace with my father in private."

"I cannot, Evelyn," Nick said. "If he awakens—"

"I will shout down the stones from their mortar. I vow to you, no one wishes vengeance for my father more than I." Her voice was firm, pained. Bitter. "Go to your wife, and leave me."

Nick walked to the stone steps, pausing at the bottom as if he walked to a gallows. How could he begin to apologize to Simone for his harsh words? How could he right things between them?

Nicholas did not know, and so he turned from the steps without climbing the first one and left the hall, shamed regret dogging his heavy footfalls.

Chapter 21

Once inside the stables, teeming with men and horses outfitting for battle, Nick sought a full rain barrel. He removed his belt and sword and set them aside, stripped off his ruined tunic, and dunked himself to the waist in the cold water. Rising with a harsh gasp, he scrubbed his palms over his skin, raked his fingers through his stiff hair. He dipped into the water twice more to rinse the filth from him. When he rose again, he realized he had not thought to bring a drying cloth or clean shirt, and the breeze through the stable cut him to the bone. He cursed, shook the water from his hair.

Something soft prodded his lower back, and when he turned, he saw Tristan, a length of linen in one hand and a dingy undershirt in the other.

Of course, Nick thought darkly. *Leave it to my brother to swaddle me like the babe I am.* He jerked the linen from Tristan, muttering a curt thanks.

"The monks have gone," his brother confided.

Nick tossed the now-damp cloth over a half wall and took the shirt. He shook it out: stained and rough, but clean. "Good," he said as he pulled the woolen garment over his head. He continued as he attended to the lacings. "I need not their greedy interference while we wait to see if Handaar wakes." He picked up his sheath and withdrew his sword.

"They are not the only ones taking their leave of Hartmoore, Nick," Tristan said, stepping closer.

Nicholas snatched the damp towel from the wall and began wiping at his blade. He glanced at his brother. "Oh?"

"Yea. Some of the nobles—" Tristan halted, looked around, lowered his voice. "Lord Bartholomew has convinced them that you brought the raid on yourself. He's spoken of reporting to William."

"Bartholomew's fat mouth concerns me not, Tristan," Nick said, swiping his blade clean. "William will not give his wagging tongue a moment's consideration. Wallace Bartholomew is greedy and envious of Hartmoore."

"That may be," Tristan conceded, "but he does hold the ears of some of the other nobles. Many have already sent their wives and servants away, and a few have spoken outright of taking their men and leaving as well."

Nick paused, his sword in one hand and his sheath in the other. "They cannot do that," he said. "Should it come to battle, 'tis the lords' duty to fight. To desert would be treason."

Tristan shrugged. "I've done what I can to stay them, but Bartholomew is relentless."

Nick sent his sword down into its sheath with a ringing hiss. "I do not need your charity, Brother."

"Charity?" Tristan drew his head back and gave a humorless laugh. "My God, Nick—I thought I had a healthy dose of pride. 'Tis not out of charity that I speak to the other lords—I'm trying to prevent us from going into battle ill-matched. Who can know what we shall face at the border? If more than a few of the nobles withdraw their support, we could very well be outnumbered and slaughtered, as all at Obny were."

Nick's blood turned to ice. "It shan't happen."

"Will you at least—"

"Nay," Nick interjected, not wishing to continue this disturbing conversation. "I must return to Handaar. Leave it, Tristan, all will be well."

Tristan seemed ready to press his case when his attention

was drawn over Nick's shoulder to the stable's entrance. Nick saw his brother's jaw harden, and he turned.

Lord Bartholomew and two other elder nobles had entered the structure and were now walking briskly down the main aisle, looking rather smug.

"Bartholomew!" Nicholas called. His anger rose when one of the nobles gave him a nervous glance but did not slow. "*Bartholomew!* I am speaking to you! Halt!"

The man did stop and turn, but said nothing, only looked at Nick in his haughty manner. The stable quieted noticeably.

"To where do you hie?" Nicholas demanded. "We do battle soon, and your outfit is needed."

"I think not, FitzTodd," Bartholomew replied. "I'll not sacrifice my men because you were too arrogant to keep watch over your demesne. I warned William in London this would happen."

"Are you holding me responsible for Obny's loss?" Nick asked quietly.

"Bloody right I am," Bartholomew sneered. "We shall see what William thinks of his darling now, eh?" Bartholomew took a step forward and spat on the stable floor. "A young fool who has married a madwoman and must cling to a brother not of his blood to hold his keep in check. Old Richard turns in his grave."

"You son of a bitch," Nick growled. "You tell William what you would. *You tell him.* And I will be there to see your head part with your body for treason."

Bartholomew chuckled and shrugged. "We shall see, shall we not? In any case, you must be overjoyed to have the lovely Evelyn back at your side. Shame you had to get her sire killed to make her return to you."

Tristan lunged for the smug man, causing Bartholomew to scramble backward, but Nicholas stayed his brother.

"Get from my sight, vermin," Nick said, his whole body shaking with rage and humiliation. "When next I see you—and I vow, I will see you soon—'twill be upon the eve of your death."

Bartholomew laughed and gave a mock bow, and the two nobles he'd entered with approached, leading their own mounts as well as Bartholomew's gelding. The codger took the reins and swung up to mount.

"Good day, FitzTodd," he said solicitously before spurring his horse from the stables. His two cronies gave chase, and from beyond the door, a faint rumbling was heard. Nick and Tristan approached the stable yard, and at the sight they beheld, Nick felt as though he'd been kicked in the gut.

No fewer than four score men had retrieved their battle mounts and were now crowding toward the barbican. Nick turned his head to the doors of the great hall, where servants ferried trunks from within and gowned ladies and their maids took seat.

Behind him, Tristan cursed. Nick set off in a trot toward the group of soldiers. He entered the fringe of the crowd of riders, holding both arms aloft.

"Hold! All you men, hold!" he shouted, jerking at trappings. "You and your lords are bound by fealty to me! You must stay and fight! Would you let the Welsh rape your countryside? Terrorize your towns and slaughter your people with no recompense?"

But the riders pulled free and moved closer to the gates. A queer feeling began to spiral in Nick's stomach, a sensation like nothing he'd ever felt before.

Panic.

A young soldier slowed his horse and looked down at Nicholas. "'Tis sorry I am, milord," the man said. "But Lord Bartholomew has put the fear into us—he says we canna win." The lad winced, looked about furtively. "I doona wanna die, milord. I gots a woman what needs me—and a bairn comin', too." He nodded, as if he'd just made a decision. "Godspeed ye, milord."

Nicholas could do naught but stare after the young man as he rejoined the exodus through Hartmoore's gates.

That is ridiculous, Nick thought wildly. *We have—had—*

nearly five hundred armed men. No Welsh village could best us. Why can they not see that?

He turned in a slow circle to face the keep, his body buffeted by horseflesh and spurred boots. Old Lord Cecil Halbrook was talking with Tristan, and both men looked concerned. The cacophony of soldiers and thudding hooves, jingling tack and rumbling cart wheels, throbbed in Nick's ears, coated by an underlying buzz, as if a mammoth bee circled his head.

He began walking toward Halbrook and Tristan, his legs tingling curiously. When he neared enough for the man to hear, he called out, "Not you as well, Cecil."

"Good night! Do not even think it for a moment, my boy," Halbrook replied in his hearty baritone. He clapped Nick's arm. "My men do not number many, but they are yours to command."

"Not all flee, Nick," Tristan said. "Lord Halbrook has spoken to many of the others, and they still stand with us."

Nick looked to Cecil, and the man nodded. "Bartholomew is a pompous braggart and not well liked."

Nicholas thought in silence for a moment. "How many do we keep?" he asked both men.

"Oh . . . er, quite a few, I'd say," Halbrook offered, looking to Tristan.

His brother's cheek twitched. "Not quite half."

Nicholas turned to watch the rear of the departing cowards so that Tristan would not see the uncertainty in his eyes. Dusk was upon Hartmoore now; purple clouds crowded the slate sky and the air swelled with cold. A fat rogue raindrop splashed on his cheek, cold and shocking.

This cannot be, he thought absently. The situation was most dire. He knew not if Randall would reach the king in time, and if he did not, with their numbers cut by more than half, a battle likely easily won would become a bloody contest on foreign soil. It could not get worse.

But when he heard his mother's frantic voice calling for

him from the hall beyond, Nicholas felt 'twas about to become infinitely worse indeed.

Hartmoore's maze of corridors was unnaturally deserted, and Simone assumed that most of the guests had retreated behind closed doors to escape the solemn and mournful atmosphere descended upon the festivities since Nick's return from Obny. Simone was grateful for not having to dread encountering one of the spiteful courtiers, but neither were there any of Hartmoore's servant's about—all of them taken to hovering about the great hall, tending to their masters and waiting just as eagerly as the family for a sign from Lord Handaar.

Simone knew what she had to do. She would fetch Didier from the old woman and, after warning Lady Genevieve, she and Didier would somehow get to London and beg mercy from King William. Nicholas could have his annulment. She had nowhere else to go after that save France, and then she would tell Didier the truth about their father.

But not yet. God forgive her selfishness, but she could not imagine letting Didier go now, when she needed him so. She had no one left.

"Lady Simone, there you are," a voice from behind her said, and Simone's nerves were stretched so that she jumped and gave a frightened yelp.

She turned to encounter Lady Haith, Isabella in her arms.

"I just came from your chambers," Haith said, eyeing her closely. "How fare thee?"

Simone tried to smile. "Much better. I was looking for you as well, actually."

Isabella squawked.

"Yea, my darling, your bed lies near," Haith said to the child with a nuzzle to her cheek. She looked at Simone. "She has eaten her fill and now wishes to sleep, the wee piglet."

Simone creaked out another smile. It faltered, then fell.

"Lady Haith, where is Didier?"

"'Tis the very reason I sought you," Haith said gently. "Come," she urged, gliding past Simone to turn a far corner.

Haith obviously knew Hartmoore's corridors better than Simone, for she had to nearly run to keep up with the redhead's strides. They ended up in a corridor adjacent to the wing that housed the lord's chambers and paused before a door. A resounding crash echoed from within the room, causing Simone to jump.

"Good heavens! Who is in there?"

"Minerva. And Didier, of course." Haith glanced down at Isabella and smoothed a hand over her downy head. Already the child slept. She looked back to Simone. "Brace yourself."

Simone followed the woman through the portal with a frown. "Why would—?" Her words fell away when she saw the state of affairs going on in the guest chamber.

The old hag was reclined comfortably on the wide bed, covered with furs. Simone's breath caught in her chest as the icy air in the chamber reached her lungs. Near the high ceiling, a large circle of normally inanimate objects flew in wild swoops—a candelabra, a pitcher, one leather slipper, the chamber pot—Simone could not see each object clearly in their dizzying flight. She shrieked and fell backward as the chamber pot broke rank and flew toward her, shattering inches from her feet.

Simone looked to Haith, who had casually crossed the chamber and was now depositing Isabella in a low, wooden crib that seemed to glow with ethereal light. "Lady Haith, what is this?"

But before Haith could reply, Didier appeared before Simone's face. The boy's apparition, usually very robust and real, was hazy and gray. Didier clutched at his white feather with both hands and looked at Simone with crazed eyes.

"Sister! You must make her leave!" His voice echoed and hitched, and Simone noticed that Didier appeared to be soaking wet, although no water pooled at his—

His legs ended in a shadowy fog some inches above the floor, and Simone became truly terrified.

"My God, Didier!" Simone whirled to face the old woman on the bed. "What are you doing to him?" she demanded.

"Now, lass," Minerva said, "doona fear. 'Tis quite normal." She turned her attention back to Didier, and her eyes darkened. "Alright, lad, get back to it, now, and quit scarin' yer sister."

She flicked a gnarled hand, and Didier flew backward from Simone with a hellish cry that made Simone's heart ache and her flesh crawl. Didier now hovered near the ring of objects high in the air, and he seemed to be spitting and growling and gnashing his teeth.

"Stop this immediately!" Simone said in a harsh whisper, striding on shaking legs to the side of the bed. "Can't you see you're killing him?"

The old woman cocked one spidery eyebrow.

Simone growled in frustration and turned to Haith, just now crossing the room. "Lady Haith, please!"

"There's no helping it, Simone," Haith said. She looked to Minerva. "Fighting it, is he?"

The old woman snorted and rolled her eyes.

Haith took hold of Simone's elbow and gently steered her away from the bed just as an ornate silver chalice hurtled to the floor where she'd been standing.

Didier wailed, and Simone gasped as a carved armchair near the hearth began to first wobble on its delicate legs and then rise into the air.

Minerva tsk-ed from her lounge on the bed. "Ah-ah, lad. I think not." She waved a hand at the bobby chair, and it returned to the floor, once more stilled.

Simone struggled to swallow the rather large lump in her throat. "I fail to see how this . . . this torture is helping him."

Haith sent her a sad little smile. "I know it is unsettling to witness, but in order for Didier to move on, we must first discover why he remains. Which means he must revisit the moment of his death."

Simone felt her anger bloom, and she spun to face the old woman again. "You did not tell me this is how it would need to be done! How could you make him suffer so when he's already been through so much?"

"If I would have told you, would you have gone through with it?" Minerva demanded. "Nae. Ye wouldna. And it's not pain yer witnessing here, lass—'tis fear, plain and simple. The boy's frightened of the something or someone that caused his death, and he's usin' up all his energy to prevent seein' the moment he passed."

"Release him, Minerva," Simone commanded.

The old one looked at Simone as if she'd just sprouted another head. "Nae, lass. Stopping it now will only delay the inevitable." She smiled, almost proudly, at Didier as he continued to twist and howl in the air. "He's makin' *progress*."

"I need him with me, now," Simone said. "You can continue with this some other time."

"You need him?" Minerva mocked. "What fer? To fetch yer slippers?"

Haith gasped. "Minerva!"

"Doona scold me, faery," the hag warned, sitting up against her pillows. "This young boy needs be freed from the bonds that hold him, and our young baroness here need not think so highly of herself."

"I am the lady of this keep," Simone growled, her words sounding surprisingly sincere to her own ears. "And I demand that my brother be returned to me!"

"I'll not be havin' any of it, lass," Minerva said, and then pursed her lips and turned her head away.

She could not leave Hartmoore without him. Would not.

"Didier," Simone said, turning her attention to the writhing phantasm hovering near the beams. "Didier, come with me now."

The boy slowed his rolling tumbles and fixed her with his chilling gaze, gray, like frozen flames. Terrified hope flashed there, and Simone flew to the chamber door. "Come, Didier—'tis alright," she cajoled. "Let us be away from here, just you and I." Her voice rose, whistling and high pitched. "I . . . I'll read to you!"

The boy's apparition swooped from the ceiling, and for a

moment Simone was filled with thrilling hope. But Didier halted abruptly halfway to the door. "*No-o-on!*" he wailed, and was jerked back into the air as if attached to a trebuchet.

"Let him go!" Simone screamed and, beyond all reason now, charged the old woman on the bed, ready to scratch her black, glassy eyes from the wrinkles in her cheeks.

Haith's strong grip halted her. "Simone, stop! Stop!"

"You don't understand—he's all I have," Simone sobbed, fighting against Haith's hold until she was free. She looked to the ceiling and Didier was gone. "Where did he go? *Didier!*"

"He's just gone dim, lass," Minerva offered in a mild tone. "Worn out from the struggle is all. He'll brighten up again in a bit."

Haith laid a gentle hand upon Simone's arm once more. "Why do you not return to your chamber, Simone. You've had a trying day and—"

The faint calls of a woman were heard beyond the chamber, growing louder.

"Ah, nae," Minerva sighed. And then she raised her face to the ceiling, her eyes closed, and began to speak. "Go in peace, Handaar Godewin. Go in peace, old warrior. We shall meet again."

The calls from the corridor grew louder still, and now the sound of running footfalls could be heard. The pounding on the door caused Simone to jump, and she knew, she knew when the cold molten fear bubbled in her stomach, what would lay beyond.

"Baroness! Baroness! Lady Haith!" The panicked calls were clear through the thick door, and the pounding began once more.

Simone looked to Haith, but the woman only stared at Minerva. Simone crossed to the door and swung it wide, revealing Genevieve's maid, Rose, weeping and wringing her reddened hands.

"Oh, God's mercy, Baroness," the girl wailed. "Do come quick! Lord Handaar . . . he's awake and—" She broke off on a hiccough. "You must come!"

Chapter 22

Nick ran into the great hall, Tristan close behind. He saw the crowd of people clustered together before the hearth, and he prayed he was not too late.

He shouldered his way through the group, and when he gained the center, his heart kicked against his ribs. Evelyn knelt at Handaar's side, her smile wide and bright, threads of tears sliding down her cheeks. She held Handaar's hand to her bosom and leaned close, whispering then listening.

Handaar's eyes were open, the blue rings of iris rolling around in bloodshot whites, trying to focus on his daughter's face. His lips moved, but his voice was too low for Nick to hear. Beneath the black fur covering his body, Handaar's midsection was grotesquely swollen. A chilling sweat broke over Nick's face and chest and back as he dropped to his knees beside Evelyn.

"—your mother," Handaar wheezed, "so proud. Beautiful girl."

Evelyn did not take her eyes from her father, and her smile never faltered, though she hiccoughed on a sob. "I know, Papa," she said, her voice stretched.

"Should not have let you . . ." He gasped a weak breath. ". . . Withington. Not happy there."

"But it's alright now." Evelyn gave a strained laugh through her smile and sniffed, rubbing Handaar's palm roughly between her own. "You'll be well soon. I'll stay and tend you—I'll not leave you again, I swear it!" Nick heard a croaking in her chest.

Handaar closed his eyes briefly, opened them slowly. The smell wafting up from the old warrior was black, so black. "Nick? Where . . . ?"

Evelyn grabbed Nick's arm, her short nails sinking through his woolen shirt, into his flesh and breaking the skin. With surprising strength, she pulled him into Handaar's line of vision. "He's here, Papa, see?" Nick could feel tiny rivulets of blood run down his arm, Evelyn's voice insanely cheerful. "Say hello to Papa, Nick."

"Hand—" Nick had to clear his throat, for it felt as though it had swollen shut. "Handaar, tell me about the raid."

"Nick," Handaar wheezed. "Obny is well. Fear not."

Nick's stomach clenched. Within the crowd, soft weeping was heard. Nick thought absently that it was his mother.

"Handaar, you must try to remember. Obny was attacked. Tell me what clan so that I might avenge you."

"Well . . . all is well," Handaar breathed again.

Nicholas squeezed his eyes shut, fought the burning there. Would the old man die before disclosing the names of his attackers? Handaar was so confused—Nick did not think he could bear the guilt if he could not repay the savages who had destroyed Obny. If need be, he would lay waste to all of Wales.

Then Handaar spoke again. "Don'gal."

Nick edged closer until he could smell the rot in Handaar's sighing breaths. "Was it Donegal?"

"Yea-a-a," Handaar breathed, and his eyes closed.

Nick's heart stopped. "Handaar?" He felt Tristan drop to his knees at his side, laying a heavy arm across Nick's shoulders. Evelyn drew a squealing breath.

But then the old warrior's blue orbs appeared once more, bright and snapping. He spoke slowly but clearly.

"Came to us," Handaar wheezed another shallow intake of

breath. "Don'gal. From the east." Another wheeze. "Disguised. We opened . . . the gates. Didn't know."

"Oh, Handaar." Nick felt he would weep. At his side, Evelyn began a fast string of whispered prayers.

Nick wrapped his fingers around the man's hand, still held tightly in Evelyn's. "I will right it, Handaar. I vow to you now, on my very life."

"I know," Handaar sighed, and his dry lips, blistered and scabbed, twitched in a weak smile. "Richard . . . proud. *I'm proud.*"

Nick felt Tristan's arm tighten around his shoulders. He squeezed Evelyn's and Handaar's clasped hands, and then let go.

"Eve. Eve," Handaar breathed, and his palm stiffened in his daughter's grip, the fingers straightening, trembling, and then curling once more over her hand.

"I'm here, Papa," Evelyn said.

Handaar's eyes swam toward her face, seeming to roll over her features aimlessly.

"Beautiful girl," he whispered, his breath crackling wetly in his throat, and a tear slid from the corner of his eyes although he had not blinked. "Love you."

Evelyn sobbed. "I love you, Papa!"

Handaar's eyes rolled away for an instant, showing their whites, but then came back to Evelyn's face. "Love you . . . love . : . you. Love . . ." And then he spoke no more.

"Ohh," Evelyn moaned. "Papa? *Papa!*"

Nick shot to his feet, knocking away Tristan's arm as Evelyn's shrill scream shot the close silence. The crowd gathered around Handaar moved back a pace en masse with a horrified hush. Nick's lips tingled and buzzed, and the floor beneath his feet began to undulate.

"Nay, Papa!" Evelyn screamed. Nick blinked and the woman came into focus, gripping Handaar's face and shaking it. "Papa, look at me!"

"Evelyn," Nick called to her, and his voice sounded rusty and worn. She continued to shake her father, and Nick reached for her. "Evelyn, stop. He's gone." His hand grasped her shoulder.

At his touch, Evelyn stiffened as if doused with icy water. An animalistic squeal came from her, and then, in an instant, she was on her feet, snarling and screeching and flailing at Nicholas with her claws spread wide.

"*You son of a bitch!*" she screamed, and the nails of her right hand dug into his cheek. "He loved you and you killed him!" Her hands were small iron fists now, and she swung at Nick, her blows landing on his face and chest.

Nick struggled to take hold of Evelyn's arms, and he pulled her against him.

"I hate you! I hate you!" She jerked within his embrace, but Nick held firm, her words doing more damage than the trio of gouges in his cheek, now leaking warm blood.

"I hope you die," she sobbed. "I hope you die and burn in Hell for what you have done."

Nick closed his eyes as Evelyn's forehead dropped to his chest and she sagged against him, a keening wail drawing from her open mouth. Nick tried to swallow against the crushing weight in his throat. He held Evelyn up, his chest spasming, and dropped his chin to the crown of her head.

Simone stood elbow to elbow with the group gathered around Handaar, tears rolling down her cheeks as she witnessed the grief of the people before her. Her heart ached— yea—from seeing the tender way Nick held the woman, how he'd accepted her blows. But the tears on Simone's face were not from self-pity but from a sadness, so deep, for Nicholas.

Simone knew what it felt like, losing someone you loved so dearly. And then being blamed for the death. She could taste Nick's pain, thick in her mouth, like a rancid honey.

And Simone realized how much she truly loved him. It did not matter now that he loved Evelyn. It did not matter that he chose Evelyn over Simone. Nicholas had brought Simone to Hartmoore, shown her what happiness could be like, if only for a few short days. If she was not destined to live her life as his wife, to give him all the love she had until her last breath was drawn, she would give him what she could, while she could. After what Armand had done, she owed him that much.

She turned to the maid, Rose, at her side. Drawing the girl close, she whispered, "Have water sent to the lord's chamber for his bath."

"Aye, mum."

Then Simone stepped forward and, as if Nicholas sensed her, his head turned. Evelyn still cried weakly into his undershirt. Nick's red-rimmed eyes locked on hers, and she could feel the pull of him, the hungry, insatiable grief eating away at him.

Genevieve approached the couple. "Oh, my darling," she said, her voice hitching. She seized one of Evelyn's arms and pulled her from Nick into her own embrace. Evelyn went willingly, clinging to the dowager baroness, her sobs renewed. "Oh, Evelyn, I am so sorry."

Nicholas faced her now, his arms hanging limp at his sides.

"Did you learn of Obny's attackers?" Simone asked softly.

He nodded, his eyes searching her face. His shoulders were slumped, the corners of his full mouth sagged, and the curling locks of damp hair trembled against his cheek. He was in shock, standing amidst the disaster in his own hall, and Simone knew that, at any moment, he would falter.

It would not do for his people to see him in this state. Nicholas would not want that. And so neither did Simone.

Within the circle of mourners, Tristan and Haith began to take control. Haith gave low commands to several maids, calling for supplies to be brought to prepare Handaar's body. Tristan ordered several of the soldiers to prepare a pyre. On the morn, Handaar would burn in a warrior's glory.

Simone drew a deep, silent breath and took Nick's hand. To her surprise, not only did he let her seize him, his fingers curled around her own tightly. She tugged. Nicholas followed.

* * *

They did not speak as Simone led Nicholas through the maze of corridors to his chamber. The few servants they passed stepped to the side with their eyes downcast in deference to the sorrowful event below. Some bowed, some whispered quiet blessings as Simone pulled Nick along. He acknowledged none of them, walking a half step behind Simone, and she was left to smile reassuringly and murmur thanks for the both of them.

Once she had opened the chamber door, Nick released Simone's hand and walked to the huge four-poster bed to sit on the edge of the thick ticking. His forearms were braced on his thighs, his hands dangling between his knees, and he stared at the floor. Simone closed the door and leaned back against it for a long moment.

What was done could not be undone. Her heart squeezed at the sight of him, so distraught and quiet. She remembered with bittersweet sadness the night they'd met at the king's birthday celebration—how reckless and handsome he'd been. How sure of himself, bold and without a care for propriety. To see him so beaten hurt her worse than the inevitability of losing him.

Simone straightened and crossed the wide chamber to Nick's formidable carved wardrobe. She removed his long, fur-lined gown and then turned toward the bed. He had not moved.

"My lord," she said softly, laying the robe at his side. When he did not respond, Simone reached down on either side of him and grasped the hem of his undershirt. He looked up, puzzlement creasing his forehead.

"Lift your arms," she commanded, pulling up on the shirt.

He looked at her blankly for a moment longer, then raised his arms, and Simone slipped the snug garment from his body.

The servants bearing water came soon enough, and Nicholas walked behind the dressing screen, his robe crushed in one hand. As they filled the tub, thunder rumbled beyond the keep and lightning stuttered on the walls. Simone busied herself by helping Rose light two braces of candles, turn back the bed coverings, and stoke and feed the hearth until it blazed.

When the servants filed out, the chamber was filled with dark corners, flickering candlelight. The crackling hearth backlit the copper tub before it, steam rising lazily and carrying with it the scent of sandalwood. Rain crashed down on Hartmoore. Simone threw the bolt on the door.

When she turned, Nicholas was stepping out from behind the dressing screen, his deep blue robe clutched shut with one fist. Simone crossed to him and took his hand once more, leading him to the tub. She walked around behind him, reached up on her toes, and grasped the collar of his robe.

Nicholas stiffened and looked over his shoulder. "Do you not wish to leave before I disrobe, Simone?" he asked gruffly.

Her pulling at the garment was the only answer she gave. The robe slid down Nick's back. She laid it aside as Nicholas stepped into the tub with two dull plops. She moved away while he seated himself to retrieve a low, three-legged stool. Pulling it to the end of the tub behind Nick, she sat, her body turned slightly toward him, her hands folded in her lap.

Nick sat as still as a statue in the tub, his bare knees drawn up. The firelight to his right cast him in a study of red and black and gold. He stared down at the water.

At first, Simone thought he had coughed. But then a truer chord entered the sound, and she looked up to see his head resting on his forearms, braced across his knees, the sides of his chest heaving. The choking sound came from him again, and Simone knew that Nicholas wept. She let him be for several moments, sitting behind him on her stool while her own tears flowed and the thunder rolled across the stone keep.

Then she wiped at her eyes and rose from the stool, picking up a square of linen and shaking it open. Simone dunked the rag into the water behind Nick and reached for the cake of soap. She began to wash his back—long, soothing passes with first the soap and then the rag, while he shuddered beneath her hands. After a moment Nick quieted, and Simone set the cake and the rag aside, reaching now for the dipper crafted from a hollow gourd.

She filled the dipper and poured it carefully, slowly, over Nick's back, watching the water ripple and shine across his muscles. Again and again she poured, each time drawing the water higher until his hair was wetted. Simone retrieved the soap once more and lathered Nick's hair, her nails raking his scalp. She glanced at his face: his eyes were closed, his lashes spiked and wet against his cheeks, the red scrapes from Evelyn's assault branding him. She looked away to rinse his hair, slick it back from his forehead with her fingers.

Nick looked up at her, water dripping from his nose, his brow, his chin. There was a question in his eyes, one that Simone could not answer.

"Lean back," she ordered softly.

Once he reclined, she picked up the soap and the rag and began to wash his body, careful not to meet his eyes lest he see the love she held for him. She would not allow him to feel pity for her this night.

She soaped and rinsed his arms, down to his long, thick fingers, the laden cloth sliding easily over his skin. Then his chest, his stomach, her hand swirling through the light crop of hair between his nipples, down the ripples of his abdomen, around his navel. Nick's breathing was heavier.

Simone felt tiny beads of sweat spring on her brow and upper lip. She dunked the rag again and moved to the end of the tub to attend his feet and legs, and she could feel him watching her through the curtain of steam. He propped first once foot, then the other, on the tub's rim while she washed him, the only sounds in the room the snapping flames and the splash of water.

He replaced his leg in the tub, and Simone let loose the cloth beneath the water to float away, unseen.

Gaining her feet, she moved to the opposite end of the tub and retrieved a longer length of linen. She held it toward him in both hands like an offering, and Nicholas rose from the tub with a roar of cascading water, his gaze never leaving her face.

He reached for the towel as he stepped from the bath, but Simone moved it out of his reach, rising up on her toes to rub the towel across his arms, back, chest. Down his stomach, around to his sculpted buttocks, his manhood, his legs.

She tossed the damp cloth over the stool and then took Nicholas by the hand once more, leading him to the turned-down bed. He climbed into it obediently, and Simone tucked the furs around him.

He grabbed her hand when she would have moved away.

"Will you stay with me, Simone?" he asked, his voice sounding rusty, tired.

At first she thought Nick was asking if she would stay at Hartmoore, as that was the worry eating at Simone's own mind, but then she realized he meant only for the night. For the first time, Nicholas was asking for her comfort, and Simone would not deny him.

She gave him a smile and walked to the opposite side of the bed. Removing her kirtle and slippers, she slid in beside Nicholas, wearing only her thin underdress.

He pulled her to him, turning her so that her back was pressed up against his chest. Simone sighed and closed her eyes as his arms came around her.

"Thank you," he breathed against her hair.

Stupid, stupid Evelyn, Simone thought, willing herself not to cry at the tenderness in his voice.

"You're welcome," she replied. She knew that on the morrow, she would be gone, and before she went, Simone wanted Nick to hear what no one had told her after her mother's and Didier's deaths. "Handaar's death was not your fault, Nick."

He stilled, his mouth against her scalp. "It is . . . loyal of you to say."

"Not loyal. True."

He was quiet for a long moment. "Simone," he began, "Lady Evelyn is my responsibility now. I—"

"I know." Simone was trying to memorize his scent, the feel of his chest warm through her underdress, the safeness of his arms about her. "We all must do as our honor would persuade us."

If he thought her answer strange, he said naught of it. He was quiet again, the only sounds in the chamber the crack and hiss of the fire. Then he kissed her shoulder. "I'm glad you came to me tonight. After . . . after I tend to Handaar on the morn, we will leave for battle."

But Simone could not entertain such dismal conversation. She would be gone when he returned, on her way back to France. "Let us speak not of it, Nick," she said gently. "Please."

She felt him nod.

Some time later, Nick's breathing became deep and even, and she knew he slept.

"I love you, Nicholas," she whispered to the dark room. "And I am sorry."

Chapter 23

Nicholas led the battle party away from Hartmoore, with Tristan at his side, in the pitch black before dawn. Behind them lay the curling whips of smoke from Handaar's funeral pyre, drying the dampness on Nick's face into black smudges.

The rain had stopped, leaving a crystalline damp in the cold air. Nick could smell snow in the frigid wind. They rode slowly, their ranks numbering not quite three hundred, and the party was quiet, the horses' tack muffled with batting and rags to disguise their approach of the border. The lack of conversation between men was due not to fear but to the early hour and the cold—every man who was riding that morn longed for the impending battle, craved revenge. They would ford the Wye just before daybreak and take Donegal's village by surprise.

Nick's own silence, however, stemmed from his thoughts of the time he'd shared with Simone only hours ago. His heart beat a heavy, steady rhythm in his chest—Simone was his. The way she had given of herself, so tenderly, to comfort him after Handaar's death amazed him. He had wept in her presence, a fact that still brought a gruff heat to his face, but she had not turned from him. She had not looked upon him with pity or scorn for his failings.

Nick had told her clearly that Evelyn was now his

responsibility, and she had understood. It was a great relief to Nicholas that there would be no friction between the women until Nick could discover what was to be done with Evelyn. If she wished to return to the priory, so be it. If not, he would secure her release and find her a husband to care for her.

The memories of his behavior the past months shamed him, and he wondered how he could have been such a fool. He loved Evelyn—aye, how could he not?—but he was not in love with her. Had never been in love with her.

As Handaar had said, there was a difference. And Nick saw that difference clearly on this foggy, frigid morning, riding over his marches to battle.

He loved Simone. He was *in love* with his *wife*. After his revenge on Donegal was meted this day, he would return to Hartmoore a new man. Armand du Roche was no more. There was naught to stand in the way of a happy future now. Nicholas mused that he may even become accustomed to his wife's young ghost—after all, Didier did keep things interesting.

But Nick's carefree mood was not to last.

"Nick, we should stop," Tristan said at his side.

"Obny's ruins lay just beyond the next rise, Brother," Nick said mildly, slowing Majesty and turning toward Tristan. "We'll pause there before crossing the Wye and be upon Donegal by sunrise."

"Nick," Tristan insisted, "I do think you should reconsider. I—"

Tristan's argument was cut short as the flaming arrow sunk into the frozen dirt, only the length of a man's height from Majesty's hooves.

The watchman called out, too late. "Sire, ahead!"

Nick raised his eyes to behold a line of lighted torches cresting the rise beyond Obny—more than three score, it seemed.

He heard Tristan move closer to his side. "It is what I was trying—"

"Shut up, Brother," Nick said roughly, his stomach turning. Had he moved Majesty forward, that arrow would have likely ended up in Nick's chest. He wheeled his horse to face their approaching party of soldiers. The heavy rumble of weapons being drawn, arrows being knocked, caused his heart to pound—the sounds of impending battle.

"Hold, men!" he shouted. "Stand your ground!"

Simone knew Nick had gone before she opened her eyes, feeling his absence from the wide bed they'd shared like a missing limb. She opened her eyes and turned her head.

The bed was indeed empty.

Before she could succumb to the despair she felt, a soft rap sounded on the door, and Simone hitched the covers higher over her thin gown. "Come."

Evelyn Godewin entered the chamber in her drab habit, and Simone stiffened. How dare the woman intrude on this place, taint the one precious night she'd shared with Nick by the nun's very presence. Did she expect to begin moving Simone's things from the room now that Nicholas was gone?

"Lady Simone." Evelyn curtsied, and her eyes flicked about the room like a pair of birds, taking in Simone's discarded kirtle, the half-empty tub and wet floor, the gutted candles.

Let her look, Simone thought viciously. *Let her see and think what she would.*

"Is aught amiss . . . ?" Simone said with frost in her tone. "What are you called now? Sister? Dedicant?" Simone clutched the covers to her and moved to sit on the edge of the bed.

A frown swept across the woman's pale face. "Evelyn, if you please, my lady." She took a hesitant step into the room. "I came to apologize for my behavior." She swallowed. "I knew not that Ni—*the baron* had taken a wife, and I have offended you unforgivably. I beg you, though, that you might see the reasons behind my actions and show me mercy."

Simone stared at the woman, knowing in her heart that she should allay her fears. After all, did she not love Nicholas as well? But Evelyn could not love Nicholas as Simone did, else she would not have abandoned him.

Simone rose from the bed, her coverings draped around her, and crossed to the trunk that held her mother's journals. She lifted the lid and withdrew the paltry coin and heart-shaped key. She looked at them, lying in her palm, while Evelyn continued to fight the tense silence by further explaining.

"I cannot help but feel responsible for . . . for Obny," she finished on a hitching whisper. "You see, had I not fled to the priory—"

"Had you not fled," Simone interrupted, turning, her fist clutched around the two small, metal objects, "you would be in my very place now, would you not?"

Evelyn paled beyond white, and Simone felt a spasming of her conscience. But her hurt and anger were not considerate of Evelyn's own grief. Yea, the woman had lost her father and her home, but had Simone not lost all that as well? And more? What else must she be forced to give up?

Simone threw the key and coin at the woman. They hit her and fell to the floor with a gay tinkle.

"I read. Your letters," Simone hissed.

The two women stared at each other for several moments, understanding passing between them wordlessly.

"You love him, don't you?" Evelyn asked quietly.

"Collect your belongings and get from my sight, *holy woman*," Simone mocked. "You will have him soon enough—what do you care of my feelings?"

Evelyn bent and retrieved the coin and key from the floor. "Lady Simone, 'tis not my intent," Evelyn began, rising and holding forth a beseeching, trembling hand. "Please—"

"*Go!*" Simone shrieked, using the hand not clutching her coverings to shove Evelyn backward toward the door. "Get from me and leave me in peace!"

Evelyn stumbled against the wall, her eyes wide as she beheld Simone. "Forgive me, Lady Simone," she whispered. "Please." Then, in an instant, she was out the door and gone.

Simone choked on the wild sob lodged in her throat. Forgive her? *Forgive her?* When it had been Evelyn's own stupidity that had driven Nick to despair, left Handaar alone at Obny? And now Nick was perhaps already in the thick of battle, possibly never to return. Forgive Evelyn, when 'twas Simone who would ensure that Nicholas and Genevieve would be safe from Armand, giving Evelyn exactly what she wanted? What she didn't deserve?

Simone let the covers fall from her body as she crossed to the trunk containing her mother's gowns, swiping at her face with her fingertips. She pulled out a scarlet kirtle trimmed in black.

She would right this situation once and for all, this very day. The tangled, bloody knot binding Nick and Simone— through Genevieve and Armand—would be severed and the loosed ends of their life together cast to the wind, like wayward feathers.

Simone saw Lady Genevieve turn the corner of the corridor ahead of her, and her heart began to pound like a war drum. She tried to swallow her fear.

"Lady Genevieve!" she called, breaking into a skipping trot after the woman. "My lady, wait!"

In an instant the woman reappeared, her face drawn around a curious smile. "Good morn, Simone. Do you come to break the fast with me?"

Simone finally reached Genevieve, and although the journey down the corridor had not been a long one, she was breathless. "Nay," she said. "But I need to speak with you, my lady. 'Tis most urgent."

"Oh?" The blond woman's bloodshot eyes narrowed, and Simone could see the toll that preparing Handaar's body through the long night had taken on her. "What is it?"

Simone gripped the parchment in her hand more tightly, and Genevieve's eyes went to it.

"You are in danger, Lady Genevieve." Simone paused. "But I think you already know that, don't you?"

Genevieve's eyebrows lowered. "In danger? Why, Simone, I'm sure I don't know what—"

"I know that you were married to my father. That he was the one who took Tristan from you." Her words fell and bounced like the blade of a guillotine in the quiet corridor. Genevieve was as still as the moon and twice as pale as Simone continued. "And I know that it was he whom you thought you killed in France."

Genevieve stepped closer to Simone, gripped her upper arm with slender fingers. Her whisper was fierce. "You would do well to have a care for whom you tell your suspicions to, Simone."

Simone shook her head and held forth the parchment in her hand. "Then tell me I am wrong," she challenged.

Genevieve stared at the offered page for a long moment, the very ends of her hair trembling. Then she snatched it from Simone, as if her courage would leave her if she did not. The woman unfolded the long page and skimmed the words. Genevieve took a miserly breath. She looked directly at Simone.

"Would that I had hit him harder."

Simone felt her chin begin to tremble, so relieved was she to have the danger at last called by its ugly name. "He's come for you," Simone said.

Genevieve only nodded, and then looked up and down the corridor. "I'll tell you what I know. Let us go to my chamber, where we will not be overheard."

Simone nodded, and the two women linked arms and turned once more toward the wing that housed Nick's own rooms.

"I am concerned, Lady Genevieve," Simone whispered, now that the truth was unleashed, unable to keep council with her own dark thoughts. "With Nicholas gone, who will protect you if Armand—"

"Do not think it, darling," Genevieve said. They were nearly upon the dowager baroness's rooms. "He cannot reach me at Hartmoore. Nicholas has left guards, and Armand is but one man. A madman, at that."

Simone could not push the itching worry from her mind. "Nicholas will hate me when he finds out," she whispered.

Genevieve gave her a tired smile and drew her into an abrupt embrace. "Nay. Nay, he will not. 'Twas I who should have told him." Then Genevieve released her and pushed open the chamber door.

Simone followed the lady in, and so she saw the rush of movement too late to save the dowager baroness or herself.

The chamber door closed quietly on the empty corridor.

Nicholas could not mistake his first man's white-blond hair catching the light or the bright colors of the king's royal guard as the sea of riders rolled like a wave over the land toward him and Tristan. Randall had fulfilled his duty, and well.

Nick's first man and a single guard pulled away from the mass of soldiers and gained the small rise with ease. Nick glanced eastward at their outfit and was darkly pleased to see no fewer than one hundred of William's soldiers mingling with his own.

The officer spoke first. "How many of the vermin?" he asked, nodding toward the west.

Nick followed the man's gaze; with daylight fully upon them, no telltale torchlight could be seen. The crest of the knoll appeared empty. "Mayhap three score."

The general grinned a sly, slippery smile. "'Twill be a victory most swift, my lord—with his majesty's battalion, we number over four hundred."

"Indeed," Nick concurred quietly, still looking toward the western horizon. "Good knight," Nick said, swinging his horse abruptly to face the trio of me.

"Sire?"

"Take your men to Wheatley posthaste and arrest Lord Wallace Bartholomew under my accusation of treason. He and his men abandoned the battle when he knew full well it was imminent. Take him to William and tell the king this. I will follow after battle to give my testimony."

"My lord?" the general asked. "You do not wish for us to stand and fight with you?"

"As you said, 'twill be a battle ill-matched, and I have a desire to beat Donegal with the men whose lands and people they defiled." Then, for no reason he could lay name to, Nick turned to Tristan. "What say you, Brother?"

Tristan gave not an instant's hesitation. "I agree."

Nick felt his chest expand at his brother's easy answer, but he was spared an awkward moment by the king's man.

"As you wish, Lord Nicholas. Good battle, my lords. God-speed." After a seated bow, the man turned on his horse and rode toward the army behind them.

Randall said, "Sire, shall I make ready the men?"

"Yea," Nick replied. "Once the king's soldiers depart, close ranks along the ridge. I want the bastards to see the hell they have called down upon them before we attack."

Randall left to do his lord's bidding, and Nick turned to his brother. "My thanks, Tristan, for supporting me before the king's man."

"I've always supported you, Nick," Tristan replied easily. "Mayhap I've not always agreed with your choices . . ." He let the statement dangle in the breeze and dismounted to begin checking his horse's tack.

Nick snorted and then he, too, dismounted, mirroring Tristan's actions. "You constantly refute my judgment, question my abilities."

"I've never questioned your abilities. Only your reasoning."

"You went so far as to coerce William into seeing me wed," Nick said, ignoring Tristan's protest.

His brother looked across both horses' saddles. "You regret making Lady Simone your wife?"

Nick met his gaze. "Nay."

Tristan sent him a cocky grin.

"But 'tis no matter—you behave as if I cannot tell wrong from right." Nick jerked Majesty's bellystrap tighter.

Tristan gave a put-out sigh and was silent for several moments before he again spoke. "Do you remember when first we met?"

Nick pulled on his chain coif, tied it beneath his chin. "Of course."

"'Twas on the precipice of a battle not unlike the one that now lays before us," he said. "I knew no more of you than I do of the Welshmen we will soon fight. 'Twould have been my right to refuse your aid for fear of being deceived. In truth, I did not yet believe our mother was not the monster of my youth."

"But you knew that we were brothers."

"Precisely." Tristan had fastened his own coif and was now pulling on his gauntlets. "And so your men joined mine. And when I would have jeopardized Haith's safety by rushing at my adversary, 'twas you who held me back."

Nick only grunted, untying his helmet from his saddle.

"And yet, I did not rail at you for your interference; I did not scold you for your lack of faith in my less-than-clear judgment."

"'Tis not the same," Nick grumbled.

"Is it not?" Tristan seated his own helmet on his head. "I owe you a great debt, Brother. And I'll repay that debt until I deem it fulfilled, whether 'tis to your liking or nay. You helped me to regain my demesne, my woman—my family. I would see you keep that which you already have."

Nick shook his head and pulled himself up into Majesty's saddle, the loud creaks of armor and battle trappings somehow comforting. 'Twould do not good to argue with the stubborn lout now, and in truth, Nick was more than a little shaken by his brother's sincere speech.

Perhaps his brother did not think him a complete failure.

But it baffled Nick how Tristan could believe he owned Nicholas a debt of any kind. Tristan, who was self-made, assured, who kept close council with the king. The notion was ludicrous to Nick.

The two brothers faced the Welsh border as the ground

beneath their mounts rumbled with the approach of their men. Nicholas looked to Tristan a final time, grinned, and held out his hand.

"It looks as if you will soon have your opportunity to repay me, Brother. Keep count of the men you lay low—'tis my wager I'll kill thrice more than you. If you surpass my number, your debt shall be forgiven."

Tristan seized his arm and laughed. "I'll take that wager. But keep close count—ciphering is not your strength. Mayhap you will end up the one indebted."

As their men closed in at his back, Nicholas could have no idea how much the battle would cost his brother.

Chapter 24

Had Simone had more than an instant to assess the situation, she may have handled it differently. But the dull thud of Armand's fist connecting with Genevieve's temple, sending the woman limp to the floor, and the arm about her own waist, a filthy hand stifling her scream, sent her into a panic.

She flailed and bucked and kicked her heels at her unseen captor while Armand stared hungrily down at the unconscious Genevieve. "Oh, Genevieve, forgive me, my love," he crooned, his words slurred.

Armand's right eyelid twitched frantically, drawing nearly closed, and his cheek hitched in a crazed grin. His hair had come undone from its usually messy tie and lay thin and greasy against his filthy tunic. Armand looked as though he'd been sleeping outdoors for days. Finally, he looked at Simone, but his words did little to comfort her.

"Portia?" he whispered with a dawning horror, but then reality shook him from that terrifying possibility. "Ah, Simone. You so resemble her in that gown—you gave me quite a start for a moment." And then he cackled, as if this were the most humorous thing he'd ever heard.

Simone had ceased her struggles, but her stomach heaved from the very stench of the unseen stranger holding her. She feared the telltale saliva filling her mouth, a herald of the vomitus that would follow did she not soon draw a clean breath. Her eyes watered, her nose clogged.

Armand looked at her conspiratorially. "Will you promise to be quiet if I allow Eldon to release you?" he asked in a loud whisper.

Simone gave a jerky nod.

"Let her go." He gave the command in French, and Simone hurled herself from her captor, gagging and swiping at her mouth.

She turned and beheld a large man, thick with fat and muscle and covered in what looked and smelled like dung.

"You must forgive Eldon's hygiene," Armand tittered. "He's been hiding behind the stables, practically in the midden heap for days, awaiting the right moment."

"I know what you did," Simone gasped. "I know, Papa! How could you? How could you do that to her, to an innocent boy?"

In one giant step, Armand was upon her and had slapped her face so hard that Simone fell to her backside. Her nose cleared for an instant and then clogged again with warm blood. Armand stood over her, his entire body trembling and his tics twisting his features into what he had become—a madman.

"Have a care for your lively tongue, Simone, lest I *rip it out!*" He lowered his voice with visible effort, growls and whines issuing from his throat, and then he shook his head violently as if to clear it. He stumbled down into a crouch over Simone, and she could not help but shriek.

"I knew not that the b-boy was in the stables that day! You, you, *you* were to t-take him to the Beauvilles, far away—away from what I had to do. *You* killed him!"

At first, the words Armand spoke made no sense—Simone had been talking about Lady Genevieve and a young Tristan. But then Simone knew, and that awful knowledge wedged in her throat like a dry hunk of bread—she was unable to swallow it or cough it up.

Armand had set the fire that had killed Simone's mother and Didier.

Her own father was a murderer.

He grabbed her with his one good hand and shook her as he continued. "That boy was my only flesh and b-blood! Never, ever, never would I have harmed the shortest hair on his head! *My boy!* M-mine!"

He dropped her back to the floor and rose, and Simone finally comprehended what he'd said to her.

"Didier was . . . he was your only flesh and blood?"

"Oh, *oui, oui, oui,*" Armand scoffed. "Of course. I would think you had figured it out yourself by now, clever—clever as you think yourself to be. I was barely conscious when I wed your whore mother. I can only assume that beggar— peddler—whoremonger—bastard Renault got on her. 'Tis why she was so eager to wed me—her family would not allow her to marry the peasant. But then she was with child, and very much in danger of being tossed out"—Armand did a fancy, hitching jig—"of Saint du Lac on her fattened arse!"

"Uncle—" Simone tried to swallow. No longer uncle. "Jehan is my father?"

"Oh, who can ever really know?" Armand shrugged and smiled. "I can assure you, though, 'twas not I. Why, when you were born, I could not even take myself with my own hand!"

Simone's breath left her, and she twisted to the side to brace herself with one arm and threw up on Lady Genevieve's floor. When she was done, she reached up for the coverlet on the bed and wiped her mouth.

Thank God. Thank God. I do not come from him.

"*C'est répugnant,*" Eldon grimaced.

"As though you should pass judgment, Eldon," Armand tsk-ed. Then Simone heard his gleeful laugh and a rifling of parchment, and Simone knew he had found the marriage decree, still clutched in the lady's hand.

"Ah-ha!" he crowed. "*Merci,* Simone. I knew you would prove useful one day!"

She turned onto her bottom once more, reluctant to have

him at her back. Armand was grinning like a fool and scanning the wrinkled page. He looked at Simone.

"She tried to poison me, you know," he said, as if imparting a great secret. "Your whore mother. She gave me a modicum of care after . . . after . . ." He glanced at Genevieve and winced, as if his words pained him. "After my accident. She thought I would die. But I did not!" He raised a fist high in the air and looked about the chamber as if he had a grand audience.

Armand's face spasmed around his wide smile, and he blew air through his lips to right his features before continuing. "I did not know who she was when I gained consciousness, and when I learned that we were wed, I thought her to be my ally." He threw back his head and laughed, and Simone cringed at the braying sound. "But then I would vomit after she fed me. My bowels turned to water. Pardon, Eldon," he said when the man moaned. "I quickly discerned that she did not want me to live. I needed play sicker than I was—nearly starved—until I was well enough to move about the keep on my own in secret."

Armand dropped to one knee and reached out a hand to gently stroke Genevieve's hair. "But by then Portia knew about you, my lady. She began stealing the coin from Saint du Lac so that I could not fund my search for you. Oh, my fondest love. I could not have that, now could I? I had a son, then, Genevieve. To replace the one you lost."

True fear began to grow inside Simone as she realized how deeply disturbed Armand du Roche was. "What are you going to do with us?" she asked.

"Us?" Armand's eyebrows twitched. "I'll do naught with *us,* you nosy little whore's spawn. A ship and crew await me on the coast. My lovely bride and I shall return to France forthwith. I'll give the king back his coin, and then we shall spend the rest of our days making love at Saint du Lac."

"But, Genevieve isn't your wife," Simone whispered.

"Oh, *oui, oui, oui!*" Armand smiled broadly. "She is. We were wedded and bedded before . . ." He waved toward his head. "You know. And now that her husband and my wife have sadly passed"—he winked at Simone—"'tis as if all these years, they never happened." He snapped the fingers of his good hand.

"What about me?" Simone asked, swallowing the vicious panic his mad explanation planted in her. "What will you do with me, Pa—Armand?"

Armand scratched at his ear like a dog and then looked thoughtfully at her. "Well, I certainly cannot leave you behind to sound the alarm to FitzTodd. And I most certainly cannot have you return to France and disrupt my bride's adjustment to her new home with your wild tales." He wiggled his nose. "So you shall accompany us to the coast. Once we have set sail, you may crawl back to FitzTodd and tell him what you please." He winked at her again. "Or I may take you with us just so I can throw you overboard."

Simone's stomach flipped over. Armand may be quite mad, but he still possessed a deadly cleverness. If he made it back to France with Genevieve, they would both be under the protection and laws of the French king and Nicholas could not touch them. She had no choice but to go along with Armand's insane plan and pray that Nicholas returned from battle soon and could track them, that he could somehow discover where Armand had hidden his ship.

"I'll be no trouble to you, as long as you do not harm Lady Genevieve," Simone said.

"Harm Lady Genevieve?" Armand drew back, offended. "Why, I would never do that, you stupid girl. Never, never, never. And I have complete faith that you'll be no trouble at all." He rose from the floor. "For if you are, I'll kill you in an instant." He showed Simone a terrifying smile.

He turned to his smelly accomplice. "Let's be off and away, then, Eldon." Simone gasped as he drew back the long tapestry along one wall, revealing Nick's boyhood passage. She had hoped that Armand would wait until nightfall to flee, possibly affording enough time for someone in the keep to discover them.

Armand flicked a hand at Simone as he spoke to Eldon again. "You take that one. Watch that she doesn't vomit on you again. You're enough of a mess as it is."

Donegal had played him well. When Nick's battalion had formed and moved over the rise, they were presented with the sight of well over two hundred Welshmen, in battle gear and crude war paint. His stomach clenched for a moment, and he wondered that he had not made a deadly mistake in sending the king's soldiers away.

Their numbers were nearly even now.

As if Tristan could read his thoughts, he said, "No help for it now, Nick. We shall triumph."

Randall drew his horse even with Nick's. "Any final orders for the men, my lord?"

Nick stared at the milling Welsh forming their ranks for several moments. He thought of Simone, her warm smile, her scent, how her arms had held him. Yea, they would triumph, for he had his love to return to, at last. A life to build.

He looked to his first man. "Fight like hell, Randall."

"Aye, Sire." Randall's horse sidestepped away, and Nick turned Majesty to face his men, raising his sword in the air. The ranks quieted, the sounds of nervous mounts and shushing mail dissipating, and Nick waited until all the men mirrored his pose. Majesty pranced anxiously beneath him, then whinnied and gave a half rear, ready to be away. Nicholas drew a deep breath.

"*For Obny!*" he cried.

His call was met with the blast of a horn and the return battle cry of his men. Nick felt his blood rush into his ears as he wheeled Majesty about, and he and Tristan raced toward the border, the D'Argent sapphires sparkling in the dull sunlight.

Genevieve had awakened and was well enough to sit her own mount for the day's long, slow journey, her horse teth-

ered behind Armand's. He'd bound her feet, a clear indicator
that he suspected she would attempt escape should the opportunity present itself, but he'd left her hands free, a courtesy of
his deluded mind. Genevieve swayed from time to time upon
the beast, giving Simone a fright, but Armand constantly
twisted in his saddle to monitor the lady's condition and
seemed genuinely overjoyed to be able to look upon the
woman.

Simone enjoyed no such liberties. Both her ankles and
wrists were bound beneath the long cloak, but Simone gave
it no thought.

She could not keep Nicholas from her mind—was he well?
Unharmed? Had he triumphed over the Welsh? Horrifying
images of Nick lying on some cold battlefield, covered in
blood, kept prying at her mind, but she would not allow them
entrance. Could not. She had to have faith that Nicholas
would return to Hartmoore, safe and whole.

Any alternative was unthinkable.

By late afternoon, the weather had improved to a balmy
breeze, with brief splashes of sunlight spilling through broken
clouds. They had passed no other travelers on the forest road
to their right, and the crisp crackling of leaves and the sweet
titters of the gray and brown birds overhead were the only
sounds accompanying the horses' footfalls.

Then Genevieve broke the silence.

"Armand, how . . . how did you find me?"

He was quiet for a long moment, so that Simone thought
he would not answer. When he did finally speak, 'twas not to
address the lady's question but to pose one of his own.

"Do you recall the night we met, my love?"

Genevieve stuttered. "O-of course I do."

Armand chuckled indulgently. "*Non.* I think not. You were
too enamored with your young viscount to pay me any heed
that eve."

Genevieve glanced over her shoulder at Simone with a
look that seemed to say, *Listen, and you shall learn what I
had not the chance to tell you.*

Armand continued. "You were . . . *rapturous*. I had never seen hair so golden, like spun silk. Your blue, blue, blue eyes," he sighed, and his shoulder jerked spasmodically. "I vow I fell in love with you that very night. You were kind enough to me when we were introduced, but I was only a lowly under-lord and had not the title or riches of your paramour." His voice turned bitter, cold, and his slur increased. He looked back at Genevieve, the skin around his mouth drawn tight. "He fathered your son, did he not?"

Genevieve held her head high. "He did."

Armand faced forward again. "I had better fortune when next we met, weeks later. Your viscount was absent, and 'tis this instance that you most likely recall."

"At my parents' home," Genevieve supplied. "My father brought you to me."

"*Oui,*" Armand said, obviously pleased that she remembered. "You were at the age that he would soon see you wed, and I, cocky youth that I was, pressed my suit with him. I told him that I would make my wealth in service to the king." He looked back at her again, and this time his face was happy, lost in the memory of that night. "You wore gold that eve; you were radiant—like a small sun, or a star . . ." His eyes took on a faraway look, and he turned back in his saddle. "I was over-joyed when your father gave me his permission to present myself after I had earned my worth. You did not seem dis-pleased with this either."

"I was not," Genevieve admitted, to Simone's great sur-prise. "My father was a hard man with a heavy hand. Al-though I indeed had pinned my hopes on . . . another, he was to be married soon. I longed to be away from my father."

"Ahhh . . ." Armand said quietly. "It makes sense now. Your actions. But you can understand why I was so enraged when I returned."

"You were gone nearly nine years, Armand."

"Through no fault of my own!" he bellowed, his voice sending the birds overhead scattering to safety. "I had . . . I was . . . I—" he paused, shook his head violently. "I risked my life to earn enough wealth that your father would grant me your hand."

"I did not wed."

"Because the lout denied you and your son!" Armand accused. He halted his mount and turned it sideways, blocking Genevieve's path. "You lay with him in hopes that he would wed you instead, did you not?"

"I was young. I thought perhaps—"

Armand silenced her explanation with the back of his hand, and Simone could not help but scream. Armand did not so much as glance in her direction, but instead watched Genevieve sway and grab for her pommel.

"Little whore," he spat. He pointed his horse forward again, only to glance back a moment later. "How fare thee, my love?"

"I am fine," Genevieve choked out from behind her hand.

A chill raced over Simone's body at the blatant display of madness. Armand obviously no longer had control over his impulses, and it worried Simone greatly. With this erratic behavior, he was likely to kill either woman at any time, without provocation or warning.

"It would have been perfect for us," Armand continued. "Because of your indiscretion, your father was as eager to be rid of you as you were to be away from him. No one would have you, save me. Your dowry was to pay the taxes on our home. I even went so far as to remove the taint of your bastard."

"His name is Tristan," Genevieve said sharply, and Simone cringed. "You stole him from me!"

"You stole my c-coin!"

"'Twas *my* coin!" Genevieve accused. "I thought my son was dead. I thought *you* were dead!"

"Yea, well, 'twas actually the king's coin once we were wed." Armand glanced over his shoulder. "Calm yourself, lovely wife—you're becoming overly distraught. In any matter, you nearly killed me in your revenge, and your son has since been returned to you. I met him in London, you know, although I did not know 'twas him at the time. Ox of a man."

Genevieve did not answer, and Simone's stomach turned at Armand's blasé retelling of the abduction of Nick's brother.

"When the king heard of my . . . misfortune, he took pity on me and paired me with Portia of Saint du Lac. Her parents were recently dead, and her family's home would have passed to the crown did she not wed. The king bid her care for me until I was well in exchange for keeping her place in her home. I did not know she was already with child by a common shop-keep, Jehan Renault. It would seem that is a pattern with me, is it not? Wedding women who have born another man's child."

Genevieve turned to look back at Simone, shock evident on her face. Simone could do naught but return the lady's stare.

Armand continued. "What with the beggarly funds Portia allowed me, I scoured all of Europe looking for you, my sweet, to no avail. But then!" Armand said in a loud whisper, holding one finger aloft. "Fortune did smile upon me, at last. As I passed the eve in a tavern in Paris, an old deckhand re-galed me with a tale of the loveliest woman he'd ever seen. 'Hair of gold,' he said. 'Eyes like a tropic sea.' She was scared, fled France on their ship in the dark of night. And I knew it was you, my love. I knew, at last, where you had flown to."

"But how did you know where to find me?" Genevieve insisted. "How did you know of Nicholas? After I married Richard, I spent my days at Hartmoore, rarely traveling to London at all."

"A delightful coincidence, I assure you," Armand chuck-led. "In truth, when Simone wed your son, I had no idea you were his mother. I only discovered it after they had departed London for your home. I arrived as quickly as I could, to see it with my own eyes, my sweet, my most precious treasure." He halted his mount abruptly. "Here we are, then. This should do nicely."

Simone had been so enraptured by Armand's macabre tale that she hadn't noticed the forbidding square tower of Withington's bleak convent through the trees. She knew the inn lay just beyond the fringes of wood, but this was still too far—Armand would never let her out of sight long enough to reach the inn.

Armand dismounted and walked to help Genevieve down. "We'll rest here awhile. Once night has fallen, we'll pass through the village and be on our way."

Eldon appeared at Simone's side and unceremonially dragged her off her horse and dumped her against the nearest tree. Genevieve joined her there, her hands having been secured.

"Eldon and I shall set about procuring us a repast," Armand said, bowing before Genevieve as if she were royalty and then turning to join the other man who was gathering wood for a fire.

"Armand," Simone called. When he paused, irritation clear on his twisted face, she asked, "Might our restraints be loosened? I have need to seek some bushes."

"I think not, little sneak," Armand tsk-ed and wagged a finger at her. "Once we have seen to the preparations, Eldon or I will accompany you. We are too close to the village for you to be traipsing about the woods unescorted." He smile was oily, insincere. "Who knows what mischief you might encounter?" And then he moved away from them.

Simone looked to Lady Genevieve and saw the woman's cold, deadly eye on Armand. With the dried blood at her mouth and her hair askew, the woman looked more than a little crazed herself.

Haith entered Minerva's chamber at Hartmoore, Isabella fussing in her arms. Her great-aunt lay sleeping, propped on her bolsters, and Haith was struck by how small and frail she looked. Two fat candles barely lit the chamber in the early evening gloom, and out of the corner of her eye she saw the gray phantasm that was Didier tumbling through the air toward her. She instinctively threw up a warding hand, and the silvery mass flew back into a far corner of the bedchamber, causing Haith's breath to frost and her heart to beat faster.

Isabella wailed.

"I know, lass, I know," Haith cooed distractedly. She approached the bed and touched Minerva's shoulder. "Minerva," she called softly. The old one stirred and mumbled a bit of unintelligible Gaelic. "Minerva."

Her eyes fluttered open reluctantly. "Och, what is it, faery? The lad's nearly worn me out."

"I know, I'm sorry," Haith said, trying to keep her composure. "Have you seen Lady Simone or Lady Genevieve? I've searched the whole of the keep and can find them not. Genevieve's chamber was bolted from within, but she was not there."

"Sweet Corra, lass, I've no idea—I was sleepin', in case you didna notice," the old one growled. "I havna seen either of them since yesterday." Isabella's insistent cries interrupted her. "What's amiss with the wee one?"

"I don't know. She won't—" Haith shook her head and bounced the baby to no avail. Her cries became more piercing, and although Haith was indeed concerned over the whereabouts of her mother- and sister-in-law, another worry was near to eating her alive, and she could no longer hold her silence.

"Minerva, I need your help." Haith swallowed, rubbing at the phantom streak of pain in her bosom. "I think something has happened to Tristan."

Chapter 25

They were winning the battle, driving the Welsh back toward the border, and with every swing of his sword, Nicholas felt Handaar's spirit strong within him. Each hot splatter of Welsh blood healed, in Nick's mind, Handaar's wounds, as if they had never been. Each body he left lying lifeless on the ground slowly filled the void in his heart at having to take the old warrior's leg, to watch him die in Hartmoore's hall. Nick felt vindicated, invincible, forgiven, as he plowed through the enemy in the fading afternoon light.

"*Aaaiiee!*"

The high-pitched yell came from behind him and then the blow to the middle of his back, bowing Nick's body forward. His breath whooshed from him as he fell, and he quickly rolled to face the second blow he knew would soon follow.

A Welshman, covered in blood, toppled toward him, a thick club in one hand and a short ax in the other, the latter raised high over his head. The beast gave another battle scream, his teeth bared in a bloody grimace.

Nick had the strength only to raise his sword, its hilt butted against the frozen ground. The Welshman fell upon it, turning his battle cry into a gurgling screech. The ax somersaulted through the air and bit into the dirt a hair's breadth from Nick's ear with a whisper and a dull thunk.

The enemy slid down the length of Nick's sword until he lay prone atop him, and Nick gave a mighty shove to the side and pulled his blade free. Spirals of color were beginning to dance before his eyes when his paralyzed lungs finally drew breath, and he lay there for precious moments, gasping.

"That was rather close," he wheezed aloud, and then laughed. The pain in his back turned his chuckle into a groan. "I'll be pissing blood for a fortnight after this battle, you bastard," he muttered to the dead Welshman, still staring at Nicholas in frozen surprise.

The sounds of combat were lessening now, and Nicholas knew 'twould only be a short time until they ceased completely. He struggled to an elbow, sheltered by the hulking body of the dead man, and looked about the battlefield before gaining his feet.

The sun was beginning to set beyond the Welsh foothills, turning black the blood-soaked slope where they fought. Already, crows picked their way through the dead bodies littered about, and even though some Welsh still doggedly engaged in hand-to-hand combat, Nicholas could see that most had fled or were fleeing.

"*Crane!*" The cry came from far off, and Nick turned, seeking he who had called, his eyes scanning the fallen bodies and fighting men.

"*Crane!*" The voice cried again, and Nick's head turned toward the border, where the sight he saw caused his blood to slog to a frozen stop in his veins.

Llewellyn ap Donegal stood on his spindly legs mayhap a hundred yards up the slope from Nicholas, his short, fat sword raised high. To the left of the Welshman stood two of his fellow bastards, holding a third man between them. The prisoner was on his knees, helmet- and coif-less, blond hair glinting golden red in the sinking daylight.

'Twas Tristan.

"The battle is mine, Crane!" Donegal bellowed and drew back his sword.

"*Nay!*" Nicholas screamed and bolted toward the men, his

legs feeling as though they were mired in a thick bog, his arms pumping slowly, too slowly.

Donegal drove his sword in a downward arc into Tristan's chest, the scene a study of black outlines. The men holding Tristan released him, and Nick's brother collapsed onto his side. Donegal braced a foot against Tristan's shoulder and withdrew his weapon.

The Welshmen turned and ran, disappearing over the crest of the ridge before Nicholas was halfway to his brother.

By the time night descended upon Hartmoore, those still in residence moved in a fog of panic. All of the guests of the wedding feast had fled, whether to battle or to their own homes, frightened of the strange happenings and bad omens that seemed to have wrapped black arms around the grand stone castle and squeezed.

Rose and Tilly, Genevieve's personal maids, along with Haith, had scoured every corner of the immense keep and grounds looking for the missing women, and now they gathered around the lord's table with the old witch, Minerva.

Evelyn sat at the opposite end, alone. She was neither included nor blatantly discluded from the conversation, and so she merely watched and listened, her hands folded over her rosary against the scratchy brown wool of her habit.

Tilly, the younger of the maids, wept openly. "I just don't know where they could have gone off to," she wailed. "None have seen them all the day!"

Evelyn's conscience spasmed, and she thought for an instant of admitting that she had seen the Lady Simone that morn, but her cheeks warmed at the idea of explaining the circumstance. Lady Simone despised her, and Evelyn could not fault the beautiful woman for her feelings. She prayed for Nick's safety and that Simone was also safe and well.

As if she somehow knew her thoughts, Minerva glanced down the table at Evelyn and frowned. The old woman terrified Evelyn.

"There's naught we can do about it now, lass," Minerva said, not unkindly, and Evelyn was glad the old one's focus was no longer on her.

"Minerva is right. We must wait for Nicholas and Tristan to return." Haith stared down at the babe in her arms, smoothing sweaty curls away from her forehead. Isabella lay sniffing and gumming a wet, honeyed rag. Both mother and daughter had red noses and mottled cheeks. Haith looked up at the maids. "Off to bed with you both. I'll wake you should we receive any word."

When the maids had left the hall, Haith lowered her voice. "Won't you try again, Minerva? I beg you." The redhead brought her hand to rest over her heart. "This pain in my chest . . ."

Minerva sighed and withdrew a small, fur-covered sack from the folds of her skirt. "Very well, faery, but 'twill be naught but more of the same, I can tell you."

Evelyn gripped her rosary tighter as the old woman muttered a singsong verse over the bag and withdrew three stones, lining them up on the tabletop. To Evelyn, they resembled small chips of bone.

"Ye see?" Minerva asked Haith. "'Tis as it was when last I asked."

Haith leaned forward, peered at the objects. "The Death stone—it worries me."

"But the Good Fortune stone is also present." Minerva gathered the pieces in one gnarled hand and dropped them back into the sack with little clicking sounds. Evelyn let out the breath she hadn't known she'd been holding.

Minerva continued. "And you know as well as I, the Death stone doesna always mean *death*. Oft times it means simply"—the next words the old woman spoke seemed whispered directly in Evelyn's ear—". . . a *new beginning*." Evelyn shivered. "Now, best you do as you bid the maids and seek your bed."

Haith dropped her forehead into her palm, and Evelyn could see her shoulders shaking. She didn't understand this cryptic witchery and had no desire to learn of it, but she felt pain at this woman's obvious worry over her husband.

"I'll not sleep," Haith sniffed.

"You must try, for the babe. She canna keep her wee eyes open." Minerva reached across the table, and Haith placed her palm in the old woman's.

"Alright," Haith whispered. "Good night, Minerva." She rose from the bench and blinked when her eyes fell upon Evelyn, as if she'd just realized the woman sat at the table with them. "Good night, Lady Evelyn."

Evelyn gave her a smile and a nod. "Good night."

When Haith was gone, Minerva dropped her own head into her palms, and Evelyn could see that she had paled. The ends of her frazzled gray hair drooped.

Evelyn cleared her throat. "Pardon me, Min—Minerva," she asked, and the old woman angled her head sideways to peer at her. "Are . . . are you ill?"

"Am I ill?" Minerva gave a low chuckle. "Nay, lass. Just old. Old, and verra, verra weary."

"Oh." Evelyn did not know what else to say.

Minerva continued to stare at her for several moments, almost through her, it seemed to Evelyn. She had the insane urge to cross herself.

"And what of you, Sister Eve?" she said at last. "Will you return to your convent now?"

The mere suggestion caused Evelyn's throat to burn. She managed to croak, "Nay. Never. That place is not . . . not *good.*"

Minerva nodded as if she completely understood. "So you'll stay on at Hartmoore, then, will ye?"

Evelyn frowned. "I don't know what else to do. I don't *want* to stay here—Lady Simone resents me, and although I know Nic—Lord Nicholas—would not refuse me, I feel I have caused him irreparable heartache."

"Aye. Ye have."

Evelyn nodded. "I wish . . . I wish that I could just go to sleep, and when I awoke, I would be far away from this place, these memories. Where none knew of me and where I could start my life anew."

"Do ye, now?" the old woman asked.

"Yea." Evelyn looked directly into the witch's eyes, and her stomach clenched. *God, forgive me for what I am about to suggest.* "Minerva, can you . . . can you do that?" she half-whispered.

"Not in the way yer thinkin', lass," the old one said with a wry smile. "But mayhap we can help each other all the same."

Excitement and fear tangled in Evelyn's stomach. "How?"

Minerva gained her feet slowly, as if it pained her to do so. "Soon enough. You just hold yer tongue and be ready should I give you the word, ken?"

Evelyn did not understand at all and, in truth, could think of one hundred things less frightening than giving over her future into the hands of an old, sarcastic sorceress.

But she promised, "I'll be ready."

And she meant it.

Chapter 26

Nicholas moved his feet, one in front of the other, by rote, his breaths ragged in his chest, heaving in and out like old, rotted bellows. He had walked through the night from Obny, but he would not be spelled by any man. He would bear the litter that carried Tristan's body back to Hartmoore, each and every step his paltry penance. His eyes never wavered from the easterly horizon, his pace never slowed.

With each numbing footfall, his own tormented thoughts spurred him on: My brother's blood is on my hands. My brother's blood is on my hands. The phrase was rhythmic, tormenting, and constant, circling Nick's mind like the scavenger birds they'd left at the battlefield.

And it was naught but the truth. Too well and too recently did Nick know these circumstances in which he found himself: covered in blood, returning to Hartmoore with a body on a litter. He thought of Lady Haith, of beautiful innocent Isabella, of his mother, and a pain seared his chest and stole his breath for a beat of time.

The litter hitched and jerked behind him, and Nick called out without pausing, "He who causes my brother to fall shall, too, meet the ground by the length of my own sword."

"Aye, Sire."

"Apologies, my lord."

"Not to worry, Sire."

"Quit being such an arsehole, Nick. I told you I could sit a horse if you would but listen to me."

Nick did not slow. "And then you would bleed the rest of the way out. Shut your mouth, Brother, and enjoy the ride, you ungrateful pile of dung."

Tristan gave a weak chuckle, then asked, "Have any of you good men some ale? This arduous journey has given me quite a thirst."

Nick heard a commotion behind him and a murmured thanks from his brother. Then an "oof" and a grunt, and then finally a growl.

"Might you at least stop *running* for a moment?"

Nicholas hitched up the litter again and proceeded to climb the slope leading to Hartmoore's wall. "We're nearly there."

A cry went out from the wallwalk atop the barbican, and Nick wanted to sigh with relief. Soon the portcullis would raise, the gates would swing wide, and his mother and Haith and Minerva would be at the ready to care for Tristan. For although his brother lived, the wound he had suffered was most deadly.

Donegal's short sword had indeed struck Tristan in his chest, the point landing halfway down the left side of his breast and traveling nearly to his hip. Thanks to the chain shirt he'd worn, the blade had not laid Tristan's chest wide. So though the garment had saved his life, it now posed a serious threat.

The mighty blow had gouged the metal fabric deep into Tristan's chest, mangling the links and tucking them neatly within the ragged wound. Nick suspected several of his brother's ribs were broken, and when he'd attempted to pull the mail out of the already swollen and purpled flesh, a wash of blood had flooded down Tristan's stomach and he had screamed and grabbed at Nick's arm.

"My God, Nick! Leave it," he'd croaked. "There is a better nursemaid than you awaiting me at Hartmoore."

They were nearly upon the gates, and Nick looked anxiously ahead. Not for Haith or Minerva, or even his mother, but for Simone. This time, when she came to greet him, Nick would take her into his arms properly. He would kiss her and tell her that he loved her and that he would spend the rest of his days making her—and Didier, if need be—happy.

And now the gates were opening, and Lady Haith dashed through them, sobbing Tristan's name.

The next people to pass through the barbican were two men—strangers to Nicholas. And although he did not yet know it, Nick was about to make the acquaintances of Jehan Renault and Charles Beauville.

The blackness within the thick wood through which Simone and her dubious companions traveled was so deep, Simone could not see so much as the head of her mount. If not for the frequent sheets of terrifying lightning, flashing every other heartbeat it seemed, 'twould have been like traversing the floor of a deep, dark ocean.

It was as wet and cold as the sea as well. The wind howled maniacally, and the rain mixed with sleet drove sideways, like cold, stinging needles through Simone's drenched and ice-crusted clothing. She fought to keep her seat, keep her face averted from the onslaught, keep her hopelessness at bay. Her nose, cheeks, fingers, thighs were numb, and she had stopped shivering hours ago. They had been riding through the storm since the previous night, and Simone was tired, so tired . . .

Armand's shout seemed a faint whisper in her ears, and when she raised her head, eyes squinted against the freezing rain, she knew that they had arrived at their destination.

The wood opened up before the quartet, and it was as if the party was poised on the very edge of the earth itself. Four large men, on foot and wearing black rain-slicked capes, stood before Armand, shouting back and forth between them. But beyond the men lay the black and tempest sea, far, far below.

She looked back to the boiling water, foaming and lashing

at the sky, and saw a low, single-masted ship anchored far out in the bay and floundering in the storm's grip. To the right of the cliff, in the valley of the bay, the charred and decrepit remains of some ancient keep leaned and yawned wide its old bones, defying the storm. Tiny pinpoints of light bobbed within and around the broken structure, and Simone wondered how much shelter it could provide.

Here, she thought, *here is where my fate lies. On the shore of this unknown coast, I will either die or be left behind to what mercy God would have on me, for surely there will be no aid for us now.*

Armand's arm swept in an arc, signaling Eldon to follow him as the four men dropped over the rise to the ruined shelter. Lightning illuminated Lady Genevieve for an instant, and Simone saw the woman's face clearly, desperate resignation making her appear haggard, and ill, and very defeated.

Simone's horse lurched forward through the thick mire, and she peered down over the edge of the cliff as they traversed the narrow, muddy trail, down, down to the violent mating of shore and water. When the lightning flashed again, the wet, red cliffs closing in around them seemed to run with blood.

As much as Nick wanted to press on, they had no choice but to stop and rest. A raging storm had swept down upon him, Jehan Renault, and Charles Beauville just after they had passed through Withington and turned south and, besides the fact that Nick was exhausted and the old Frenchman looked unwell, the wind and black, icy rain had made it so that Nicholas could barely make out Didier's feather, hovering limp and dripping above Majesty's head.

The three men crowded into a copse of old, thick cedars, and Nicholas strung a small tarp between the branches to give them a modicum of shelter. The fire they so desperately needed was a failure, doing little more than smoldering in the wet needles and mingling its acrid smoke with the chilling fog.

None of the men spoke, uneasy and reluctant allies each, but settled against the crumbling trunks for what little rest they could gain in the crashing fury of the storm. Neither Jehan nor Charles had bothered to inquire as to how Nicholas knew which direction to go, and Nick had not volunteered the information.

They would not believe him any matter.

Oh, Simone, how I have wronged you, Nicholas thought.

Armand du Roche was the man who had condemned Tristan to a youth of hell. The very man Genevieve had fled France for, believing she had killed him. And now, years later, Armand had come for Nick's mother, his deluded mind holding the woman as some fantastic prize—his treasure.

The two women Nick valued most in his life were in the clutches of a madman. A murderer, who had killed his own wife and the boy he'd thought was his son.

Nick felt he had wronged Didier as well—the boy who was no longer a boy. And Tristan. And Evelyn. Was there no one his selfish pride had not battered? In the instant he had witnessed what he'd believed to be Tristan's death, Nick had realized that his brother had been correct in his chastising those many months since Evelyn's betr—

Nay, not betrayal, Nick corrected himself. Since Evelyn had honored her mother's dying wish.

What a fool I have been. He readjusted himself against the tree. When he'd first seen Simone, he'd known that never had there walked upon the earth a more beautiful woman. She had enchanted him, confounded him, frightened him, and ignited within him a passion so deep that he had never felt half its equal in his life. And yet, when it was commanded that they should wed, Nick had railed at her, at Tristan. He'd kept prostitutes on the eve of their wedding.

He'd not believed her when she'd confided in him.

He'd abandoned her, with no explanation, time and again. In London, in Withington, at Hartmoore.

He'd ignored her pleas for help, when her mother's journals had warned of the very disaster they now faced.

And while he'd been so determined to be offended by the way others perceived him, he'd lost Obny and Handaar.

He'd nearly lost Tristan in battle, without telling his brother how much he valued his guidance and support. His friendship.

Nick looked back on the man he'd been the past several months, his faults and misdeeds spread out before him like a soiled cloth. It was not the man his father had raised to succeed him, and Nicholas was shamed.

But no more, Nick thought, a fire struck deep in his belly. *I will right this. I will make amends. I will be the man my father would have me be, the son my mother deserves, a worthy brother.*

Before Nicholas had departed Hartmoore, Tristan had seized his arm as the men readied to move him to an upper chamber.

"Avenge me, Brother," he'd whispered, and Nicholas had been shaken to see the glassy wetness in his brother's eyes, the pain of a young boy still hiding deep within the fierce warrior. "Make Armand du Roche pay for what he has done and bring our mother home."

Nick had sworn it.

He thanked God for Jehan Renault's and Charles Beauville's arrival, for bringing the truth so that Simone could be freed from the guilt she carried, so that Nicholas could strive to rid his family, once and for all, of the specter of gloom that dogged their memories.

But he also feared the Frenchmen's presence, knowing full well they planned to persuade Simone to return with them to France. His blood ran cold, not from the sleet that pelted him but from fear. He squeezed his eyes shut and prayed.

Simone, please give me the chance to be the husband I should have been all along.

Nicholas felt a fluttering against his right fist, holding the wet blanket around his shoulders.

Didier's white feather.

"Wake me in a pair of hours, lad?" he whispered, and the feather bobbed heavily, up and down.

Yea.

Nick opened his fist and rested the back of his palm on the sodden ground. The feather fell down into his upturned hand.

Nicholas gently closed his fingers over the small, weightless drift of fluff and felt a queer tingle against his shoulder, just above his elbow. He closed his eyes.

The man slept, not knowing—or mayhap he did—that Didier du Roche kept vigil at his side, his small hand in Nick's, his head pressed against his arm.

Haith shooed the soldiers from their chamber and now sat near Tristan on the bed, laying their daughter against his unwounded side.

She was so relieved to see the even rising and falling of his chest, to see him frowning in the deep sleep he'd fallen into as soon as he was placed upon the bed. Isabella, too, slumbered peacefully at his side, contented to have her father returned to her at last.

He would live. Haith's eyes filled with grateful tears. Minerva had worked her magic once again.

The old woman was tired now, and Haith had felt a stab of guilt at seeing her great-aunt so pale and bowed, her usually lively footsteps shuffling and hitched. Didier had fatigued her these last days, and the exertion of healing Tristan had exacted a heavy toll. Haith tried to rub the worry from her mind.

She can rest now, Haith told herself. *Soon we will return to Greanly, where she will be her old, cantankerous self.*

A soft rap sounded at the door before it opened a crack, and the old Scotswoman herself poked her frazzled gray head into the room.

"Faery?" she called softly. "May I come in?"

"Of course," Haith answered, a smile easing across her lips as Minerva limped inside the chamber, wearing her old black cloak. *She must have caught a chill,* Haith thought, and then frowned to herself. She could not have Minerva falling ill.

Minerva shuffled across the floor, eyeing father and daughter with her own smile. She eased down on the mattress next to Haith.

"Sleepin' like babes, the pair of 'em," Minerva said proudly.

"Yea." Haith nodded, and looked at her aunt. "What are you still doing about, Minerva? 'Tis late and you need your rest as well. I did not like the sound of that cough earlier."

Minerva shrugged a bony shoulder. "I wanted to see you, 'sall. All of you together." She reached out a crooked finger and stroked the baby's arm. "I'll have my rest soon enough, faery."

Haith frowned again. Something was amiss. She could smell its foul odor as if it were a pot of boiling horehound root. She reached out a wrist and rubbed it over Minerva's forehead and cheeks. "Are you feeling ill?"

The old woman ducked away, chuckled, then rose from the bed. "I'm nae ill, I'm nae ill. I'm only tired."

Haith was unconvinced and watched the old woman skirt the bed and come to stand near Tristan's head.

A smile increased the wrinkles of Minerva's face as she smoothed a palm up over his forehead and across his hair. She left her hand there and leaned down to kiss his brow.

She whispered against his skin, "Keep well, my boy. Care for my lasses. You have my heart."

Minerva straightened, and a shiver of hot–cold panic slithered through Haith. The old woman returned to Haith's side and eased back down onto the mattress.

"Minerva, I don't like how you're behaving—it's frightening me."

"Doona fear, faery," Minerva soothed. "Naught is amiss. In fact, all is quite right." She reached beneath her cloak and withdrew the fur sack containing her precious rune stones. Minerva looked at the weighty purse for a long moment before taking Haith's hand and placing the bag in her palm. "I want you to have these, Haith," she said mildly.

Sorrow gripped Haith's heart as she felt the soft fur against her skin, Minerva's fingers wrapped firmly about her own. And Haith knew.

The old woman was dying.

"Minerva" was all Haith could manage to choke.

"Shhh." She smiled sadly and brought her other hand to Haith's cheek, the smooth, leathery palm so gentle and cool. "Let us not speak of it, lass. I mean for there to be nae sorrow between us now."

"Let me stay with you, care for you," Haith croaked, her throat feeling dry and twisted like driftwood. "If you rest—"

But Minerva simply shook her head. "I'll be gone from Hartmoore by morn, to find my way back to where my *spirit* can rest." She dropped her hand away from Haith's face and twisted to look at Isabella. She pressed her fingertips to her thin, trembling lips and then reached out to touch the babe's cheek.

"You will grow to be a fine woman, Isabella Buchanan D'Argent. Heed your dreams, and they will serve you well."

Haith could not hold back her sobs. "Minerva, you can't go—what shall I do without you? What shall any of us do?"

"Och, now," the old woman said gruffly, and pulled Haith into her arms, her head on Minerva's flat bosom. "Ye'll do just fine, lass," she soothed, stroking Haith's hair while she cried and clung to Minerva's worn gown. "You are a healer in your own right now—you doona need me any longer."

"But I *do*," Haith insisted, each hiccoughing breath earning her Minerva's familiar smell. She wanted to breathe deeper, hold the scent in her lungs forever.

"Here now—sit up an' dry your face." Minerva took her shoulders gently and moved Haith away, wetness in her own black eyes. She fished up the hem of her cloak and smoothed it over Haith's cheeks. "This is what I want, Haith. What I need. I've been from my home for many a year, and I've longed for it so. Do you ken?"

Haith did not want to answer. She wanted to keep Minerva here with her, forever, in this very room, if need be.

But she was no child to give voice to those selfish desires. Minerva had sacrificed her own life to come to England many, many years ago and had stayed, first with Haith's mother and then with Haith. She would not deny this woman her final wish, not when Minerva had asked for so little in her long life, and not when Haith loved her so very much.

She swallowed. "I understand." She would be strong for Minerva because she sensed that the old Scot needed it, but tears still rolled down her cheeks, and Haith felt as though she were a young girl once again, frightened and unsure.

"There's my lass." Minerva smiled and glanced down at the fur sack still clutched in Haith's hand. "You use those now, and care for 'em."

Haith nodded. "I will."

"*I know ye will,*" Minerva whispered with a fierce smile. She leaned in, placed her palms alongside Haith's face, and kissed both her cheeks softly. She pressed her forehead to Haith's, and both women closed their eyes. Outside the keep, thunder rumbled.

"I do love ye, faery."

A great, shuddering gasp rocked Haith, stopping her heart for a moment, an eternity. And when she opened her eyes, Minerva had simply vanished, the ghostly warmth of the old woman's palms already fading from her cheeks.

Evelyn was waiting in the night shadows just inside Hartmoore's gates on shaking legs, the reins of two horses gripped in her hand. She had pilfered the required supplies from Hartmoore's kitchens, God forgive her theft, and divided them up between the two packs on the beasts.

Thunder rolled across the land like evil laughter, and then a bolt of lightning lit the surrounding hills, causing Evelyn to jump. She had never been so frightened in the whole of her life. She tried to soothe the horses lest the guards on the wall above hear.

An odd tinkling sounded behind her, and Evelyn turned to see the old witch striding swiftly toward her, her black cloak billowing in the sudden gale.

"You've done well, Eve," Minerva said as she neared, eyeing their mounts and supplies.

"How are we to get through the gates?" Evelyn asked as she helped the old woman onto her horse by making a low stirrup out of her linked fingers.

"Doona fret about that, now," Minerva answered, taking easy control of the nervous beast. "Just gain yer mount and let us be off—we've no time to spare."

So Evelyn did as she was told, and in a moment a thunderous wind washed through the bailey, splintering the broad oaken beam and blowing one half of the gate open. The portcullis beyond, oddly, was already raised.

"Yah!" Minerva yelled in her warbly voice and kicked her horse, bolting through the open gate and into the storm beyond.

Evelyn leaned into her mount's neck, very much aware of the rain-muffled shouts of alarm from the guards above her. "Follow Minerva, eh, boy? Can you hurry, please?"

And in an instant, Evelyn, too, was galloping through the dark barbican, following a dying old witch northward to their destinies.

The open half of the gate swung closed after Evelyn with a crash that drowned out the thunder.

Neither woman would ever see England again.

Chapter 27

The deepest interior of the ruined abbey, the remains of a great hall, was mostly intact, its rotted, ancient wood withstanding the brunt of the storm's fury. But the rain rippled down the walls in sheets and dripped from the roof beams and poured through gaping holes, giving the shelter the atmosphere of a damp sea cave.

Sputtering torches dangled haphazardly around the walls in crumbling, crooked iron holders, and a large fire snapped and sputtered directly in the center of the spongy floor. Ragged holes hid amongst shadows in the rotted boards, grinning back black nothingness. Simone felt as though she and Genevieve had been dropped into the midst of a nightmare.

The two women huddled together near the fire, their wet, heavy clothes plastered to their bodies. They sipped warm, watered wine from crude wood bowls and tried to remain as inconspicuous as possible. Since their arrival at the coast, Armand had seemed to grab a firmer hold on his sanity and now spent his time talking with one group of seamen or another, discussing the storm, the sea, the viability of setting sail.

The day had dawned hours ago, but the skies were still black as night, the storm roaring vitriolicly at them, unrelenting. Simone thanked the heavens for the violent weather—she knew 'twas the only thing keeping Armand and his captives on English soil.

"We must set sail by nightfall," he said to the captain, a swarthy man with hard eyes. "'Tis unsafe for us to remain here." He suddenly stomped over to Genevieve and grasped her chin, turning it toward the man as if in proof. "Look at her—she is unwell!"

Genevieve indeed looked quite ill. Her face was chalky, with bright, hot coals in place of her cheeks and dark hollows around her glassy eyes. She did not struggle against Armand's touch.

But the captain would not be swayed.

"To put out to sea now would mean death for us all," he said. "Even should the storm subside, seas are high—we would be dashed upon the rocks or swept out to the open waters." He shook his head and spat. "We'll wait. A day or two, mayhap."

"*We cannot wait!*" Armand bellowed, stomping his feet in time with his words. He shook his head violently, as if to clear it, his eyes wild. "Am I not p-paying you the exorbitant price you demanded? Are you not obligated to heed my wishes?"

"A dead man can spend no coin," the captain reasoned, un-perturbed. "You are lucky I agreed to this insanity, any matter—it is past the time to be making the journey across the Channel. Dangerous. Be content that we should even attempt it. But not this night," he added.

"*Aarrgghhh!*" Armand bellowed, snatching at his hair. He mumbled under his breath for a moment, and then his gaze swung toward Simone, and her heart stopped.

"I'll g-give you the girl," he said to the captain. "Do we leave as soon as the weather clears, high seas or nay, you may keep her and do with her what you wish. I've no need of her any longer."

The captain chuckled. "I reckoned I'd take her any matter," he challenged Armand. He shot Simone a lecherous grin full of nasty promise. "But we'll depart only at *my* word—I'll not lose good men to cater to your reckless haste." Then he left

Armand sputtering, tossing Simone a wink as he passed out of the hall and into the storm beyond the keep.

Simone let out her breath. One of the guards—or deck-hands, Simone did not know who was who—a filthy, fattened man with matted hair holding a wineskin in cloth, leaned over Genevieve with a grotesque smile, and Simone's stomach turned at the nearness of him.

"More wine, milady?" he gurgled, holding forth the vessel.

Genevieve nodded jerkily and held up her small bowl with unsteady hands.

The guard reached out a scab-covered paw and swiped at Genevieve's breast. "Oh, beg pardon," he minced.

Simone shrieked and threw her bowl at the man's head. "Get away from her, you monster!" she screamed.

The guard dropped the wineskin and batted Simone's bowl away, his eyes narrowed. "I'll have your backside for that, little whore," he growled, and advanced on Simone, his hands outstretched into filthy claws.

But, to Simone's surprise, Armand intervened. "What is this? What is this?" he demanded, grabbing the guard's shoulder and spinning him about.

"The bitch threw her cup at me," the man said. "I was just tryin' to give 'em summore wine, an'—"

"That is a lie!" Simone said. "He touched Lady Genevieve!"

Armand looked at Genevieve, crying soundlessly. "Is this true, my treasure?"

Genevieve nodded, not bothering to look up.

Armand's face erupted in a spattering of twitches, and he shoved the guard backward, causing him to stumble. "How dare you, you, you—unworthy maggot!" He pushed the guard again and advanced on him. "You touched my wife? My bride? My t-treasure?" He shoved the man once more, and Simone noticed that the guard's feet were coming perilously close to one of the largest, yawning holes in the floor.

"I did not!" the guard denied, shaking his head frantically. "I did not! You didn't see it! I didn't touch her!"

"Liar!" Armand shouted, and gave a final mighty shove

at the man's chest, sending him tumbling backward into the hole.

The guard's scream was cut short by a wet, ripping sound. Armand seized a torch from the nearest wall and held it aloft over the void. A group of men gathered around the hole, some grimacing and turning away.

"You'll not touch her again, now, will you?" Armand laughed into the hole. "Not with your guts all spilled about willy-nilly!"

Genevieve gave a soft moan and leaned into Simone, and Simone wrapped her arms about the lady.

"I'm going to die, Simone," Genevieve said in a crackling whisper. "Either here or at sea, and in truth, I would rather it be here."

"Shh," Simone whispered into the woman's wet hair, slick and cold like icy seaweed. "You'll not die. Just rest, my lady. I'll watch over you. Just rest."

But Simone did not know how either of them would survive. Genevieve was in no condition to travel in haste should they devise a way to escape the keep. And where would they run? Armand had navigated thick forest for most of the journey to the coast. As far as Simone knew, there was not a village or a hut for miles and miles. They could never escape on foot.

A day, mayhap two, the captain had said. Would that be enough time for someone to track them? Simone closed her eyes against the despair she felt. She was only fooling herself—they'd left no trail to follow. It was too far, the coastline of England too vast, and Simone knew it.

Against her breast, Genevieve slept fitfully, and for that, Simone was glad. She let her tears fall, thinking of the boy she'd left behind at Hartmoore. She hoped that, if the old witch could not help Didier find peace, she would let the boy keep his company with her. At least he would have someone who could see him, talk with him. Keep him from being lonely.

"Oh, Didier," Simone whispered, her tears leaving hot

trails down her cheeks as she let her eyelids block out her horrifying surroundings. "I am sorry I failed you."

"There's no need to cry, Sister," the voice said matter-of-factly in her ear, and Simone froze. "Or is that rain dripping on you? It *is* rather damp in here."

Simone opened her eyes and turned her head and there he was, sitting cross-legged beside her.

"Didier?" she whispered. "Is it really you?"

He gave her a mischievous grin. "Of course it is. The baron waits in yonder wood with Oncle Jehan and Charles. They're having a row about who should come and rescue you and Lady Genevieve." He looked down at the woman and frowned. "Is she ill?"

"How—how—" Simone brought the hand not holding Genevieve to her mouth, hysterical hope threatening to spin the hall into dizzying nothingness. Nicholas had come! He'd used Didier to find her!

He's come for his mother, not for you, a hateful voice of reason said to her, but Simone did not care. He'd come, which meant he was safe.

"Yea, Didier," she croaked. "She is quite ill."

The boy's face was solemn, thoughtful. "I am very sorry to hear that. She is a nice lady." Then he looked around the room, touching his thumb to each of his fingers.

"What are you doing?" Simone asked, ducking her head behind Genevieve's.

"Counting." He scrunched up his face. "Lord Nicholas bade me see how many men were about. Sister, what is ten and six and ten?"

"A score and six," Simone answered, dazed, her mind still reeling. "But how will you . . . ?"

"We have a plan," the boy said simply. He popped onto his feet. "Wait here. I'll be right back."

"Didier, wait!" Simone said, a bit loudly. She did not want to be left alone again.

But Didier was already gone and Armand was approaching,

looking highly agitated and rubbing at himself as if he were a hound beset by fleas.

Looped around his crippled forearm was a long, dirty length of rope.

"What are we waiting for, FitzTodd?" Jehan demanded for the tenth time since they had spotted the abandoned abbey below. The relentless rain dripped from the man's hood. "If Simone is indeed in yonder keep, she is in great danger! Let us go now, before it is too late for her or your mother."

"I agree," Charles Beauville said in an accusatory manner that set Nick's teeth on edge. "Why have we traveled this long distance if you have no plans to approach Simone's abductor?" He raised a sparse, effeminate eyebrow. "I cannot blame you for your fear, but—"

Nicholas growled, at the very ends of his patience with the haughty Frenchman. Nick seized the man by the back of his neck and thrust him forward to the very edge of the wood, Charles Beauville scrambling on the tips of his toes to keep up.

"See you those lights, you pompous idiot?" he demanded, releasing Charles. "They are *torches*. Armand is not yet so deluded that he would attempt this deed alone. Do we charge blindly ahead, we shall put the women in more danger than they already are, and die ourselves." Nick spread one arm toward the lair. "But, do you have a death wish, please, be my guest."

Beauville paled, and his mouth gaped open and shut like a fish's.

"He's right about that, son," Jehan intervened, coming to stand between the two younger men as the lightning flashed. "We must think this through, if only for Simone's sake. But FitzTodd"—Jehan turned his slender face, the boning, the eyes so like Simone's, toward Nick—"I fail to see how standing about will garner us the information we require."

Nicholas turned from the men and scanned the steep track

below. Still no sign. "We've a spy within the very den," he said over his shoulder.

"A spy?" Charles squawked. "Why did you not say something? Jehan, I—"

"Who?" The old man ignored Charles, touching Nick's shoulder. "Who else would know where to find her? Who would aid us?"

Nicholas looked at Jehan, saw the desperate hope in his eyes, the pleas for Nick to confirm the old man's greatest fear and also his wildest hope.

He knows, Nick thought. *Whether Simone confided in him or nay, this man knows.*

"Who do you think, Renault?" Nick said, not unkindly. "Who, indeed, would care enough for Simone to travel all this way? Who could gain entrance to the abbey without being detected?

"Who bears Armand a grudge greater than any of us three?"

Jehan's prominent Adam's apple bobbed up and down, and the old man's eyes welled. "Didier?" he choked.

Nick nodded.

Charles gave a strangled, wild sound and stepped forward once more, his face the color of the foam on the beach below. "That's quite enough, FitzTodd! I know not what game you play, but I'll not stand for it!"

Nick looked at him mildly. "Have you finished?"

"I—I—" Charles stuttered, and then closed his mouth in a prim line.

"Good. Then listen well." Nick spoke calmly and evenly, but Beauville must have seen the cold murder in his eyes, for he glanced at the old man and retreated a step.

"Simone told me how you betrayed her. How she confided in you and you not only refused her but branded her a madwoman," Nick said. "As much as it shames me to admit it, I, too, did not believe her claims of Didier's spirit." He paused, making certain he looked directly into Beauville's eyes. "Until I saw proof of him with my own eyes."

"You are . . . insane," Charles said in a high-pitched whisper.

"Nay. And neither is Simone. Do you hope to persuade her to return to France, you'd do well to reconcile yourself to having the ghost of an eight-year-old boy watching your every move."

"*Non! Non!*" Charles shook his head. "It cannot be! You say these things only to make me not want Simone. But I do! Nothing will ever make me not want her!" The man spun on his heel and walked away from Nicholas and Jehan to stand alone, farther into the wood.

"Forgive him, FitzTodd," Jehan said. "He is levelheaded to a fault. He simply cannot fathom that—"

"I care not," Nick interrupted. "I am shamed to have disbelieved Simone. Now that I see what a fool I was, I have little tolerance for Charles's petty fears. If he loves her as he says he does, he would believe her as well."

Jehan peered at Nick, realization lighting his proud, tired face. "You love her, then?"

Nick turned away, toward the trail once more. "Of course."

"I see," Jehan said quietly. He joined Nicholas at the edge of the wood. "Mayhap Simone will not be returning to France as I had hoped."

"Mayhap," Nick said. Then he saw a tiny swatch of white floating in a jerky, arcing manner up the trail. "In any case, we shall soon know—Renault, your son approaches."

Nick heard the man's sharp gasp. "There?" he whispered as the feather drew nearer.

"Yea." Nick looked down at where he guessed the boy's head to be. "Are Simone and Lady Genevieve inside, Didier?"

The feather moved up and down. *Yea.*

"Are they well?"

Up and down—*Yea.* Then, side to side.

Nay.

Jehan looked to Nicholas. "What? What does it mean?"

Nicholas shook his head, frowning. He continued to address the boy. "Are—are they both alive?"

Yea. Yea, yea.

Nick's heart began beating once more. "Guards inside?"

Yea.

"How many?"

The feather moved to swirl around Nick's fist, and he held his palm out. The feather rose up on its tip in Nick's hand and began tapping against his skin.

"*Mon dieu,*" Jehan breathed.

Then the feather withdrew. "Twenty-six," Nick said. "Are you certain, lad?"

Yea.

"Very well." Nick turned to the old man and checked his sword on his hip. "I'm going down to get them. In the storm, I'm certain I can sneak in without being detected." He glanced toward Didier's feather. "Are the women bound?"

Nay.

"Good. Jehan, stay here with the horses. When you—"

"I am going with you," the old man declared.

"Nay, you're not." Nick walked to his mount and retrieved a short dagger from his pack. "When you see us coming, be ready to help me with the women. From Didier's answers, one of them may be injured, and we'll need hurry."

"FitzTodd." Jehan seized Nick's arms, stopping him when he would have passed. "You cannot do this alone."

"No offense, Renault, but you would do naught but slow me down. And I'll not be alone." Nicholas gave the man a clap on his shoulder. "Didier will be with me."

"At least take Charles," Renault pleaded. "He is young, strong . . ."

Nick ground his teeth together. He did not want the prig's help. More likely than nay, the poor excuse for a man would get them both captured. Or wet himself.

Probably both, Nicholas decided.

"Oh, Beauville," Nicholas called to Charles, still standing with his back turned toward them, obviously deep in thought. When the slight blonde started and turned, Nick said in an unabashedly condescending tone, "Didier and I are off to storm the keep. Would you care to join us?"

"Go to Hell, FitzTodd," Charles said, his voice trembling, eyes wild. "I'll fetch Simone while the fiends are disposing of your body!" He turned away again.

Nick looked at Jehan with a shrug and a wry smile. "He doesn't fancy a siege just now."

Jehan frowned, glancing at Charles for a moment. "FitzTodd—*Nicholas*—" he tried. "I beg you—"

"Nay." Nick offered the old man his arm. "You may wish me luck, though."

Jehan took Nick's hand, gripping it firmly in both of his. "God's blessing upon you. *Both*." He glanced at the feather, which swayed side to side quickly, as if the boy was waving.

Nicholas nodded, and pulled free from Jehan's hands. "Let us be off, Didier. I'll need for you to cause a distraction. Listen closely . . ."

Jehan watched the large man knit a path along the edge of the wood, out of sight from those in the ruin beyond, the tiny white feather bobbing along at his hip. They faced great danger bravely, while he and Charles waited behind like helpless maidens. Jehan looked again at his young countryman, and his frown deepened.

They both had stood aside for too many years. He checked his weaponry and then followed the baron's tracks.

Chapter 28

Nicholas crawled over the icy, jagged rocks on the seaside of Armand's lair, Didier's feather clutched in the sweaty creases of his hand for safekeeping—and for luck. He felt a narrow ledge of wet, sandy soil above him and pulled himself up to rest with his back against the rotten and water-swollen timbers, stifling as best he could his gasps for breath. He looked down the way he had come: nearly a sheer drop to the sea, the waves crashing against the rocks as if in frustration that he'd not fallen.

Then, to his right, scrabbling footsteps, the skittering of loosened pebbles sliding down the seacliff. A lanky, olive-skinned man in loose-fitting chausses stepped around the side of the abbey, his carefree whistle abruptly ending when his eyes met Nick's.

"Qu'est-ceque c'est?" the man demanded in a surprised voice, but Nick quickly shot out one booted foot, collapsing the man's knee in on itself with a sickening crunch.

The swarthy man opened his mouth to scream, and Nick swiped his leg at the man's ankles, sending him over the cliff edge, his cry of pain and fear fading quickly in the swell of the roaring surf billowing up from the sea.

Nick's heart pounded, and he waited for a warning cry to be raised, for another man to investigate. But no one came.

From within the keep, he heard a crash, followed by alarmed shouts in French. Nick took several deep breaths, in through his nose, out through his mouth. Then he leaned to his left to peer around the side of a jagged timber, where once a wall had protected the rear of the abbey.

The first thing Nick saw was Simone and his mother, clinging to each other on the floor near the center of the room, and Nick's heart pounded so that it competed with the rushing surf below. Both women appeared battered and bedraggled; Simone's hands were bound and Genevieve looked feverish, but they were both alive and whole.

Nick's joy was blotted out by fury as Armand stepped near the women, his arms outstretched, shouting, shouting . . . what?

"'Tis naught but the wind, you fools!" Armand turned in a dragging circle, and Nick saw a handful of French guards skirting the wall of the room, their eyes drawn to where Nick could not see.

"Return to what you were doing!" Armand bellowed. "'Tis naught but the Christing wind—*aaaghh!*"

Nick's eyebrows rose as a flaming torch went cartwheeling through the air past Armand and toward the group of guards, bouncing a shower of sparks off one man's shoulder and making him squeal and dance.

Good show, Didier.

"'Tis the spirits of the monks!" the assaulted guard whined in French. "They are taking their revenge for our trespass of the abbey!"

"Oh, you giggling milkmaid," Armand scoffed, but Nicholas could see the sweat pouring down Armand's face even from this distance. "There are no such things as spir—*Christing Hell!*"

Another torch spun by Armand, glancing off the madman's ear, and now the previously singed guard spun and wrenched at the abbey's poor excuse for a door, pulling it completely free from the frame and tossing it aside. The guards rushed through, shoving and trampling each other in their haste to exit.

"Where are you going, you moronic imbeciles? I'm paying you to see us to France! You cannot desert us!"

Armand threw his head back and actually howled with rage. Nick grinned maliciously and eased closer to where the wall ended in a gaping hole. He peered down the length of the hall.

The only persons inside now were Armand, Simone, and Genevieve.

And Didier, of course.

Nick slid his feet in until he could perch on his haunches and began to slip around the edge of the wall.

He never saw Eldon bring the hilt of a dagger down upon the back of his head, but for an instant, Nick surely felt it.

Didier was tiring, but still he wrestled with yet another heavy torch on the wall when Eldon appeared around one side of the hall's rear wall, dragging a large object behind him.

The large object was Nicholas.

Simone could not help but scream, jolting Lady Genevieve out of her uneasy rest.

"See what I've found lurking about, my lord," Eldon said mildly, dragging Nick on his stomach by both wrists. Nick's eyes fluttered, and a trickle of blood ran from above his right ear and down his cheek and jaw.

Eldon dropped Nicholas into a pile at Armand's feet and then reached to his belt, withdrawing a pair of weapons and tossing them to the floor with a clang.

For the longest time, Armand stared down at Nick, as if he could not quite place him. Then he dropped to his haunches, watching Simone's husband as he groaned and stirred. Armand glanced up at Eldon.

"Anyone following him?"

"Nay, my lord. He was quite alone."

Armand stood. "Hmmm. How did you find me, FitzTodd?

Hmm? How?" He nudged Nick's cheek with a booted foot. "Answer me!" He nudged harder, and Nick's head rocked against the wet and filthy floor.

Armand drew back his foot again, this time farther, as if he would truly kick him in the face.

Genevieve struggled away from Simone. "Stop, Armand! Do not!" she shouted in a hoarse voice.

Armand paused, turned to look at the woman. "Do you think to command me, wife?"

"He is my *son*," Genevieve pleaded. "I beg you . . ."

Simone's eyes went to the far end of the hall, where Didier still struggled with the torch. But by now the boy was so dim that he could not even grasp the weapon, let alone budge it from its iron fixture. He swiped at it, again and again, looking back over his shoulder worriedly at Nicholas, but with each attempt, his small hand only passed through the torch.

Armand stared down at Genevieve, the right side of his face drawn to nothingness, the eye looking as though it had been plucked out and the lid sewn up tight. His right fist was mangled into a lump of thorny flesh.

He at last fully resembled the monster that he was.

"Very well," he said, his words a slithering slur. He looked to Eldon. "Get the remainder of the rope." He stabbed his claw toward the gaping hole in the floor where the guard had lost his life. Then his arm raised, indicating the half-rotted beam leaning over the cavernous void. "Str-r-ring him up, string him up! I'll not have him interfering."

Genevieve choked. "Nay!"

Nicholas stirred as Eldon seized him once more. "Kings'men follow me, du Roche," he said, his words mumbly and awkward. "Shurrounded."

Armand laughed as Nick was dragged near the hole in the floor. "No army of any size could penetrate yonder woods. 'Tis why I chose this very location! Hidey-hidey—only by sea could they think to reach me!" He danced a sick, stumbling jig to the missing wall just as a bolt of lightning stabbed the sea, illuminating the turbulent waves. "Methinks they'd be drowned should they try!" He thrust a triumphant claw into the air.

Simone felt frozen in place, utterly helpless to do anything but watch. Didier had said that Jehan and Charles had also come—where were they? Dead?

Where, indeed, was Didier?

Then she saw him, faded and gray, slinking along the wall behind Armand. He had given up on the torch and was resorting to throwing small pebbles and bits of crumbling wood at Eldon, who had bound Nick's hands behind his back and now slipped a crude noose over Nick's head.

"Armand!" Simone shouted. "You have what you want! I beseech you, spill no more blood in the name of your madness!"

Nick's head came up at the sound of Simone's voice, and he looked around the hall blearily, as if searching for her.

"Madness?" Armand spun on Simone and in three great, dragging strides was upon her, lifting her with one hand beneath her chin. Genevieve skittered away. "You speak to me of madness? Am I mad, Simone?" He shook her, his fingers biting into her throat, and she beat her bound wrists at his arm as her airway was pinched closed. "La-lala-la! Oh, Armand is *insane!*" he mocked her. "*You* speak to people who do not exist! *You* drove your betrothed away! All I want is what is due me, what has been stolen from me, denied me, these many years, and I'll not be denied any longer!"

Tiny pebbles and detritus from the floor bounced off Armand's head and back, but he paid it no mind, releasing Simone and looking toward Eldon.

"Raise him!"

"Nay!" Simone screamed through her abused throat as Eldon tossed the rope over the dripping beam and proceeded to pull back with all his weight. Nick rose to his feet slowly, stretching his body and neck as long as he could make them, rising on his toes. His feet scraped forward, and with a gurgle he swung out over the pit and rose, higher, higher. The beam creaked and moaned.

"I daresay, FitzTodd," Armand said, then chuckled. "I do hope that beam does not give out." He aimed a finger dramatically downward.

Nick's face was reddening, and his eyes rolled toward his feet. He quickly returned Armand's glare and kicked his legs.

The madman looked back to Simone, raising a palm to one side of his mouth as if he parlayed a bit of gossip. "*Spikes.*" He jerked his head toward the hole and wiggled his eyebrows. "Must have been the dungeon at one time. Convenient, *non?*"

Eldon looped the end of the rope around a rickety support beam two, three times and then stepped away. Simone could hear splintering wood.

"He'll fall!" Simone cried, and struggled to her knees. She looked wildly for Didier, but he was nowhere to be seen.

"Oh, *oui,* 'tis likely." Armand nodded. "Or, he'll strangle. It makes no difference to me."

Simone gained her feet and began hobbling toward the support where the rope was slithering, slithering slowly as it unwound from the spongy wood. Nicholas gurgled and kicked. Eldon stepped toward her with a menacing growl, but Armand waved him off.

"Leave her. She has not the strength to hold him and 'twill keep her occupied until the wood fails and drags her in."

Simone reached the rope and looped it as best she could around her hands and bound wrists. She leaned back with all her strength, and the beam creaked louder.

"Simone," Nick gasped, "let go!"

"Nay," she sobbed. "I'll not let you fall!"

"Armand!" Genevieve's voice, trembling and weak, rang against the howling wind. "Cut him down!"

Simone looked to where the lady's voice had come. Genevieve had crawled to Nick's discarded weapons and unsheathed a small dagger. She now held it to her own outstretched wrist.

"Cut him down or I will end my life this instant," she threatened, her face an alabaster mask, eyes glittering gray ice.

Eldon looked from Armand to the lady, as if unsure what he should do.

"Genevieve, my treasure," Armand soothed, his eyes wide. He stepped toward her. "There is no need—"

"*Stay back!*" she screeched. "One step further and I will slit my wrist—I swear it!"

The rough rope was slipping through Simone's palms, dragging bits of skin with it. She felt as though her hands were on fire and that her spine would snap before the beam. From where she stood, she could see the tall, tree-high timbers standing upright in the pit, their ends whittled to crude, vicious points. The body of the unfortunate guard was skewered halfway down a spike, like a fish over hot coals.

Simone leaned back harder.

Perhaps it was because he was insane—or simply because he was foolish—that Armand took another step toward Genevieve. "My love, my heart . . ."

Genevieve sunk the tip of the blade into the milky white skin of her forearm, and blood, rich and thick and red, sprang forth.

"*Non!*" Armand screamed and quickly backed up a step, his good hand clutched to his chest. "You cannot! Genevieve—not after I have waited this long for you." Tears actually began to run down Armand's cheeks. "All that I have sacrificed—all for you!"

Genevieve glanced out of the corner of her eye. "Eldon . . ." she warned.

The man froze in his stealthy creep.

"Get away, you fool!" Armand bellowed, waving his hands. "Away, away, away!" His face was as crimson as Nick's now.

Simone heard her own sobs as if they came from outside her body, and her vision was blurred by tears. She could do naught to clear them from her eyes, save for toss her head and blink.

"Cut him down," Genevieve said again. She paid no heed to her blood, dripping onto the floor. "Cut him down, and I will accompany you back to France without a struggle. I swear it."

Armand's one usable eye narrowed. "How am I to trust you, tricky woman, when you are just as likely to sneak upon me and bash in my skull again with any common object?"

Genevieve's gaze did not waver. "I swear it on my sons' lives."

Armand backed down into a rickety chair and glanced anxiously toward Simone.

"The girl comes as well," he said. "I would have my own leverage lest you renege on our agreement."

Above Simone, Nick's struggles were weakening.

Genevieve looked to her, the question in her eyes.

"You will let him live?" Simone gasped, her palms burning like liquid hell against the rope that held Nick aloft. All she could think of was Nicholas, warm and safe.

"Of course," Armand insisted. He smiled a crazed grin and beckoned to Genevieve with his claw. "Let him down," he called to Eldon. When the man hesitated, Armand shouted, "*Let him down before my wife bleeds to death!*"

Eldon approached, and once he took hold of the rope, Simone could finally unclench her raw fingers from their death hold. She fell onto her knees, shaking.

"Drop the blade and come to me, Genevieve. Now."

Across the hall, the dagger clattered to the floor and the lady crawled to Armand, still seated in the chair as if it were a throne. Simone watched as Armand leaned forward and drew Genevieve's limp upper body onto his lap. He took the side of her face in one large palm and kissed her cheek, cradling her head before gently moving her aside as he rose from the chair.

Eldon lowered Nicholas down, pulling him away from the pit and letting him collapse on the floor. Simone scrambled to him, her fingers tugging the rope from around his neck and pulling it over his head, her fingernails splitting and bleeding.

"Nicholas?" she gasped, turning his face toward her. His

eyelids fluttered open, showing bloodshot whites. "Nick? *Aaghh!*" She screamed as Armand seized her from behind by her hair and dragged her to join Genevieve. He flung her against the other woman. Then he slapped both women, in turn.

"Whores. Christing, bloody, bleeding whores!" he muttered. "After all I've done for you both, this is how you repay me."

Simone looked up to see black rage coursing just beneath Armand's skin, rippling his flesh as surely as if a demon lurked inside him, watching the proceedings with glee.

Spittle flew from Armand's mouth, his words running together like a Latin mass. "I gave you my name, you ungrateful-bastard-common-born-bitch! Filthy gutter scum, spawned of Christing slime! Look how well you've wed because of me!" He flung his withered arm to indicate Nicholas, still and quiet on the floor. "A bloody, Christing, fucking *baron!*

"*And you!*" Armand spun to Genevieve, still clinging to the seat of the chair, too weak to move away to safety. Her arm was smeared shades of red and brown with her own blood. "I risked my very life to please you, only to return to find you'd born another's son! I wed you anyway, though, didn't I? Tried to better your station, make your mistakes"—he snapped his fingers—"disappear! And you tried to *kill me* for it!" Armand was sobbing now, as he limped toward Genevieve. "I should kill *you!* I want to . . . I want to crush your throat in my hand until you are dead! After all these years of searching, searching, searching . . ." His head jerked on his neck, and he screeched in demonic rage. "I sacrificed my only son! My beloved boy! My Didier! For you—*all for you!*"

"Not your son, du Roche," a male voice rang out.

Chapter 29

Simone's head swung to the far side of the hall where Jehan Renault stood, a slender sword in hand.

"Renault?" Armand whispered.

"Not your son," Jehan repeated. "*My* son. Mine and Portia's. You killed them both."

Armand shook his head furiously, his twisted features a blur. "*N-non! Non!*" He stabbed his claw toward Simone. "That one! That one is yours! Didier was *mine!* I laid with your whore!"

"You laid with Portia when she quickened with my child," Jehan said. "You were drunk, she seduced you, thinking you were too ignorant to know. And she was correct."

"*Non!*" Armand gripped his head with both hands. Snot ran into his gaping mouth as he moaned.

"*Oui.*" Jehan stepped closer.

Simone skittered to Nicholas's side as quickly as she could. She saw that he was awake, and when she reached him, Nicholas rose up on one elbow.

"My hands, love," he whispered.

Simone quickly undid the ropes, ignoring her throbbing fingertips and keeping a wary eye on Eldon.

When his hands were free, Nick untied Simone's wrists and

then rolled silently away from her. She watched him gain his feet, steady himself, and move stealthily along the wall.

When she looked back to her father and Armand, she saw that Didier now stood just behind Jehan.

The time had come for Didier to know the truth.

"Tell him, then, Armand," Simone taunted. "Tell my father how you set the fire that killed Portia and Didier. Tell him!"

"*Oui,* Armand," Jehan encouraged. "Confess your sins before I send you to Hell."

"I did it! I did it!" Armand screeched, ripping at his hair until wispy clumps floated to the floor and twisting his back as if he fought off a lash. "It was what she deserved! She would take my son! My coin! My very treasure! All that I had!"

The temperature in the decrepit hall fell like a stone through fog. Simone could hear the tinkling crackle of rainwater freezing in place on the old timbers, could see the frost creep round her legs and across the floor, an icy wind swirling over its blue-slick surface.

And then Didier stood between his two fathers, facing Armand. The boy's eyes glowed an awful red.

"You set that fire? You set it? You? *You?*" With every word, Didier's voice became clearer, his form more vivid to Simone.

And when he said, "You killed my mother?" Jehan gave a choked sob.

From across the room, Simone heard Genevieve whisper, "Oh my dear God."

"*Didier?*" Armand asked hoarsely, his twitches suddenly stilling. He squeezed his eye shut and then opened it, looking closely. "Am I dead? Where am I?"

And then Simone realized that all in the hall could see her brother, hear him as clearly as Simone did.

"You killed my mother?" Didier asked again, advancing on Armand.

Eldon stood rooted to the floor facing away from Nicholas, as if he looked upon the very devil, his face devoid of any color.

Armand backed up, bumping into his chair, and he fell against it as if he could no longer stand. His words were nearly unintelligible through his gray and twisted mouth. "She was going to take you from me, boy. I—I had plans to bring *you* with me to England—not Simone! We were to complete my quest together! My son at my side!"

Armand's chair flew through the gaping void in the rear wall, and Armand squealed and staggered upright.

Didier took another step forward. "You killed my mother." It was no longer a question.

Armand backed up another step, skidding on the ice-crusted dagger Genevieve had dropped. "Didier, I did not know you were there! Not until after . . ."

The dagger spun away from Armand, coming to rest directly next to Nick's foot.

Eldon was slowly unsheathing his sword, aware of himself enough to eye Jehan with murderous intent.

Nicholas bent and seized the blade, then his eyes found Simone's and seemed to say, "Do not look." But she did look, could not help but look as Nick crept up behind Eldon, covered his mouth with one hand, and slid the dagger into his ribs all in a mere blink of time. Then Nicholas turned the man neatly aside, letting Eldon slide into the pit.

The smell of smoke suddenly burned Simone's nostrils, and she looked back to Didier. The boy had opened his mouth impossibly wide, and in an instant the sounds of the storm beyond were gone, replaced by the hellish din of a fiery inferno.

"*Non. Non, non, non,*" Armand moaned, sidling backward once more. He was through the rear wall now, and the silent, silvered rain beat down upon him.

Within the icy abbey, invisible flames crackled, walls that were not there collapsed, ghostly horses screamed and kicked at their stalls. There was a sizzling, like pork on hot iron, and then the sound of a boy's voice—Didier's voice—crying, "*Maman! Maman!* Wake up! We must get out! The door is too heavy for me to open! *Maman!*"

Armand screeched and then slipped backward, his arms

windmilling wildly. The sandy loam beneath his feet gave way and he dropped, catching himself on a jagged rock with his good hand. In a blur, Didier had passed through the hall and now stood over him, looking down.

Simone scrambled to her feet and ran, slipping and skidding over the ice-slick floor, to the edge of the cliff, sleet and wind stinging her face. Didier stood at her side, his mouth still singing the awful dirge of the stable fire that had taken his and Portia's lives.

"Simone," Armand cried up to her. "My daughter—will you not save me? Will you not save the man you called Papa for the whole of your life?"

"You were never my father, even when I thought you to be," Simone said, and she stepped behind her brother, placed her palms on Didier's bony shoulder. She could *feel* him, his heat, his vibrating fury.

Didier snapped his mouth shut with a loud click and the sounds of the hellish blaze ceased, as did the very wind and rain buffeting the cliff and the abbey. Even the sea was silent as Didier looked at Armand.

"Let go," he said in a quick, low voice.

Armand's fingers unclenched and he fell away from them, backward, into the black. He did not scream.

The next sound they heard was a dull thud, then two more, then another. Then, as if the world exhaled a long sigh, the sounds of the ocean returned.

The skies began to clear. There was no sign of the French ship, once anchored in yonder bay.

'Twas as if it all, like a terrible dream, had simply gone away.

Didier turned, smiled up at Simone, and her breath caught in her throat—he was so beautiful.

"Sister," he said, holding up his arms to her.

"Didier," Simone croaked, and dropped to her knees, wrapping her arms about him tightly, smelling him, closing her eyes.

Didier pulled away and looked into her eyes. "The baron fetched me."

Simone nodded, smiling through her tears. "I know."

Didier nodded, too, then glanced over her shoulder. His eyes found hers once more, their pure, green depths filled with uncertainty. "Uncle Jehan is not our uncle."

Her smile grew wider. "Why do you not go and see him?" She turned on one knee and placed her arm around his skinny waist.

Jehan had not moved. He still stood several steps away, his sword in one hand, its tip touching the ground. Tears wet his face.

"Didier?" he said gruffly, and his sword fell to the ground with a clang.

And then the boy ran, his small feet slapping the damp floor, and launched himself into Jehan's arms.

"Papa!"

"Oh, my boy! My boy!" Jehan turned around and around. "How I have missed your sweet face!"

Simone saw Nicholas, crouched now at Genevieve's side, his arm bracing her shoulders. The lady cried quietly into her hand, and Nick glanced up at Simone. She could not fathom the emotion on his face—was it relief? Sadness? Regret?

Jehan stopped spinning, and Didier leaned back in the old man's arms.

"Can you stay?" Jehan asked tentatively, as if he knew the answer before he voiced the question.

Didier shook his head. "I miss *Maman*."

"Of course you do, my boy, of course," Jehan whispered fiercely.

"Papa?" Didier asked.

"*Oui*, my son?"

Didier poked a finger into his father's chest shyly. "Have you anything to eat?"

Simone could not help but laugh out loud, and she was surprised when she heard Nick's chuckle.

Jehan set the boy on his feet slowly, reluctantly, and reached into a pouch on his belt. "Well, what have we here . . . let's see—oh! Do you fancy a sweetmeat?"

Didier nodded and took the small piece—little more than a crumb, really—popped it into his mouth and chewed. He closed his eyes, his gamine face enraptured. After he swallowed, his eyes opened. "Thank you."

"You are most welcome," Jehan said, crouching down. "Now, tell me, how long—"

Didier silenced him with a hand over his lips and shook his head.

"Now?" Jehan whispered.

Didier nodded. He kissed the old man's cheeks, and Jehan crushed his son to him.

"I love you, my boy. I always have and I always, always will. Kiss your *Maman* for me, eh?"

"I will." Didier gave Jehan one last smile and then turned to Nicholas and Genevieve. "Farewell, lady," he said politely. "You are very kind."

"Farewell, Didier. You are very clever." The dowager baroness summoned the brightest smile her deteriorated condition would allow.

Didier's chest puffed out. He looked to Nick. "Thank you for letting me ride Majesty, my lord. I very much enjoyed it."

Simone saw Nick's thick, corded neck, already ringed with bruises, convulse. He cleared his throat. "I am sorry I did not believe in you, Didier."

"'Tis alright, Baron." The mischievous grin Simone knew so well lit his face and shone bright, brighter than the morning sun. "I did not believe in you either."

Nick snorted and held out his hand, a show of respect from man to boy. In Nick's palm was a dirty, crumpled, dingy-white feather.

Didier's thin shoulders straightened, and he slapped his hand into Nick's.

Nicholas pulled the boy into his arms, engulfing Didier in his embrace, and pressed his lips to the crown of the boy's head.

"I am in your debt," Nicholas whispered.

Didier pulled away. "Farewell, Baron."

And then Didier turned to Simone once more, and she did not know if she could bear the crushing weight of love she felt, if her eyes could withstand the sight of him, so brilliant and pure. She felt heavy and light at the same time. Didier walked to her, tugged at her hand so she knelt before him again.

Simone sighed a quick breath. "Well, we've had quite an adventure, have we not?" she asked lightly.

Didier nodded, his eyes wide. "I should say so."

Simone laughed and took his small hands in hers. "Didier, I wish that I would have been a better sister to you when—"

But he was shaking his head at her, giving her a silly frown. "Simone, you are my best friend. You always have been." He threw his spindly arms about her neck, and Simone squeezed him like it was the last time.

It *was* the last time.

"'Twas never your fault," he whispered in her ear. "Love you."

"Love you," Simone whispered back. She released him slowly, smoothing her hands over his unruly hair, down his neck, over his arms, memorizing the feel of him. "Where do you go?" she asked.

Didier shrugged, smiled. Then he gestured toward the rear of the hall, where the sun sank over the horizon, casting the placid waters in shimmering washes of magenta and orange.

"*Out there,*" he said simply, a touch of awe in his voice, and Simone could see the anxious excitement to be away flashing in his eyes.

But she feared for him. "You . . . you won't become . . . lost?"

"Oh, *non,* Sister," he assured her, and held out one fist to her. Grasped between his fingers was his once-white feather. "I have this."

Simone nodded, and tried to smile as she glanced at Nicholas. His jaw was set, his nostrils flared. Simone looked back to her brother, feeling as though her heart were being squeezed in a mighty hand. A hand the size of an eight-year-old boy's.

Didier glanced at the missing section of wall and then back to Simone, almost shyly. He leaned forward, whispered, "May I go now, Simone?"

She fought past the sob in her throat, and a hot, fat tear splashed onto her bodice. "*Whenever you wish, my love.*"

"Farewell, Sister."

Simone could not say it, and so she simply smiled.

Didier turned on his heel, and Simone gained her feet to watch him. With a delighted giggle, he burst into a run through the hall, fast, faster, and his laughter broke loose of him and swelled. Through the gaping hole in the rear of the hall he raced, and as he leaped off the edge of the cliff, his arms outstretched, Nick's feather in his small fist, Simone heard him call out "*Maman!*"

Then, in a blink, he was gone.

And Simone knew he was at last free.

"Simone! Simone!"

She heard the running footfalls, the delicate inflection of her name being spoken by a native countryman. But she did not turn. She could not seem to take her eyes from the view of the sea, the mellow sun taking this horrible, wonderful day away from her.

But then arms snapped around her, pulling her into an embrace, and they were not Nick's arms.

"Simone, *mon dieu!*" Charles gasped and then held her away to look into her eyes. "I saw the ship smashed upon the rocks and I thought . . . I feared . . ." He broke off, appearing genuinely terrified, and crushed her to him again.

"Release my wife, Beauville." Nicholas's voice brooked no argument.

Charles turned but left one arm about Simone's shoulders. "Simone is coming home to France with me and her father. I love her and I want to marry her." Charles looked down at Simone, his eyes still fearful. "I do Simone. I love you."

"Simone is already married," Nicholas said mildly, helping Genevieve to her feet. When he was assured that she could stand, he approached the arrogant Charles. "But if she wishes to return with you, then it is her decision to make."

A murderous look flitted over the Frenchman's angular face. Charles looked to the old man, approaching beyond Nick's shoulder. "Jehan?" he called, as if seeking the elder's aid.

Simone's father walked past Nicholas looking fragile and ancient. He came to stand before Simone, took both of her hands, and moved her a step away from Charles. "Give us a moment, son." He smiled at Simone. "My darling."

Simone was radiant. Her hair bedraggled and snarled around her face, dried blood and smears of dirt on her cheeks, her gown now black and ruined.

Nick thought she had never looked lovelier.

"You are my father," Simone said wondrously, and then embraced him.

And that was when the first real prickling of fear pierced Nick's heart. This was Simone, with the father she'd always craved. Jehan loved her, had loved Portia and Didier. Even Charles Beauville had done naught but shout his love for Simone from the moment he'd come to Hartmoore. And Simone had been without that particular comfort from anyone for quite some time.

Including myself, Nick thought.

Simone drew away with a little hiccough. She touched Jehan's face and smiled before turning to Nick's mother.

"Lady Genevieve?" she asked, as if unsure how the woman would receive her.

"Oh, Simone!" Genevieve and Nick's wife collapsed against each other. "You brave, brave girl. Brave girl!" she insisted. "I owe you my life, and the life of my son."

"Nay." Simone leaned back. "'Twas you who saved us all."

She glanced down at his mother's wrist, now wrapped in a strip of dirty underdress. "Is it very bad?"

"Just a scrape," Genevieve assured her. She looked at Nick, her gaze tired but intense. "Simone refused to leave me. She had chance to escape, time and again, but would not go. Without her, I think I would have given up."

Nicholas caught his mother's meaning easily. Simone had risked Armand's madness, her own life, to ensure the safety of his mother. He looked at her.

"'Twould seem I owe you a great debt as well, Simone."

She stared at him for a long moment, and Nicholas felt his control of the situation slipping through his grasp.

"You own me naught, my lord."

And then Nick was terrified.

Tell her, you great buffoon, he said to himself. *Tell her you love her and that, as your wife, she will return home to Hartmoore with you.*

Nay, he argued. *I have done too much telling and not enough asking for far too long.*

Yea, he loved her more than his own life, but because of that, he would keep his word and let Simone decide.

"What say you then, Simone?" Nick asked, wishing they could be alone but needing her answer given freely, before all. "Will you return to France?"

She seemed to think for a moment, her fingers twisting in the skirt of her gown.

Jehan stepped forward. "Simone, would that I could have you with me after all these years, but you are a woman now and you must decide your own way. If you wish to stay, I have . . . I have your mother's coin safe in London."

"Coin?" Charles snorted rudely. "Think you she cares about coin, Jehan? She needs a husband who will care for her, a home!"

"Hold your tongue against such slander of my person if you please, Charles," Jehan reprimanded in an offended tone. "The coin is hers any matter, and she should know it is at her disposal."

The blond man drew his prissy self up. "I meant you no—"

"Will Evelyn stay at Hartmoore, my lord?" Simone's soft query cut Charles's empty apology short.

Nick's eyebrows rose. "Unless she has returned to the convent—"

"She's not," Charles squawked eagerly, "and you well know it. She was at Hartmoore when you returned from battle."

"Interrupt me again," Nicholas warned, "and I shall toss you off yonder cliff. You did not seem so concerned about Simone's welfare while you cowered in the wood."

Charles's face turned red in the dwindling light of the dripping hall. "I was merely waiting for—"

"Oh, do shut up." Nick turned to Simone and said solemnly, "Yea, Evelyn is still at Hartmoore." He paused, saw Simone's face fall. "I shall send her away should you but breathe it."

"Nay," she answered quietly. "Nay, Nicholas. There has been too much . . . too much," she finished simply. "You never wished to marry me and since you have, I've brought naught but heartache to your family." Nick opened his mouth to refute her, and Genevieve did as well, but Simone continued on quickly. "I very much wish to be with . . . my father. I—I miss . . . my home."

The words cut Nick so deeply, he had the urge to look down and see if there was blood on his chest. Still he could not help but ask, "You would return to the people who shunned you?"

"For the people here did not?"

Nicholas had no answer for that.

She huffed a little sigh. "I think it best for us both if we seek the annulment discussed in London. I will return to France and . . . and marry Charles as my mother wished. You will return to Hartmoore, and things will be as they were meant to be before . . . before Armand."

Nick wanted to scream in rage and pain. He stepped forward and seized her hands, heated and marred from where she'd held the rope that had held him aloft. She loved him. She must!

"Simone, are you certain this is what you want?" he asked, silently begging her to change her mind.

"Please, do not touch me," she whispered. Nicholas flinched and dropped her hands. "Yea, 'tis what I want."

Nick felt the room tilt for a moment, saw Charles smirk, heard his mother's little mew of sorrow. And then Nicholas had no choice but to close himself off. He gave Simone a stiff little bow.

"Very well. I must travel to London on another matter, regardless." Nicholas looked to Jehan because he could no longer stand to see Simone, Charles's arm again about her shoulders. "You may accompany us, if you wish. I am certain the annulment will be issued posthaste once William learns the details."

"*Merci,* Lord Nicholas," Jehan said. "Your offer is very kind. Of course we will accompany you."

Nick nodded, and then quit the hall at a brisk pace, passing into the darkness, grateful that it would hide his grief.

Chapter 30

It took the party three days to make the trip to London, and the whole of the way, Simone felt as though she were slowly dying. She and Nicholas spoke not a single word to each other, and as far as Simone knew, she was already dismissed from his life.

She spent her nights between Jehan and Genevieve, her days on horseback, trying to avoid conversation with the now buoyant and loquacious Charles. It seemed each word out of her soon-to-be-husband's mouth sent long, jagged splinters into her head. He tried to be humorous; he was juvenile. He tried to be attentive; he was annoying. He tried to talk with Simone about their future and she was completely disinterested.

She missed Didier.

She missed Nicholas.

When she could, Simone passed the long hours conversing with Lady Genevieve and Jehan. The two elders of the group got on surprisingly well, and oft times Simone enjoyed merely listening to the pair talk of France and children, food and politics, but never about Simone leaving England.

And never, ever about Armand.

They had passed through a cluster of humble cottages on the first full day of travel, and Jehan had used his most excellent skills to trade one of the French guardsman's mounts for supplies and articles of rough, but clean and sturdy, peasant garb. They all seemed much more comfortable in the humble clothing, save for Charles, who had refused a change of clothes in favor of his fine tunic and chausses. He hadn't been nearly as dirty as the rest of the party, any matter, merely wet.

So now he smelled of mildew, even if he did sport fine embroidery.

The afternoon on which the small band of travelers passed through the gates of London town came all too quickly for Simone. Although she'd been in the city only once, it seemed memories reached out their soft fingers from every corner, plucking at her endlessly.

There was the inn where she and Armand had stayed, where she'd first learned she was to become Nick's wife.

There was the market where Nicholas had gifted Didier with his beloved feather.

There were the steps to the abbey, which she'd ascended with Nicholas on the day they'd wed.

And as guards approached to take charge of their mounts, as they made their way to the king's receiving chamber, as they waited in tense silence for word on whether William would see them, Simone felt her resolve to leave Nicholas slipping through her fingers like water.

Nick led the audience from the king's receiving room with his back stiff and his jaw clenched. By the morn, the documents would be procured, and it would be as if Simone had never been his wife.

In writing, any matter. Nicholas knew no mere piece of parchment, no matter how royal, would ever be able to erase his black-haired pixie from his heart.

The party was met in an antechamber by a prissy manservant.

"Lord FitzTodd," the man intoned, his head tilted so far back that Nick could see up his nostrils. "His Majesty bade me show the Ladies FitzTodd to their chambers, while you attend the sentencing." He sniffed in Jehan's and Charles's direction. "We regret we cannot accommodate the whole of your party."

"What is this?" Charles demanded. "I'll not be separated from my betrothed!"

The manservant drew back with a sneer.

"She's not your betrothed yet, Beauville," Nicholas snapped, and then wanted to bite off his own tongue at his possessive tone. Nick simply wanted to take Charles's head from his shoulders. He knew he could do it. It really wouldn't take much effort . . .

Jehan interrupted Nick's dark fantasy when he took Simone's hand. "I shall have some items sent for your comfort, my dear. Is there aught in particular that you desire? Anything at all . . . ?"

"*Non,* Papa. *Merci.*" She gave him a wan smile.

"Very well." He kissed her forehead. "I shall see you on the morrow."

Charles approached Simone after Jehan had moved away, but she averted her head at his advances. "Charles, please. Do not."

Nick could not help but smirk at the man's discomfiture.

"Good night, my love," Charles said smoothly, and gave a dramatic bow. "Sleep with the angels."

And then the two men were gone.

"This way, if you please, my ladies." The manservant swept an arm before him.

Genevieve kissed Nick's cheek and gave him a sad smile before following the servant.

Simone looked to Nick like she desperately wanted to say something. In her rough, plain gown, her long, dark hair in a simple plait, her huge green eyes sparkling like emeralds in a clear stream, she was a figure in a fantastical painting, and Nick wanted very badly to touch her.

Instead, he bowed. "Lady Simone . . ." and then he stopped, swallowed. He did not know what to say to her, since he could not say what he felt. "I wish you . . . contentment in your new life."

Nicholas thought he saw Simone flinch. "Oh, it is an old life, that," she said. "Thank you for tolerating me and my family, my lord. *Adieu.*" She turned, and her soft leather slippers made no sound as she joined his mother and the servant and was just . . . gone.

Nick did not know how long he stood there, staring at the spot he'd last seen her in. He also did not know how he had managed to muck up their very last moment together.

He finally headed for the Tower to witness Lord Wallace Bartholomew's execution, an event that suited Nick's mood perfectly.

Perhaps if Bartholomew made too much of a fuss, Nick would stick his own head on the block instead.

Simone wanted to be anywhere other than where the king's servant had shown her to. A rented room in the city, France, even the ruined abbey on the coast. But, oh God, not here.

She stood in the center of the very chamber she and Nicholas had shared when last they were in London.

Oh, the cruel irony of it all.

Simone tried to ignore her surroundings, washing the dust from herself in the small bowl in the corner. She tried not to see Nicholas washing in the same bowl, drinking by the hearth, sleeping in the wide bed they'd shared.

They had been together more in this room than at any other time in their short and soon to be dissolved marriage.

By the time the servants knocked on the door, bearing Jehan's gifts, she had cried for over an hour.

The soft night rail, robe, comb, and plain gown made her smile though, and after a young maid had set the tray of food on the small table, she requested a proper bath.

Now the fire burned low in the hearth and, her damp hair combed and the light night rail draping her body, Simone approached the bed as she would a gallows. She climbed in quickly, lay down, and squeezed her eyes shut.

* * *

Nick had considered passing the remainder of the night at the tavern where he'd been drinking. There were wenches aplenty plying their trade, but the thought of sharing his body with a woman other than Simone sickened him, even as far into his cups as he was. Since he'd been blessed by Simone—yea, blessed, dammit; he was drunk and could be maudlin if he so wished—he knew it would be a lifetime before he could seek another's bed and not see Simone's flawless milky skin, hair black as a raven's wing, her sweet face smiling up at him . . .

Nick groaned and staggered against the corridor in the guest wing. Bracing himself with his shoulder, he looked around blearily.

This door? Or that? He cursed bitterly.

Like a proper phantasm, the king's personal servant appeared, a smug smile on his smooth face.

"Good evening, my lord," the man smirked. "Might I show you to your chamber?"

Nick grunted and pulled himself away from the wall, following the slender man a short distance down the corridor. Nick could not help but wonder which door Simone slumbered behind.

After a short jangle of keys, the door swung open on a dark, glowing chamber. "Here you are, my lord. Good night."

Nicholas stumbled in, and the door closed softly behind him. He stood in the center of the room and groaned when he realized where he'd been interred.

'Twas the same chamber he'd shared with Simone.

Nicholas struggled out of his tunic and hurled it across the room with a great yell. The garment tangled around a chalice and sent it clanging to the floor.

"Damn her!"

Then he heard a gasp and a single word asked in an unmistakable female voice.

* * *

"Nick?"

Simone sat up in bed, clutching the covers to her chest. At first she'd thought the intruder was a dream, and then she'd feared she was being accosted. But when she'd looked closely at the masculine outline, she could have no doubt of the visitor's identity.

He spun around, quite unsteadily, she noted. He'd obviously been drinking.

Nick seemed to peer into the murky shadows of the bed and then, to Simone's amazement, he chuckled. "Either this is the cruelest dream I've ever had or I am infinitely more pissed than I had intended."

Simone couldn't help but smile in the dark, her heart pounding. What did he want?

Oh, please God . . . let it be me.

She cleared her throat. "I thought you were an intruder— what . . . what are you doing here, Nick?"

He shook his head as if to clear it and gestured with a thumb toward the door. "The manservant . . . wrong room, obviously. Er, I . . . *oh, hell!*" He scrubbed his hands over his face, sighed. He looked so tired. "I apologize for the intrusion. I'll find another—"

"Don't go," she said before she could stop herself, and then felt her face flame. Perhaps she could sound a bit more desperate. "I . . . I wasn't asleep," she added quickly. "'Tis late, Nicholas. We both need our rest and . . ." Was she truly saying these things or had Minerva once more taken control of her mouth?

Then Nicholas cocked his head, looked at her in that manner he had, and she knew that her thoughts were her own.

"Any matter," she continued. "'Tis not as if we've never shared a bed before. Completely innocently, of course."

Nicholas continued to stare at her. "This is true. But I have no wish to make you uncomfortable, Simone. Are you certain this is wise?"

"Nay," she answered truthfully.

He stepped closer to her, and Simone could see the outline

of his body through his thin undershirt, the firelight behind him causing him to glow.

"It *is* a large bed," he said at last.

Simone bit her lip. "Plenty of room."

He walked to the side of the bed—*his side* of the bed. "A bed of that size, 'tis unlikely we'd even touch."

"Highly unlikely," Simone agreed. "And we'll both be gone at first light, any matter."

"Bright and early," Nicholas said. He was staring at her hungrily now, his shoulders jerking as he kicked off his boots. "Perhaps we could talk a bit, since you seemed to be having trouble sleeping."

"Yea, let's talk." Simone felt gooseflesh spring over her arms as if coaxed by his gaze. "How . . ." She cleared her throat. "How did you find Lord Bartholomew's execution?"

"Oh, quite lovely." Nick pulled his undershirt over his head. "Simone, I want you."

Her breath left her in a combination of a sob and a laugh. Those words . . . priceless.

"We're no longer married, Nicholas," she said, the argument sounding inane and empty to her own ears.

"I beg to differ," Nicholas murmured, his hands dropping to the ties at his waist. "Although on the morrow we will go our separate ways, until the dawn's light, you are very much still my wife, and I would take this night to love you as I should have loved you all along."

Simone's body trembled, her stomach clenched. *Oh, thank you God. Thank you, thank you, thank you . . .*

She held the coverings aside, inviting him in with a smile.

Thank you, God. Thank you, thank you, thank you . . .

Nick went immediately to her, gripping her tiny waist through the thin gown with both hands, taking her mouth and kissing her like he would devour her.

And she kissed him back, first holding his shoulders and then wrapping her arms completely around his neck.

"You taste . . . like . . . Heaven," he mumbled, his tongue flicking out to taste her lips. The effects of drink had left him, but Simone's intoxicating presence left him drunker than before. He nuzzled her neck, pushed her gown off her shoulder with his cheek, tasted her there.

She sighed, arched into him. "Nick. Oh, I have missed you."

"And I you," he replied, dragging the hem of her night rail up her leg and over her hip, clutching her buttock and pulling her against his erection. "I am so sorry, Simone. All the wasted time, and now you'll be gone from me."

"Shhh," she whispered, kissing his neck where the shadows of bruises ringed him still. "There is no help for what is past. Let us be content with tonight, as if there were no tomorrow."

He raised his head to look into her eyes. "I love you, Simone. Is that not enough to make you stay?"

She smiled sadly, and again Nick thought she looked as if she wanted to say something. Instead, she ran her hand down his front to grasp his manhood and rub it over the hot length of the cleft between her legs. Nick gasped and jerked.

"It is enough for tonight," she said.

Anger filled him then, mingled with his raging love for the woman beneath him. He stared down into her face—so beautiful, so filled with passion—and sat back on his haunches. "Whose gown is this?"

Simone frowned. "What?"

Nicholas reached the fingers of both hands into the neckline of her night rail, skimming the fair skin over her collarbone. "Is this one of your mother's gowns?"

"Nay," Simone said warily. "Papa had it—"

Nick ripped the bodice into two halves, cutting off her explanation with a cry and revealing her two pale globes of breasts, perfectly round and topped with dark, raspberry nipples.

He dropped forward, his mouth drawn to first one nub of puckered flesh and then the other, and Simone sighed and arched against him. He pulled his head away with a slurping sound, and her breast jiggled back into its perfect fullness, the pale skin covered in gooseflesh.

"Are you cold?" he whispered.

Simone gifted him with a slow, sly smile. "Nay, my lord," she said. "I am on fire."

Nicholas growled deep in his throat and moved backward on the bed until he was bent over her. Grasping the two ragged edges of her gown, he completed the separation and caught his breath at the delicate perfection of her body. He clambered to cover her, and she welcomed his kiss, welcomed his hand between her legs.

"Touch me, Nick," she pleaded against his mouth, and moaned, and Nick obliged her, sliding a finger into her tightness. She pressed upward against his hand.

Nick was shaking so that the very bed beneath them trembled in syncopation with the thunder beyond the chamber. He wanted to please her, wanted to sate her desire before taking her maidenhead, but the sight of her naked body, the sound of his name on her lips, the feel of her hot wetness surrounding him was too much for him to bear.

"Simone," he said into her neck, "I cannot wait."

"Then do not," she sighed.

It was all the leave he required. He withdrew his hand from between her legs and swung over her, pushing her thighs wide with his own. Simone spread her arms on the mattress, a symbolic welcome, an offering, and the delicate lines of her ribs heaved with her breaths. Nick took himself in hand and leaned forward, wedging himself at her opening. Then he balanced on all fours. Simone ran her fingertips down his ribs, his waist, to grip his hipbones.

He looked into her eyes. "You will feel some pain."

She shook her head and smiled.

"You will," he insisted, "but only this first—"

Then Simone pulled at his hips and arched into him, and Nick lost his words. He was barely in her and Simone cried out softly. She bucked again, and Nick sank slightly deeper.

She stilled with a gasp when Nick felt her maidenhead pressing against him.

"Shhh," he soothed, dropping to his elbows on either side of her head. He brushed the hair from her face, kissed both her eyes, her lips. He reached down and drew first one of her hands, and then the other around his neck.

"Let me," he murmured against her mouth.

He withdrew his length from her slightly, rocking his hips back and forth, stretching her. He withdrew more, then sank in only slightly deeper. Over and over he did this, entering and withdrawing an inch at a time, bumping her maidenhead harder each time, quickening his little thrusts. Simone's pants as he pushed at her drew Nick's seed to its very limits.

"Oh, Nick," she moaned, pressing her nipples into his chest. "Please, oh, please . . ."

And then he pushed his entire length into her fully, harnessing what little control he possessed to not stay seated and explode within her. He withdrew immediately and then entered her again, long, even, firm strokes, relishing the tight gauntlet of her, feeling her every shudder and pulse. He pushed into her, felt her pubic bone through the soft flesh of her mound, ground into her, and felt his release starting.

"Oh God, Simone," he groaned. He slid his arms under her shoulders, crushing her to him. She opened her legs wider. He had never felt on the verge of something so profound as he did now with this woman. His woman, his wife.

She panted his name as his pace increased, and Nicholas could feel her tightening in rushing waves around him.

"Tell me, Simone," he demanded through his teeth, striving to hang on to his release a beat longer. "Tell me!"

"I love you, Nick!" she said clearly, and then Simone gave a cry as her climax rushed over the both of them, and Nick felt himself push deeper still within her.

"I love you, Simone," he panted. "Do you hear me? I love you."

And then he spilled himself into her, forever and ever, it seemed, and for a moment he was the happiest he'd ever been.

* * *

When Nick had finished loving her, he surprised Simone by pulling her close, turning her so that her shoulder blades nestled against his chest, sheltering her in his arms just as he had on their last night at Hartmoore. Simone sighed and closed her eyes, feeling warm and heavy and sated and safe. The musky perfume of their lovemaking hung within the heavy drapes, cushioning the sounds of the fire's snapping and amplifying their slow, heavy breathing.

"This changes naught, does it?" he asked, his deep voice rumbling low over the crown of her head.

Simone didn't want to answer. Didn't want to destroy the easy peace of the moment. But he deserved a response.

"Nay," she said quietly. "You did not think it would, did you?"

"In truth, I thought it might." His thumb drew slow circles around her navel. "Does he make you happy, then? Charles? You can forgive him for what he did to you?"

How could she tell Nicholas that Charles most definitely did not make her happy? That each moment in his presence since he'd arrived at Hartmoore sickened her? 'Twould sound like a plea for Nick's pity, and Simone was tired of being an object of pity or scorn. A burden. A pawn.

Since her mother's and Didier's deaths, she had been naught but a means to an end to each person in her life: Didier's link to the mortal world; Armand's leverage to gain England and his mad treasure; Nick's compromise to placate his family and his king. She had been used not for herself but for others to gain what they truly wished. Didier had wanted Portia; Armand had wanted Genevieve; Nick wanted Evelyn. But no one had seemed to care what Simone wanted, and no one at all wanted *her*.

Except Jehan. Her father wanted her, wanted what was best for her.

'Twas novel to be desired, valued, finally for herself and

not what she could help gain. Nicholas had said he loved her, but could she believe him?

Nicholas nudged her. "Simone? Do you sleep?"

"Nay." She was quiet a moment longer. "My father needs me." She felt him stiffen slightly behind her, and she knew her words wounded him. She wanted to apologize, but could not.

Better for her to leave Nick now, perhaps angry with her, than to stay and have him resent her in time. He would forget this little pain, and mayhap even one day remember her fondly.

"Can I fetch you anything?" he asked after a while. "A cup of wine? Something to eat?"

She shook her head. "I think I'll go to sleep now."

She felt his lips press her hair, and it made tears well in her eyes. "Good night, Simone," he whispered, his breath warming her scalp.

Simone swallowed, drew a slow, shallow breath. "Good night, Nicholas."

Chapter 31

Nick fell into a desperate, exhausted slumber, Simone still in his arms. And he dreamed.

He was in Withington once more, on the journey from London to Hartmoore with Simone.

The damned convent! How could he have forgotten its proximity to the inn?

Because it truly did not matter, his present-self reminded him. You are not in love with Evelyn. You love your wife. When you are with Simone, you think not about Handaar's daughter. Only when you see aught which reminds you of Evelyn does your pride pinch you.

That made sense to Nicholas, but even so, he was still in Withington in his dream, and he let the memories carry him along until he was once more seated against the ancient oak beyond the inn, wine jug in hand.

A small, white feather circled and swooped toward him.

"Ah, young Didier," Nick said in the dream. "Chastity itself. I would think you'd be sitting faithfully at your sister's side, preventing me what little comfort I have in this world."

The wine jug was dispatched down the hill and into the river, and then the feather began swaying and bobbing, Didier's first attempt at communication.

Are you a boy . . . ?

Is it about the accident . . . ?

Do you remember what happened . . . ?

And then Didier's feather fell to Nick's lap, dripping and matted, and Nicholas was plunged into the dark, icy cold of the boy's memories, deep, invisible water seeming to close over his face.

Didier, did you drown?

But this time, in Nick's dream, the details were more vivid. Through the boy's eyes he saw not darkened countryside but water all around him, dirty, fecund water rippling with red and gold, burning his nose and throat as he choked and gasped. *Don't breathe, don't breathe . . .*

Horses screamed, from far away it seemed, and the whole world rumbled. Heat was all around him.

Blurry wood inches away from his nose, rough-hewn boards shaped into a V.

And hard fingers clamped around the back of his neck like a skeletal claw, holding him down, down, down in the water.

His struggles ceased.

His mouth opened.

The water and the pain faded away into nothing, nothing, and he was floating, weightless.

Didier, did you drown?

"Didier!" Nicholas sat up in bed with a hoarse cry and looked around wildly.

He was in the guest chamber at the king's palace. Sunlight streamed, bright and painful, onto the floor. Nick looked to his right.

Simone was gone.

His eyes flew about the room. No sign of her remained but a lone piece of parchment on the table, and Nicholas knew it was the annulment decree. 'Twas as if she had vanished from his life. As if she, and Didier, had never been.

"He did not die in the fire," Nick said aloud, as if to test the statement. "He . . . he *drowned*."

Nicholas tried to string together all that he knew in his sleep- and fear-clouded mind.

The boy was in the stable when Armand set the blaze, but Armand had sworn he hadn't known Didier was inside.

When Simone had told Nick the tale of her brother first coming to her after his death, she'd said he'd been dripping wet.

The water, and the wooden boards shaped into a V. A trough, perhaps?

The hand on the back of his neck . . .

Armand hadn't known he was in the stables, and Portia was already dead.

Someone else had been in the stables, someone who did not want Didier to escape.

In an instant, Nicholas knew.

He sprang from the bed to dress, praying that the ship that would take his wife away with a murderer had not yet set sail.

Simone stood at Jehan's side as the crew of his ship crawled over the docks and up the plank like insects, carrying freight and supplies. The sun blazed as if to spite her sadness, and the seabirds called mockingly, swooping and taunting her with their freedom. The sea swelled and hushed, its smell rotted and decaying here.

"Did you sleep well?" Jehan asked, searching her face with concerned eyes. "You are very quiet."

Simone tried to smile at him, but it pained her head and so she gave up. "I'll be fine."

She tried to push the image of Nicholas as she'd left him this morning from her mind. The way his hair had smelled when she'd kissed his cheek one last time.

"Where is Charles?" she asked her father, seeking to cover up the bittersweet memories with something distasteful.

Jehan gave her a conspiratorial look. "He's off to make a purchase. A gift for you, he said, to cheer you on the voyage."

Simone sniffed. She knew she was being unfair, but she

didn't care. There was naught he could buy her that would bring her comfort.

And with Saint du Lac's coin, no less. Yea, she had given her permission for Jehan to hand over Portia's coin to Charles. She would marry him once they returned to France, and Simone cared little for riches tainted with so much blood and heartbreak. But still, his ready use of the funds irked her. Already Charles had spoken of improving Saint du Lac. A larger hall, a bigger stables to replace the one lost in the fire. Simone cared not.

In truth she did not care to return to Saint du Lac at all. Jehan had tried to converse with Simone about her mother, to defend the woman, but Simone would not have it. She felt infected, sickened by her mother's lies, the lies that had kept her and Didier from their true father, kept them all tethered to Armand du Roche.

But until they returned to France and she was married to Charles, for the whole of the voyage, she would simply be Simone Renault, daughter of a wealthy merchant. And then she did smile a bit and squeezed her father's arm.

"Oh, there he is now," Jehan said, and gestured across the docks to where Charles weaved in and out of the crowd. The sunlight glinted off his blond locks, turning them an obscene yellow, and he smiled broadly, carrying a long, leather-bound package under one arm and waving to her with the other.

Simone noted darkly that he had managed to procure a fine new tunic since the previous day, and for some reason that nagged at her as she stood awaiting him in the plain, simple gown her father had sent.

"Are we set to board?" Charles asked, coming to stand before them. "Good day, my love."

She did not reply, although when he leaned in to peck Simone's cheek she allowed it.

"We were but waiting on you, Charles." Jehan beamed and gestured toward the odd-shaped parcel. "What have you there?"

Charles winked at Simone before answering. "Oh, naught

but a small token of affection for my betrothed." He wagged a finger at Simone. "And there shall be no peeking, lady. 'Tis to amuse you after we set sail, and I shan't have you ruin the surprise."

Simone had to struggle not to roll her eyes. "I shall try to restrain myself."

A shadow flickered across his face, but he covered it with a bright smile. "I'll hold you to that."

Jehan intervened on the awkwardness. "The bosun's just given me the signal, young people. Let us board and be off. The quicker we begin, the quicker we arrive."

Simone thought she would vomit with each echoing step up the plank. Once they were aboard, England and Nicholas would be but a memory. The last place she'd seen Didier, the first place she'd met her father.

The first and last time she'd been in love.

They paused just inside the ship's railing, waiting for the queue to disperse, and Simone turned her head to gaze back at London. Its gray buildings, its sooty air, its raucous, odiferous docks.

"Good bye, my love," she whispered.

"What say you, Simone?" Charles asked, his brows drawn together.

"Naught," she answered, looking at him and then glancing away as they moved onto the ship's deck. "I said naught."

They watched the deckhands toss down the mooring lines, and the ship slipped smoothly out to a calm sea. The winds were brisk and miraculously strong in their favor.

They would reach France quickly.

Charles led her down to Jehan's own cabin, a courtesy to Simone from her father. The room was quite small and cramped, the low ceiling seeming to press down upon even Simone's diminutive height. The cot against the wall was narrow and bowed, its ropes stretched beyond their ability to recover. Two plain wooden chairs and a table bolted to the floor were the only other furnishings, crammed at angles to two of Simone's own trunks strapped to a wall. The cabin was dark and dank and smelled of dried seawater.

Simone shuddered.

Charles lit a lamp and gestured for her to sit on the edge of the bed. She chose a chair instead. He shrugged with a good-natured grin and sat across the table from her, placing the parcel between them.

"First, allow me to say," Charles began, "that I know the past year has been . . . difficult for you, Simone."

She did not answer. Difficult?

He cleared his throat. "And mayhap I did not support you as I should have, when . . . when you confided in me about . . . about . . ." He trailed off, clearly uncomfortable with the subject matter.

Simone arched one brow. "About what, Charles? About Didier? My brother's ghost?"

The man paled in the dubious light of the lamp. "Er . . . *oui.* He's gone now, though, is he not?"

"Unfortunately, he is." Just the sight of Charles so discomfited made her sick to her stomach. Coward.

"You're certain?" he pressed.

She merely stared at him until he blushed and cleared his throat.

"Very well." He pushed the package before her. "Then mayhap this will comfort you in your . . . your loss."

Simone didn't want to undo the twine holding the leather around whatever lay inside. For some reason, she broke out in a cold sweat at merely wondering what was within. But she drew it nearer and plucked at the string.

"I do hope you like it," Charles urged. "I'm rather proud of myself, I'll admit."

When are you not? Simone thought cattily.

After unfolding first one flap of leather and then the other, Simone gasped at the package's contents. Her hand flew to her mouth.

A short wooden sword, tiny leather shield, and a leather coif lay before her—a soldier's kit, made for a little boy.

With a single white feather laid across it all. Simone's breath caught in her chest.

Charles frowned, picked up the feather between his thumb and forefinger as if it were an insect. "How did that get in there?" he mumbled, and then tossed it away.

"Charles, it—" She took the kerchief he offered and blew her nose. "It's perfect." And Simone thought, for just a moment, that if Charles Beauville could have purchased this for her, life with him as her husband may not be as hellish and unbearable as she'd feared.

He was not Nicholas, but then again, what man was?

"You like it, then?" Charles asked, leaning forward with a pleased grin.

Simone ran her hand along the smooth, wooden sword blade. "I do. I love it."

"I am glad." A pause, and then, "Perhaps one day *our* son might find sport with it."

"Perhaps." Simone picked up the small coif, and a handful of feathers drifted to the floor. Simone huffed a small, bemused laugh, but Charles only muttered about the ill-kempt shopkeep and his habits.

Simone looked at the coif for a moment and then set it aside with a little frown. "How could you ever think to seek this out? How could you know how much it would mean to me?"

"I know you, Simone, better than you think I do." He gave her a sly wink. "I was determined to secure one before we set sail. It cost me a great deal, but when I saw how deeply you still grieved, I wanted you to have some small thing to remember him fondly." He reached out and took her hand. "Since Didier's own playthings were lost in the fire, I thought you would appreciate this."

"And I do, very much," Simone assured him, and then as she smiled at Charles, her blood froze in her veins. Her smile fell from her lips.

Charles leaned forward, a concerned look on his face. "Simone, what is it?"

"How . . . how—" She stopped, tried to fight past the tightening in her chest. "Charles, how did you know Didier's soldier things were with him in the stables?"

The man drew back as if she'd punched his nose. "Why, you told me."

But Simone was already shaking her head. She pulled her hand free and stood. "Nay. Nay, I did not."

"I'm certain you did, Simone," he insisted, his eyes narrowing. "How else could I know?"

She continued to shake her head, backing toward the small cabin's door. "I told *no one*," she whispered, a panicked tear sliding down her cheek. "Only Nicholas. How could you know, unless you . . . unless you were there." She gasped. "You were!"

In an instant, Charles's face had changed into a twisted mask of fury. He bolted from the chair and leaped toward her.

Simone screamed and turned, grasping for the door handle, but Charles was already upon her, pulling her from her escape and flinging her onto the narrow bedstead.

"You don't understand," he gasped, coming toward her with his palms out. "Didier was not supposed to return to Saint du Lac. He was supposed to remain with you—safe at my home!"

Simone scrambled backward into a corner of the cot. "You knew what Armand had planned," she accused. "You let him kill my mother, and you let an innocent boy die!"

Charles crawled onto the cot. "You must stop saying such things. Listen to me, Simone, Portia lied to you your entire life. She was not a good mother," he insisted desperately.

"Get away from me!" Simone shrieked, kicking at him.

Charles flailed at her legs, grunting. "Would you *stop?*" He tried to catch hold of her, finally seizing her ankles and jerking her onto her back. He leaned over her, and she tried to slap at him, push him, but he pinned her to the thin ticking.

"I was only trying to secure our future," Charles said,

breathing heavy. "I knew what Armand had planned, *oui,* but there was naught I could do to stop him. I didn't know that your mother had hid Saint du Lac's fortune in Marseilles with Jehan—I wanted to be assured that Armand would not abscond with our coin in search of his treasure."

"*My coin!*" she spat at him. "Mine! Did he see you in the stables, spying? Didier? Did Didier see you after Armand had set the fire and locked my mother's body inside?"

"Shut up, Simone," Charles warned.

"He did, didn't he?" She was crying now, but she barely noticed. "He asked you for help and you let him burn so that Armand would not know you were witness to his crime!"

"Nay, love—Didier did not burn."

The low, rumbling voice broke through Simone's hysteria and drew both her and Charles's attention.

Nicholas stood in the narrow doorway, his sword drawn and pointing directly at Charles's back.

Chapter 32

Charles choked. "FitzTodd—how—?"

"Nick!" Simone screamed, and resumed her struggles.

Nicholas stepped into the cabin, filling it with his murderous presence. "Back away, Beauville."

"This is none of your concern, FitzTodd," Charles said, jerking Simone in front of him as if to shield himself. "She is no longer your wife!"

The imbecile, Nicholas thought before stepping forward and simply pulling Simone to her feet. He drew her tight to his side, and she buried her face in his chest.

"You did not let Didier burn alive," Nick continued calmly. "After he saw you, you held him in a water trough until he drowned. You had to rid yourself of him quickly, else you would have also perished in the fire."

Simone's head raised and she looked up at Nick, her face stricken. "The water," she croaked. "How did you know?"

"Didier told me, love," Nick said gently, touching a forefinger to her lips. "Long ago in Withington, and again last night, after we made love."

Simone looked to Charles, the truth breaking over her pale face like a black storm cloud. "'Tis why you refused our betrothal, labeled me as mad—when I told you Didier's spirit came to me, you feared he would tell me what you'd done and that I'd tell others, Armand. But if everyone thought me mad, no one would ever believe me."

Nick nodded. "And 'tis why he did not fly to your rescue at the ruins. He knew that Jehan believed in his son's ghost. If Didier's spirit did exist, Charles didn't want to be found out and ruin his last chance at gaining you—and your coin—for himself."

Charles sneered and shook his head. "'Twas never about you, Simone—only the coin. When Jehan came to me after you had flown to England, he told me 'twas he who was guarding your mother's coin, that he was your true sire. I need that coin—Beauville Castle is near ruined!"

Simone's eyes narrowed. "You'll never get it. Never!"

"Get up, Beauville," Nick commanded, gesturing with his sword. "King William's ship and guards wait. You'll be held accountable for what you have done."

Charles did get up, but he began to chuckle. "Oh, certainly. And how will you prove my guilt, FitzTodd? By telling your king that a ghost helped you solve the mystery? You'll be laughed out of London!"

"We shall see," Nick said blithely, and moved Simone away from the doorway to let Charles pass.

Jehan Renault waited just beyond the door in the small corridor, and from the look on the old man's face, he'd heard clearly all that Charles had confessed.

"Jehan." Charles blanched when he saw the man. "Fitz-Todd lies! I would never—"

Jehan slapped Charles, twice, three times, until Charles's lip was split and bloody and the man had raised his hands to his face with a cry. "I called you *son,*" Jehan choked, and then spit in the murderer's face. "Get above," he commanded, shoving him toward the stairs.

Nick pulled Simone behind him, her tiny hand gripping his. Once they had gained the upper deck, he saw that it had been deserted as he'd asked. A quick glance at King William's ship, now some distance away, showed the same—an empty deck.

No witnesses.

Beauville turned, bewildered. "What is this, FitzTodd?"

"'Tis your trial," Nick said simply. "And Simone and Monsieur Renault are to be your judges."

Then he gestured to the long plank affixed to the side of the deck, leading only to empty air and the deep blue sea.

Simone looked up at Nicholas. "I don't understand."

Jehan spoke. "I do, Daughter. Charles is correct on one point—no one would ever believe our tale about Didier. 'Tis likely the scum would be found innocent and set free."

"Nay," Simone cried. "He must pay!" She looked to Charles, and was pleased to see the fear in his eyes. "You must pay for what you have done!"

Jehan approached her and took her arms. "And that is what Nicholas has given us, darling—the opportunity to mete our justice, here. Now."

Simone looked to Nicholas again, to see if he would refute what her father was saying.

"We can take him back to London, if you prefer, Simone," Nicholas advised. "We can try to convince William that he gave a full confession. I'll not force your hand. But before you make your decision, I want you to know that I will abide by whatever choice you make." Nick's eyes matched the blue of the calm sea beyond his back, holding Simone's gaze.

He continued. "I love you, Simone. My pride—my own foolish insolence—has nearly cost me all. I hope it has not cost me what I value most. You have given me that which I never knew I lacked, or even needed. You have shown me the meaning of unselfish love—love for my family, my mother and brother. Passionate love, like I have for you. I never knew its meaning until you came into my life. I have no pride now—I lay it at your feet."

Simone did not want to bring up this thing, not now, when Charles awaited his fate. But she felt that she and Nick stood on a precipice, on the very edge of a future that would be spent either apart or together, and she would not let herself hope against all reason. Not yet.

"But what of Evelyn?" she asked at last.

Nicholas frowned. "What of her? I do not love Evelyn, Simone. I never have."

"She loves you," Simone said quietly. "I read the letters she sent you—she regretted her choice of the convent and wrote for you to send for her so that the two of you could be married."

Nick shook his head. "It matters not. I love *you*. I always will, until the end of my days."

Simone swallowed. "Are you certain, Nick? Very certain?"

"I love you, Simone," he repeated, slowly and deliberately. "More than anything or anyone. I want you to stay with me in England and be my wife forever. I want to marry you again. Will you come home with me? Please?"

"I most certainly will," she whispered. Simone walked to Nicholas, raised up on her toes, and kissed his lips. "I love you, Nick," she said, looking directly into his eyes.

Then she turned to face the blond man cowering against the ships rail, and Didier's gamine face sprang to her mind. His huge laughing eyes, his mischievous smile, his love of a good prank, his pure heart.

Charles had stolen that from Simone, from Jehan. And she knew that they could never convince anyone else of the fantastic events surrounding this tragedy.

"Step onto the plank, Charles."

"*Non!*" he croaked, his gaze flitting nervously to the long, bowed board. "*Non!* I cannot swim!"

Simone raised her eyebrows. "Well then, mayhap you can breathe underwater."

Charles eyes grew even wider. "Of course I cannot. You know I cannot!"

She felt Jehan come to stand at her other side.

"And neither could Didier," Simone said quietly.

Jehan drew his long, slender blade, and he and Nicholas advanced on the man.

"*Non! Non!*" Charles screamed, looking around wildly for

aid. But of course, there was none for him. The front of his chausses darkened with urine.

Nick motioned toward the plank. "You can walk under your own power, like a man, in acceptance of what you have done, or we shall cut you down and throw your body overboard," he said, herding Charles to the opening in the ship's railing. "'Tis your choice."

"I will not!" Charles insisted, his voice cracking. "I'm sorry! I shall return to France and never see any of you again—I swear it!"

Jehan's blade flickered. A slash of red appeared on Charles's left cheek, and he screamed.

"We'll not see you again, any matter," Jehan said. "But the only way you'll reach France is in a fish's belly. Now, go."

"Simone, please!" Charles begged, backing gingerly onto the board. "Have mercy on me!"

She could feel all three sets of eyes on her as she stared at the man who had murdered Didier.

"Nay," was all she said.

She heard his shrill scream and the great splash as his body hit the water. And although she did not watch as Charles drowned in the cold, vast sea, she listened eagerly to every gasping breath, each gurgle and cry to the very last, wrapped in Nick's arms with her eyes closed, Didier's face clear in her mind, until Charles was no more.

Epilogue

Christmas Day, 1077
Hartmoore

The feast was superb—all of Hartmoore gathered in the great hall to the sounds of music and laughter, the smells of holly and tallow candles, roast bird and savory pies. Simone sat at Nick's side at the lord's table, her hand resting on her still-flat belly beneath her kirtle. To the other side of her sat her father, laughing and talking with Lady Genevieve, as was his habit the past two months.

Only Tristan, Haith, and Isabella were missing from the festivities, having gone back to Greanly shortly after Nick and Simone's wedding. Nick's brother had healed remarkably quickly from his wound, and Haith had been anxious to return to their home. Simone noticed a distinct change in her sister-in-law since Minerva's . . . departure? Death? Simone was still unsure as to what exactly had become of the old woman. But Lady Haith was different now. Still the same caring, intuitive woman, but now with a rather intense air about her.

And her eyes, Simone noticed right away, had changed from a clear, crisp blue like Nick's and Tristan's to that of a deep night sky—almost black.

Any differences Nicholas and Tristan had between them were put to rest upon Nick's return to Hartmoore, and the large blond man had actually wept in his mother's arms when he learned that Armand was at last dead. Nicholas had played a major role in accomplishing what Tristan, in all his years of battle and wars, could not. Simone knew that the brothers' bond was tempered now and would never be broken.

Evelyn Godewin was nowhere to be found at Hartmoore, causing somewhat of an awkward moment when the monks from the priory returned for the dedicant. Simone felt a twinge of remorse at the way she'd treated the poor lost woman, but Nick had assured her that Evelyn was searching for her own destiny—something that had always seemed just beyond her reach. It could not be had at Obny, or with Nicholas, and certainly not at the convent.

Simone hoped the woman found it, whatever it was she sought.

As for Jehan Renault, Simone's father had decided to stay on in England with his daughter and son-in-law. France now held too many dark and painful memories and he hoped to start anew, building a life with his daughter and her family, and possibly—Simone and Nick suspected—with Lady Genevieve as well.

With her father's help, Simone had slowly begun to forgive Portia for her duplicity. She better understood now her mother's motives—Portia had simply tried to give Simone and Didier respectable lives and had fully planned to reunite her children with their father and the man she loved with all her heart. She had never expected Armand to live out the year when she'd wed him, and would not have, Jehan assured Simone—ill health or nay—had she but known what a madman he was. Portia had done her best, and Simone could not fault her for that. Her mother's journals and gowns were now lovingly tucked away.

"Do you tire?" Nicholas leaned over and whispered in her ear.

She turned to nod at him. "A bit. Would you mind?"

He immediately stood and helped Simone to her feet. They called their good nights to all as he led her up the curving stone stairs. Once in their chamber, they undressed and climbed into bed to nestle in each other's arms.

"'Twas a lovely feast," Simone sighed, snuggling her nose into Nick's chest.

"Mmm," Nick murmured. "You are lovely."

Simone smiled. She could never have imagined herself so happy. Blissful. Complete. *Wanted.*

She thought Nick may be falling asleep, but curiously, she was no longer tired. "Have you given any more thought to a name for this babe, husband?"

Nicholas stirred, kissed her collarbone, and his words were deliciously muffled against her skin. "How do you fancy Olivia for a girl?"

She tilted her head back and kissed his mouth. "I like it very much. And if it is a boy?"

Nicholas looked into her eyes. "I was thinking"—he kissed her again, his hands roaming her back—"perhaps"—his hands moved lower—"Didier."

"Do you not think that may be a bit confusing?" She ran her hands through his hair.

"How so?" Nick murmured, dropping his mouth to her neck.

"Well," Simone broke off, tapping Nick on his shoulder. When he raised his head, she pointed a finger behind him, and he craned his neck to look.

A single white feather bobbed around the end of the bed.

Up–down–pause. Up–down–pause.

Nicholas groaned, and Simone couldn't help but giggle when her husband said, "Didier, we can *see* you."

She listened for a moment and then laughed aloud before saying, "My lord, Didier rather fancies the name Willy for a boy."

Nick looked toward the feather warily and then back at his wife, as if he suspected a bit of mischief was afoot.

Simone didn't have the heart to tell the poor man he was correct.

GREAT BOOKS, GREAT SAVINGS!

When You Visit Our Website:
www.kensingtonbooks.com

You Can Save Money Off The Retail Price
Of Any Book You Purchase!

- **All Your Favorite Kensington Authors**
- **New Releases & Timeless Classics**
- **Overnight Shipping Available**
- **eBooks Available For Many Titles**
- **All Major Credit Cards Accepted**

Visit Us Today To Start Saving!
www.kensingtonbooks.com